GLITTERBALLS

★

MICHELE HOWARTH

Girl from the North Country

Illustrations by Michele Howarth
Designed and Typeset by Richard de Pesando

Set in Garamond and Rustica

First edition 2024
ISBN 978-1-0687577-0-9 GlitterBalls (Paperback)

Girl from the North Country

Published by Girl From The North Country
www.michelehowarth.com

EX-LIBRIS

Girl from the North Country

For Elliot

MICHELE HOWARTH

INTRODUCTION

★

'Fancy a Vesta?'

MICHELE HOWARTH

1978

★

Sometime between the birth of the world's first IVF baby and Jim Jones blowing out his brains in Guyana. Sometime between *The Hair Bear Bunch* and *Granada Reports*. Sometime between masturbating into a face flannel and noodling on his guitar, seventeen-year-old Neville 'Howie' Howden's mother shouted, 'Fancy a Vesta?' up the stairs. And, in that moment, Howie's planets lined up like Ray Reardon's snooker balls. A stellar pop career launched off the back of a rehydrated ready meal.

1980

✳

Sometime between the eradication of smallpox and the discovery of who shot JR. Sometime between *Tiswas* and *Auf Wiedersehen Pet*. Sometime between masturbating into a face flannel and noodling on his guitar, nineteen-year-old Neville 'Howie' Howden's frenetic, amphetamine-fuelled debut single 'Fancy A Vesta?' bolted straight up the charts – bagging seven weeks at the top spot for post-punk rascals You!Yes!You! There was no denying it. Queenie Howden had fired the starting pistol on her son's dazzling career. It was a legend he'd dined out on many times in the intervening years, though he'd always glossed over her lifelong refusal to eat 'that foreign muck'.

2019

★

Sometime between Prince Philip totalling his Land Rover and fire engulfing La Notre-Dame de Paris. Sometime between *Good Morning Britain* and *Fleabag*. Sometime between masturbating into a face flannel and noodling on his guitar, fifty-eight-year-old Neville 'Howie' Howden's karma rocked up to bite him on the arse. As his mother's coffin trundled through the crematorium curtains, it was his stellar pop career that was going up in flames, to the cymbal crashes and *thud thud thud* of the chorus of his breakthrough hit.

PART ONE

★

Mid-March, 2019

THE BIG I AM

★

Howie had never relished the journey north. Despite touring the globe for the best part of four decades, dividing his time between properties that lay empty for most of the year, it was those 200 miles from his home in Surrey to his birthplace of Stockport he found the most gruelling of slogs. And never more so than on that miserable, wet, mid-March day. As his mother lay on her hospital deathbed, Howie – worse for wear and possibly over the limit – had dragged his heels to be with her. His reluctant drive up the inside lane of the M6 had seen him rarely exceed sixty miles per hour in a car engineered to reach 200. Dementia had wiped Queenie's memory of her two adult children, and there was a part of Howie – a large part – that couldn't see the point of a bedside vigil. He dearly hoped his sister Jean would call to inform him of his mother's demise, and so gift him the opportunity to turn back home.

Fame had buffered him from most of life's grisly realities, so he'd been relaxed about passing the familial buck of his mother's care to Jean. He'd rarely visited the nursing home where Queenie had spent her final years. It wasn't something he was proud of, or something he'd ever share, but seeing his mother's vulnerability scared him. He hadn't the emotional intelligence to process distress. Early success had triggered a chronic case of arrested development and, with his relationship on the rocks and his manager off his rocker, he was struggling to negotiate such a huge life event alone.

There'd been quite a stir when he'd swaggered down the ward, guitar case in hand, collar up; his faux nonchalance at odds with the squeak from his leather trousers. The noise of his Cuban-heeled boots, clippy-cloppy on the linoleum floor, harmonised with his open-mouthed champing on a fresh stick of gum. His eyes, still pink from the previous night's excesses, were invisible behind mirrored shades. But mostly people had focused on his hair – an asphalt-black travesty of the dishevelled mop that had once been his crowning glory. A trademark look that had screamed frontman, much to the annoyance of his equally ambitious bandmates. But though his boyish floppy fringe had thinned, Howie still had the strut of youth. The charisma that had helped secure his stardom was undiminished by the ageing process, even if his fatty liver and enlarged prostate were a bleak reminder that time stands still for no one.

Though Howie was far from conventionally handsome, there was a roguish twinkle about him – something a skilled surgeon had managed to preserve when trimming away the more jowly aspects of a face that, while having nothing going for it on paper, had somehow achieved Serge Gainsbourg levels of dissolute cool. Deeply lined from too much downtime spent around hotel pools, he had a bust-nosed rakishness that women had found irresistible, and a generation of men had tried to emulate. And while staff, patients and visitors had craned to get a better view of this mythical creature – part rock-god, part twat, depending on the angle – a ripple of *He's shorter than I thought*, cut through with a flat, northern *Who does he think he is? The big I am*, had travelled around the room. Fortunately for Howie, a touch of work-related deafness ensured he'd heard none of it. His presence had energised the ward, and he felt it in his bones.

POOR CHOICES

Eddy hadn't relished the journey north. Touring the globe for the best part of four decades had killed the wanderlust he'd embraced as a younger man, and never more so than on that day. Those 200 miles from his hotel in London to his home in Manchester were proving to be the cruellest of slogs. As Queenie lay on her hospital deathbed, Eddy Katz – worse for wear and possibly over the limit – had washed up in a bad place, emotionally and geographically, somewhere off the M1. Victim of fragile mental health and a rail-replacement bus service. He had no idea whether Queenie was alive or dead, and being out of phone battery and luck had complicated an already wretched predicament. Eddy had been Howie's manager for the best part of forty years, a longevity peculiar in their industry and the most enduring relationship of either of their lives. Under normal circumstances he would have been at the hospital to help shield his client from a public eager to intrude upon private misery. But there was nothing normal about his circumstances. And maybe nothing would be normal again.

Eddy stood jacketless and soaked, hitch-hiking in the pelting rain, on the grassy verge of a motorway slip road. His hair, a bit mad professor since he stopped visiting the barber, was wrapped in a scarf. He had a nice face, crumpled and affable; one which presented a complete lack of threat. It looked sad in repose, which was often, with the brown eyes and long lashes of a Hallmark card spaniel. It was the kind of face that saw women sit next to him on public transport, a face that suggested he wasn't one of the lads, but could be, to women, that rarest of things – a platonic male friend.

He twanged an elastic band on his wrist. A cognitive therapist had advised he should do this each time he had a negative thought. But for Eddy, whose thoughts ping-ponged constantly between dread and despair, it was the psychiatric equivalent of being handed a step-stool to scale a prison wall. His empty stomach gurgled. There was little trace of Dungeness crab left in his system, yet it was still repeating on him. Memories of the night before, of poor choices and rotten company, came back to him in a mortifying jumble.

Eddy's intolerance for seafood had first come to light when eating potted shrimp on a class outing to Morecambe. But his flouting of the kosher laws of his school and parents' kitchen hadn't been the subversive teenage stunt he'd envisaged. His infamy wasn't secured by his rebellion, but by soiling his trousers on the coach home. An ignominy he never lived down and for which his parents and teachers had little sympathy. So it should have come as no surprise that a lapse in vigilance while dining with Howie would cause a similar disgrace – a digestive haunting that threatened to conjure his mother back from the dead, just so she could tell him *I told you so*. But the crab wasn't the worst of it. His broken glasses, missing jacket and fishy burps were a reminder of terrible foolishness. The kind of idiocy that sees late middle-aged men subject to police attention, press scrutiny and female rage. For Howie there'd never been anything that a fat cheque, a non-disclosure agreement or a course of penicillin couldn't make go away. But there'd be no such easy fixes for Eddy. The motorway stretched out before him, but it felt like the end of the road.

SIX STONES OF NOTHINGNESS

Even before Howie's arrival at the hospital, there'd been a buzz of anticipation, stoked by his sister Jean, who never missed an opportunity to crowbar his name into whispered conversations with the nursing team. News of Queenie's celebrity son had whipped around the ward faster than the winter vomiting bug. The older nurses sang the hook of an early hit, but it meant little to the junior staff, who just shrugged and asked why he hadn't paid for his mother to be cared for privately. Because, although she had the curtain swished around her in a half-hearted attempt at privacy, Queenie would breathe her last to the clatter and babble of life on an underfunded and overcrowded NHS geriatric ward.

Reeking of cigarettes, Howie had been staring at his phone from the moment he'd sat down with his guitar, alongside his mother's bed.

'Are you going to give us a tune?' Jean asked.

But Howie ignored her. It was a rude but deliberate tactic to disengage with her humming of show tunes and forensic reminiscences of a childhood he could conjure up only in monochrome. Jean stood, looped her bag over her shoulder and pulled her chunky, hand-knit jumper over her ship's decanter bottom.

'I'm going to spend a penny,' she mouthed.

But he didn't look up. His lack of interest in his sister contrasted sharply with his preoccupation over the whereabouts of Eddy. He had a bone to pick with him. Their night on the town had turned ugly and it would appear Eddy had gone to ground. *Bono wouldn't put up with this*, he thought. He checked his texts, but there was nothing. Just a coded message about a bag of draw and a waxed pussy sext from an acquaintance he'd reached out to earlier when hoping to sweeten his stay in the north. Knowing he'd lined up drugs and premier league sex improved his mood considerably.

Howie contemplated his mother. Under the thin hospital blanket, she seemed little more than a tuft of white hair and an empty catheter bag. Cocaine and nicotine withdrawal caused his knee to bounce, and the tremor created ripples in the jug of water on the bedside table. He genuinely found it impossible to associate this tiny, desiccated scrap of a bird with the pinched-faced dynamo who'd brought him up single-handedly. Rarely seen without a head full of plastic curlers, anchored by setting lotion and pins, and immovable under a hairnet, she'd put in a forty-five-year stretch on the cold meat counter of Stockport's indoor market. He had little memory of her leaving the house at five-thirty every morning, but he did recall being looked after by Jean – just a schoolgirl herself – until his mother returned late each afternoon, ciggy in the corner of her mouth, jellied meat under her fingernails. He remembered how she'd squeeze him to her bony body, her work overall scratching against his young boy face. His nose pressed into the acrid tang of pickled eggs, breaded ham and stale tobacco. The ash from her Embassy cigs sprinkled over his regulation short back and sides like icing sugar dusting a Victoria sponge. He cast his mind back to the teatime dread of the stall's leftover fare; the potted meat, the moulded brawn in aspic or that worst of all offals, tongue. He recalled how she would regale them with stories of the immigrant customers she begrudged having to serve. How scandalised she was by the women who wore saris under the coats and cardigans that protected them from the chill of a country not always forthcoming in its welcome. It felt like a hundred years ago and, in terms of the distance Howie had travelled since those days, it might well have been.

While he mulled this over, Queenie – silent and motionless since his arrival – slowly raised both arms from beneath the covers. Her hands balled into fists, as though primed for a bare-knuckle fight.

'Fuck,' he whispered.

She tilted her head, and her toothless mouth gaped open in a mute, Edvard Munch scream. Her cheeks were hollow, her waxy skin as yellow as an unloved houseplant. Unable to bring himself to touch her, he patted the bed. 'It's okay. I'm here,' he said.

Queenie remained silent.

'It's me, mum. It's Howie.'

Nothing.

'It's me,' he said, before whispering, 'Neville.'

Howie's nerves jangled as his mother became restless. His pulse quickened, along with a wave of regret about the lines of coke he'd tooted in the hospital car park. The hard edges of the plastic visitors' chair cut into his hands as he gripped the seat. There was nothing in his lived experience to prepare him for this moment. Suddenly, taking a loud, diabolical glug of air, Queenie sprang to life, and pedalled her twiggy legs as though falling from a great height. Her cannulas threatened to dislodge from her stick-thin arms as she flailed about like some malfunctioning marionette. Kicking off the covers to reveal a shrunken, shrivelled, mummified Queenie of the Cold Meat Counter, swaddled in a polycotton nightie.

'SHITTING NORA!' Howie shouted, jumping up. His chair clattered backwards through the curtains and the plastic water jug bounced off the bedside cabinet, spilling all over the floor.

Then, in Queenie's final, never-to-be-forgotten last headfuck act on earth, she opened her flinty eyes wide and wild – and, like a macaque monkey in a tourist hotspot, she grabbed Howie's hand, yanking him to her. So close that he could feel her acetone breath on his face, her too-long nails embedded into the palm of his hand.

'I know who you are,' she said, her growl liquid with the secretions that gurgled in her larynx like a badly clogged drain.

Every fever dream, zombie movie and acid flashback resurfaced to punch him in the kisser. He tried to prise back her fingers as she hissed and rattled like a boiled-dry kettle, brown frothy sputum bubbling into her mouth and down her chin. And then she was still.

Howie stared at the six stones of nothingness that a few seconds earlier had been his mother. The rest of the ward, the rest of the world beyond the hospital curtain, carried on as though nothing had happened. A strange, parallel universe, with a clattering tea-trolley and a patient complaining about a too-hard jacket potato.

He placed his hand on top of the blanket. 'Phew,' he said.

PART TWO

★

Late-March, 2019

THE SOUND OF MUCUS

*

If the mourners thought 'Fancy a Vesta?' an inappropriate choice for Queenie Howden's funeral, then Howie was unaware, steadfast in his conviction it was what she would have wanted. Jean had maintained their mother was a Frank Ifield fan and that she'd wanted to be seen off to 'I Remember You'. But Howie overruled her, and so 'Fancy a Vesta?' it was.

While Jean blew her nose under the net of her pillbox fascinator, Howie stamped his heel and mouthed the words to the chorus of his breakthrough hit. His mirrored shades reflected his mother's coffin, with its white chrysanthemums spelling out 'MUM'. Jean would have preferred a 'MOTHER', or even a 'QUEENIE' but, at fifty pounds a letter, Howie had vetoed the extra expense. He flinched as his sister took his hand, her screwed-up wet tissue a snotty barrier between their familial flesh. Being this close to his family and past unsettled him. It was a reminder of everything he'd escaped once 'Vesta' had become a hit in fourteen countries.

If Howie inhabited a glamorous otherworld from those gathered there that day, then his girlfriend, Stina Q, appeared to come from a different planet entirely. This long-limbed Swedish-Eritrean beauty towered above the congregation, Howie included. Her height made ever more extraordinary by the knotted head wrap that enfolded her hair. As poised as Jean was lumpen, and pencil-slim in Helmut Lang, Stina radiated a sublime, if slightly coached elegance she'd gained from her years in the modelling industry. It was unfortunate then, that Howie and Stina's young daughter Viola resembled her father's side of the family.

'That's a Howden conk,' Queenie had said when first presented with her newborn granddaughter. It had been a fleeting moment of clarity from a woman lost to the fug of Alzheimer's.

As the service reached its conclusion, Howie sat rigid while Jean gripped his arm, yelping and whinnying like a farm animal in distress. To be in such close proximity to her famous brother in public was a rare event, and Howie couldn't help but think she was milking it.

'You're frightening Viola,' he said, with just the ten milligrams of Xanax he'd necked before the service stopping him from ripping himself from her grip.

Viola, her lazy eye covered with a large patch, stared at her Auntie Jean through googly spectacles, trying to compute this adult anguish. But if being around family wasn't ordeal enough, there, right behind Howie, was the icing on the cake. Eddy Katz; slumped and sobbing, nursing a *Whizzer and Chips* shiner of a black eye, his face as creased as his suit. The sound of mucus being shovelled up a grown man's nose was more than Howie could bear, and he glowered over his shoulder to silence him.

The two men hadn't seen or spoken to each other since their night out in London two weeks earlier, and the hostility between them crackled and sparked like arcing power lines. As they locked eyes a huge snot bubble ballooned out of Eddy's nostril, and popped like a giant FUCK YOU.

RUM BABA

Like a sprinter anticipating the starting pistol, Jean stood at the window, hands on her saddlebag hips, braced for action. Despite Queenie outliving most of her peers, speculation that her famous son would be in attendance had secured a healthy turnout at the crematorium and Jean was hopeful the gathering at her bungalow would draw a similar crowd.

As the first of many cars turned into the cul-de-sac, she burst into action. Ripping cling-film off trays of finger food with the zeal of a newly qualified beauty salon waxer. The frenetic activity causing circular sweat stains under her armpits and inflaming the fungal infection that a too-tight bra had aggravated under her bust. She hurried between the kitchen and lounge, pushing aside Agnieszka, the Burgess's domestic help, who was struggling to put away a cylinder vacuum cleaner and all its attachments.

'Chop chop!' Jean said to Agnieszka, while rapping on the kitchen window to her husband, Gordon, who'd been sent into the garden on a final dog poo hunt.

'There!' she shouted, pointing. 'Strewth.'

He spotted the turd and turned to smile at his wife, tipping his imaginary hat in a casual salute.

A mahogany cabinet, home to Gordon's golfing trophies and Jean's collection of royal family knick-knacks dominated the Burgess's lounge. The display provided a talking point for the chattering ghouls who filed into the room, killing time before the arrival of Jean's very own royal. Because it wasn't every day Howie came to visit. In fact, in the twenty-five years Jean and Gordon had lived in that quiet corner of Romiley, Howie hadn't visited at all.

'That's not our Neville's car,' Jean said, elbowing her way to the window as Howie pulled up outside. 'Our Neville drives a sports car. Like James Bond.'

But there was no mistaking it was him. His arm dangled from the passenger-side window of the small yellow hatchback, ciggy in hand, his eyes unreadable behind mirrored shades. Gordon, tasked with the removal of a strategically placed parking cone, was already out front, directing Stina into the space like an aircraft marshal bringing a jumbo jet into land. Jean watched from the window.

'Ever the gent,' she whispered as Gordon opened the driver's door and offered Stina his hand.

A general buzz of male excitement broke out over Stina's never-ending legs, while the women waved at Viola, a large child who appeared older than her four years, wearing a fuchsia-pink puffa jacket that matched the atopic dermatitis that covered much of her face.

Jean barged out to greet them – a cacophony of talcum powder and static, crackling polyester and chafing pantyhose. Casper the dog plodded behind, his tail wagging with as much enthusiasm as a fourteen-year-old morbidly obese Labrador could muster. Howie remained in the car, drawing heavily on the cigarette which he held between his middle and ring finger, in the style of a French intellectual. Jean relished this opportunity to give her brother her undivided attention. She opened the car door and offered him her hand.

'Where's your car?' she said ventriloquist style, through clenched teeth.

'Long story,' Howie replied, his rebel insouciance hindered by the bright yellow Peugeot. He exited the vehicle with a languid stoop as spectators in the bungalow expressed surprise over his height. Jean cupped his face in her hands and his dark glasses lifted from his nose.

'I've got your favourite,' she whispered. 'Rum Baba.'

GRAB-RAILS

Howie felt unsteady as Jean led him by the hand into the hallway, passing the gold disc he'd gifted her after much lobbying. It was a more measly gesture than it appeared. An inconsequential award from a minor territory, hung pride of place next to a graduation photograph of Gavin – the only visible memento of Jean and Gordon's absent son. His decision to settle in Sydney a geographical demonstration of his need to escape parental disapproval of his lifestyle and husband.

Trepidation, Mogadon, and the heady combination of hyacinths and hard-boiled eggs caused Howie's knees to buckle. But he was in little danger of toppling as Jean threaded her arm through his and frog-marched him into the low-ceilinged lounge – offering a glimpse of what it must have been like to cross her path during her long career as a store detective.

'Everyone! This is our Neville,' Jean announced, with the ham she'd brought to many a light operatic production.

A chorus of excitable 'Hello, Our Nevilles' rippled around the room. Howie offered a polite *namaste*, as Stina and Viola were swallowed up into the flabby-armed quicksand.

With the exception of some of the more elderly guests, grappling with the challenges of eating off their laps, most of the mourners were standing. Howie was directed to sit in Gordon's chair – a bottle-green leather, deep-buttoned scroll-winged affair, perfectly in keeping with his gentleman's club aspirations. Howie scanned the room, expecting to see Eddy. Their relationship was in crisis, but Howie needed him to act as a buffer between himself and these people. But there was no sign of him. Instead, a smiling, bearded, white-haired man with a home brew belly caught his eye and nodded. Howie nodded back, clueless.

'Neville,' the man said, his voice as large as his girth, a plate of food in one hand, the other outstretched to greet him. 'It's been a while.'

He was heavy-set, with the kind of physique that suggested he might be prone to blocking toilets. Howie stayed seated, overshadowed and miniature in comparison, and shook his hand.

'Bill Ellis,' the man said.

Howie's brain cogs whirred, but there was nothing. His blank expression betrayed the need for a prompt.

'Unsworth Road Juniors.'

Finally, Howie recognised something unchanged in this person's jovial face.

'Oh, Christ. Unsworth Road. Bill. Yeah man.'

'It's been a while.'

'Totally,' Howie said, his mid-Atlantic drawl recasting it as *toadally*. 'Bill. Billy Bumfluff. Wow. The only kid in juniors with a moustache.'

Bill laughed, stroking his white Father Christmas beard, flecked with flakes of puff pastry. 'I got a Philishave for my twelfth birthday.'

Howie was glad for this benign interruption to the discomfort of the wake. He'd always liked Bill and his family.

'Sorry about your mum, Neville,' Bill said. 'I saw quite a lot of her. I installed her walk-in bath.'

Howie didn't know anything about a walk-in bath. 'Really? Cool.'

'And the grab rails. Before she went into the home.'

Howie didn't know anything about grab rails either. Insights into his mother's frailty unsettled him. He'd never modified his teenage view of her as a sinewy little powerhouse in a bri-nylon housecoat. Feisty and able-bodied. Indestructible, somehow.

'How's your dad doing?' Howie asked.

Bill shook his head. 'Ah, the asbestos got him.'

Howie whistled.

'Yeah. He was only fifty-two,' Bill said.

'Shit. Sorry man. What about your mum?'

'Same thing. From shaking out dad's overalls of an evening.'

'Wow.'

'Yep. The boilermakers' curse.'

The Boilermakers' Curse. Cool song title, thought Howie. *A bit Nick Cavey*. He wondered if he should jot it down.

The two men chatted, comparing memories of their neighbourhood.

Of a place with little through traffic and no parked cars; a childhood unchaperoned; playing footie in the street until called back home by folded-armed mothers on scrubbed doorsteps. Howie had no beef with Bill and was saddened to learn of his parents' fate. The news may have come over thirty years after the fact, but he remembered Mrs Ellis being especially kind to him, perhaps recognising the stigma of single-motherhood that earmarked him out as different. But mostly he was bothered that Bill appeared so fucking old. Being jerked back through time – exposed to these parallels – troubled him. It seemed incomprehensible that he was the same age as Bill. He felt exactly like he did at sixteen. Even if his enlarged prostate was telling him otherwise.

ON SHPILKES

Eddy Katz had poor spatial awareness at the best of times. And never more so than when parking. So, with one eye swollen shut and his right wing mirror missing, it was hardly surprising he'd polished off the Flymo while reversing into his garage. Not that he was arsed. Running over the lawn-mower was the least of his worries.

Without bothering to check the damage, he turned off the engine, lit a spliff and attempted to pull himself together. Increasingly ill at ease in groups of strangers and mildly phobic about outside catering, Eddy had ducked out of the funeral reception. He knew small talk would aggravate an already irritable bowel and his fractured eye socket would draw unwanted attention. So, after Queenie's service, he'd slipped away, arriving home at the arse end of an awful fortnight and sliding towards the end of his tether.

Eddy had always been a fretful kind of guy – predisposed to trouble with his nerves as his late mother used to say in English, or '*on shpilkes*' in the Yiddish she would dip in and out of at home. But of late, Eddy's workaday anxiety, depression, irrational fears, neuroses, daytime nail-biting and night-time teeth-grinding, had shuffled up to make room for two new kids on the block. Those evil twins – paranoia and psychosis.

There'd been little in the way of merriment growing up in the Katz household. Barbra Streisand, Sammy Davis Jr. and a profound sense of dread had been the background hum to his upbringing. Emotions had been heightened but largely negative, and the young Eddy had been steeped in his parents' vigilance and melancholia. Intense parental love manifested itself as something fretful and oppressive, the whispered implication that 'It' could happen again colouring every social interaction outside of the family home. Eddy's father Leo was distant, silent and sad, while Ethel, Eddy's mother and catastrophist in chief, was convinced someone or something might rob her of her boy if she didn't monitor his every move, every minute of the day. But Eddy's paranoia was founded in neither marijuana nor the Final Solution. He had fucked up. There was no way he could face Queenie's wake. More to the point, there was no way in his current frame of mind that he could face chewing the fat and pretending everything was okay with Howie fucking Howden.

WHERE'S EDDY?

All eyes were on Howie as Jean bustled about, barking at Agnieszka to keep the tea flowing while she slopped sherry trifle into bowls, her swollen feet oozing from her patent leather court shoes like freshly baked bread. Gordon sported a double-breasted blazer complete with embroidered crest and brass buttons. Howie wondered if this was how they dressed on their Brexity cruises. He'd never had much in common with his sister, but the dissimilarity had never been more stark than when sitting in her lounge in his mirrored shades, his hair primped and freshly tinted. The gunmetal blue of his tattooed hands complementing his chunky rings and chain bracelets that quivered ever so slightly. His tremor payback for the hard spirits, cocaine, marijuana, over-the-counter and prescription medication that pumped like a steam train through his veins.

Howie felt more exposed than ever following Billy Bumfluff's departure. He watched as Bill gave Jean a comforting hug and overheard her thanking him for everything he'd done. Howie felt an unexpected prickle of propriety over his mother. He hadn't bargained for this sense of estrangement and was sheepish that others had come forward to support her when he hadn't stepped up himself. He watched as Gordon mingled among the guests – never once missing an opportunity to put his arms around the shoulders of the men or waists of the women, giving Stina an extra little squeeze while flashing Howie a cheery wink. Howie couldn't believe Eddy had left him to fend for himself. His social unease causing him as much discomfort as his recently broken veneer. He had no idea how to work this room or trade in this brand of small talk. His comfort zone ended at the perimeters of his celebrity and the gates of his Weybridge driveway.

'What do you call a barmaid in a push-up bra?' Gordon asked, gatecrashing his brother-in-law's body space to exploit the imagined comradeship between two red-blooded males.

'Go on,' Howie said, recoiling from Gordon's malodorous breath.

'A brass half-empty.'

Impervious to Howie's non-committal nose snort, Gordon raked his fingers through his Reg Varney hair and gave Howie a conspiratorial nudge before moving off to circulate, relishing his role as mine host. Howie ran his tongue over his stump of a tooth and sank back into the chair, wishing he'd taken something stronger to cushion himself from the full force of Gordon and Jean's bonhomie. But he reasoned there was no controlled substance on the planet more trippy than listening to one of Gordon's blue jokes a mere three inches from his face.

All of the remaining guests were strangers to Howie, except one, Tony Dunn, the office PA, who was sitting next to the buffet, feeding crisps to Casper from a side plate. Almost twelve weeks earlier, Eddy had gone over his head and employed Tony on a three-month trial. Howie resented the easy relationship they enjoyed and was still in a sulk about it.

Tony was looking unusually formal in an ill-fitting black suit and tie. Howie ruminated that all that was needed was a fedora and she'd be a dead ringer for John Belushi. Her appearance disturbed him. He preferred his girl-on-girl action to be of the Playboy Bunny variety; the type of lesbians who want a man to join in. Real-life lesbianism unsettled him. And Scouser Tony, with her quiff, tats and ear spools, her doughy belly and her uneven gait, unsettled him a lot.

Tony caught Howie's eye and offered a friendly nod.

'Where's Eddy?' Howie mouthed.

She shrugged and shook her head. Howie had made no effort to get to know her. He'd already lined up a replacement and was counting the days, conscious that he should terminate her contract while it was still legal. *She probably knows her rights*, he thought. *She looks the type.*

WANDERING HANDS

Stina had bristled at Gordon's playful little squeeze, his salmon-paste breath hot on her neck as she stood at the buffet. But it came as no surprise. He'd given her one of his special hugs the first time they'd met, backstage at one of Howie's gigs. Not wanting to make any waves, Stina hadn't told Howie she'd felt a hardness press against her. But she'd been in similar predicaments often enough to know the best way to defuse the situation was to play along, to keep it light. She knew these guys could flip from hail-fellow-well-met to insults and threats in the blink of an eye. She smiled broadly, stepping back to break free from his unwelcome embrace. Gordon hitched his trousers, popped a profiterole into his mouth and strutted away, pumped up and triumphant.

Stina didn't turn to check on Howie to see if he'd noticed the exchange. He'd been in a foul mood, ever since she and Viola had got to the Manchester hotel that had been his home since his mother died. She helped herself to a congealed egg mayonnaise sandwich she had no intention of eating, and checked Jean's carriage clock for the time that stood still. She longed to open a window, to inject some oxygen into the airless room.

Hoots of laughter rang out above the boisterous chatter, the volume rising in tandem with blood alcohol levels. Queenie's death may have come as little surprise, but Stina found the jollity discourteous. She imagined it would take just a few more top-ups from Gordon's drinks trolley and the whole room might erupt into the hokey-cokey. Her modelling career may have taken her all over the globe, but nowhere on the planet felt as alien as this corner of Little England, with its whiff of soft biscuits and xenophobia. She clutched the gold locket she wore around her neck, the one that housed tiny photos of her parents – her beloved *mor* and *far*. She tugged it from side to side along its chain. Their timber home, bordering an Uppsala County nature trail and steeped in linseed oil and parental love, felt a world away from Jean and Gordon's crowded lounge. It was an unusually bright spring day in the north-west of England, and one to be embraced in this greyest of countries. Stina looked out at the rotary clothes dryer, packed away in its protective cover, and remembered her mother's clothes line, tied between spruce trees. That glorious sight of bedding billowing in the breeze, the brilliant white sheets a dazzling contrast against their falu red home, painted with the pigments of the copper-laden land and russet soil of her childhood. She watched as a blue tit flew from a bird feeder. She'd never felt more cooped up, more yearning for the land of her birth, than when standing in that room, avoiding Howie's stinky mood and Gordon's wandering hands. Stina was overcome with homesickness. She missed that part of Sweden that she'd left as a teenager, when at seventeen, she'd embarked on a new life in London, with only her parents' broken hearts and her mother's *knäckebröd* to remind her of home. Her melancholy intertwined with the looming requirement to apply for settled status, forcing an issue which she had so far chosen to avoid. She felt affronted by the new legislation. Belittled by this obligation to apply to live in the country in which she paid her taxes. To seek permission to stay with her British partner and British child. It was a country from which, on this most awful of days, deportation would have come as a blessed relief.

Stina looked at her daughter, lying on the floor, chatting to Tony and stroking Casper. Viola's comical, helium, little-girl voice carried above the low-pitched murmur of the room.

'Bebisbjörn?' Tony said, looking at Viola's teddy. 'That's a good name.'

'It means "baby bear", in Swedish.'

'You speak Swedish?'

'*Ja.*'

Stina smiled. It was reassuring to see Viola confidently interacting with a stranger. She worried about her so much; this four-year-old child in a seven-year-old's body. She dreaded her starting school full-time. She knew her height and her eye patch would single her out and make her a target for the bullying that had blighted her own schooldays. The dog soon tired of Viola's vigorous petting and flapped about in a struggle to rise.

'Come on old man,' Tony said, as she and Viola helped Casper to his feet, allowing him to mooch off towards the kitchen, breaking off only to scoot his backside along the burgundy and gold medallions, swirls and swags of the carpet.

Tony and Stina's eyes met. They pulled the same *oops* expression, bonding over the awfulness of both the occasion and the elderly dog's impacted anal glands.

JUST SOME BLOKE

★

Howie watched as Tony limped around the table, piling her paper plate high with finger food. Stina, graceful and impeccably mannered in any social setting, appeared to be chatting effortlessly with Jean's friends and neighbours, while Viola lay on the floor beneath the table, chewing her hair, hugging Bebisbjörn and breaking wind. Jean bent down, huffing and puffing, to hand the child a fairy cake, peeling off the paper case and carefully licking her fingers.

Howie found it extraordinary that his sister was just six years his senior. The age gap felt generational. How could someone whose childhood ran parallel with the sixties, whose teenage years would have exposed her to disco, funk, soul, R&B – someone over a decade younger than Anita Pallenberg for fuck's sake – be so unapologetically uncool? It both bewildered and annoyed him. Because somewhere, in the depths of his psyche, Howie feared that rubbing up close to his sister might burst the bubble. That he'd be found out. If the twenty-four-year age gap between himself and Stina validated his rock god status, then Jean's stout arse confirmed an unspeakable truth.

He wasn't special.

Strip him of the expensive clobber, the private dentistry, the Mid-Atlantic accent, and the catwalk model girlfriend, and he was just some bloke from Stockport. A glance around the room confirmed his worst fears. If he was sex and drugs and rock'n'roll, then this lot were plug-in air fresheners, company pensions and a Jeremy Vine phone-in on Radio 2.

Howie excused himself and went into the back garden for a toke on the spliff that had been calling him ever since they'd pulled into the cul-de-sac. He lit the dimp and checked his phone for word from Eddy. But there was nothing. He took a drag on his spliff and his mind wandered to thoughts of a woman he'd recently hooked up with. She had everything. Young and beautiful, with no gag reflex, she'd provided saucy respite from the drudge of funereal obligations. He had plans for this one.

From where he was standing, he could see Agnieszka in the kitchen. He walked towards the open back door to get a better view, watching as she bent to stroke Casper, stretched out across the floor like some giant, fermenting, bratwurst. Howie took in the scene, contemplating Agnieszka's behind as she chatted to the dog in Polish. He scanned the outline of her knickers through the overstretched fabric of her baby-pink leggings. By squinting his eyes ever so slightly he could visualise her buttocks naked. *Nice,* he thought, as he drew heavily on the last dregs of his spliff.

A FUCKING MESS

Eddy dabbed his face with a tissue. He was under strict doctor's orders not to blow his nose, for fear of compromising his orbital floor fracture. He looked in the rear-view mirror and wondered if anyone had noticed he hadn't shaved. His stubble and Albert Einstein hair might look fashionably dishevelled on a more cocksure kind of guy; his swollen black eye could even signal alpha male. But he just looked a fucking mess.

Eddy hadn't expected Queenie's funeral to hit such a nerve. But it didn't take much to reduce him to tears these days. Everyday tasks felt insurmountable and he was spending more and more time in bed. He'd lie awake wired, looping thoughts – then, minutes before the alarm was due to go off, he'd fall into the blackest sleep. He never woke refreshed. Instead he'd be nauseous and exhausted, drenched from chronic night sweats and consumed with self-loathing.

Eddy was aware of Queenie's mean streak. Of an anti-Semitism so entrenched that she would introduce him as 'our Neville's jew friend' without a shred of shame. Yet he'd still gone the extra mile for her. In a curious way, the association fulfilled a need in both of them. For Eddy, it had been a clunky attempt to address the fraught relationship he'd had with his own parents. He'd spent his life locking horns with Ethel and Leo, while trying – and failing – to please. For Queenie, Eddy was a cock-eyed connection to Howie: a son too squeamish and distracted to notice how she was navigating the indignities and expense of old age. It had been Eddy who'd quietly organised the standing order that fed into her account for all those years. A modest, but useful sum that the business could well afford. He considered it a benign form of embezzlement. It was one of the many things he covertly put in place to ensure Howie did the right thing by proxy, because he knew the likelihood of Howie doing the right thing off his own bat was pretty much zero.

At the crematorium Eddy had turned off his phone. He suspected he'd be in trouble for sagging off Jean's soirée. And, sure enough, sitting in his car, he heard the *ping ping ping* of missed calls, voicemails and texts when he switched on his mobile. Also, scattered among them, were calls from Tony.

Tony had brought a much-needed cheerfulness and humanity to the workplace. Sometimes Eddy felt she was the only person who gave a shit about him. Because underscoring all his disillusionment with the music business and with Howie was the wretchedness of living in the death throes of his marriage to Una Coyne, his wife of twenty years. The binbags piled high in the garage, full of his belongings, were a bulging testament to just how bad it had got.

It had come as little surprise when Una had refused to accompany him to the funeral, and Eddy knew better than try to persuade her otherwise. So it had been Tony who'd put an arm around his shoulders during the service – an act of tenderness he'd found excruciating. But the only affection he craved was from Una. Kindheartedness from anyone else highlighted just how little warmth was coming his way at home. Eddy was desperate for reassurance, for some demonstration his wife still loved him and that everything was going to be okay. But perhaps she'd never really loved him and nothing would be okay again. He'd always been fearful that she would leave him. Now he feared she'd already gone.

MY FRIENDS CALL ME HOWIE

★

Howie watched as Agnieszka went about her business, laying out cups and saucers on a tray. He considered her to be a fairly attractive woman, the kind who brushed up well – she was maybe mid-thirties, in an apron that covered what he computed to be C-cup breasts. He cleared his throat. Agnieszka jumped, startled to discover she was being observed. Casper struggled to his feet to consider, through cataracts and advanced nose blindness, what had caused this unexpected charge in the atmosphere. Howie flicked the remains of his joint onto a pretty cluster of lily-of-the-valley and strolled towards her, beaming. A diamond in his tooth glinted in the sunlight as he outstretched his hand to introduce himself.

'You must be Agnieszka.'

Agnieszka appeared flustered as he shook her hand for a beat longer than customary.

'Yes. Hello. Neville.'

Howie grinned, his Hollywood smile fucked up by his broken veneer. He liked her accent. Accents were a turn on.

'My friends call me Howie,' he said.

SKITSTÖVEL

★

Stina watched as Howie flicked the butt of his spliff into the flower bed, and wondered what Jean and Gordon would think when they found it during what were clearly – judging by the tidiness of their borders – forensic weeding sessions. Feeling alone and unprotected, her eyes darted, praying Gordon would keep his distance while Howie was out of the room. But there he was, true to form, aiming a salted peanut at a middle-aged cleavage, the recipient hooting with laughter. Stina had never been more relieved to be wearing a dress with a boat neckline or more grateful for her flat chest. She watched as he continued on his rounds, topping up people's drinks, never once missing an opportunity for one of his special back rubs.

'*Skitstövel,*' Stina whispered to herself. Always reverting to her native tongue when grappling for that extra-special insult.

She had become Stina Q at sixteen, dumping her given name on the say-so of a model agent who insisted that she *lose the Qvist*. It was the first of many changes which Kristina Qvist had had imposed on her during her career. Lanky, knock-kneed and with feet so large that the legend of Bigfoot had gifted a hated childhood nickname. '*Storfot*'. *Stina Storfot*. Towering above her peers, she was easy pickings for the bully boys and girls who delighted in tormenting her, most especially over her hair. No one knew what to do with the coils which her mother paddle-brushed into a halo of frizz; that hairdressers, more used to limp, straight tresses, would butcher. Then, as if to confirm the universe loves a joke, as puberty triggered yet another growth spurt, Stina was prescribed spectacles with thick lenses and ugly frames that didn't flatter her, purchased from a small-town optician who offered little choice.

Not only did Stina feel a freak in her community, but she also felt like one at home. She'd been adopted as a newborn, adding a further layer of complexity to her core belief that she was a misfit who didn't belong. And though there had never been any secret surrounding her start in life, it wouldn't have taken a rocket scientist to work out that her family weren't genetically related. Because while her parents might have been the sweetest couple in the province, they were also possibly the shortest. And the whitest. Like a pair of woodland sprites with skin so pale as to be almost translucent, and with eyelashes as white as their hair.

If Stina's mixed-race heritage wasn't enough for her to stand out in racially homogenous, rural Sweden, then growing to six foot guaranteed it. So no one had been more surprised than she was when, at fourteen, a model scout approached her during a school trip to Stockholm. The woman had spotted something extraordinary in this gawky teenager with badly ironed hair; her angular face a picture of bashfulness and acne; her gap-toothed smile hidden behind her hand.

All the idiosyncrasies that had brought Stina so much grief – the hair, the height, the teeth, even the massive feet – were seen as attributes by the scout who recognised in Stina that rarest of prizes: the catwalk/editorial crossover. She was soon signed up, despite her parents' misgivings and tears, and contracted into promises of life a million miles from the rural backwater that had been her childhood home. Word of Stina's good fortune divided her community into two camps: those who were full of envy, whose behaviour became even more hateful: and those who, bewitched by her upgraded status, wanted to be her best friend. She wasn't sure which was worse, and she was bright enough to recognise these as opposing cheeks of the same two-faced arse. This new-found popularity did nothing to alleviate her loneliness and isolation, and genuine attachments felt further from reach than ever. Overt racism burrowed below the surface, leaving the indignity of everyday micro-aggressions to endure. Focus was still directed on her appearance. No one valued her good nature or had any interest in her intellect. But for the most part they had, at least, stopped mocking her feet.

AN END GAME

★

While he hadn't the stomach for Tony's concern, Eddy felt it churlish to tell the one person on the planet who showed him compassion to eff off. He was under no illusions that, while he'd been hamstrung by disenchantment and chronic fatigue, it had been Tony who'd been running the office. The prospect of losing her was yet another worry to add to his festering heap of woes.

Tony's previous employment in the nursing home was ideal training for a job in the gorgeous industries. Eddy had clocked her during his visits to see Queenie. He'd admired Tony's work ethic and good humour, and reasoned that having wiped adult bottoms in the real world, she would be equipped to wipe them metaphorically at the sharp end of Pop.

'I'll give you double whatever you're earning here,' he'd said, arbitrarily picking a wage out of thin air.

'I'm earning fuck all.'

'Okay, I'll triple it.'

'Will there be a swivel chair?' Tony had asked.

'Consider it done.'

'Can I wear what I want?'

'We're very informal,' Eddy had said, mindful that Tony looked incongruous in her work tabard.

'And I'll need to bring me dog,' she'd said, on a roll.

Eddy had faltered for a second, trying to figure out the implications of having a dog in the office.

'He's dead friendly,' she'd added, as though fearing she'd gone too far.

'What sort is he?'

'A big daft thing. A rescue. Some sort of lurcher. Looks like he's been made out of pipe cleaners.'

'Fuck it. Why not.'

And so their cheerful negotiation had continued, with promises of petrol allowances, designated parking spaces and flexible hours.

He pressed the remote control on his key fob, and a shaft of sunlight flattened as the garage door lowered. A wave of anxiety crashed over him and he snapped the elastic band on his wrist. He took a long drag on his spliff and held the pungent smoke in his lungs, glumly ruminating on how exciting it had been before Howie traded credibility for celebrity. They'd been a right pair of chancers. Surviving on little more than mischief and ketchup sandwiches. Bluffing their way to success with brass neck and northern swagger.

But although the drift into mainstream pop had afforded middle-of-the-road success, any creative satisfaction had melted away as Howie migrated from John Peel to Dave Lee Travis, before finding a permanent home on *Steve Wright in the Afternoon*. Howie's later songs had failed to garner the critical acclaim of his early work, but his long-standing female fan base were reliable as bums on seats, and his back catalogue provided a decent income through occasional use in adverts, TV and films. But Eddy had found himself sidelined by Howie's money men: wily characters who struck deals in private members' clubs, and on golf courses and grouse moors. They'd invested Howie's wealth into offshore tax avoidance schemes – his money helping to fund the construction boom that had thrown up bland office blocks and identikit housing estates on brownfield sites across the north-west. Howie, seeing his wealth accumulate with little input or effort, had done nothing to counter it. He seemed happy to be the cash cow for the sycophants and Yes Men who'd burrowed their way into his life. Eddy had become the only person prepared to stand up to him. The only person in Howie's circle brave enough to say *no*. He knew it was an endgame.

BROTHERLY

There was no small talk among the women who'd cornered Stina, now voicing incredulity over Prince Harry's choice of wife.

'I give it six months,' said a trebly voiced woman, wearing a diamanté crucifix that drew the eye to her sun-damaged décolletage.

'Once she's had the sprog, she'll be off,' said another, a chipmunk-faced curtain twitcher, brandishing a bad attitude and a ham sandwich.

Stina's mind ran a mile a minute as she tried to process the subtext of this exchange. 'They seem to be very much in love,' she said, a little too loudly, with an out-of-character sharpness.

The women raised their drawn-on eyebrows. Their mean little cabal had clearly been stung by the pushback, and they moved away from her as one homogenous pack of ghastliness to seek out allies more accepting of their world-view. Stina trembled at the exchange, dizzy from these women targeting her, the only person of colour in the room. She clasped the edge of the table as she looked out of the back window, and tried to regain her composure. It had been a horrible couple of weeks. She welled up and a big fat tear escaped down her cheek. She brushed it away with the back of her hand. It bothered her that Eddy hadn't shown up. She'd always found his presence reassuring. He could manage Howie's moods in a way that she, his girlfriend of five years, could not. She hadn't known Howie and Eddy to fall out before. Not like this. Their relationship had often been boisterous and sparring, but always brotherly. Now they were barely speaking.

Stina glanced over at Viola, who was chattering away to Tony. They hadn't been formally introduced but Stina had already warmed to her, seeing how at ease she was with her daughter and how kind she was to the old dog. She'd clocked the tenderness Tony had shown Eddy at the crematorium and recognised the sincerity of her concern. Stina felt in desperate need of a friend in the room. Someone who wasn't going to touch her up or steer the conversation around to immigration. She caught Tony's eye.

'I'm going to the loo,' she mouthed.

Tony nodded and smiled, before turning her attention back to Viola. Stina was relieved to find someone she could entrust with Viola's care while she took a breather. Someone happy to play with the girl. Someone relaxed about engaging with her, in a way that Howie was not.

BOTTOMS UP

With a louche stoop, Howie returned to his armchair, Jean having policed it in his absence. Gordon stood over him, smelling of Imperial Leather, antibiotic cream and fetid scalp. He grinned broadly, a little flurry of dandruff fluttering from his head like a lightly shaken snow globe.

'Sherry, Neville?' he asked, waggling a bottle of Bristol Cream, his mouth full of crisps and bad dentistry, reflected in Howie's mirrored shades.

Howie took the whole bottle.

'Bottoms up,' Gordon said, winking. He trundled off, clinking his drinks trolley around the room.

IN THE DOGHOUSE

It mightn't have been obvious from his dishevelled appearance, but Eddy was a perfectionist at heart. It was this unbridled attention to detail that had, in no small way, helped propel Howie to success. But in recent months, even more so in recent days, his obsessiveness had turned sinister and inwards.

Sometimes, often in the early hours, when the quiet of the house amplified the racket in his head, when haunted by threats both real and imagined, Eddy's thoughts would turn to taking his own life. This process of rationalisation had at first tiptoed, then galloped, gaining traction as the scumbags of his psyche came out in force to cheer him on. These ruminations, once easily overridden by love for his family, had mutated into something twisted and malign. He took solace from the idea that he could jump ship at any time and, true to form, he'd meticulously schooled himself in the ins and outs of this grisly business. There wasn't an aspect of doing himself in with which he wasn't familiar. He could reel off famous and obscure deaths. And often did. Killing the mood in social settings.

Given the dismal state of their relationship, it hadn't been hard for Eddy to persuade himself that Una would consider his passing a stroke of luck. His parents were dead and his only sibling, a sister, lived a conservative life in Israel and would doubtless be relieved to have her embarrassment of a brother out of the way. He reasoned that his daughter, Joni – that beloved miracle baby who'd arrived late in his life and against the odds – would be better off without him. This mangled hypothesis was confirmed by her adolescent withdrawal. Her silence and the secrecy, her retreating to her room, proof of his redundancy. He dreaded his daughter's journey into adulthood and felt unqualified to navigate her through. And Howie? Well, Howie always fell on his feet. He probably had some other manager lined up. He felt certain a whispering campaign had destabilised his influence and that Howie had some Yes Person waiting in the wings.

Eddy tried to get a grip. He couldn't risk going indoors in such a state. Una had little enough patience with him at the best of times. But now, after what had happened, any concern she might once have harboured was as dead as a Hays Code kiss. He twanged his elastic band and attempted a breathing exercise to calm himself. But he couldn't remember the correct sequence and held his breath when he should have released it, hyperventilated, almost passed out and relit his spliff instead. It wasn't the first of the day. It wasn't even the first that afternoon. Or indeed since he'd parked up. He knew he'd been hammering it lately, but weed took the edge off the jitters. Unfortunately, it did nothing to combat the joylessness of his every waking minute. While his marriage had been floundering for as long as he could remember, this time things were different. He was well and truly in the doghouse. And deservedly so. He'd fucked any attempt at reconciliation with Una.

The shrill bell of his phone caused Eddy to start.

Una.

He stared at the screen and attempted to compose himself. But neither his spliff nor his elastic band were cutting it. He took a puff on his inhaler, and tried to sound casual and unruffled. But his voice was high-pitched, his nose bunged up. Like SpongeBob SquarePants with a nasty cold.

'Hiya.'

But it wasn't Una's familiar Irish accent that greeted him. It was Joni, using her mother's phone. Joni, named after Joni Mitchell. A smart kid. Twelve years old, but already sounding like a weary teenager; accustomed to navigating tensions in an unhappy household. She'd always been a deep-thinking, frowning child, and had inherited her father's body clock and her mother's cynicism. Her discovery of goth had perhaps been inevitable. Her hair was dyed as dark as school would allow it and her Lydia Deetz home-cut fringe perfectly set off her bring-on-the-apocalypse face.

'Mum wants to know where you are,' she said, her voice weighted with the burden of the go-between.

'I'm outside. Two minutes. Promise.'

But Joni said nothing. She'd become distracted. Her mother, in the background, was detailing something unfolding outside of their home –

some drama beyond the closed garage door. Eddy ended the call. He knew the game was up. All the confusion, the mess of the previous couple of weeks fell away as his options vaporised, leaving him with only one choice. Such clarity was a blessed relief. He switched on the engine. But the universe was determined to have the last laugh. The radio blasted into life with Howie fucking Howden dirging his way through the intro of 'Begin the Beguine'. The single was a lacklustre track off a phoning-it-in covers album, and Eddy had taken little professional pleasure from it making it onto the Radio 2 playlist.

'Fuck's sake,' he gasped, his hand reaching for his heart.

He jabbed the radio's off-switch. There was no more thinking to be done. The sound of the engine ticking over accompanied the sinister calm.

'I'm done here.'

Eddy lowered the window. Slowly the garage filled with fumes. He closed his one good eye, blew his nose properly for old time's sake, relaxed and laced his hands onto his lap. He was ready to embrace oblivion.

PART THREE

*

Mid-March, 2019

A THOUSAND SPEED BUMPS

✴

Two weeks earlier, word had come through of Queenie's hospitalisation. It shouldn't have come as a surprise to Eddy. Her frailty meant that even the smallest of accidents or ailments could domino into a medical emergency. But she was a tough old bird, who Eddy had believed would somehow go on forever. The news wrong-footed him. As he contemplated Howie's brief text, informing him that Queenie was dying, another pinged up.

WILL DO NORTON

Howie was publicising his Swing Classics album, *Call Me Unpredictable* – a toe-curling vanity project that Una had renamed, without even hearing it, *Call Me Feckin' Predictable*. The promotional tour was kicking off with an appearance on *The Graham Norton Show*, a high-profile gig to be followed by the usual round of fluff-piece newspaper interviews and tame daytime TV chats. Eddy was dreading it. He was normally expert in wriggling out of these things, the shine having long since worn off chaperoning Howie on promos. But on hearing the news of Queenie's bleak prognosis, he immediately, and without fully thinking it through, agreed to join him to ensure every last detail of his rider was fulfilled, from the Indian head massage to the bottle of 1999 Barolo.

The following morning, when the horrible realisation that he'd committed to accompanying Howie had sunk in, Eddy had lain curled in bed, the duvet pulled over his head. He hadn't slept for more than fifteen minutes, but erratic sleeping was nothing new. It was the reason he'd abandoned the marital bed. Una was a light sleeper and early riser; he was an insomniac with acid reflux. So between him waking her when coming to bed late, and her waking him when she got up early, it made sense for them to sleep apart. This lack of intimacy appeared to suit Una. It certainly suited the dog.

During one of many attempts to win over his wife, Eddy had agreed to them getting a puppy. And so it was that Chakakhan – named for her ability to hold a note – had come into their lives. She was a rescue Chihuahua with a pitiful history – two kilograms of unhinged malevolence. From day one, Una had been devoted to the animal and was rarely seen without her pop-eyed gremlin with its puppy-farmed overbite in a papoose slung around her chest. Maybe it was pre-homing abuse that could explain the aggression this tiny creature directed towards men and towards Eddy in particular. But in private and in therapy, Eddy wondered if the dog was acting out Una's subconscious desire to keep him at arm's length. Could Chakakhan be a canine manifestation of Una's hostility? The dog's misandry evidence of man-hating lurking beneath the surface in his wife? It was true that Eddy had been allowed only stolen kisses since Chakakhan came into their lives. His anti-social hours and Una's snappy-toothed breast plate had impacted greatly on their sex life, and rare moments of intimacy had been conducted to the furious yodelling of Una's cuckolded dog-baby locked outside their bedroom door.

Eddy pulled himself up in an attempt to ease the discomfort in his chest. He felt as though he was breathing through a straw. He scratted about among the detritus piled on his bedside table for his asthma inhaler, knocking paperbacks, pens and an open bottle of Gaviscon onto the floor, the pink gloop glugging onto the carpet unchecked. His sty of a bedroom smelled like a stale bread bin. He hadn't changed his bedding in an age and the once-crisp bottom sheet had become discoloured and baggy. He shook his inhaler and breathed out. *Perhaps it's lung cancer?* he thought. That particular worry had perturbed him for at least thirty-five of the forty years he'd been smoking pot. He pressed the top of the canister and sucked in the meds. Eddy may have been actively suicidal, but it turned out that fostering a death wish did nothing to ameliorate his hypochondria. A Google search down a doom-and-gloomy rabbit hole of symptoms and prognoses, only heightened his concerns. But this discomfort in his chest wasn't something antacids or inhalers could fix. This was heartache of the romantic kind.

Over the years, as Una had become increasingly taciturn and hard to read, Eddy had wondered if she was seeing someone else. But, afraid of the answer, he'd been too fearful to confront her. He knew once that particular genie had been let out of the bottle he'd never be able to stuff it back in. His paranoia led to some low-level stalking and he'd sneaked a look at her texts, but they'd thrown up no clues. He'd once tried to follow her car, but his driving was erratic at the best of times and he was way too distracted to keep his eye on both her and the road. He'd ended up in a bus lane, none the wiser about Una's imagined infidelity and sixty quid worse off in fines. He thought couples' therapy might help, but he'd ended up going to sessions alone. He wondered whether she needed space and tried keeping his distance, but she seemed visibly cheered to have him out the way. This served only to fuel his neediness. But there was no comfort to be found in the arms of a woman so prickly you could've planted her in the garden as a blackthorn hedge.

While living in this toxic state of affairs was hellish, there were transient moments of clarity, when Eddy dared peek at life as a single man. He would get a cat, he thought. They made him wheezy, but he didn't care. He just wanted something to hug. Sometimes, when a therapy session had gone well or when the SSRIs fleetingly kicked in, he'd imagine life with a new partner. One with softer edges. A little less brittle. In rare, but wildly optimistic moments, he even dared believe he might have a functioning sex life again. But these glimpses of a brighter world were short-lived. His stomach would turn to water at the prospect of losing Una and becoming a part-time dad to Joni. He'd even miss that effing dog.

Eddy forced himself to get up and open the window to inject some air into the room. His small overnight bag lay open but unpacked on the floor. He gazed out at the cherry blossom fluttering to the ground in the breeze. The garden was lovely but, daffodils aside, he couldn't identify a single plant in it. He'd had nothing to do with its creation, bar settling the inflated invoice of a local landscaping firm. This gentrified Manchester suburb – too hip for footballers, too bohemian for corporates, but popular with fashionable creatives – provided easy pickings for those looking to profit from the Chorlton-cum-Hardy glitterati. Eddy knew he'd been ripped off – it happened a lot once people discovered he worked in the music business – but he'd settled the bill without argument. He hadn't the stomach for a fight. *Good luck to them*, he'd thought, and chalked up the piss-take to experience, while making a mental note never to use the firm again. A lone magpie rattled across the garden. Eddy, always susceptible to signs and omens, made a *puh puh puh* spitting sound. An OCD tic picked up from his parents in their attempts to ward off the evil eye.

His phone pinged. It was Tony, texting to remind him to remember his train tickets. She knew when to nudge him and he appreciated these gentle prompts. But the prospect of a day and evening spent in Howie's company, knowing he'd want to hit the town after recording the show, stretched out in front of him like a thousand speed bumps. A wave of melancholy swelled around him. He peered down to the patio, trying to fathom if the drop onto the stone slabs would be enough to end it all. It was unlikely. He'd read a grisly account about femurs telescoping though pelvises and concluded that winding up a depressed paraplegic would be just his fucking luck. It wasn't the first time Eddy had considered jumping. He'd even done a recce of a multi-storey car park, but it had looked too brutal. He didn't want to be splattered on the pavement next to the smokers and vapers outside a Wetherspoons. For his pulped remains to become some viral internet sensation. Beachy Head had offered a more romantic option. He could make a day of it. The thought of a holiday-suicide combo got him thinking about going the whole iconic Lover's Leap hog. Of travelling to the USA and chucking himself off the Golden Gate Bridge. But ultimately, his vertigo had put an end to such scenarios. Not being able to jump to his death because he had a fear of heights was much the same as ruling out slitting his wrists on the grounds that it would hurt. Because while the prevailing opinion may be that suicide is a coward's way out, Eddy had come to the opposite conclusion – that topping himself would take bottle.

PIPE DREAMS

There was no love lost between Una and Queenie. Una's suspicion that Queenie harboured anti-Irish sentiments was a reasonable assumption, given her poisonous world-view. Yet the prospect of her death and subsequent funeral loomed large. Una knew Eddy would want her to accompany him, but her loathing of Howie couldn't be overridden by social niceties. Being in the same room as him was unthinkable. She was aware that her animosity made life awkward for Eddy, but she wasn't cut out to play the dutiful wife. She was a hair's breadth from lashing out at Howie and couldn't trust herself not to. Not even at a funeral. She knew this antipathy wound Eddy up. It was a great bone of contention between them, and Eddy often reminded her it was Howie who cash-flowed their lives. But that wasn't how Una saw it. As far as she was concerned, Eddy had earned every last penny working for that bastard. Una had seen the work he'd put into strategising Howie's career; how he'd micromanaged every twist and turn, how he'd delegated work to other people, only to double-check they'd done it, then do it all over again himself. She knew the toll this had taken on both their relationship and his mental health.

'No one gets to the top by themselves,' she'd argued, during one of their many spats on the subject. 'Even Bowie had help, whatever your man might think.'

'Leave Bowie out of this,' Eddy had said, sitting at the kitchen table, finishing off a bowl of breakfast cereal at two in the afternoon.

Una knew she was dangerously close to stepping over a line by taking a pop at one of Eddy's heroes, but she was furious enough not to give a shit. She'd been loading the dishwasher at the time and was paying little heed to the crockery that she was chucking in. The clatter of plates echoed her rage.

'I mean it. He hadn't a pot to piss in when Angie styled him, it was Ronson's missus who came up with the haircut and his manager bankrolled him when he was skint.'

'So what? It was all about Bowie's talent.'

'Yeah, but take away their contribution and instead of Ziggy Stardust you've got some bloke with pipe dreams and bills.'

'Bollocks,' Eddy said, holding out his empty bowl.

'It's not bollocks,' she replied, snatching it from his hand and throwing it into the dishwasher with such force that she may as well have been at a Greek wedding. 'He had brilliant people styling him and supporting him, sticking their hands in their pockets. Most people don't have that.'

'So you're saying if he hadn't had a great haircut, he'd have ended up a greengrocer or something?'

Una leaned back against a kitchen unit and rubbed her temples.

'What I'm saying,' she said, slowly, as though English wasn't Eddy's first language, 'is he was lucky to have those people, on his side, at that stage of his career.'

Eddy drew breath, about to say something.

'Don't you dare tell me that people make their own luck,' Una jumped in, before he could say anything.

He clamped his mouth shut.

'Talent doesn't always rise to the top,' she continued. 'That's what gobshites with charmed lives want people to believe, to keep up the con. You'd think good fortune would make these feckers humble and generous, but it never does. It makes them mean. They can't wait to pull the ladder up behind them. They won't give anyone a leg up, because half the fun is feeling like they're on top. Thinking they're winners in a world full of losers gives them the horn. Smug pricks, showing off their swimming pools in feckin' *Hello* magazine...'

'Bowie never did *Hello*.'

'I'm not talking Bowie, you clown! I'm talking about arseholes like Howie. They don't give a bald bollock about the talent that slips through the net. They blame them. They think it must have been their own stupid fault.'

'Bowie was always destined for success.'

'That's fairy-tale shite peddled by feckers who've done all right for themselves. The world's littered with wasted talent, Eddy. What about all the Bowies we never got to hear, because there was no one rooting for them? Who didn't have people like you, worrying everything into place, twenty-four hours a day, seven days a week?'

'They're all working as greengrocers, if we follow your logic.'

'They're everywhere, Eddy. Serving us in cafés, cold-calling us, teaching our kids, driving our buses, wiping our arses...'

Eddy looked like a baffled owl, but he knew better than to say anything while Una was in full flow.

'It does my head in. All those Ziggy Stardusts just left to rot.'

'There was only one Ziggy Stardust, Una.'

'Fucking hell, Eddy. Never mind The Man Who Fell to Earth. Bowie should have written a song about you, the man who missed the point.'

Una kneed the dishwasher door shut, and the crockery and cutlery clattered inside. Chakakhan hopped backwards as she barked at Eddy.

'What is your point?' Eddy said, with one eye on the dog.

'My point is, had it not been for those people who championed him, Bowie would have been a one-hit wonder with a bad perm.'

Eddy and Una hadn't spoken for days afterwards, and Bowie was added to an increasingly long list of subjects that were off limits. But had Eddy been a little less stoned and a little more aware of his wife's thwarted ambitions, he might have realised the bitter exchange hadn't been about Ziggy Stardust at all, but rather Una's own wasted talent. Because, despite their comfortable lifestyle, Una's dreams and ambitions had withered to nothing over the years. She'd given up on her acting career, despite industry excitement over early promise. Maybe she hadn't had the best representation to steer her forward or, perhaps, being Irish had unnerved the executives who preferred their talent more winsome English rose. Or was it because once she'd hit her thirties there hadn't been so many parts for women, and by the time she'd reached her forties there'd been hardly any at all? Whatever it was that had caused her career to flounder, once baby Joni came along, nobody noticed her throwing in the towel. But it quietly saddened her that her career had come to nothing and she was financially dependent on her husband. And, unlike with Eddy, there had never been value placed on her talents or her time.

Some of this was ticking over in Una's head as she checked out at the supermarket, her noise-cancelling earbuds helping drown out the bleeps from the barcode reader and the chatter of her fellow man. She spent a lot of time ruminating. Eddy had said her silences unsettled him. But Una's skeletons, stuffed away at the back of closets, revealed themselves only in her brooding and downbeat appearance. Middle age had rendered her invisible to young people and the opposite sex. But that was no hardship. She preferred it that way.

Once she'd cleared away the crockery and plastic packaging from a previous customer, Una sat by the café window, with a too-bitter coffee, under LED lighting and a small cloud of gloom. There was nothing about her that suggested a life lived on the periphery of showbiz. The dark glasses she sometimes wore indoors were to stave off migraines, her cropped no-nonsense wash-and-go hairstyle was silver at the temples, her slight frame obscured by baggy sweatpants and an oversized top. If she went into the sun, her hair would lighten and her face would break out in freckles, but her pale skin suggested she was happier indoors.

Una gazed out at her car, strategically parked so that she could check on Chakakhan. Their unremarkable estate had been chosen solely for its dog-crate-sized boot space. They'd been a one-car family ever since Eddy wrote off his Honda by rear-ending a static caravan. Una was afraid that the dog might be stolen if she dropped her guard – an unlikely scenario, given the yapping and snarling issuing from the vehicle.

She thought about Eddy. That morning, dropping him at the station, she'd hesitated when he'd leaned over to peck her on the cheek. His breath had been acrid from skipping breakfast and not having cleaned his teeth, and Chakakhan, crated at the back, had gone berserk at the suggestion of intimacy between them. Una had pulled away, and clearly – by the look on Eddy's face – had wounded his feelings.

'Mind yourself,' she'd said, as he got out of the car.

But he hadn't responded and had taken off without eye contact. She'd watched as he joined the throng. He was a weary presence, in amongst the hurry and excitement of the other travellers, more stooped than she'd realised. The first male in his family to reach 5'10", but seeming diminished. Una had wanted to run to him. He looked so vulnerable, jostled slightly on the escalator by a young person with a backpack almost as big as themselves. But it would have taken too long to find somewhere to park and already the queue behind her was impatient for her drop-off space. So, Una had driven away, troubled by a sense of foreboding and the all-too-familiar feeling of having fucked things up again.

SHE HAD A PLAN

✴

Tony's previous employment in the dementia wing of a nursing home may have had its challenges, but it was kids' stuff compared with the day-to-day tap dance she had to do around Howie's ego and Eddy's mental health. And though it wasn't what she'd planned when graduating with a master's in music, it was an interesting stopgap while she figured out how to realise her quiet ambition of winning a place in the horn section of an orchestra. But mostly she enjoyed being, for the first time in her life, on the inside of a tent pissing out. She was on good wages and had become, by default, her own boss. Eddy's hours were erratic. He rarely showed up before midday and that was if he showed up at all. It was a perfect arrangement, as far as Tony was concerned, especially as it meant she no longer had to sleep in her car. Because five and a half months previously, a calamitous chain of events had rendered her homeless. No zero-hours contract in the care sector was ever going to dig her out of that hole. So, squatting an office, in a converted mill in the old garment district of Manchester, was a no-brainer for this twentysomething, who was two years out of college and up to her eyeballs in debt. She had few possessions beyond a library card, a large dog and a dented tuba. Her knackered Ford Escort, with 200,000 miles on the clock, was almost the same age as herself.

Although too inhibited by her slight disability to enjoy the basement gym, Tony took advantage of the showers during the week; a stand-up wash in the third-floor toilets sufficing when the gym was closed at weekends. There was a small fridge and microwave in the office, and a communal rooftop garden. When Tony couldn't be bothered driving to the launderette, she'd wring out her undies in the sink. Her tuba in its case was covered in a throw and semi-camouflaged behind a Swiss cheese plant. Everything else was either in her car, behind the sofa or in a holdall ferreted away beneath her vast desk. The same desk behind which she sat on her Herman Miller swivel chair, working long long hours, breaking off only to read library books, or to watch tuba solos or ethical porn on the MacBook

Eddy had presented her with on her first day at work. She'd recoiled from the offering, clueless how to accept it. Wondering what the catch was, her mind blown when she realised there was none. Each night she'd burrow down in a roll-out sleeping bag on the huge, squidgy sofa that doubled as her bed with Fazakerley, her grateful rescue dog, plastered alongside. His being passed around student homes in Fallowfield, then left tied to the railings of a vacated house at the end of a summer term, had created an attachment to Tony she found absent in the human realm. Eddy was too preoccupied and off the ball to suspect anything, and either the security guards hadn't noticed her working day was unusually long or were turning a blind eye to someone who took the trouble to remember their names.

Tony saw it as a temporary arrangement. But her credit rating was shot, rents were prohibitive and being a dog owner narrowed the field considerably. Even so, she had a plan. Living in the office meant she had zero overheads. She was funnelling every spare penny of her earnings into ridding herself of debt. For the first time in her adult life, she had some prospect of her gaining control of her finances. All she had to do was keep her head down and keep the job. Perhaps she could have found somewhere to live if she'd been willing to share, but she'd learned the hard way that the only thing worse than sharing with strangers was sharing with friends. And while her current set-up wasn't ideal, all it took was a sobering dog walk into town, where wretched human flotsam was washed up into doorways, to snap her out of self-pity.

'Don't forget your tickets,' Tony said on the morning of Eddy's London trip. She'd tried to persuade him to have them delivered digitally to his phone, but his argument was that he was just as likely to lose his phone as he was to lose printed tickets. Perhaps more so. Tony accepted he had a point.

'Oh, shit. Thanks,' he said.

She could hear he was breathless, but Tony put it down to his age. He felt ancient to her. Perhaps breathlessness was to be expected at sixty-three. His stories of the seventies; of three-day weeks, telephone party lines and bell-bottom flares, felt as distant as the Gunpowder Plot or the sealing of the Magna Carta. She didn't know anyone else as old as him. Even her own parents were younger, and she hadn't seen them for years. But despite the age gap between herself and Eddy, they had the kind of easy relationship she had failed to accomplish with her peers.

'You sound knackered,' she said.

'I didn't sleep well. It's okay. I'll have a kip on the train.'

'Well if you need anything, call. I'm going to have me haircut, but I won't be long.'

Keeping her hair immaculate was one of the few indulgences Tony allowed herself. Once a month she went to a Turkish barbers, where she could get her pompadour undercut made super-sharp for a tenner.

'I'll take me phone,' she said.

'Tony, it's fine. Take as much time as you want. Seriously.'

It would be easy for Tony to take advantage of Eddy's relaxed approach to her work day, but she had no intention of taking the piss while her boss was out of town. She wasn't wired that way. Not even on her birthday.

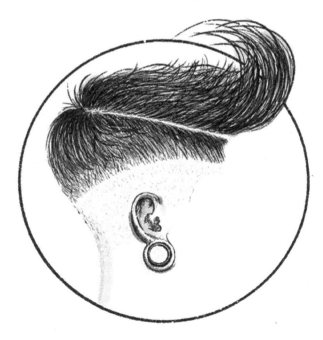

JUST IN CASE

★

Eddy discovered the ecstasy pill while checking he had his wallet – a neurotic tic that saw him patting his jacket pockets at least once every fifteen minutes, despite being sat on the train. He couldn't remember how old it was or even if it had been through a cycle at the dry cleaners, but the prospect of spending an evening in the company of Howie, of being subjected to his post-TV adrenaline rush would be unendurable without some form of narcotic. It wasn't Eddy's drug of choice. It wasn't the gloom of the comedown that bothered him – gloom was business as usual – but he was mindful of a ruined city break, a supposedly romantic weekend with Una in Verona, on which he'd necked 100 milligrams of MDMA in the hope of introducing a little *amore* into their flagging sex life. Instead, it had kicked off a particularly nasty flare-up of his IBS and he'd spent the entire two days twatted and bloated, shitting for England in the en suite.

Eddy looked up from the book he was finding impossible to concentrate on and glanced around the carriage. His fellow first-class passengers were the usual smug bunch – mostly loud talkers, puffed up with the promise of extra leg room, complimentary trolley snacks and a cast-iron guarantee of separation from the hoi polloi by a strategically placed buffet car. He offered his empty cup to a passing steward, who poured him a drink from a large thermos jug and handed him a packet of three Digestive biscuits. The tea was stewed and had the peculiar burnt tang of yesterday's coffee so familiar to the train travelling elite. The steward moved on and Eddy caught the eye of the passenger opposite.

'It's hardly the Orient Express, is it?' he said, to the well-groomed middle-aged woman with coral lipstick and matching nails.

She flashed him a look that suggested she wasn't joining in, pushed her reading glasses up her nose and returned to her broadsheet newspaper. Eddy's toes curled in his shoes. He looked at his hands, at his horribly chewed-off fingernails, and had an unwelcome flash of insight into how he must appear to his fellow passengers. He was in dire need of a haircut and, despite a cursory wipe with a wet flannel, he hadn't bothered to clean his teeth or shave. Down the front of his jumper – stretched a little snugly over his let-himself-go paunch – were spliff burns and the rubbed-out dribble from a long-since-eaten soft boiled egg. His waxed Belstaff jacket would have looked the business on anyone else, but Eddy looked as though he'd slept in a bin. He'd made the woman opposite uncomfortable and it embarrassed him. Eddy felt the unwelcome flutterings of a panic attack but was mindful to not freak out coral-lipstick lady with his breathing exercises. He discreetly twanged his elastic band and pretended to read *The Siege of Stalingrad*, while tearing a corner from a page and wrapping the pill, embossed with the beaky-faced grin of Daffy Duck. He secreted it away in his pocket. For later. Just in case.

MEREDITH PRUITT

Tony recognised her immediately from the walk. She had a lightness of foot that gave the impression of being carried along by a helium balloon; that she might, at any second, leave the ground and float away. It was so different from Tony's heavy, lopsided lollop, and one of the many things she'd found attractive about her.

'Meredith Pruitt,' she said, barely perceptibly, but just loud enough for Fazakerley's ears to twitch at the whispered name of a once-adored human.

Tony stood back a little from the office window, studying every detail of her ex-girlfriend's demeanour and vivid, deranged wardrobe. In happier times, Tony had adored Meredith's whimsical style, but now, emotionally distanced at the third-floor window, it occurred to her that Meredith looked like she'd mugged a five-year-old. Her neon green tulle skirt, billowing in the spring breeze, revealed knee-length striped socks and scuzzy white trainers. An oversized baby-blue teddy fur bomber jacket hung off her shoulders, along with a child-sized bumblebee backpack. Tony noted her hair colour had changed again, this time to an ice-blonde, and was held back from her face with a Mickey Mouse-eared headband. Meredith was gazing at the old mill conversion, almost to the spot where Tony was watching with a mouthful of cherry Bakewell she was unable to swallow. She ducked back. This was the first time she'd clapped eyes on Meredith since she'd walked out on her five and a half months ago.

Tony Dunn and Meredith Pruitt had become a couple when a mutual love of good causes and flesh had thrown them together at a burlesque charity fundraiser. They had little background in common. Tony had been bounced around the Merseyside care system, whereas Meredith was very much a Home Counties daddy's girl. It had been a whirlwind romance, but there had been no question in Tony's mind that, in Meredith, she'd found the love of her life. Within days of their meeting, Meredith had moved herself into Tony's spartan room in a grotty Fallowfield houseshare, bringing with her a mountain of frou-frou, sparkle and fairy lights. And so began an intense, if short-lived, skew-whiff love affair.

Meredith was untroubled by the kind of insecurities a childhood of upheaval had hard-wired into Tony, and Tony's deep-seated belief she wasn't good enough for her girlfriend distorted the dynamic of their relationship from the start. Short and curvy, with a hearty laugh that broadcast to the world how at ease she was in the space she inhabited, Meredith was quite the Bambi-eyed beauty. Unlike Tony, who had learned to be wary, to ruffle no feathers, to tread lightly – which was ironic, given her uneven gait. A badly healed growth-plate fracture had left her with a pronounced limp, a lifelong souvenir of the parental neglect that had seen her fetch up in the care system as a mute child.

Though unnerved by the volume of Meredith's tat, Tony absorbed all of the frippery into her north-facing back bedroom. Her monastic cell was instantaneously reimagined into a Hello Kitty-Dodge City bordello mash-up. Meredith bulldozed over all of Tony's carefully constructed boundaries – her austere decor, neatness and routines all evidence of those institutionalised, formative years. But Tony's accommodating of this madcap intrusion into her space suited Meredith, who wasn't used to negotiating her way through life and had none of Tony's need to please. Tony's every waking moment was spent counting her blessings, that she'd found herself with this cutie. By contrast Meredith, having been treasured her entire life, took Tony's adoration for granted and felt under no obligation to pull her weight emotionally, financially or on the domestic front. She'd enjoyed all of the safety nets of a doting, well-off family and, unlike Tony with her long hours at the nursing home, she could afford to be laid-back when it came to earning a living. It was a privilege that spilled over into a feeble work ethic and a hit-and-miss track record of contributing to rent. But despite investing wholeheartedly in a fairytale future, Tony knew, on that day five and a half months ago, as she'd stepped over a pair of tennis socks discarded on the stairs, that it was over.

It had been five and a half months since Tony had walked in on Meredith in bed with their housemate. Five and a half months since she'd heard the full-blast music and the joyous whoops from the two women on the other side of the bedroom door. Five and a half months since she'd opened the door to the sweet-sour hit of jasmine bath bombs and groin sweat. Five and a half months since she'd walked in on Meredith, bellowing along to '*Shape of You*' – off-key, but with gusto – her arms outstretched in the Glastonbury sway, revealing bright blue armpit hair and scant consideration for the neighbours. Five and a half months since she'd witnessed her lover, naked except for a pair of Halloween head boppers, grinding her foof on the face of that second-year sports science student. Five and a half months since she'd watched, paralysed and rooted to the spot, as the pumpkins on springs boinged about Meredith's peony-pink hair in perfect synchronicity with her bouncing bosoms. Five and a half months since Tony had been confronted by the stark-naked, super-toned body of that housemate – a so-called friend – with her muscular legs spread gymnastically wide, showcasing a Harry Potter tattoo and a completely hairless front bottom, her face now squished under Meredith's flange. Five and a half months since Tony knew, as Fazakerley barked at the din of her screaming and Ed Sheeran's *oh-i-ing*, that all was irreparably lost. Their relationship couldn't survive this snapshot of Meredith's exuberant betrayal, of being cheated on in glorious X-rated Technicolour. It had been five and a half months since Tony fled with her library books, tuba and dog – wretched and instantly homeless – to sleep in her car in the suburban back roads of Prestwich and Whitefield, moving on each time the Neighbourhood Watchers got wind of the battered old Ford Escort blighting their leafy streets.

There'd been no communication between them since. Tony had ditched her old number after Meredith sent a text, using Tony's shift work at the nursing home to justify her infidelity. Tony's new SIM card was as empty as her love life. She hadn't heard one word about Meredith, having withdrawn from their wider social circle, a deliberate knee-jerk act of self-preservation. Tony had been crushed by Meredith's duplicity, but during that five and a half months she'd made a pretty good fist of piecing together some semblance of a life. She may have been grieving for her aspirations of the settled domesticity denied to her growing up but, conversely, her screwed-up background had instilled in her a resourcefulness that had helped her survive those first few wretched weeks. The devastation had felt familiar and strangely comforting. She was accustomed to being let down by humans, and her trust issues had turned out to be spot on. She was in no hurry to re-engage with her self-obsessed peers. She was better off sharing her life with her dog. So, her expectations had been low when Eddy, her shambolic angel, bailed into her life. He'd rescued her. Because although the office wasn't exactly a room of one's own, it was at least a roof over one's head.

All of this was now flying out of the very window she was peering from. She had hoped never to hear Meredith Pruitt's name or see her face again. Yet, there she was in the street below, in that off-the-beaten-track part of Ancoats, swanning up and down the pavement, 'like she bleedin' owns the place,' Tony said to Fazakerley.

The dog rested his chin on his front paws, and looked at her, showing the whites of his eyes, vigilant to this change in her mood.

Meredith turned her back to the building. She tilted her head, one hand flicking her hair over, her other arm held out in front of her, taking what Tony thought could well be her millionth selfie. Tony ducked back from the window, indignant at this encroaching on her turf. Her stomach did somersaults at the unwelcome arrival of her ex back in her orbit. She leaned forward to take another look. But Meredith had gone.

FUCK IT

Howie hadn't appreciated being bumped off the top spot on *The Graham Norton Show* – the music interlude going instead to an unexpectedly available Harry Styles. So, as Eddy sat in the green room, chewing his nails, watching the interview streamed live, the best he could hope for was that Howie wouldn't be the object of playful teasing. All hope died when Miriam Margolyes came out and made a beeline for him, ruffling his carefully coiffed hair. Eddy rummaged in his pocket and found the pill he'd secreted on the train.

'Fuck it,' he said, throwing it into his mouth and swigging it down with glugs of Howie's 1999 Barolo.

ONE OF HER HEADACHES

✴

Una was having one of her headaches. A real blinder. Perhaps it had been the bitter supermarket coffee. Or perhaps it had been the stress of another trying day. Either way, she needed to lie down, in the hope of easing the tension she held permanently in her neck.

It felt neglectful to go to bed before Joni but, with Chakakhan under her arm, Una groped her way upstairs in the dark, faltering at her daughter's bedroom door, aware the days of simply walking in were over. She knocked and waited for a response.

'What?'

Una despaired at Joni's new-found talent to make one simple word sound like a complaint. She poked her head in, apologising for having to go to bed so early. But Joni didn't seem especially fussed about her mother's predicament, or in any hurry to help out.

'Kay,' she said, from high on her platform bed. She was almost invisible, save for the glow of her laptop.

It seemed Joni could barely be bothered to form complete words these days, let alone sentences. And not for the first time Una wondered where her baby had gone. The funny kid who'd skipped everywhere had been replaced by this secretive, surly interloper who stomped and banged doors and confided in friends instead of her mother. This new distance distressed Una. But her neediness seemed only to ramp up Joni's determination to keep her mum at arm's length. She increasingly felt like a spare part, whose only discernible use was as a provider of goods and services. She knew this was irrational, that she'd probably been every bit as charmless herself at Joni's age, but none of this changed the fact she grieved the loss of something she knew was impossible to preserve. She shut Joni's bedroom door and, in need of a little unconditional love, gave Chakakhan a kiss on the head before gently letting her onto the floor. The dog knew the drill and trotted off to Una's bedroom to take her place on what, once upon a time, had been Eddy's side of the bed.

THE DUMPLINGS

✱

By the time Eddy and Howie settled at their table at The Jambhalabar – a velvet-rope nightclub a stone's throw from the Strand – Howie's sulk, sustained by alcohol and cocaine, had bedded in for the evening. He'd been itching to get away from the TV studios, giving the slip to the half-dozen female fans hanging around the exit. Eddy, on the other hand, his oxytocin levels on the up, had kept the car waiting and taken time out to engage with the bunch of jolly fiftysomethings – fans who'd grown up with Howie and who were thrilled to have this impromptu attention from someone, anyone, in his entourage. They were a small selection of the usual faces: Angela with the dimples and the husband in the nick; Julie from Brum with the flat-ironed hair; the Two Sues; Death-Stare-Maureen; and bubbly little Cheryl who had special status in the group, having shagged Howie back in the eighties. Just the once, but with the private shame of herpes to prove it.

The venue was a regular haunt of Howie's. A place in which, as a favoured investor and VIP, he was guaranteed priority service. The high-backed, deep-buttoned banquette at the back of the room was his preferred spot. It gave him a discreet but clear view of the comings and goings, while Eddy, sitting opposite, shielded him from inquisitive diners. Eddy didn't like to eat this late as a rule, but the ecstasy had left him unusually sanguine about rich food and acid reflux. He was rolling. Any residue of bleakness and fatigue had dissolved in the cab on the way over. He looked around the room, studying his surroundings. He'd been to the restaurant before, but never fully appreciated the sumptuous Buddhist temple decor, as though imagined through Widow Twankey's knicker drawer. He felt a rare sense of achievement.

'We've come a long way.'

Howie looked at him. It wasn't like Eddy to be so upbeat, so self-congratulatory.

'Yeah man, toadally,' he said. 'It's a step up from cider and hashish in

Hulme.'

Eddy felt a surge of affection and leant over and squeezed his arm.

'They were the best of times.'

Howie pulled away and Eddy sat back in his chair, still staring, still grinning. He took a puff on his inhaler. Proximity to his client often caused his chest to tighten, something he put down to the residual dander from Howie's three Norwegian Forest cats – and not, as Una had once speculated, because Howie was as noxious as leaking landfill.

'You're very loved. I hope you know that,' Eddy said.

Howie signalled to a female server that he was ready to order.

'Oh,' Eddy rummaged in his pocket. 'I forgot. One of the Sues made you something.'

Eddy pulled out a pebble, primitively painted with the message *HOWIE ROCKS* in childlike, primary colours. He placed it in front of him.

'And what am I supposed to do with that?' Howie said, pushing it back across the table.

'It's a play on words,' Eddy said, giving it a little pecked kiss before putting it in his pocket. 'A lot of work's gone into it.'

Howie studied this curiously loved-up stranger. 'Why do you even talk to them?'

'Who?'

'The Dumplings.'

'Oh mate, they're harmless.'

'To you maybe. They fucking haunt me.'

Eddy screwed up his eyes and contemplated this for a second or two. Then, unable to counter the effects of his cheeky little truth drug a moment longer, he asked, 'On a scale of one to Morrissey, just how determined are you to alienate your fanbase?'

Howie jutted his jaw and locked eyes with Eddy. 'Excuse me?'

'Mate, they just wanted selfies. Five minutes out of your life. That's all it would have taken. Harry Styles managed it, and he had dozens...'

The female server Howie'd called over had been at his side in a beat and, without consulting his dining partner, he placed their order.

'The Dungeness Crab. Twice.'

Howie sniffed loudly as he watched the young woman walk away. His eyes lingered on her backside, shimmering in a kingfisher-blue cheongsam. He turned back to Eddy.

'I don't want them at gigs.'

Eddy was caught up in the moment, not fully engaged, having tuned into the background music. 'Who? Waitresses?'

'The fucking Dumplings. Every gig, every telly, there they are. The same fucking faces leering up from the front row. Every. FUCKING. Time,' he said, the word *fucking* cutting through the babble of the room.

Diners turned, surprised by the raised voice. Eddy closed his eyes, clicked his fingers and swayed along to a Nitin Sawhney track, miming to words he didn't know.

'Their devotion is the most beautiful thing.' Eddy opened his eyes and outstretched his arms towards Howie. 'Embrace it.'

'It's alright for you. You don't have to look at them.'

Eddy assumed the appearance of someone mulling this over, and adopted his best pretending-to-think face. But his mind had floated off elsewhere. Somewhere less unkind. Somewhere where Dumplings get their selfies and Howie gives them the time of day. Howie looked across at the waiting staff, with their identikit long blonde hair and their figure-hugging culturally appropriated uniforms. He turned back to Eddy. 'Jagger wouldn't put up with it.'

Eddy sighed. 'They turn up of their own volition. At their own expense. You can't ban them.'

'They make me look bad.'

Eddy leaned forward, beckoning Howie towards him and whispered, 'Be careful what you wish for. Colonel Gaddafi surrounded himself with beauties and he ended up buggered with a penknife.'

Howie slapped the table, causing the cutlery to bounce. 'Sort it out, Eddy.'

And with that the DJ turned up the music, flipping the vibe from the hum of evening to the throb of late night. In normal circumstances, Eddy would have gone back to his hotel to bite his nails and stare into the abyss. Instead, the two men sat in silence. Howie scanned the club while Eddy twiddled with this cutlery, attempting to stifle an urge to cha-cha-cha onto the dancefloor.

THE EXACT MOMENT

★

While lying in bed, waiting for the pain meds to kick in, it occurred to Una that she hadn't heard from Eddy since she'd dropped him at the station that morning. Though the days of them being in almost continual contact had long since given way to something more perfunctory, it was unusual for Eddy not to touch base. She lay still, the dreaming dog squeaking and twitching on the pillow beside her, and tried to pinpoint the exact moment her marriage had died. Had there been a particular day on which it could have been saved, if either of them had the inclination to do something about it? Or perhaps things had been disintegrating for years?

Una knew neither of them had been particularly attentive to the other's needs. Both had been too quick to take the hump. Simmering resentments had eroded something that had once been relaxed and playful. There'd been no shock betrayal, just a shift in priorities when Joni was born. Eddy's 3am jetlagged clattering in the kitchen, his too-loud music, his mile-a-minute babble and bullshit phone calls had been incompatible with new parenthood. She wondered how other people managed it. She knew couples who'd become closer when they'd had children. It had consolidated them as a family. Maybe it'd had something to do with her struggle to get pregnant and then to stay pregnant. The quiet carnage of miscarriages. They'd both been unable to articulate how awful these losses were to those friends who appeared to fire out babies like targets at a clay pigeon shoot. In the end it had been an unremarkable, early morning fumble that had culminated in Una becoming a first-time mum at forty-two, and Eddy a first-time dad at fifty. And if, as it had turned out, Una and Eddy found it hard to relax into parenthood, it had no impact on their capacity to love their unexpected gift of a daughter. So why, she wondered, given all they had, weren't they happy?

The medication eventually worked and Una fell into a fitful sleep, fully expecting to be woken by a text from Eddy, telling her what time she could expect him home.

ABRACAFUCKINGDABRA

Eddy was too busy accompanying the pounding drum beat – pit-a-patting his cutlery on the table, tinging the glassware with his dessert spoon – to notice Raoul Zazou, owner of the Jambhalabar, budging up next to Howie. But, as Eddy had often mused, Raoul always seemed to appear from nowhere, materialising like some malevolent genie. He was a slight man of indeterminate age, whose wide vowels suggested links to Essex. He was hyper-groomed, spray tanned and shaven-headed, with threaded eyebrows and a moustache so thin you wondered why he bothered. He always had his shirt buttons undone, exhibiting an oiled chest as hairless as a dolphin. His appearance betrayed nothing of the power he exerted over many a high-profile celebrity, and his talent for extracting money from the rich and famous had never ceased to amaze Eddy. Raoul had even once tried to tap him up for £30,000 to sweeten some Portuguese property deal that involved a local mayor and a *pastelaria*. But, as comfortably off as he was, Eddy wasn't in that league. He didn't have £30K swilling about to sink into some questionable transaction involving crooked government officials and *pasteis de nata*, and Raoul hadn't bothered him again.

Raoul leaned over to give Eddy a perfunctory shake of his hand. His sudden appearance caused Eddy to start. 'Fuck me,' he said. 'Abracafuckingdabra.'

But Raoul's focus, as always, was on the money. And in this instance, the money was Howie. Normally Eddy would prickle at the conspiratorial nature of their whispered conversations, but right at this moment he didn't give a flying fuck. All Eddy wanted was to dance. Had Eddy been sober, had he not taken the E, he wouldn't have known what to say to the two young women Raoul had beckoned over to join their table. But Eddy was far from sober and a long way from both his home and a moral compass. His depression had lifted along with his inhibitions, and he welcomed the opportunity to throw shapes on the dance floor. Maybe even with a woman who, despite her orthodontic braces, had the most enchanting face he'd ever seen.

OOM-PAH-PAH

*

The mid-March evenings were surprisingly chilly, but Tony didn't care. She loved being up on the roof, alone, after everyone had clocked off. She shivered and zipped up her jacket, keeping her eye on Fazakerley as he mooched about, cocking his leg against the big concrete planters filled with ornamental grasses. He was an easy dog, friendly without being in your face, but she knew it would only take one person to tramp through Fazakerley poo, for the goodwill to evaporate.

Tony unwrapped a half-eaten slice of cherry Bakewell. It had been a difficult day. The sighting of Meredith had rattled her, and had spoiled what should have been a low-key, but pleasant enough birthday. Having distanced herself so effectively from her past, she'd had no one to share her day with, but she'd still woken feeling pretty Zen, planning to treat herself to her favourite tart from her favourite café, and looking forward to her hair cut. It hadn't come up in conversation, and she hadn't dared broach the subject, but she'd have liked to have gone to London with Eddy. To be at the TV studios on her birthday would have marked the day out as special. But it probably wouldn't have been possible, not with a dog to consider and she knew Howie would never have allowed it.

'He's such a prick,' she said to Fazakerley, who was staring at the unfinished tart and watching as she picked out crumbs from the tinfoil.

Tony checked the time. It was getting on for midnight. She stuffed the ball of foil into her pocket and gave Fazakerley's head a ruffle. 'It's me birthday soft lad. What did you get me?'

Fazakerley pawed at her arm. She pulled out the screwed-up ball from her pocket and showed it to him.

'It's all gone mate. Sorry.' Knowing the clock was ticking on her special day, she took her tuba from its case, carefully lifting it with both hands, she buzzed, stretched and licked her lips before wiping them on her cuff. She was dedicated to her tuba and fitted practising around Eddy's erratic hours with a mute indoors or without constraint up on the roof each evening.

The area was still commercial, the residential drift having not yet reached this quiet part of Ancoats, and the northern drone of the brass instrument provided a mournful backdrop to a part of England that had seen more than its fair share of sorrow.

Tony warmed up with a few pitch-perfect long tones that segued into a slow, mournful *Happy Birthday To You*, then signed off with an improvised oom-pah-pah flourish. A couple of people in the street below clapped and whooped 'HAPPY BIRTHDAY!'

Tony shouted her thank yous, and the street again fell silent. She felt horribly alone. She pulled out the mouthpiece and wiped it before laying the instrument back in the brand-new case she'd blown a whole wedge of her wages on – a birthday treat and a rare indulgence for someone with such church mouse proclivities. She checked her phone. It was midnight. She set off back to the office, wheeling her tuba case with Fazakerley by her side, and embarked on her twenty-fifth year feeling cheesed off and unloved.

'Fuck you Meredith Pruitt. Fuck you.'

A FAMILY MAN

★

Howie was a hands-off dad. His limitations as a father evident in his interactions with Viola, who he'd struggled to bond with from the moment of her dramatic entrance into the world, courtesy of a ventouse delivery. The miracle of birth had been marred by him witnessing his daughter being sucked out of Stina's birth canal by a contraption that wouldn't have looked out of place in the back of a plumber's van.

Already a father to two adult sons, Howie had lost contact with his first-born as a toddler, while the mother of his second child had bailed even before the twelve-week scan. His parenting of Viola was informed by his own upbringing in the sixties – the absence of his feckless father providing a reason, if not an excuse, for some of his shortcomings.

Howie's estrangement from his previous children hadn't registered with Stina when they'd first got together. Those relationships had felt like ancient history to a woman born a few years after the first of his sons and a few years before the second. But, as she settled into motherhood, she became curious about her predecessors. Beverley Eccles, a local girl, pregnant at seventeen and the only woman Howie ever married. Stina had seen just one picture of her, in black and white, cut from a photo booth strip: a laughing teenage mum with synth-pop asymmetric hair. Howie and Bev, squashed together– happy and gurning – his face a little fuller. His keeping the picture safe, tucked away behind his driving licence, suggested a nostalgic streak she wasn't familiar with. The floppy fringe that became his trademark was already in evidence. He was holding their son Scott – a podgy Renaissance angel of a baby with a big head and tight curls, and a Howden nose that gave him more than a passing resemblance to Viola. The emotional punch the picture packed had taken Stina by surprise. It had been quite the jolt to come across this crumpled piece of her partner's history. It was a bittersweet snapshot of Howie's former life at the beginning of the You!Yes!You! years. A relic of a family that hadn't stood a chance against the pressures of celebrity and success.

If Bev had been the Cynthia Lennon of Howie's back story, then the narrative would follow that Ninette Plouffe, a lingerie model from Perpignan, would be the Yoko Ono. This disastrous and short-lived public coupling was perceived as the cause of You!Yes!You!'s acrimonious split, and the reason behind Howie deciding to ditch the band to pursue a solo career. This simplistic hypothesis, beloved of fans and tabloids, cast Ninette as a scheming witch while failing to examine Howie's lack of obligation towards the guys who'd been with him from the start. The truth, had anyone cared to scrutinise, was that some years into success, his bandmates had come to represent – just as his first wife had done – something parochial and unhip. He saw them as his backing band, and their constant ribbing – a throwback to their schooldays – got right on his superstar tits. So Howie surrounded himself with guns for hire, musicians he could pick up and drop as the fancy took him. The act became polished and slick, middle-aged and middle of the road, and lost all the chaos and grit that had been at the beating heart of its relevance and appeal.

When Stina had first hooked up with Howie, there had been no shortage of people queuing up to inform her of the mistake she was making, reminding her of the many women who'd passed through his life and his bed. He was a Casanova, beloved of the tabloids, whose exploits had helped sell papers to a public who were both envious of, and titillated by, his exploits. But to Stina, Beverley and Ninette were different. They'd mothered Viola's half-brothers, and as such they had a connection. The maintenance payments may have long since ended, but the gagging orders that underscored them would be in place in perpetuity. But if Howie felt any yearning to reconnect with his absent sons, he didn't voice it. And Stina knew not to go there, suspecting he'd be sensitive to criticism over the one area of life in which he'd failed.

The mothers of his sons aside, his relationships had followed a predictable rock-star pattern. Few lasted long and perhaps it had only been Stina falling pregnant, so early on, that had seen their relationship inch towards its five-year anniversary. Stina had embraced this change in her circumstances, and believed that Howie would do the same. She'd always yearned for a large family, and had dreamt of adopting and fostering a huge brood to offset the loneliness she'd felt as an only child.

'What? Like Mia fucking Farrow?' he'd said, dismayed, when she'd voiced the idea.

This bubble had burst as decisively as the condom that had brought Viola into the world, and his vasectomy, undergone without her knowledge, was testimony to his dissent.

On the morning after the Norton gig, as Stina cleared away the breakfast things, she pushed the reasons Howie hadn't returned home the night before to the back of her mind. Now wasn't the time to track him down and tackle him. His mother was on her deathbed and he had a long drive ahead. Viola sat at the table, her eye freshly patched, her red face shiny with moisturising cream, chattering away to Bebisbjörn the teddy and her queue of soft toys, lined up for their morning roll-call. Stina fed Cantona, Ferdinand and Ronaldo, Howie's enormous, long-haired cats, mixing their food with the costly supplements he'd sourced from across the globe. Their coats were glossy from daily brushing – a routine that Howie carried out uncomplainingly. His devotion to these creatures was a revealing insight into his capacity to nurture, his attentiveness all the more perplexing given his limitations as a parent. Stina was rushing a little, assembling Viola's lunchbox, bunching her hair into two fat space-buns, determined to get her off to school before Howie returned to collect his car. That damned car. She should have known when he'd bought a two-seater sports car in the days following Viola's birth, from a dealership favoured by footballers and costing as much as the average house price, that Howie wasn't going to cut it as a family man. Looking back, she wondered whether she should have seen the writing on the wall and walked out there and then. But she'd been young and idealistic enough to believe their baby would change him and that she could make it work.

DRAGSVILLE

✴

As the minicab crossed over the Thames, Howie checked his watch, reluctant to return home while Stina was around. He knew she'd be caught up in all the domestic stuff associated with getting Viola off to nursery – a routine he found 'dragsville'. He decided to stall for a while, and have a ciggy. He was disgruntled at the prospect of having to drive to Stockport and grumpier still about the young Slovak model Raoul had set him up with at the Jambhalabar – a sexual disappointment that had prompted him to fire off a text to a female acquaintance in Manchester, informing her he'd be in town overnight. She was a long-standing and dependable fuck – a little older than he was used to, but super-toned, discreet and undemanding and could always be relied upon to make herself available at short notice. *Maybe*, he thought, *she could bring a friend*? It had been a while since he'd had a threesome and the thought cheered him. The disappointment of the previous night offset by the promise of something more animated from his playmate in the north.

FERMENTED HERRING

★

Eddy had no idea of the time. His sand-dry eyes were glued shut by eyelashes clogged with the dust and debris of a night on the town. The room was in darkness, but the clatter of the maid's trolley in the corridor and the wet buzz of traffic outside suggested it was raining and that he'd overslept. He ran his tongue over his fuzzy, unbrushed teeth. His throat parched from sleeping with his mouth wide open. He tried to lean over to the bedside table to feel for his phone, slapping around in the tangled sheets like a porpoise caught in nets, his useless arms dead weights from sleeping too long in the same position. His guts spasmed and squished as pins and needles signalled the blood flow returning to his numbed limbs. He tried to assemble the jumbled fragments of the night before. But remembering brought little consolation. It would appear the pseudo pan-Asian decor of the Jambhalabar had invoked a long-forgotten disco hit, buried deep in his subconscious, and he'd danced the Kung Fu to Every. Single. Song. His karate chops and kicks emptying the dance floor.

Eddy lay still, processing his embarrassment and the scratchy discomfort of his bare buttocks on the hotel mattress. The airless room was rank with the stench of his breath, which smelled of fermented herring and tasted even worse. His swollen mouth didn't feel right, as though his lips belonged to someone else. He was massively dehydrated, but in the dark and without his spectacles, or the energy to raise himself off the bed – a glass of water remained an impossible dream. Eddy was paying the price of being an out of condition sixty-three-year-old, of staying up too late, of drinking too much and of taking a drug that lowered the inhibitions he'd spent his entire adult life studiously embracing.

He kicked the sheets away and in doing so knocked some plates that had been stacked on the bed onto the floor.

'BASTARDS,' he shouted at the crockery as he tuned into the discomfort of a fork prodding his kidneys.

Eddy patted the bed, hoping to find his phone and spectacles.

He needed to work out the logistics of getting home, even though, right at that moment, he couldn't work out the logistics of getting off the bed. He draped an arm over his eyes to cut out the small chink of light coming through the edge of the heavy-lined curtains and prayed his pounding headache might soon ease. Slowly, as his faculties gained a little strength, he became aware of a damp discomfort that had so far gone unnoticed, masked as it was among all the other discomforts vying for his attention. Eddy had wet the bed.

Wobbly legged, dizzy headed and struggling to configure the layout of the unfamiliar room, he pulled himself upright. He was clothed from the waist up and bare-arsed from the waist down. Stepping on, and tripping over, the scattered contents of his overnight bag and the remains of a room-service meal he had no memory of ordering, he trod on something hard, which snapped underfoot.

'Fuck's sake.'

He bent down and recovered his broken spectacles, the movement nudging his bowels. He only just made it to the bathroom in time and collapsed onto the toilet seat, his rectum trumping like the rat-a-tat-tat of automatic machine gun fire. Within seconds, the ill-fated Dungeness crab was returned to the sea as a smooth, turdy bisque, whistled off to its watery grave by Eddy's tremulous mewling.

He sat on the toilet, slumped, sweating and about three pounds lighter, until the feeling began to disappear from his legs. He knew he had to scrub up, sort out this sorry mess and set off home. He also knew this was hopelessly ambitious. Everything hurt and, with dreadful inevitability, slow heaves began to signal his body wasn't done with expelling the previous night's merriment. Eddy projectile vomited with such force that his nose-spew pebble-dashed the opposite wall of the bathroom.

Finally, after purging his system from both ends, Eddy was spent. He pulled himself up, using the toilet roll holder as leverage, his sorry reflection in the bathroom mirror confirming the worst. He looked as if he'd been in a fight. And maybe he had. He ran his tongue over the crusty mess on his upper lip, the ferrous taste confirming it as dried blood. He filled the sink and dunked his face into the water, holding it under, and considered the feasibility of drowning himself. A few airless seconds confirmed it as hare-brained an idea as it had been to chaperone Howie.

Shivering, he fumbled his way through the bedroom to open the curtains just wide enough to locate his phone. He balanced his one-armed spectacles on his face, the backs of his eyeballs throbbing as he twitched the curtain to cast a shaft of light over the pit of a room. It looked like a crime scene. He squinted to make sense of the fuzzy shapes, strewn pillows and bedding. There was a picture hanging crooked on the wall, an overturned table lamp, an upturned chair and the shadowy figure of a barefoot young woman huddled in the corner, her thin arms wrapped around her bony knees. She looked at Eddy, standing in the half-light, wearing a shirt and an inside-out pullover, yet butt naked from the waist down.

'Where is my friend?' she asked.

SOBER ENOUGH

✱

There were no parked cars along the kerbs of this exclusive postcode, each residence having ample driveways behind electronic gates. Howie knew that a minicab, with its engine idling, would be conspicuous in this leafy suburb, so instead he asked the driver to pull up in the car park of the golf club, adjacent to his home. He preferred using minicabs, rather than traditional black taxis. He found their drivers, often Asian and sometimes new to the country, less likely to know or care who he was, which was perfect when sulking around. Travelling incognito added to the clandestine thrill.

He reasoned that while he might not be sober, he was sober enough. He would set off north before Stina returned from her Friday morning hot yoga class, so avoiding any scrutiny over his whereabouts the night before. Right now, he needed the house to himself, to decompress, to have a shower, a coffee and a smoke, to wank into a face flannel and to noodle on his guitar without having to listen to his morning-person girlfriend, or his high-pitched, in-your-face, soon-to-be four-year-old child.

Already, despite the early hour and the rain, there were men trailing golf carts for the first tee-off of the day. Howie had never understood the attraction of such an unsexy, plodding game, enjoyed by ruddy-faced men in pastel slacks and Argyle pullovers. But Raoul had badgered him to join a club, expounding how much business took place on the fairway. Howie had booked lessons.

He waited and watched until Stina drove past, conspicuous in her bright yellow car. He could see Viola, on her booster seat in the back, waving her arms as though conducting an orchestra, and felt a pang of fatherly pride. She loved music. She was already able to pick out tunes on the piano. Just one plinky-plonky finger, but she clearly had an ear for it. She was such a funny kid. Always so freaking cheerful despite the skin and eye patch. These moments of connection with his daughter troubled him. He felt destabilised by brushes with parental love.

He coughed, self-conscious about welling up, and glanced up to check the cab driver wasn't watching him in his rearview mirror. He knew Stina was disappointed in his shortcomings as a father, but he couldn't risk attachment. Not after losing Scott.

He hadn't blamed Bev for leaving. It was a fair cop. Her finding out about his infidelities when Scott was just a toddler was bound to end badly. In many ways he was relieved. You!Yes!You! had taken off. 'Vesta' had been a success, spawning further hits. It had been like winning the lottery. But way, way cooler. He was so fucking pleased with his twenty-two-year-old self. But he hadn't bargained for the sex and drugs of rock'n'roll to see him estranged from his first-born son indefinitely – a situation entirely of his own making. Bev remarrying and his son bonding with his stepfather had triggered juvenile emotions that saw him flouncing out of his young boy's life. But unbeknownst to anyone, not even Stina, he'd kept an eye on Scott's career as a chef. His son's face regularly cropped up on the Instagram feed of the fashionable Manchester restaurant that Howie would studiously avoid when in town. Celebrities, with their arms around the kid with the Howden nose, would point at this bashful culinary boy wonder. Scott hadn't cashed in on his father's name and Howie noted, with sadness, that he'd taken his stepfathers' instead.

When Howie's second son was born ten years after his first, his limitations as a parent had become engrained. Lucas being born in another country offered a physical and emotional distance that Howie chose to embrace. The child speaking French as his first and only language was the perfect excuse for dropping contact. He felt no connection to this son he'd never met and found the lack of attachment liberating. It was a stratagem he'd tried, and in many ways succeeded, to employ with Viola.

Given his relationship history, he'd never imagined his romance with Stina to last beyond the first few months. Her beauty and her public profile had bolstered his ego for sure, but his falling for her was a novelty that had confounded him. He had, genuinely, for a short time anyway, believed their future could be monogamous. But it required a level of commitment he soon found burdensome. And even though the surprise pregnancy pulled them into a coupling that suggested permanency, he'd always had one eye on the door. So these sporadic feelings of tenderness towards Viola, of his heart swelling with paternal love, were not welcomed.

'Okay,' he said, to the cab driver, as the yellow car disappeared from view. 'All clear.'

SILLY COW

✱

With her head rested on her folded arms, Tony had fallen asleep at her desk and had woken with a perfect indentation of the stitched sleeve seam of her hoodie imprinted on her cheek. She was stiff and groggy, in yesterday's clothes, and nursing the disappointment of a rubbish birthday. Seeing Meredith the day before had poked at buried feelings and she had, against her better judgement, felt compelled to scrutinise her ex-lover's Instagram feed. This hadn't been the cathartic exercise she'd needed it to be. She'd been hoping to figure out some plausible reason why Meredith was hanging out in the back streets of Ancoats, away from the buzz of bars and eateries. Perhaps her motives for being down this side street were legitimate, but Tony knew her well enough to have grave doubts.

Tony reasoned that, as cyberstalking went, it was fairly innocuous. It was hardly an invasion of privacy given Meredith appeared to have no desire to keep anything in her life to herself. There seemed to be no situation too intimate, no photograph too revealing, no chain of thought too vapid that would stop her from telegraphing it to the big wide world. There was nothing she wasn't prepared to share through an endless stream of revelatory online posts. Tony had hoped Meredith would appear to be as miserable as she had been over the previous months. But selfie after pouting, laughing, drinking, dancing selfie gave the distinct impression that Meredith was having a ball.

When in the first throes of love madness, Tony hadn't spotted it. But now, her more critical eye noticed that every photo Meredith had ever taken had featured her own face, centre stage. There wasn't a vista or spectacle too magnificent for Meredith to photobomb; no sight too majestic, no scenery less of a feast for the eyes than her own pouting mush. The only photos Tony posted were of Fazakerley or her tattoos, though she'd deleted the one of Meredith drawn as Betty Boop. Inked onto her calf just weeks into their relationship, it felt foolish now. Meredith's tattoos were understated, pretty and floral – sprigs of daisies at her ankle, a butterfly on her shoulder, an astrological glyph for her star sign on her wrist – though with 'Libra' spelled out underneath, for avoidance of doubt. Tony's doodle-pad body, by contrast, had the aesthetic cohesion of a fridge covered in magnets. It was partially out of self-consciousness and partially out of self-preservation that she never posted portrait shots on social media. She had no desire to connect with her past. She didn't want to hook up with or be tracked down by anyone, even if it meant spending birthdays alone. But she was annoyed at herself. She'd been doing so well, and now here she was, miserable again, Meredith having fucked up her sleep and her day. The dog hadn't been walked, twenty-five years old felt ancient and her homelessness filled her with shame.

Tony studied a picture of Meredith turned to camera, squinting in the searing sunshine. She was wearing a saffron-yellow sari, her hair citrus-lemon, her face a little sunburnt and a red bindi spot had been painted between her brows. Out of focus and over her shoulder there was the fuzziest hint of a blurred, white structure that, on closer inspection, turned out to be one of the marble minarets of the Taj Mahal. But it was the most recent photo that had jumped out at her at 2am, having drunk too much coffee and comfort eaten her way through a whole packet of stale water biscuits. It was Meredith, smiling broadly into the camera, her ice-blonde hair flopped over one eye. Tony searched the photo, hoping to detect some hidden sadness, some regret about her lost love, but instead there was just the aching familiarity of a face she'd once treasured. It pained her to see the sweet cow's lick in her eyebrow, the nose piercing, the Blythe Doll eyes with her trademark flicked eyeliner. Meredith was never without her make-up, not even in bed. In the early days of heartbreak, when Tony had been trying to find positives in the wreckage of her love life, she'd taken consolation from no longer having scuzzy pillowcases, encrusted with the mascara Meredith hadn't bothered to remove before bed. But, studying this photo, Tony recognised the backdrop as her office building. In fact, had the photo been examined forensically, there might even have been the blurred outline of Tony herself, observing her ex-lover with a look of pursed-lipped indignation. Tony read the hashtags: #ancoats #selfie #mybestlife.

'Silly cow,' she said, breaking into another packet of past-their-sell-by-date biscuits, while checking her phone to see if there had been word from Eddy. But there was nothing.

YOU BROUGHT ME

★

'Who let you in here?'

Eddy caught sight of himself in the full-length mirror. His reflection gave a horrible insight into the vision he was presenting to the young woman, hunched in the half-light of his hotel room. He was shivering and clammy, stood a few short feet away from her, cupping his genitals in the gloaming. His brain short-circuited as he tried to make sense of his situation – he grabbed the pissy bed-sheet with one hand while shielding his privates with the other, whipping the bedding around his bare-arsedness as a makeshift sarong.

The young woman said nothing. She rested her forehead on her knees. Her bare arms were folded, hiding her face.

'Excuse me. Who let you in here?'

She looked up at him, appearing baffled by the question, her straight, dark, shoulder-length hair clipped away from her face with a single kirby grip. Her smudged make-up gave the appearance of a half-finished water colour sketch. 'You brought me,' she said, her Eastern European accent heightening her teenage indignation. A spaghetti strap from her flimsy dress fell from her shoulder onto her matchstick arm.

'Do you have a cigarette?' she said

Eddy caught a glimpse of her orthodontic braces. 'No I fucking don't.'

'A roll-up?'

He didn't – and, even if he had, he wasn't sure she was old enough to smoke it.

'Who the fuck are you?' he said, focusing in on the teddy bear pendant that hung from a silver chain and rested on her jutting collar bones. Yet all he could think, through a muddle of panic and revulsion was, HOW OLD IS SHE?

'Iiris,' she said, as though this was something he ought to know. 'With three eyes.'

'What?'

'Iiris. It sounds like ears. *Eeear-is*. But it is spelled with three eyes.'

Eddy stared at her, unable to fathom what the hell she was talking about.

'Not the English Iris. *Eeeeris.*'

Eddy held out his palms and shook his head.

'With three eyes,' she added.

'I'll give you the money for a cab,' he said, scanning all the surfaces for his wallet, fearful this stranger may have robbed him. He spotted it on the bed, lying open next to his phone, complete with debit card and cash. He took out a twenty-pound note.

'Here.' He held the note out towards her, but again she buried her face in her knees and folded arms. He took out another note in the forlorn hope that waggling another twenty quid at her would solve his predicament. But her head was still hidden, her arms wrapped around herself, her hands seeming way too big for her tiny frame. She reminded him of an Egon Schiele painting, but the connection only served to disturb him further. *I'm going to end up on a fucking register*, he thought.

'Here, for a taxi,' he said, silently imploring her to take it.

She remained motionless. Eddy looked at her bony shoulders and felt a momentary pang of paternal concern. Una was a slight woman, but her weight seemed to be controlled by a fast metabolism and rage. This person looked borderline malnourished. He offered another twenty-pound note, then another, but still she didn't move.

'Get yourself some breakfast too.'

The thought of eating triggered a memory from the night before. Of being in the restaurant. Of Raoul bringing two young models, new into town, to their table. Still clutching the sheet around himself, Eddy sat down on the bed.

'Fucking Raoul.'

He recalled the other girl now. She was equally as thin, equally as young. Both of them rangy and knock-kneed. Like baby giraffes.

'I don't want to state the bleeding obvious, but have you tried phoning your friend?'

She looked at Eddy. 'My phone is gone.'

'Tell me your number and I'll ring it. It's probably under all this crap.'

She methodically reeled off her phone number, as though learnt by rote in English classes. Eddy tapped it into his phone. It went straight to voicemail.

'Did you leave it in the restaurant maybe?'

She shrugged.

Eddy felt a rising irritation – the same annoyance he experienced when Joni didn't seem overly concerned about taking care of expensive things. He looked at his phone, aware he may have missed calls and messages.

'Fucking hell. One per cent.'

No sooner had the words left his mouth than the screen turned black as the battery died.

'Maybe it is in the taxi,' she said, pausing and glancing about her. 'With my coat.'

Eddy winced. The taxi. He remembered now. He knew he had no business being in a taxi with this girl-woman.

'And my bag,' she added, without drama.

Eddy had a memory of Howie cosying up to the other one, the fairer-haired of the two. Of her sitting next to him on the banquette, holding a wine goblet that seemed as large as her head. Howie's body was turned towards her, full-on attentive, leaning in to top up her glass. All ears he was. Eddy knew what that signified. Howie only listened intently when drugs or sex were on the cards. It had been an age since he'd shown any interest in anything Eddy had to say.

'Your friend took her,' she said. 'Howie Rocks.'

'Howie Rocks?'

Iiris picked up the pebble, painted by one of the Sues, from the floor beside her. She held her arm out straight, the stone flat in her palm.

'The old man with the boat.'

I've got a little houseboat in Chertsey, Eddy remembered hearing Howie telling the young woman as she stood, a good foot taller than him, his arm around her waist as she wobbled, unsteady on her five-inch heels. As chat-up lines went, it had served him well. A succession of young women had made their way to that little houseboat in Chertsey – the age gap widening as Howie got older. For Eddy – a man who'd met the parents of every one of his past girlfriends – the number of women who'd passed through Howie's bed was beyond comprehension. It was definitely scores. Probably hundreds. More likely thousands. He presumed Howie had long since lost count.

A GALLANT GESTURE

★

Iiris had discovered the remains of a joint in one of the pockets of Eddy's Belstaff – the jacket he'd given her to protect her from the rain and to lessen his embarrassment as they'd walked through the hotel foyer. He'd insisted she take it, as her slip of a party dress – semi-indecent in the cold light of day – gave scant protection from the downpour. She had thought it a gallant gesture, but was perhaps too unworldly, too guileless, to have noticed Eddy's unease as he hurriedly checked out from the hotel, the unauthorised late check-out landing him with an extra day's fee.

He'd given the bill a quick once-over, astonished at what he'd managed to rack up, courtesy of room service and the mini-bar. *I don't even like Pringles*, he'd thought. But he'd paid up regardless, eager to draw a line under the whole dreadful episode. He'd thrown the jacket around Iiris's shoulders and chivvied her out through the lobby. They made a dubious couple – him, haunted and hungover, a slouchy, unkempt late middle-aged man, his untucked shirt hanging below his jumper, a split lip and broken spectacles sitting at a wonky angle on his face; and her, rangy, barefoot, bare-legged, trotting on tippy-toes, holding the jacket at her throat with one hand, and carrying strappy heels and a pebble with the other, her bra-less nipples prominent in her flimsy dress.

There were no black cabs to be had in this weather, so Eddy made some cursory excuses before taking another note from his wallet and pressing it – to the raised eyebrow of the hotel doorman – into Iiris's hand.

'Sorry, I'm late for my train.'

Iiris said nothing. She took the money, her face expressionless and impossible to read, the cold causing the peach-fuzz hair on her bare arms to stand on end. Eddy was halfway down the steps before he glanced back.

'Take care,' he said, wincing. The rain already trickling down his neck.

Iiris watched as he scurried away in the direction of the tube station then melted into the throng of people dashing about in the downpour. She dropped her shoes onto the ground – the seen-it-all-before doorman held an oversized umbrella over her as she wriggled her dirty feet into her inappropriate footwear, pulling the back straps carefully over the blister plasters on her heels. She pushed her arms though the sleeves of the Belstaff, in an attempt to stop shivering. The jacket – a little tight on Eddy, since inactivity and anti-depressants had caused his weight to creep up – swamped her and fell lower than her tiny dress. She stuffed the 'Howie Rocks' pebble and the notes Eddy had given her into a pocket for safe keeping and discovered the skinny, bent remains of a half-smoked joint. The doorman turned his head away, pretending not to have noticed. She held it between her first two fingers as she snapped and unsnapped the jacket's many pockets, checking for a lighter – rifling through the bits and pieces Eddy had failed to take in his rush to cover her up. She took out a small, leather travel pass holder that contained his over-sixties railcard. Iiris looked inside at a photograph of a young girl tucked behind the return portion of Eddy's train ticket back to Manchester, along with the small, square sachet of an extra-lube condom.

CITY 'TIL I DIE

★

In a railway carpark, log-jammed by a fleet of coaches, and with neither shelter nor waterproof clothing, Eddy stood in the steady rain, his jumper as sodden as his spirit. Until that moment, he'd managed to hold it together, despite his train terminating unexpectedly at Milton Keynes. Damage to overhead wires at Nuneaton had put paid to the relative comfort of first-class rail travel and pitched Eddy up on that greatest of all levellers, a rail-replacement bus service. He scanned the mayhem, rooted to the spot by a weariness that wasn't entirely due to lack of sleep. His missing jacket and ecstasy comedown were a punishing reminder that he wasn't cut out for hedonism. He watched as a frazzled steward called out instructions and was drowned out by the ticking-over of coach engines and the rumbling wheels of suitcases sploshing through puddles in the potholed tarmac. Eddy stood on the sidelines, bewildered, incapable of throwing himself into the mêlée. Not only had his jacket not made it out of London, but neither, on checking his trouser pockets, had his asthma inhaler. He gingerly bent and pulled a scarf from his holdall, wondering what it would cost to have an Uber drive him the 150 miles home.

'This way mate.'

Eddy felt a hand touch his arm. A smiling steward with a rosy-red apple of a face and lovingly coiffed Clint Boon hair took his holdall and gently guided him through the throng.

'Mind your backs.'

The sea of passengers parted and moved aside, eyeing the chaotic-looking older gentleman who had been singled out for special treatment. Eddy was profoundly grateful yet baffled by the kindness. The steward leaned into him and Eddy flinched at the hot breath on his ear.

'You've got to help a Blue.'

Eddy was confused by the reference, but the steward – Glen, according to his name badge – winked and playfully tugged at Eddy's Manchester City scarf, and pointed to a small, enamel MCFC pin on his own lapel.

Eddy felt soothed. Coming from a provincial city obsessed with football, he knew these tribal connections could be as effective as a masonic handshake, and was relieved to find himself taken under Glen's protective wing.

'Come on, let's get you sorted.' Glen knocked on the door of one of the coaches and beckoned the driver to open up. Eddy thanked him as best he could, the kindness threatening to undo him. 'No worries mate. City 'til I die,' Glen said, handing the holdall back to him.

Eddy stumbled up the steep steps of the coach, clutching his bag and stomach, worried both might empty over the floor. He turned to give Glen a little wave. But he'd already disappeared into the crush.

DIRTY BASTARD

★

Parked up at the far reaches of the service station car park, Howie let down his window. Splots of rain hit his hand as he held a cigarette at arm's length, and watched as people ran to take shelter inside. He felt safe, parked this distance away. He took a long draw on his ciggy and braced himself to look at his phone, hoping there would be word from Jean. But there was nothing. He didn't know if he could do this. To drive up to Stockport to watch his mother die.

He was surprised there'd been no communication from Eddy. It was unusual for him not to return his calls – but even more unusual was Howie's enthusiasm to speak to him. He was fascinated to know what happened after Eddy left the Jambhalabar with the young Estonian. He'd never known him to cop off like that before, and felt a pleasing sense of satisfaction that someone who was normally so maddeningly faithful, had taken a tumble from the moral high ground. Howie tried him again, but his call went straight to voicemail.

'Dirty bastard,' he said, smiling to himself.

Thinking about Eddy took his mind off both his dying mother and the young Slovak model he'd taken back to his houseboat – whose number never made it into his phone and whose name he'd already blotted from his memory. Howie had found her company tedious once he'd fucked her, so a few hours later, parked at the overground station, he hadn't been able to hurry her out of the minicab quick enough. His offhand goodbyes overrode her complaints of feeling unwell. He'd been annoyed she'd vomited into his boat's composting loo within minutes of waking. She'd been crying and he'd wanted her gone. He'd watched as she'd turned heads among the early morning commuters, her walking unsteady, and dressed for a party, rather than a crowded train to Waterloo. He noticed she seemed to be setting off towards the wrong platform but hadn't felt obliged to correct her when she'd turned to wave him a timorous goodbye. Her hair had been straggly and wet from the rain, her face apprehensive and unsure. He'd slunk back in his seat and asked the cab driver to take him home. *She'll work it out, he'd said to himself.*

ONION RINGS

✳

Eddy would have preferred to settle at the front of the coach, where he could fix his gaze on the road ahead in the hope of controlling his biliousness. But the opening of the coach doors had prompted an emboldened group of passengers to push their way up the steps with the sharp elbows of overnight campers at a Black Friday sale. Eddy found himself shunted to the back, thrust along by the force of fifty or so feral rail travellers forcing their way down the aisle with their battering-ram luggage, grabbing seats in a screwball game of musical chairs.

There was no room overhead for Eddy's bag, and even if there had been, it was unlikely he could have managed to stretch that far without something in his intestines giving way. However, squished in, between the window and a lanky young man with too long a pair of legs in too small a space, he found comfort in having his holdall on his lap. It gave him something to hold onto. He was only a hair's breadth away from sucking his thumb.

Eddy wiped the condensation off the window with his sleeve and peered out through the fog of his wonky, steamed-up spectacles. He watched as Glen jovially herded a sizeable group of vexed passengers towards a coach. Although it had been some time since Eddy had been able to tolerate the noise and crowds of a football match, dear Glen with his flat vowels and Madchester hairdo had made Eddy feel homesick for the north-west. For its familiarity. For his home. For his own bed. For Joni and Una.

Una.

Her name was like a slap. There was only one thing worse than flashing his knackers to a young woman in a hotel room, and that would be his wife finding out about it. Panic, sickness and a convenient case of transient amnesia had, until that precise moment, gifted him a mental block regarding Una and his lost night in a hotel room off the Tottenham Court Road. Throughout his entire marriage, and despite being on the fringes of sweetie shop temptation, Eddy had been pathologically faithful. His moral compass and nervous disposition kept any notion of extra-marital chicanery well and truly in check. He hadn't the constitution for leading a double life – heck, he hardly had the constitution for leading a blameless one. Eddy twanged the elastic band on his wrist and nibbled his nails.

As the doors closed and the last of the grumbling passengers settled, the coach inched its stop-start way out of the car park. Eddy wiped queasy sweat beads off his forehead with the end of his damp scarf. He was resigned to the disrupted journey ahead, relieved they were now on their way. He consoled himself that in a couple of hours they would be pulling into Stoke-on-Trent to be decanted onto a train home. *How bad could it be?* he thought.

Moments later, and in answer to his question, his travel companion – legs splayed, and with trainers the size of canal barges – proceeded to unwrap the stinkiest of cheeseburgers. Eddy pulled his scarf over his nose in an attempt to stifle the smell, but it did nothing to lessen the stench of flame-grilled flesh or the sour milk odour of his own armpits. Burger Boy ate with a slow, methodical attention to detail, licking each finger in turn, smacking his lips between every mouthful, before taking out the pickle and flicking it onto the back of the seat in front of him with a precision that suggested he had done it before.

But it was the onion rings that did it. It was the carton of deep-fried amuse-bouche, wedged between the pair of them, that tipped Eddy over the edge.

'Jesus fucking Christ, Jean-Paul Sartre was spot on.'

The youth turned his head as if in slow motion and gazed at him, his mushroom-soup pallor and droopy eyelids giving the impression of being either half-asleep or not giving a fuck. Either way, it was winding Eddy up.

'Hell IS other people.'

Eddy grabbed the onion rings and plonked them firmly onto Burger Boy's lap. The young man looked at the carton, then looked at Eddy, who found himself mesmerised by the perfect crescents of blackheads that circled the lad's nostrils. Burger Boy blinked slowly, his expression vacant, the only colour in his face being the scarlet dots of freshly picked spots. He held an onion ring slightly above his mouth and, like a gecko snatching a mealworm, he flicked out his tongue to grab it.

A couple of other passengers, with the misfortune to be seated adjacent to the pair, craned to see where the raised voice was coming from, but turned away when Eddy caught their eye. His messy hair, split lip and one-armed broken spectacles, sitting skew-whiff on the bridge of his nose, made him look slightly unhinged. And maybe he was. A ripple of unease passed through the passengers, holed up on what was turning out to be quite the nightmare journey for all of them. But they kept their heads down, pretended it wasn't happening and hoped someone else would come and sort it out for them.

AN IGNOMINIOUS CHORE

★

Having flicked his cigarette butt out of the car window, Howie stretched down into the passenger footwell, careful not to disturb his beloved Taylor guitar, which was strapped into the seat. He felt around for a bottle. The VIP need to wee was much the same as anyone else's, but a full bladder on a long car journey presented Howie with a predicament that was peculiar to the rich and famous. There was nothing dignified about pissing into a bottle, but it was preferable to being asked for a selfie in a public toilet. A furtive snap of his pop star knob could make its way around the planet before he'd time to wash his hands. Howie unzipped his trousers and directed the tip of his penis to the top of the bottle. Nothing.

When it came to bottle-pissing, Howie was a practised and skilful marksman. He'd pissed in bottles and even shat in a few plastic shopping bags in car parks and lay-bys throughout most of mainland Europe. He could, however, use the restrooms of America unmolested, as You!Yes!You! had failed to accomplish significant sales in that particular territory – something he'd blamed on Eddy, the record company, even the Americans themselves, rather than his reluctance to work such a vast landmass. Slogging away, doing college gigs and small-town venues to build up a fanbase, would have necessitated a level of slumming it he wasn't prepared to endure. But this once-nifty sleight of hand had now become an ignominious chore. Wealth had buffered him from many of life's indignities, but even he couldn't escape the march of time. He glumly wiped the after-dribble from his leather trousers, opened the door and poured the urine into the pools of rainwater encircling his car. He checked his watch. *Damn*, he thought. He was making good time.

DO OR DIE

★

As the coach crawled through the Friday afternoon traffic, a jaded steward with contoured blush, arched eyebrows and a brutal inverted bob worked her way along the aisle. The aborted first leg of the journey had been so short-lived that there hadn't been time to check tickets and it was only now, as Eddy rummaged through the bag on his knee – opening and closing zips, getting increasingly frantic with each ticketless pocket – that he realised his over-sixties travel pass holder was gone.

'Tickets please,' she said, her manner exuding all of the joylessness of someone in the grip of menstrual cramps.

'I can't believe you're doing this,' Eddy said, rooting in his trouser pockets, while the steward endorsed Burger Boy's ticket with a biro squiggle. 'If we'd wanted to travel by coach, we'd have bought coach tickets and saved ourselves a few quid.'

'You can apply for a refund if your journey is delayed, sir.'

'IF?' Eddy pointed out of the window at an elderly gentleman, with a bent back and a Jack Russell in a pushchair, plodding past the coach.

Eddy knew this shitty state of affairs wasn't the fault of the onboard crew. But whether it was lack of sleep or the chemicals still metabolising in his liver, the screwed-upness of the night before or just those damned onion rings, it was this luckless woman who found herself at the receiving end of Eddy's tether.

'On a scale of one to Adolf Eichmann, just how much of a jobsworth are you?'

The steward, possibly younger than her heavy make-up suggested, looked baffled. She may not have got the reference, but the punch still landed. She flashed a look that implied she wasn't finished with him yet and stropped off back to her seat. Eddy felt a strange sense of disconnection. The unpleasant exchange hadn't been nearly as cathartic as he'd supposed it would be. It was as though he was hovering above himself, contemplating this tatty-haired, fucked-up, old, unfamiliar stranger being impolite to an employee who was just doing their job. It would be fair to say that Eddy had, after a lifetime in training, accomplished peak self-loathing.

Passengers craned to see who the arsehole was at the back of the coach, making all the fuss. But Eddy no longer cared. Nor did he care he couldn't find his ticket. All he wished for now was a small handgun and the elbow room to blow his brains out. But not, he fantasised, before first wiping out Burger Boy, who was currently texting, the clicks of his keyboard unmuted. Fortunately for his fellow travellers, Eddy had neither a firearm nor the necessary hand-to-eye co-ordination for a killing spree. So as the coach picked up speed he sat slumped, slap bang in the centre of a Venn diagram of biliousness and humiliation.

'Where is my friend?'

Eddy looped the scene in the hotel room for what felt like the thousandth time. His stomach did an Olympic-class triple axel as the coach veered off a roundabout and onto the slip road of the motorway – the driver clearly required to meet with some unrecoverable schedule. Eddy gripped the prickly moquette of his seat, fighting the urge to puke while being serenaded by Burger Boy's nose whistle, mouth-breathing and the tinny clashing beat that pulsated from headphones placed, not over his ears, but around his neck. Fragmented memories from the previous twenty-four hours were coming back to Eddy. He wasn't sure this was a good thing.

'Where is my friend?' the young woman had repeated.

The back end of the coach swung about as it hurtled up the motorway, trying to make up lost time, weaving in and out of the heavy traffic, the headlights of the oncoming vehicles blurring against the rain and the miserable half-light of a wet afternoon. Eddy closed his eyes, leaning into the steamed-up window in an attempt to put as much distance as possible between himself and Burger Boy's jutting knees and the sound of him siphoning the dregs of his fizzy drink through a straw. He rested his clammy forehead in the palm of his hand, trying to suppress his queasiness and make some sense of the jumble of memories in his head. Please God, let him not have laid a finger on her.

'Your ticket?'

Eddy was nudged out of his brooding by the steward, back again, her face a picture of had-it-up-to-here-ness, a veritable poster girl for underinvestment in rail infrastructure. Eddy couldn't be arsed to hunt for his ticket anymore. Every movement caused an awful wave of dizziness. In the scheme of things, his lost ticket felt like the least of his worries. He passed his debit card to her.

'I'd like a TRAIN ticket to Manchester please.'

'One hundred and eighty-five pounds,' said the steward flatly.

'A hundred and eighty-five pounds? Good God. There'd be riots in France,' Eddy said, with an incredulous shake of his head, causing his brain to ricochet around his skull like the steel balls of a pinball machine. 'I've got a senior railcard. Does that knock a few quid off?'

'On you?'

'Have a guess.'

'I can't give you a discount without seeing your card.'

'Well, there's a surprise.'

If the backs of his eyeballs hadn't hurt so much, he would have rolled them, but this, at least, was one problem he could make go away. He tapped his PIN into the device and handed it back to the steward.

'Payment declined,' she said, a little more loudly than was necessary, her face the perfect marriage of triumph and disgust.

The steward held out the device so Eddy could read the screen. He balanced his broken spectacles more squarely on his nose and squinted his eyes to read it. Eddy knew he had enough money to cover the ticket, so didn't know what to be more freaked out about – not being able to pay for the journey or the possibility his account had been hacked. But there was something about the failed transaction that nudged yet another unwelcome reminder of the night before.

'I don't want to patronise you,' Howie had said to his dining companions at the Jambhalabar, holding up his hands as if to surrender when the bill arrived.

It had been classic Howie. He'd taken over ordering for everyone – choosing the most expensive dishes and the costliest wine – then sat back and waited for someone else to pick up the tab. Eddy remembered taking out his card and stumping up. It had been hundreds of pounds. Then there had been the hotel, with the 5am room service. He had no memory of drinking spirits and didn't even like Pringles, but his minibar bill alone had come to more than a continental city break. Had Eddy been sitting next to the emergency exit he may well have thrown himself out of the moving coach there and then. But, pinned in by Burger Boy, he had no practical means of escape. The steward was still waiting, her heavily lacquered hairdo as firm as her resolve. Eddy turned and looked out of the window as the coach sped past a couple sat on the grass embankment above a broken-down camper van, each with a plastic shopping bag on their head as protection from the unceasing rain. He so longed to be one of them. *Get me out of here*, he whispered to himself, and to a god he didn't believe in.

No sooner had his prayer been offered up, than the coach whizzed past a sign for motorway services. *A Welcome Break* in half a mile. As miracles went, the appearance of Newport Pagnell service station lacked the splendour of Our Lady of Guadalupe, but to Eddy, faced with the stony-faced displeasure of the steward and the consequences of ticketless travel, it was heaven sent. It was now or never. Do or die.

'STOP THE COACH!'

A shock wave rippled through the vehicle. Even Eddy was taken aback by the boom and projection of his voice and, despite it threatening to burst his brain, he couldn't resist another cathartic scream.

'STOP THIS FUCKING COACH!'

The coach wobbled into the middle lane as the driver, startled by the outburst, struggled to control the vehicle. Passengers squealed and the air turned blue with swearing, but Eddy didn't give a fuck. The steward staggered sideways, falling into the lap of an elderly gentleman, his face a mess of liver spots and confusion.

Eddy punched the carton out of Burger Boy's hand, throwing the last few onion rings into the air. The deep-fried confetti scattered over the hapless youth, who grabbed at each morsel like a toddler reaching to catch bubbles. Eddy chucked his holdall into the aisle and clambered over the lad, unconcerned about his yelps of discomfort and paying no heed whatsoever to where his heels or elbows happened to dig in.

'Sorry kiddo, needs must.'

Eddy had no plan beyond getting off the coach but, even in this moment of madness, he knew he hadn't the inner strength to endure one more second of being cooped up with his fellow man. He also suspected – if the steward's thunderous face was anything to go by – there was more than a passing chance he'd be met by the transport police at Stoke-on-Trent.

So it was that Eddy was deposited, to audible sighs of relief and a muttering Mexican wave of 'wanker', onto a grass verge at the service station. He watched with tearful relief as the coach accelerated away, engulfing him in exhaust fumes. The affront felt deserved. Eddy dropped his bag, turned and threw up into the oleaster hedging. He wiped his mouth with the edge of his scarf and tried to gather his thoughts. Without a functioning debit card and with only the cash he had left in his wallet, his options were limited. He picked up his holdall and set off, following the exit signs back onto the motorway, jaywalking along the kerb and getting more and more soaked with each passing vehicle. But he didn't care. The open road beckoned. And while hitch-hiking on the hard shoulder of this particular freedom highway lacked the dust bowl splendour of a Woody Guthrie song, he preferred to take his chances with the high-sided vehicles rather than brave the disapproval of a coach-load of passengers, bombing up the M1 to the Potteries.

JOE CUNT

Howie woke with a jolt, startled by his own loud snort. He'd dreamt someone had taken a picture of him through the side window of the car – of his head lolling back and his mouth wide open. But there was no one around in this weather. It took him a few seconds to orient himself, to take in the blur of a service station car park through his misted windscreen. He used the palm of his hand to smear an arc of vision, and his eyes focused in on a big yellow Pudsey Bear cut-out, waving at him through the rain. The remainder of the drive wouldn't take more than three hours in normal circumstances, but it was Friday afternoon, the weather was bad and Howie was doing all he could to draw out the journey, crossing his fingers for roadworks. He opened his window and a new packet of cigarettes, and lit up, taking a long drag before texting Stina to remind her to take the jacket he'd worn on the Norton show to the drycleaners. He checked the time. He'd been asleep for well over an hour. His head felt fuzzy and his stomach rumbled. The only thing that had passed his lips since the previous evening at the Jambhalabar had been nicotine, caffeine and too high a dose of the co-codamol tablets he had dispensed on repeat by a rogue private doctor whose hourly rate was as excessive as his prescribing.

He looked across at the entrance to the service station and, recalling the joys of all-day breakfasts, momentarily toyed with the idea of venturing inside. It had been such a treat, those motorway stop-offs, back in the day with the band. How ironic that the luxury success had brought to his life had been at the expense of simpler pleasures. Sitting in his Aston Martin with his piss bottle, unable to access a fry-up or have a regular wee, offered up a self-pity he needed to dump on someone. In the absence of Eddy, he phoned Stina.

'*Hej Hej*,' she said as she answered.

'I'm starving.'

'Can't you get something at the hospital?'

'I'm still on the motorway,' Howie said, failing to admit that, despite having left home a good four hours earlier, he'd still only made it as far as junction fourteen.

'Are you hands-free?'

'I'm pulled over. At the services.' There was a pause.

'Can't you get something to eat there?'

'Not without running the gauntlet of Joe Cunt, I can't.'

On a normal day, a day when Howie's mother wasn't dying, he would have expected to be scolded by Stina for using THAT word. But this wasn't a normal day, and Howie didn't feel obliged to pussyfoot around the sensibilities of a girlfriend who, he sometimes felt, was a bit too feministy.

'And anyway, I don't want to leave the guitar.'

'Howie, I'm not sure what to suggest,' Stina said, hiding her annoyance well, but not well enough.

'Oh forget it.'

Howie wasn't in the mood for her disapproval and ended the call. Within a matter of seconds, she'd called him back, but he didn't pick up. He downed another couple of co-codamol with a slug of Jack Daniel's. But his irritation was short-lived. The chime of a text, informing him his Manchester date had secured the company of an enthusiastic bedfellow, perked him up no end. He took another swig from his hip flask and set off, drumming on the steering wheel to full-blast 'Smokestack Lightning'. It took just seconds to breach the speed limit, and, cheered by the music and a now empty bladder, he WHOO-HOOED along with Howlin' Wolf as he sped towards the slip road – to his dying mother and his three-in-a-bed sex banquet. But not so fast that he didn't catch, through his rain-soaked windscreen with his wipers on full tilt, a glimpse of a man who looked the spit of Eddy. Walking towards him, along the verge of the slip road in the pissing rain, a holdall in his hand, his shirt hanging below his jumper and a Man City scarf wrapped around his head.

'Can't be,' Howie said to himself.

The man who may or may not have been Eddy caught his eye and put up his hand, as though flagging him to stop. Howie took his foot off the accelerator ever so slightly, before slamming it back down to join the Friday afternoon motorway traffic to the whoo-hooing of Howlin' Wolf.

JOY

★

Walking along the slip road with his thumb out was a far cry from the last time Eddy had hitched a lift. That had been as a beardy college dropout, during the summer of '75, with a girlfriend called Joy, who he'd not long lost his virginity to at the grand old age of nineteen.

Having flunked out of his first year of teacher training, and desperate to escape parental expectations of a fortnight's bed and breakfasting on the Fylde Coast, Eddy had hit the Hippy Trail with Joy in Istanbul and they'd travelled overland to Kathmandu. He embarked on this adventure with too little money in his pocket, and a wail of 'YOU'RE KILLING YOUR MOTHER' in his ears.

Eddy and Joy had made the journey in beat-up cars, coaches and even a double-decker London bus, but it was the hitch-hiking that came back to him now. He remembered climbing into a pick-up truck en route to Kabul. The Afghan farmer had let them sit up front in exchange for Eddy's spare pair of Levi's – a transaction that turned out to be far less attractive once they'd realised they had to share the space with an unhinged cockerel. The experience had gifted Eddy with a lifelong phobia of live poultry in enclosed spaces, but the journey had largely been magical, as the young couple straddled that sweet spot between childhood restraints and the looming responsibilities of adulthood. It had cemented his love for Joy and consolidated his passion for hashish. Sadly, their delightful, uncomplicated romance had proved less enduring than his lifelong love affair with weed.

As successive vehicles accelerated past, Eddy wondered how his life would have turned out had he and Joy set up home in Nepal. Perhaps he'd always been a hippy at heart. Maybe that was why the materialism Howie embraced so wholeheartedly had never sat quite right with him. The home comforts that commercial success brought had always been tainted with guilt. Eddy could never fully enjoy the spoils of his success in the knowledge that someone, somewhere in the world was struggling. Unlike Howie, who took great comfort and pride in knowing he was faring better than most.

Too lethargic to distance himself from the spray of passing car tyres, Eddy wondered why he and Joy had gone their separate ways. He could think of no good reason, other than silly misgivings over settling down too soon with a first love. Had it taken all these years for the penny to drop? That everything he could have ever wanted in life he'd had back then but he'd been too young, too restless, too stupid or too stoned to realise? Despite not having given her a moment's thought in years, Joy was vivid to him now, as drivers unseen and anonymous behind headlights, wet windscreens and wiper blades accelerated onto the motorway. The cheerless Buckinghamshire skies, already mournful and overcast, were closing in, but Eddy was back on the Silk Road with Joy, remembering her stoicism and good humour, and the gauzy cheesecloth dress that became transparent when the sun shone through it from behind. He'd returned home from that trip a different person to the *nebbish* Ethel had waved off. He'd severed the apron strings and arrived back – to the horror of his parents – with a rucksack full of bed bugs, a mild case of hepatitis A and an Afghan coat that smelled so badly of the goat it originated from that his mother banished it from the house. Just a few months later, now living *in sin* with Joy in a tatty red-brick Salford terrace, Eddy capitulated to his mother's demands and agreed that his father could sling the coat onto the compost heap. Perhaps Ethel may have been less triumphant about this volte-face, had she known that his agreeing to the destruction of this hippy relic wasn't out of respect for her middle-class sensibilities, but due to the arrival of punk at the Free Trade Hall.

All this was flitting about Eddy's head as he stood, thumb out, hoping some kindly driver might give him a lift to somewhere closer to home. It turned out kindly drivers were thin on the ground, and no one wanted to stop for the bedraggled guy with the thousand-yard stare and a football scarf wrapped around his head – not even the sadistic bastard in the flash car. The one Eddy thought might be about to stop. The one who slowed down only to rev up again, soaking him to the bone. For a split second he'd thought it was Howie's face peering out at him through the frantic wiper blades. Eddy had long since learned to zone out whenever Howie bored on about his vehicles, but he did half-remember some reference to a red sports car. No, it couldn't have been.

Eddy gave up. He picked up his holdall and turned back towards the service station. He had thirty quid cash left in his wallet, a dead phone, no charger, no medication and no marijuana. But most of all, he was all out of ideas.

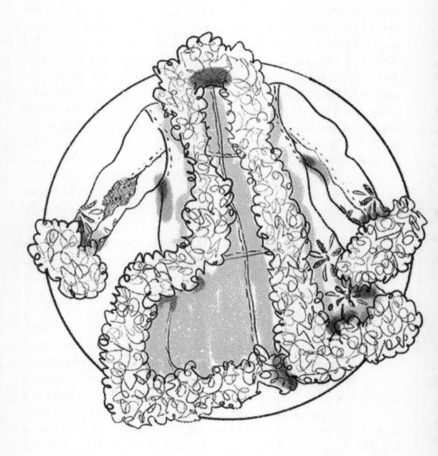

NO BUSINESS HERE

★

'Don't send her up!'

The panic in Tony's voice betrayed her alarm when reception called to say there was a young woman in the lobby, without an appointment.

'She's no business here.'

Tony's mind raced as she tried to think on her feet. Her breathing was rapid and noisy as the receptionist relayed the message, framing it a little more sensitively than Tony had communicated. Fazakerley broke off from gnawing on an air-dried trachea and sat motionless on the sofa opposite, his eyes fixed on Tony, monitoring the change in her demeanour. It was clear from the conversation that the woman wasn't leaving. It was also clear that the voice in the background wasn't Meredith's.

'Sorry, who is it?' Tony said, relaxing ever so slightly.

There was a short exchange that Tony struggled to hear.

'She's calling herself Iiris,' the receptionist said, pausing before adding, 'with three eyes.'

A QUIET WEEP

✱

If anyone had spotted Howie, parked at the far end of the hospital car park, they may have thought he was having a quiet weep – his head bowed, the back of his hand wiping across his nose. It had taken a good thirty minutes for him to bagsy the spot, away from the busy entrance and the hospital volunteer, who'd taken the trouble to flag him down after yet another circuit of the too-few spaces, and pointed out there was a park-and-ride service nearby. But Howie wasn't a park-and-ride kinda guy and though he was normally pathologically impatient, on this occasion he was happy to wait as long as it took for the right spot to come free. More time in the car park was less time on the ward, and he needed a ciggy, a toot and one of his stop-start wees before braving his living, breathing sister, and his at-death's-door mother.

Howie checked his phone again, but there was no word from Eddy. He wondered how things would pan out if he sacked him. It would be odd having a new manager, but it was time for a change. He needed someone younger, someone who could steer his plateaued career towards a more youthful demographic. He thought about the Dumplings. He contemplated how the audience had laughed at the playful ribbing he'd been given on the Norton show the night before. *Lou Reed wouldn't have put up with that*, he thought, knob poised over the top of his bottle while waiting for his flow to get going.

Howie wiped the drips off his leather trousers. He'd always had a predilection for the hackneyed tropes of rock stardom, but these days he found that when it came to after-dribble, leather was far more forgiving than fabric. He checked himself in the rear-view mirror and parted his hair flat with his hands in order to monitor his white roots, a regrowth that required touching up by Stina every fortnight to keep this tiresome proof of ageing at bay. He looked at his watch again and, with a heavy heart, accepted he had pretty much exhausted all delaying tactics. It was time to brace himself for the worst. Whether the worst was being witness to his mother's dying or simply the prospect of having to make small talk with his sister wasn't something he bothered to unpick.

He necked a Xanax, finished the dregs of his hip flask, stuffed a fresh stick of chewing gum in his mouth and walked, guitar case in hand, past a gaggle of smokers outside the main entrance to a whisper of *He's shorter than I thought* and a *Who does he think he is? The big I am.*

BINGO!

If Jean Burgess had a superpower, it was her complete lack of awareness as to how irritating she might be to others. This was never more in evidence than when she was sitting opposite Howie, on the other side of her mother's hospital bed, opening and closing the zips of her shoulder bag; sniffing, muttering and tutting each time she looked into an empty compartment.

'You don't have anything sweet on you, do you, our Neville?' Jean said.

'Nope,' Howie replied, locked into his phone screen. 'And neither should you.'

Oblivious to the dig, Jean continued to rummage, breaking off every now and again to blow her nose with the screwed-up tissue she kept tucked in the cuff of her jumper. Unlike Howie, who'd been present at his mother's bedside for barely an hour, Jean was two days in and flagging. Comfort eating while waiting for her mother to die – that slow motion slog of watching and waiting for the inevitable to happen, was playing havoc with her blood-sugar levels.

'Bingo!' she said, unearthing a toffee. She unwrapped it with an attention to detail that betrayed the carnal pleasure she took in confectionery. The toffee clacked around her mouth with such a racket that, had Howie closed his eyes, he might have thought she was dancing a flamenco. It was a pretty primitive way of controlling the type 2 diabetes she failed to keep in check. But, as she often boasted, she'd got to the age of sixty-four avoiding expert advice *thank you very much*. The toll this pig-headedness had taken on her body was another matter, but her numb feet didn't overly concern her. Even if it had led to her writing off her car in a supermarket car park when unable to lift her foot off the accelerator.

'A lot of fuss about nothing,' she'd said at the time, playing down the consternation of the shoppers whose cars had been pranged as Jean took out a whole row of tail-lights, registration plates and back bumpers. The trail of destruction had only been brought to a halt by the annihilation of a trolley park.

'Pwllheli Butlins. What year was that?' Jean had taken a small black and white framed photo off Queenie's bedside cabinet and was leaning over her in an attempt to engage with Howie.

He glanced at the photo for the briefest of seconds. 'No idea.'

She leant further over, to better show Howie the photo. 'I can see Viola in me.'

Howie poured himself a glass of water from the jug at his mother's bedside and took a glug, along with a random anti-inflammatory he'd found in his trouser pocket. He returned to his phone. It would have been easy for them to sit in respectful silence, but Jean felt compelled to fill the gaps by humming what appeared to be the entire back catalogue of Rodgers and Hammerstein.

'Are you parked in the car park, love?' she said after a little while, her lip-smacking toffee-eating reaching some kind of crescendo.

'Yup.'

'Costs a ruddy arm and a leg. I got Gordon to drop me off this morning. I told him our Neville will give me a lift back.'

'Can't.'

'It's only a hop, skip and a jump. And it would save Gordon the bother.'

'No room,' he said, nodding at his guitar.

Jean looked crestfallen. 'I could have it on my knee.'

Howie laughed. 'I don't think so.'

'Driving's uncomfortable for him,' Jean glanced at Queenie, lying flat out between them, and whispered, 'what with his cyst.'

'Oh God,' Howie said, screwing up his face and pinching the skin between his eyebrows.

'A pilonidal abscess.' Jean stretched out the pronunciation *pie-lo-ni-dul* for emphasis. 'They're quite common with driving instructors.'

Howie held up his hand, as though to stop her.

'It's all that sitting.'

'I really don't want to know.'

'He's on the list to have it drained. Been waiting ruddy months.'

Howie crossed his legs away from her and turned sideways in his chair, still zeroed in on his phone.

'I can't believe your Eddy employed that girl. All those tattoos. Ye gods. Has she been in prison?'

Howie ignored her.

'The tomboy,' she whispered, in a tone louder than her normal speaking voice. Her hands cupped around her mouth in a makeshift megaphone. 'From the nursing home. What's she calling herself?'

Howie sighed. 'Tony,' he said.

Jean shook her head. 'Bloody ridiculous. What's her real name?'

'Tony.'

'The world's gone raving mad.'

Jean zipped her bag closed and pulled herself up from the chair. She walked around the bed, touching him on the arm to get his attention. 'I'm going to spend a penny,' she mouthed, before sashaying down the ward, making it her business to catch the eyes of patients and visitors fascinated by this dumpy sixty-something woman, her pudding basin haircut perfectly framing her suet pudding face. Howie's arrival had singled her out. Had made her feel special. Jean tossed her head as though she had an imaginary mane of hair – though her trot was more Thelwell pony than catwalk horse stomp. Her entire professional life as a store detective had been about keeping a low profile and blending in, so this interest, this celebrity by proxy, was both alien and intoxicating. It was only Jean's bladder that prevented her from doing an impromptu meet-and-greet the length of the ward.

LIKE ALL MEN

★

Tony sat behind her desk, trying to give off an air of authority and professionalism to the hollow-cheeked, surly-faced young woman who sat on the sofa opposite, emptying the pockets of an oversized Belstaff jacket.

'How do you know Eddy?' Tony asked, hardly daring to hear the answer.

'I don't,' she said.

Fazakerley moved over to sniff at the little pile of belongings next to Iiris, but she shooed him away with a flick of her hand. Fazakerley's hackles may not have risen, but Tony's did. She called the dog to her side, but not before noticing an asthma inhaler amongst the debris.

'Is that Eddy's jacket?'

'He gave it me,' Iiris said, a little attitude creeping into her voice. 'I was cold.'

It disturbed Tony that this young woman was wearing Eddy's jacket. It suggested an intimacy she found unsettling. She was beginning to wonder whether she needed to re-evaluate her rose-tinted-spectacled presumptions about her boss. He'd never struck her as a letch, but perhaps she'd been naive about what he got up to when away from home. She felt angry and a little sick. She knew Howie was an arsehole, but she'd held Eddy in such high esteem. It pained her to think he might be, as instinct had repeatedly warned her, like all men.

She tapped out several texts, one after another, each more curt than the last, her thumbs bashing the keys harder and harder until she was communicating only in capital letters. Iiris lay back on the sofa, barefooted and sulky, nibbling the skin around her fingernails.

'Where you staying?' Tony asked, annoyed by Iiris's filthy feet on what was, in effect, her bed.

'I don't know,' she said, wrapping Eddy's jacket around her. It occurred to Tony that this bony young woman seemed unusually cold in the warm office.

'Look, girl, Eddy's not here. Leave me your number. I'll get him to call you.'

'I don't have any phone,' Iiris said, bored and monotone, her eyes closed. 'I must find my friend.'

Tony may only have been in her mid-twenties, but she felt the age gap widen every time this kid opened her mouth.

'What friend?'

'The Slovak.'

'What Slovak?'

Iiris opened her eyes and turned to Tony with a look of disdain. 'Zophie. The Slovak model. From Slo-vak-ia,' she said, turning away and closing her eyes again.

Tony was just a hair's breadth away from tipping over the sofa.

'I don't see what any of this has to do with Mr Katz.' *Mr Katz*, she thought to herself, *what the fuck*? She never called him that, but felt compelled to pull rank.

'Howie Rocks took her,' Iiris said, fishing about in a pocket. She pulled out the painted pebble and held it up for Tony to see.

Tony was none the wiser.

'Look, I don't know what went on in London, but you can't stay here.'

Iiris sighed heavily. 'Do you have cigarette?'

'No, and you can't smoke indoors,' Tony said, now full on hoity-toity. 'It's against the law.'

She watched as Iiris put the pebble back in her pocket and rearranged the cushions behind her head, fidgeting to make herself more comfortable. She settled back down and closed her eyes. Tony felt helpless. It was late afternoon and the building was emptying; office workers were off to pubs and bars, excited to be knocking off for the weekend. As usual, Tony had nothing planned. But even so, Iiris was encroaching on her downtime and what was, unofficially, her space. She walked over to her and took the pile of things she'd emptied from Eddy's pockets. She studied the hotel bill. It made for eye-watering reading. *He doesn't even like Pringles*, she thought. The statement was made out to the company address and this, plus a receipt from a Manchester taxi, would explain how Iiris found the office.

The return portion of his train ticket explained how she got to Manchester. What none of it answered was why.

'Did you get the train with Eddy?'

'No. He ran away.'

Tony had a creeping sense that what happened in London, wasn't going to stay in London. 'Ran away where?'

Iiris sighed as though Tony's questions were exhausting her. 'To get train.'

Tony thought about it for a moment. Eddy was pretty hopeless at anything practical, but surely he'd have had the wherewithal to buy a new train ticket? The most plausible explanation was that he was already back home. Tony tried ringing his mobile, but again it went straight to voicemail. Perhaps his phone charger, in amongst his belongings, explained his silence. There seemed to be no option but to call his landline. Tony dug about in a desk drawer for the battered old relic that was the office address book, and found what might be the number, filed under *HOME*.

'Yes?'

'Una?'

'Yes.'

'Oh hiya, Una, sorry. I didn't know if this was the right number. It's Tony from the office. Is Eddy there, please?'

There was a moment's hesitation.

'He's in London.'

Tony's heart sank. 'Oh, okay. Can you ask him to call me when he gets in?'

Tony wanted to get off the phone as soon as possible, but it seemed her call had tapped into some of Una's own concerns.

'I've not heard from him since I dropped him off at Piccadilly yesterday.'

Tony could hear Una breathing a little heavier. She hesitated. She didn't want Una to know about Iiris. Eddy might have been in her bad books, but she still had his back.

'His charger's here,' said Tony.' I think his battery's dead. But I know he set off for the train.'

'What time was that?'

Tony looked at Iiris, peeling the blister plasters off her heels. 'Erm, not sure. Sometime this afternoon? He should be back soon.'

Tony was beginning to panic. She feared that if Una carried on asking questions, she might be compelled to inform her this update had come courtesy of a teenager, who was wearing her husband's clothes. Who was hopefully over the age of consent, but whose orthodontic braces suggested otherwise.

'Have you spoken to Howie? Maybe he knows something?' Una said.

'No, I didn't want to bother him. Not today.'

Una didn't respond and Tony felt it necessary to qualify her remark. 'Cos of Queenie.'

'Oh right, so.'

They said their lukewarm goodbyes, and Tony shuddered as she got off the phone. She looked over at Iiris lying on the sofa, her eyes closed, possibly asleep, and bristled at her mucky feet, now pressed into the cushion Tony used as a pillow. She picked out Eddy's over-sixties travel pass holder from his small pile of belongings, hoping to find some clues. She recognised the photo on his senior railcard, his eyes wide, started by the flash. It had been one of the first things she'd organised for him, after berating him for not taking advantage of the discount. How delighted he'd been to feel like he was getting one over on 'those robbing bastards'.

Tony took out a passport-booth photo of an unsmiling girl, her face the spit of Eddy. She turned it over. *Joni, Feb 2019*. She liked this kid's attitude; her messy urchin-up-a-chimney short hair; her cartoon geek glasses, too big for her face and setting her apart from those girls who looked to the Kardashians for style guidance. Still in the holder was the voucher for Eddy's seat booking. Tony wondered what the other passengers in first-class must have thought of the half-dressed waif, bare-legged and dirty-footed. It must have raised eyebrows. Would this be one of those stories that one day would turn out to be a funny anecdote, something her and Eddy would have a laugh about? But her discovery of a condom, tucked behind the photo of Joni, suggested otherwise.

NO NEED FOR A CHANGE OF NIGHTIE

The door opened inwards, causing Jean to be in contact with every surface of the too-small hospital toilet cubicle. Her leg pressed against the pan as she attempted to squeeze the door over her sucked-in stomach before clattering it shut. There was nowhere to hang her bag, just two empty screw holes where a hook had once been, embellished with an old-school cock and balls.

'Ruddy vandals,' she said.

Jean was in a hurry, clamping her thighs together and clenching every muscle in her pelvic floor, hoping to swerve the indignity of a shameful accident. Her overactive bladder was a tiresome reminder of her carbonated drink addiction. Hampered by the restrictions of the space and her chins, Jean fumbled with her trouser zip, managing, in the nick of time, to turn and crash down heavily on the toilet seat, her bare left buttock sliding against the cold metal side of the sanitary towel bin. A harsh gush of piss hit the water and Jean was instantly relieved. The release of a steady hiss of gases, built up from hours of sitting and snacking at the bedside of her mother deflated her like a punctured poolside lilo.

Thankful to have the toilets to herself, Jean sat, slightly slumped, her trousers, underwear and nylon tights around her ankles, her arms folded onto the bag that rested on her cottage cheese thighs. She pulled a tissue from her sleeve and blew her nose. The events of the previous few days, on top of the previous few years of daily visits to the nursing home, were nearing an inescapable dénouement.

Jean ruminated on the enormity of the small drama unfolding on the ward. It was clear Queenie was perilously close to the end, this sad fact confirmed by the kindly Zimbabwean registrar Jean had taken an instant dislike to. The one who'd advised her not to stray too far from the hospital grounds. Who'd interrupted Jean when she suggested she might pick up some clean clothes for Queenie.

'There's no need for a change of nightie,' he'd said.

Jean stared at the door, honing in on a poster that expounded the dangers of chlamydia in the under twenty-fives. She closed her eyes and breathed slowly, aware of a dripping tap and the telltale scent of Sugar Puffs. After two days of consoling herself with prohibited confectionery, her piss was pure glucose. She made a mental note to starve herself for the next hour or so, to counter the effects of the handful of Quality Street she'd snaffled earlier from an open tin at the nurses' station.

Jean was shaken out of her brief moment of Zen by her mobile phone vibrating. She rummaged in her bag, finding it buried amongst screwed-up tissues and sucky sweets. Her stomach lurched. It was Howie. She knew this could only mean one thing, but she didn't feel it appropriate to take such an important call while sitting on the lav. She switched off her phone and sat for some moments longer, contemplating her mother's mortality, before beginning the not inconsiderable undertaking that was sorting out her undergarments and extracting herself from the cubicle.

'Okay mum, let's get this done.'

RIBBED FOR PLEASURE

★

Tony hoped the XXXL *Call Me Unpredictable* T-shirt she'd pulled from a box of merchandise would act as a makeshift dress for Iiris. But, despite its size and because of her height, the T-shirt only reached as far as her upper thighs. Iiris stood, hands on hips, cinching the T-shirt in at the waist.

'It's too big,' she said, her grumpiness chiming with Tony's own.

'It's not a fashion show,' replied Tony, the words sounding, even to her own ears, ridiculous and prim. But she was thinking on her feet. She had taken matters into her own hands. She needed this person gone.

Tony had booked Iiris into The Sharples, a boutique hotel with which the management company had an account. But, as the young woman climbed into the cab, Tony felt a pang of guilt. As glad as she was to see the back of her, she was all too aware of this Iiris's vulnerability, alone in a strange city. And, as the cab moved off, Tony didn't feel relieved, she felt awful. She slunk back to the office, troubled, unable to shake off the self-reproach Iiris's eviction had generated. She was angry at Eddy for being off-radar, for putting her in this position. But mostly she was angry about the extra-lube condom she'd found among Eddy's things which, she had noted, was *ribbed for pleasure.*

A PISS-POOR EXCUSE

★

Una was agitated. If it was true that Eddy didn't have his charger, it would go some way to explaining him not being in touch. But he could surely have found some other way to make contact. He could have called her from the phone in the hotel or borrowed someone else's, or even used a call box for fuck's sake, although, thinking about it, Una wasn't 100 per cent sure there were such things anymore. She wondered about getting back to Tony – she could probably retrieve her number from the landline – but she didn't feel comfortable drawing attention to how fretful she was over her husband's continuing absence. It felt too personal and Una was pathologically boundaried.

Una knocked on Joni's door before poking her head around, looking for some signs of life in the mess of the bedroom. Again, the only light came from her laptop screen, high on the platform bed. Building the structure from scaffolding had been Joni's idea and they had indulged her, outwardly embracing her move into adolescence while quietly mourning the shift away from the girlish pastel hues of early years towards something industrial and harsh. Though any fears it signified the end of childhood were quashed as it became obvious that giving twelve-year-old Joni the responsibility of looking after her own space had been misguided.

'There's more cans in her bed than in the River Irwell,' Eddy had said, bringing down yet another binbag full of litter.

But Joni loved her high-rise bed, with the desk underneath that she never used. But for Una it had come to symbolise the new distance between them.

'Jojo, have you heard from your dad?'

Joni peeked her head over the rail.

'No,' she said. For once there was no irritation in her voice. 'Why?'

'Oh nothing. His phone's dead. I don't think he's got a charger with him.'

A silence hung between them. Both of them knew this was a piss-poor excuse. Joni had been excluded from conversations about her father's depression, about his visits to a psychologist for talking therapies, his trips to a psychiatrist for prescription meds, or the thousands of pounds spent on alternative therapies which Una worried was money down the drain. Joni was told nothing of an overdose that had managed to both freak out and infuriate Una, or a bodged suicide attempt the medical profession hadn't taken seriously, seemingly on account of it having failed. Una hadn't wanted to burden Joni with the awfulness of what had happened. But neither did she want to keep it a dark secret. She promised herself that, if Joni did ever ask about her father's mental health, she would answer honestly. But what she failed to take into account was that Joni might never ask.

Una contemplated her options. But outside of calling the police, which felt a little drastic, there didn't seem to be anything to be done, other than to sit it out and wait for Eddy to turn up.

'He'll be on his way back,' she said. 'Go to sleep. He'll be here in the morning.'

But she sounded unconvinced, even to herself.

RESOURCEFULNESS AND FOLLY

★

Tony rang The Sharples and was put through to Iiris's room, where the girl answered in the same bored voice to which Tony had become accustomed. But at least for now the problem of her presence in Manchester was contained.

'Oh hiya, Iiris, it's Tony.'

'Is Eddy back?'

'Maybe. Possibly. Don't know. He might be at home. Have you ordered something to eat?'

'I must find my friend.'

'Okay, but meantime you need to eat. Use room service. It'll be covered by the office.'

Tony was aware this might be foolhardy; that Iiris may take advantage of her all-expenses-paid break. But she was past caring and, anyway, she reasoned that Iiris didn't look like she had much of an appetite.

'When I hear from Eddy I'll get him to call you. But can't promise anything. You've got enough money to get you back to London in the morning. There's three trains an hour from Piccadilly. It's a five-minute walk from the hotel.'

'What I do in London?'

'How do you mean?'

'My friend, the Slovak, Zophie – Zophie with a zee – she has address of model apartment. And keys.'

'A model apartment?' Tony said, imagining some kind of fleapit for sex-trafficked teens.

'It is nice. It is in Chalk Farm. But there is no farm.'

Tony sighed. 'Okay, right. You haven't the address.'

'No, but it is near a bus stop.'

'Well that narrows it down a bit,' Tony said, by now so slumped in her swivel chair that her head had more or less disappeared into her hooded top.

'Iiris, how long had you been in London?'

'Since on Tuesday.'

'So, three days. You're having quite the adventure aren't you.'

Iiris was silent.

'Iiris?'

'I must find my friend.'

It was with a heavy heart that Tony gave Iiris her mobile number, knowing, as she did, that it opened a line of communication she may come to regret. She told her to stay in the hotel, warning her that Manchester was mental on a Friday night.

'And Iiris,' Tony said, 'order something to eat.'

Tony had always looked out for the younger children in care and Iiris reminded her of kids who seemed to have no concern for their personal safety, who would wind up in perilous situations. Iiris's turning up unannounced in a strange city, using Eddy's train ticket and tracking down his place of work – all of this while coming from a country Tony would have struggled to find on a map – drew into focus that same mix of resourcefulness and folly. It bothered Tony how relaxed Iiris was, walking around semi-robed. She checked the time. Some of the big shops were open until 9pm. She took the company credit card, something she'd been entrusted with but had never used, and set off into town.

Tony dropped off the Primark bag at The Sharples' reception. She'd picked out an oversized sweatshirt and a pair of grey leggings in the hope of quashing any sex appeal that might draw the male gaze. She walked a circuitous route back to the office, her keys evenly spread between her clasped fingers to form a spiky knuckle-duster. Her journey was slowed by criss-crossing the road back and forth to avoid large groups of revellers, oblivious to the drizzle, who spilled onto the pavement outside busy pubs and bars. She hated the alcohol-induced threat in the air; the screeching and the bellowing. She wouldn't normally walk through town on a Friday or Saturday night. But she was emboldened by her bad mood.

Back at the office building, a brick shithouse of a security guard buzzed her into reception, everyone else having long since gone home. She wearily trudged past him, limping particularly heavily, her bad leg playing up in the rain. She tried to give off the air of someone forced to work late rather than someone ready for bed. But, as the elevator doors opened the guard called to her, waving an envelope. 'Any idea who this is?'

She limped over to him.

'It's been on the desk since yesterday,' he said.

It was clearly some kind of greetings card. Bubblegum pink, the name written in silver ink, in a juvenile curly script. *Tonya*. Only one person called her Tonya, her hated childhood name. The 'a' dropped long ago in favour of Tony. Only one person had the temerity to deadname her. Only one person would stick that name on an envelope and encircle the entire fucking thing with a big fucking heart. Only one fucking person. Meredith fucking Pruitt.

THE HOTTEST DAY OF THE YEAR

★

Normally Una would have been in bed by ten-thirty, settled with Chakakhan and a good book. An avid reader of domestic noir, she had a tower of grisly fiction, stacked on the floor next to her bed. Instead she was downstairs, flicking through the TV channels, trying to distract herself. It would seem no amount of checking her phone could conjure up Eddy.

The living room door opened slowly. It was Joni, wearing an oversized jumper – the perfect camouflage for the adult body she was trying to conceal.

'Have you done your teeth?' Una asked, as Joni flopped on the sofa next to her. Chakakhan budged up a little to make room, delighted to be nestled between her two favourite girls.

'I will.'

Una said nothing, overriding a knee-jerk compulsion to chastise. It was an age since Joni had sat this close to her and Una was grateful for the contact. She looked at her daughter. It pained her to see her girl going through the transition to womanhood. Physically maturing faster than her peers, her hated thirty-six inch bust singled her out for unwanted attention from the boys at school, with their goatish pleasure over a classmate wearing a bra. Even in the soft light of the table lamps, Una could see Joni was suffering a breakout of pimples, and despite the late hour and being in the privacy of her own home, she had covered them in a cakey concealer.

'What you watching?' asked Joni.

'Nothing,' Una said. 'It's all bollocks.' She handed Joni the remote control.

'Have you heard from Dad? Joni said.

'No. Not yet.'

Both mother and daughter stared at the TV screen, neither paying much attention to what was on. Joni flipped through the channels, back and forth, back and forth, before landing on *The Graham Norton Show*. Howie's face flashed up. He was in the middle of some weary anecdote about his Ivor Novello nomination twenty-five years earlier.

'Gross,' Joni said, switching away from terrestrial TV and onto Netflix.

Una was silent. Seeing Howie had packed a punch, his voice familiar and unwelcome in the room. She hadn't spoken to him in almost a decade. Not since that day. The hottest day of the year.

The Saturday festival crowd had been surprisingly responsive to an act that was something of a wild card. Shoehorned between Biffy Clyro and the Ting Tings, the mid-afternoon slot had been perfect for Howie. The crowd were just about drunk enough to get behind someone who had an ironic attraction, since they knew the music second-hand from their post-punk parents.

Una had been standing at the side of the stage with a two-year-old Joni propped on her hip, her hot child's sticky skin adhered to her own, the toddler twirling her mother's long blonde plait around her chubby little baby fingers. Eddy, a few feet away, sat on a flight case, skinning up. It was Joni's first festival, and she was lapping up the joyful atmosphere – the attention of strangers and this upending of her normal routine. Her ears were protected with noise-cancelling headphones and her skin smothered in SPF50 sun cream. Una was bare-legged, the uncommon heat only just bearable in her loose cotton dress and flip-flops. Howie was next to her, lightly jogging on the spot, shaking out his arms, cracking his neck, waiting to go on stage. He caught her eye and she smiled, the vibe as happy as the weather was hot.

She'd turned back to watch the band, her plait pulled over one shoulder, serving as a comforter and a plaything for Joni. It had taken Una by surprise when Howie kissed her on the back of her bare neck. It felt inappropriate, too intimate, but even in that moment she'd been rationalising it. *It was just a friendly peck she'd thought*. Weird, to be kissed on her neck, but still, just a friendly peck. She turned and looked at him, her face blank as she tried to work out what had just happened. Howie flashed her a big smile, the Californian dentistry jarring with his Stockport face. Puzzled, she turned back to watch the band, wondering if they'd seen. But the band were facing the audience. She glanced over to Eddy. No, him neither. He was licking a Rizla paper and rolling a joint. She looked behind her, but there was no one, and the crowd out front couldn't see into the wings. She was smack dab in the centre of the action, surrounded by thousands of people, yet to all intents and purposes she was alone. Una recognised the band's introduction. She knew Howie would be strutting onto the stage in a matter of seconds. And that's all it took. Seconds. Just seconds for his hand to be under her skirt, between her thighs, his palm shoved hard between the cleft of her buttocks, his fingers hooked into what her mother and her religion had taught her were *her privates*. It was only the fabric of her underwear that prevented full penetration. And that was it. Three seconds, maybe less, and Howie was off, swaggering onto the stage. The hand he'd assaulted her with, raised triumphantly in the air. Una was frozen to the spot, little Joni still twisting the plait around her fingers while Eddy sat on the flight case, trying to get his lighter to work.

It had been a decade ago. A decade in which she'd made sure never to be alone in Howie's company ever again. A decade in which she'd retreated into motherhood, into her home, into herself. A decade in which she'd worn her hair short – the plait she'd had since childhood swept into a hair salon's dustpan long ago. A decade in which she'd never worn a frock or gone bare-legged on any of the hottest days of the years.

That was it, thought Una, staring at the TV screen as Joni flipped through the channels. She had finally pinpointed the fatal blow to her relationship with Eddy, the exact moment her marriage had died. Because before Howie had got to the microphone, before he'd sung a note, Una had started to unravel and her marriage had begun its slow, inexorable journey towards the rocks. She'd never told Eddy what had happened. She hadn't told anyone. And so this corrosive secret had oozed into every corner of their relationship, eating its way through the soft tissue of their marriage.

She'd replayed it a thousand times over the years, trying to shape it into something fathomable. Maybe it was because she'd smiled at him? Perhaps she'd sent out the wrong message, egged him on by wearing that above-the-knee summer dress, her legs bare. Maybe it had been something and nothing, just boys being boys. It had only been seconds after all.

And it was now so long ago that she sometimes wondered if it had even happened. But watching Howie in high definition from the safety of her sofa, as he flashed his rakish, pantomime villain smile, the diamond in his tooth glinting in the studio lights, she was back at that festival. With him taking off onto the stage, turning to her, laughing, flashing his wide toothy grin; the diamond catching the summer sun on the hottest day of the year.

A PIG OF A COUPLE OF DAYS

While Una and Joni were brooding in the suburbs of south Manchester, Tony was having her own dark night of the soul a few miles away, just north of the city centre. The pink envelope remained unopened on her desk. She didn't want to touch it. She pushed it with a ruler to flip it over, noting the flap had been sealed with a lipstick kiss. There was no question about it. It bore all the hallmarks of classic Pruitt. If Meredith could have engineered some way of jumping out of the envelope, wearing little more than tit tassels and a vajazzle, the gesture would have been complete. Maybe it was the residual worry over Eddy's whereabouts or the trace of Meredith's *Daisy Dream* perfume spritzed over the envelope, or perhaps even Iiris's dirty feet on her pillow; whatever it was, Tony was engulfed by self-pity. Forty-eight hours earlier she'd been rebuilding a meaningful life. Now she was facing the possibility it had all been a wind-up. That once again, ladders had been kicked away and she was sliding back down yet another fucking snake.

Fazakerley plodded over to her and sat against her legs, his chin resting on her knee, aware that Tony was having a moment. She rubbed his shoulders, something they both found soothing. She wondered whether Eddy was home by now. Maybe Una had forgotten her promise to get him to call? She looked again at Meredith's envelope next to the neat little pile of belongings from Eddy's pockets; at the packet of anti-depressants and the asthma inhaler. Surely he would need both, though the legendary collection of Cup-a-Soups he kept in the office revealed a tendency to hoard.

Usually at this time of the evening she would take Fazakerley onto the roof for tuba practice, but there was a fierce downpour and she wasn't in the mood. Her anger at Eddy was muddled with anxiety over his whereabouts. Might he be waxy and dead on a slab? Tony crossed herself and said a silent prayer to St Dymphna. It had been a pig of a couple of days. She needed a good night's sleep but knew that, until Eddy made contact, there was little chance of meaningful rest. She checked her phone again. Nothing. She threw Meredith's envelope into the bin. And took it out again. Passing it under her nose, the perfume transported her back to the time she thought was the happiest of her life. She looked again at the lipstick seal, at the perfect red stamp of Meredith's lips, and remembered what a great kisser she'd been.

A PRAYER NONETHELESS

★

Una hadn't slept. She'd seen Joni to her room after midnight, but was too agitated to hit the sack herself. Even in this rainiest of cities, a peculiarly relentless rainstorm felt ominous and she had lain on the sofa, cupping Chakakhan to her stomach and trying, unsuccessfully, to rest.

Inevitably a headache was threatening to kick in but, with no prospect of sleeping, she'd taken her migraine medication and tried to watch TV instead. But she couldn't shake the feeling that something awful had happened to Eddy. If only they'd parted at the station on better terms and hadn't made such a botch of their goodbyes. Or their marriage. She turned off the TV. The weather showed no signs of improving. The ping ping ping of rain hitting the metal garden furniture sounded like a hospital monitor and played into her fears.

When finally the insipid early morning light began to seep through the curtains, Una opened the French window into the garden. But her attempts to coax Chakakhan outside were futile. The dog took a quick sniff of the wet air, and darted back onto the sofa. In more normal circumstances Una would have togged up in waterproofs and taken her for a walk around the block. But it didn't feel right to leave the house, not while Eddy was missing. She couldn't risk a lapse in vigilance as she believed on some weird cosmic level, it was only her wakefulness, her waiting for him, that was keeping him present.

She figured Howie would have been the last person in their circle to see Eddy, but contacting him would be the ultimate of last resorts. An admission that no amount of magical thinking was going to return Eddy home. She didn't have Howie's number in her phone, but it would probably be in the address book they kept in a drawer. An analogue back-up kept despite many of the contacts being forgotten, estranged or dead. Alternatively, she could go through Stina. She had nothing against her even if she found her choice in partner repellent. But they weren't close, and she didn't feel comfortable approaching her with something so intimate. She wasn't sure she would be able to talk to anyone without falling apart. Una wasn't an active churchgoer, but from time to time she would find herself striking deals with a god she wasn't sure existed, but from whom she took comfort. Una prayed. Not the hands together, eyes closed, head-bowed praying of her childhood. But it was a prayer nonetheless. She prayed that should Eddy be delivered home safely, she would do all it took to mend their marriage. If Eddy returned, they would rebuild a more gentle life, away from Howie. Perhaps renew their vows. Una was enveloped by a certainty this would be possible. If it wasn't too late.

SOLDIERS

✱

It was around 9am when Howie woke, naked and alone, in the hotel, his two lady friends having made a discreet exit in the early hours, his interest in them evaporating in tandem with his erection. But as anticipated, there had been no fuss or ill-feeling. These two had known the score. They had been as keen to leave as he was for them to go. They worked at the elite end of the oldest profession, and while they didn't come cheap, he'd been happy to pay top dollar for the cast-iron guarantee of sex, discretion and a swift, no-strings, thanks and ta-ra.

Howie rang room service and placed an order. He preferred to eat in hotel bedrooms to avoid the side-eyed glances of fellow diners in the breakfast room. Mornings meant flat hair and water retention, and he needed time to assemble his thoughts and his face into something more rock'n'roll. He still hadn't heard from Eddy, despite leaving a voicemail the previous evening, informing him that Queenie had died. He'd tried again on waking, regardless of the early hour, but was met with an alert that notified him that Eddy's mailbox was full. In all the years they'd worked together, Eddy had been at the end of a phone. Howie was annoyed at this lack of consideration from someone who, despite such a long bond, he considered to be on the payroll. But at least it assuaged his guilt. The planned discussions with another manager – an associate of Raoul – were becoming all the more pertinent and timely.

Howie slipped into the bathroom when he heard the rattle of the breakfast trolley outside the door. It was an old trick that saved him having to make small talk with staff while they set up his breakfast. It also saved the expense of a tip.

'Leave it there thanks,' he shouted, running taps to add authenticity to the deceit.

There was nothing about Howie or the room to suggest the frolics of the night before. Just the used condom in the bin and the lipstick on his penis. It had been a tonic, following the grisliness of his mother's death.

But now, alone in the hotel room, as he removed the silver dome from his breakfast plate to reveal a lone boiled egg, he was confronted by the realisation this would be his first motherless day on the planet. He tucked the linen napkin into his bathrobe and tapped the egg with a teaspoon, carefully picking off the broken shell so as to not lose any of the white. Just like Queenie used to do for him as a little boy. A wave of regret took him by surprise. He felt foolish to have let the years slip by, to have so rarely visited his mother in his childhood home, where she would have made him breakfast, no matter his age. But he'd been too mean with his time, too up himself, too plumped up with his celebrity status to bother. Howie buttered and cut his toast into strips. *Soldiers for my little soldier*, said his mother in his head, in the rasping man-voice that betrayed her lifelong dependency on tobacco.

Sitting in the quiet of the hotel room – his ordinarily bouffed hair lying as flat as his mood, his mirrored shades discarded in favour of varifocals, his bottom lip quivering as he dunked his soldiers into the runny egg – he longed for Eddy to call. To help stop the unwelcome sensation of mourning his mother.

FUCKING FAHEEMA

★

'How did you find me?' Tony asked, breaking her silence of five and a half months.

'I bumped into Faheema and she, like, told me?'

Tony had to move the phone from her ear, having forgotten how loud Meredith was and how her up-speak turned every the statement into a question.

'Told you what?'

'What do you think? That you'd been literally poached by, like, Howie Howden? What the actual fuck!? Amazing!'

Meredith's laughter caused Tony a prickle of annoyance. She was offended at her ex being astonished at this change in her circumstances – her disbelief that someone had recognised her worth and had taken the trouble to ride with it. 'Fucking Faheema,' Tony said.

Faheema was a former colleague from the nursing home who knew, as had all the staff, the circumstances of Tony leaving. That Eddy Katz, a regular visitor of Queenie Howden's, had offered her a job in some hip office in town. It had been quite the scandal.

'Who've you told?'

'Everyone of course!'

'Fuck's sake Meredith.'

'What? Why the, like, secrecy?'

'It's not a secret.'

'Well then.'

'Anyway, it wasn't Howie,' Tony said, compelled to say anything that might calm Meredith. 'It was his manager.'

'Same thing.'

'No, it's really not. I hardly ever see Howie. I work in the office.'

'I know. I, like, Googled the address.'

'Why?'

'I wanted to wish you a happy birthday, silly.'

'Oh. Right. Ta for the card,' Tony said, wincing.

'No worries. So do you want to go for a, like, coffee?'

Tony had started to regret calling Meredith even as she was tapping in her number – the number she'd deleted from her phone, but which Meredith had included in the birthday card. The birthday card that had, on top of a shit birthday and an even shittier couple of days, weakened her resolve.

'Meredith, why did you get in touch?'

'I thought we could catch up. It's been, like, ages?'

'Five and a half months.'

'Literally amazing.'

Tony paused. There was a lot to process, but it would appear the hurt of Meredith's betrayal hadn't been buried quite as deeply as she'd hoped. In fact, it had taken all of two minutes for it to scratch its zombie-like way to the surface.

'Won't your girlfriend mind?' Tony said.

Her intention hadn't been to sound defensive. Her plan, having agonised over it since opening the card the day before, had been to sound happy, carefree and indifferent. However, it turned out that feigning chirpiness wasn't a skill she possessed and, as often happened around Meredith, her impulse control had been compromised.

'What girlfriend?'

Tony sighed. She hadn't intended to bring up the issue of the sports science student. 'The girl with the Harry Potter tattoo.'

Meredith said nothing, but Tony was in too deep now, and was feeling very much in for a penny. 'The one with the Snitch on her snatch.'

Finally Tony had discovered the key to calming Meredith. Her voice changed, becoming grave. 'Tonya, it wasn't like that. She wasn't my girlfriend. It wasn't serious.'

'It was serious to me.'

'And anyway, I haven't seen her for, like, ages? I literally don't even, like, live there anymore?'

This news didn't surprise Tony. She'd always suspected Meredith, with her access to daddy's money, was just slumming it when she moved into the houseshare in Fallowfield.

'I'm, like, near you actually. I've got an apartment in the Northern Quarter?'

'Of course you have,' Tony said.

'Off, like, Tib Street?'

'Good for you.' Tony flinched at the thought of Meredith living so close by.

'It's nothing fancy. I'm sharing with a friend.'

Typical, thought Tony. Meredith believing herself short-changed; that her handed-to-her-on-a-plate lifestyle was never quite as cushy as she deserved.

'Oh Meredith, do me a favour. Fuck off, will you.'

'Tonya, don't be, like, like that –'

'Oh and something else, me name's TONY. T. O. N. Y. TONY,' she said, cutting Meredith off mid-blabber.

She threw the phone onto the desk and Fazakerley rose to his feet, aware he may be needed. Tony was furious with Meredith, but not as furious as she was with herself. Had she been in the habit of bursting into tears, she would have done so. But Tony'd had an upbringing in which crying had brought derision not comfort. So instead she sat with her arms folded, spinning left and right in her swivel chair, Fazakerley moving his head in synchronicity. She picked up her phone, freaked that Meredith might call her back, switched it off and hurled it – as if the phone were contaminated – across the room to the sofa.

JUST BUSINESS

★

Howie used his damp bath towel to block the gap under his hotel room door, clambered onto a side table and covered the smoke alarm with his complimentary shower cap. He opened the window the few inches it would allow and blew spliff smoke outside into the torrential rain. This normally busy area of the city was oddly empty for a Saturday morning, the weather having washed the street of weekend shoppers. He looked out from his top-floor vantage point – the most expensive suite in the hotel – at hi-vized council workers clattering down DIVERSION signs, re-routing the traffic away from surface flooding. Water bubbled up from manhole covers, the drainage system overwhelmed by a month's rainfall overnight.

Howie had planned to head back south straight after check-out, but he knew that to drive a low-slung sports car in these conditions wouldn't be ideal. And, anyway, he was tired. Boisterous sex and his mother dying had taken it out of him. Returning home to Stina's sympathy would be too much to endure. He found the weekends – which revolved around his daughter's hectic social life – a trial at the best of times, but this weekend threatened to be more tedious than most. It was Viola's fourth birthday and plans had been made for an afternoon party at the house.

'What possessed you?' he'd demanded to know of Stina, after discovering mother and daughter hand-painting invitations on the kitchen table. 'You can't have Joe Cunt crawling all over the place.'

His anger and use of the 'C' word had seen Stina spirit Viola out of the room with hurried promises of CBeebies.

'You've had parties here,' she'd argued, later that evening, once Viola was in bed, following a day of bad humour and slammed doors.

'Yeah man, with my friends.'

'Well these are Viola's friends.'

'It's not the same thing.'

'This is her home too Howie. There will only be six of them. If that.'

'Plus their fucking parents coming for a nose.'

Howie had a point. It had been an issue since Viola had started nursery – when he'd realised that any child his daughter befriended came with parents he might have to engage with. His worst fears were realised on discovering a couple of kids' parents giving themselves a guided tour of the upstairs rooms during what was meant to be a playdate. But now, thanks to his dead mother and the overnight deluge, he'd been dealt the perfect hand of extenuating circumstances. The universe had offered a tailor-made predicament that allowed him to blamelessly duck out.

Always wanting to keep his options open and never one to travel light, Howie had brought his favourite guitar, clothes, MDMA, Xanax, cocaine, marijuana, co-codemol, a nice single malt and a jumbo box of prophylactics, ramming it all into a car that wasn't big on luggage space. Hearing the next room's window open, Howie leaned forward to see a woman's hand dangle from the small gap, a cigarette between her fingers. He smiled. He saw no reason why he wouldn't be able to stretch out his little sojourn until the funeral.

Having secured the suite for the extra nights, Howie texted Stina to let her know he was staying up north. His assertion that he needed to sort things out suggested a proactive role in the organising of his mother's funeral, though he fully intended to leave all the heavy lifting to Jean. He planned to use the time to kick back, maybe even write some songs. Howie pulled on his silk harem pants and took a face flannel from the bathroom. He figured being holed up in the hotel room with his guitar, booze, drugs, internet porn and the occasional sex worker would be a productive way to spend this period of mourning. And, developing the theme further, now would be as good a time as any to move things forward with regards new management. It had been thirty-six hours since he'd witnessed Eddy – pissed, stoned and high – getting into a cab with the Estonian model. But the vicarious pleasure he'd taken in seeing him legless was now tempered by him disappearing into thin air.

'Can't have been,' he said to himself, as he found himself thinking about the Eddy lookalike who'd waved him down on the motorway slip road.

Sacking him would be unfortunate after all these years. Not that he'd do the sacking himself. He'd get his lawyer to do that. Keep it arm's length. It would be just business, after all.

POST-NATAL RESENTMENT

★

Stina had been expecting it. So it came as no surprise when Howie's text came through, saying he wouldn't be back for Viola's birthday celebrations. She slipped the phone back into her jacket pocket, the echoey screams of the under-fives swimming class masking her cursing, under her breath and in Swedish.

Stina had been taking Viola to Saturday morning lessons since she was a toddler, but although Viola's peer group had long since mastered the basics, it was clear her daughter wasn't a natural. She watched as the instructor held Viola by the hands, her legs flapping about like an albatross with an itch. But what she lacked in grace and aptitude, she made up for with enthusiasm. Not even her painful skin condition, aggravated by the pool's harsh chemicals, could put her off her weekly dip.

Stina sat among the mums and dads, and a fair few Surrey nannies, trying to control her emotions. She took out her phone and read the text again. It wasn't Howie's reasons for not coming home that upset her. Bad weather and a dead mother were reason enough. It was his fucking tone. There was no hint of disappointment or regret over not being there for his daughter. She thought about their recent argument over Viola's party and her indignation became tinged with relief. She could now host her daughter's birthday celebrations without having to accommodate Howie's rancour. She was glad he wouldn't be around in some adolescent grump, sabotaging Viola's day.

Stina looked up as a father shouted encouragement to his child. It pained her to think her daughter might go through life without her own father cheering her on. She wondered how it had come to this. That first year with Howie had been magical. He'd been loving and attentive, and she'd been smitten. The pregnancy had come as a surprise to both of them, but Stina had been happy to embrace the life change. Those months had been the most blissful of her life. The anticipation of motherhood mixed with the crazy, exhausting headiness of new love. She was certain that

149

nothing, or no one, could ever derail a future that felt so full of promise. But even though people had told her how relationships can change after children, nothing could have prepared her for the impact of a colicky baby with inflamed skin and a Hammer Horror scream. Stina's response had been to double down, to focus on the child. But for Howie, this upending of his egocentric life had triggered a rotten case of post-natal resentment. He'd stepped back so far from Viola, that he'd fallen off the paternal cliff. Stina knew the situation was untenable.

'Look, momma!' Viola shouted, allowing the instructor to briefly let go of her hands. She thrashed about, slathered in more emollient than a cross-Channel swimmer, with only armbands, foam noodles and the instructor grabbing hold of her to prevent her from a certain drowning.

'Bravo,' Stina shouted back, her vision blurred by tears. 'Well done, sweetie.'

She put both thumbs up to her daughter, her heart full at Viola's beaming face, comical in her silicone swim cap, her goggles accentuating her lazy eye. The divide between herself and Howie had never felt wider. Stina was so tired of this, of trying to be parent enough for both of them. She was just like Queenie...

The thought, which popped into her head from nowhere, horrified her. Queenie's and Stina's lives could not have been more different, yet the parallels between the two women, of their overcompensating for an ineffectual parent, came into focus. She thought about Howie's own father – a man who'd cleared off when Howie was a small child, avoiding parental responsibilities, debts and the husband of the barmaid he'd been having an affair with. She felt bad she'd been so quick to judge Queenie – the parent who'd stuck around – more harshly than the feckless *skitstövel* who'd fucked off. She felt ashamed to have blamed the single mother, the sole breadwinner, the one who'd been left to bring up the children alone.

DEAD WOOD

★

Howie wouldn't normally answer a call from a number he didn't recognise, wary it might be a snide journalist or resourceful Dumpling. But Eddy's vanishing had both angered and unsettled him. Although it had never been discussed or addressed, Howie was aware of Eddy's precarious mental health, but had downplayed his fragility, dismissing his episodic depressions as nothing a good night's sleep wouldn't fix. He'd little sympathy for a malady he believed signified weakness – so, recently, Howie had tasked Raoul, with his myriad of connections, to put out some feelers and discreetly find him new management. Because Eddy, as far as Howie and Raoul were concerned, was dead wood.

'Howie, Eddy's missing. I don't know what to do.'

'Una,' Howie said, recognising her voice straight away, even though they'd barely said a word to each other in years.

'I haven't heard from him since I dropped him at the station on Thursday,' she said, talking quickly, her voice breathy and panicked. 'When did you last see him?'

Howie knew exactly when he'd last seen Eddy. When he was leaving the Jambhalabar. Shit-faced. With the Estonian. He decided to keep that little nugget of information – along with the Eddy lookalike at the service station – to himself. Howie knew that accelerating past someone who may or may not have been his sodden manager reflected badly on him.

'I've not heard anything since Thursday night,' he said. 'He hasn't been taking my calls.'

'Oh,' Una paused, the only sound being the desperate clutching at straws. 'Though Tony did say he set off for the train yesterday.'

Howie laughed, without cheer.

'Seems she's better informed than us two then.'

'So it would seem.'

'Anyway, I was out of action. Because of mum.'

'Shit. Sorry. How is she?'

'She passed.'

'Fuck. Sorry. I should have asked. Sorry. Sorry for your loss.'

'Yeah man. I texted Eddy. To tell him. But he didn't reply.'

'Oh,' there was a break in Una's voice, 'that's not like him.'

'Toadally,' Howie said. 'Anyway, when he turns up, tell him to call me. I want to know what he's playing at.'

'Will do,' Una said, her voice so faint as to be barely audible.

Howie hadn't reflected for long after Una called. He couldn't understand why Eddy had stayed with someone so taciturn and frosty when their lifestyle was perfectly suited to playing the field. He saw Eddy's fidelity as a weakness. As a young man, Howie had read that Warren Beattie had slept with over 12,000 women. He saw this as a challenge. But he'd lost count around the 2,500 mark, and lost heart on discovering that Fidel Castro's bedpost was reportedly notched with 35,000 female souls. Howie's more recent attempts at monogamy had been doomed from the outset. While he'd managed to rein in his out of control libido during those first months with Stina – making all kinds of promises to her and to himself – his heart had never been fully in it.

Time to move on, he thought, still standing at the open window, taking a long drag on a spliff while phoning Raoul.

'Hey, how's it going brother?' he said, the words strangulated while he held the smoke in his lungs.

'Howie,' Raoul said, sounding abrupt. 'I was about to call. We need to talk.'

'Yeah man? How's things?'

'Things are fucking bad mate. Those girls from the other night? They've landed me right in it, innit.'

It took a moment or two for Howie to fathom which girls Raoul was talking about. His dying mother, his expensive threesome and his eggy soldiers had consigned the new-in-town models at the Jambhalabar two days previous to ancient history.

'No way. How come?'

'The Slovak didn't show up for a job yesterday.'

'The Slovak?'

'Howie. The one you fucked. Fuck's sake.'

'Oh, right. She was Slovakian?'

'Or Slovenian. Who fucking cares?'

'Yeah man.'

'Her flatmates say she won't come out of her room.'

'Weird.'

'And now the agency are giving me shit like it's my fucking problem.'

'Nothing to do with me, man. I dropped her at the station early.'

This didn't seem to placate Raoul. 'She says she wants to go home to Slovenia. Slovakia. Wherever.'

'No way,' Howie said, trying to sound sympathetic to Raoul's plight. But his support was half-hearted. He didn't see how it concerned him.

'I'll go round there and throw the fucking whore out onto the street myself,' Raoul said.

Howie blew his cheeks out. 'Toadally.'

'And her mate. The Estonian. No one's seen that one since she went off with Eddy.'

'Eddy? What, she's still with him?' Howie said, instantly focused as he tried to make sense of the news.

'Who knows? Stupid fucking bitches. Howie, find out what Eddy's playing at.'

'But I don't know where Eddy is,' Howie said, his voice small.

'Sort it out, Howie! I don't need this shit!'

'Yeah man. Toadally. I'll get on it.'

Howie's hand shook as he took the phone from his ear then, on the off-chance it might cut him some slack, he said, 'My mum died last night.'

But Raoul had gone. Howie shuddered from the chill breeze. He didn't like being in Raoul's bad books. Eddy may have been chief architect of his career, but it was a role that had been downgraded over the years. It was Raoul's approval he sought now. He treasured his connection to someone so fêted in fashionable circles as a fixer. The Jambhalabar was an A-list playground, a glitzy backdrop in which rock stars, film stars and even the occasional royal, could rub up against each other literally and metaphorically to keep their celebrity currency buoyant. But mainly Howie enjoyed easy access to young models, dispatched to the nightclub by prestigious model agencies, with promises of exposure and career progression. Some were starstruck, some ambitious, others bewildered, some barely out of school – but few had any real understanding of the seedy underbelly of the VIP lounge; an environment in which sexual availability would be deemed as a given; endorsed by a friendly smile, the accepting of a drink, a dance, or the wearing of a short skirt or a low-cut neckline. It was a place where there was no one to shield these girl-women from a licentious clientele. But, most especially, where there was no one to protect them from Raoul: a man so embedded in the model industry that to step out of line, to displease him or his buddies, would make for an abrupt end to their fledgling careers, and see them sent back home – ambitions thwarted and promise unrealised – to which ever part of the world they'd been scouted from.

Howie could kick himself. He knew he'd made a mistake encouraging Eddy to come along. *Fucking lightweight*, he thought. He flicked his still-smouldering spliff out of the window and banged it shut.

NO-FRILLS HOTEL

✱

Peering out from behind the net curtain of his no-frills hotel and squinting in the unexpected mid-March sunshine, Eddy was relieved to see it had stopped raining. He was thankful that the room – situated at the back of the building and buffered from the brutalism of the M1 northbound at the front – was peaceful. Yet the fine weather did little to improve his overcast mood. He took in the unfamiliar surroundings: a neat stretch of grass being pecked at by carrion crows taking a break from motorway roadkill to enjoy the fat worms offered up by the sodden ground; a new-build housing estate and its fenced-off gardens; a young girl bouncing on a trampoline, her head appearing and disappearing above the fence. It was a strange, ordinary otherworld, that jarred with the one in which Eddy was currently marooned, and from which he had no straightforward means of escape. A lone magpie swooped onto the grass and strutted around before stopping abruptly, appearing to notice Eddy watching from the window. It turned its head to the side to get a better look at him.

'*Puh puh puh*,' mouthed Eddy, letting the net curtain fall back into place as he stepped back into the room.

The previous evening Eddy had discovered that thirty quid in cash could buy a room at a service station hotel and still leave change for an egg mayo sandwich, a bag of crisps and soft drink meal deal. This revelation, along with a couple of antacids from the nice woman on the front desk, had solved his most pressing issues of shelter, hunger and acid reflux. Unfortunately the sandwich, marked down and all by itself in a Friday evening chill cabinet, hadn't sat well on his sensitive stomach. But the freebie hotel room sachet of herbal tea had helped settle his sulphuric eggy burps, and he felt marginally refreshed after having a shower.

With his toothbrush still in London, Eddy had gone to bed with his mouth tasting like a stable. In normal circumstances, he'd have felt too vulnerable to sleep naked, it tapping into anxieties of being burgled, of having to fight off intruders while undressed. But there was no normal anymore and he'd fallen into a strong deep sleep, way before his usual bedtime, and dreamed of smoking a hookah in Shangri-La, while the sun shone through the diaphanous cheesecloth dress of a rosy-cheeked rail steward called Glen.

The next morning, sitting on the end of his bed in nothing but a towel and broken glasses, he listened to the soft pad of footsteps along the corridor, of doors opening and closing, and the chat of travellers heading off for breakfast. He thought about Una. He wondered if she had noticed – or cared – that he hadn't returned home the day before. It wasn't unusual for his plans to change, but he'd always let her know. But that had been in the days when he had nothing to hide. He may not have been able to call her because of his dead mobile and mislaid charger, but it was shame, guilt and the futility of his existence that stopped him from picking up the hotel phone.

The underpants and socks he'd rinsed through the night before and laid out to dry on the windowsill were cardboard-stiff and made a crackling sound as he put them on. He hadn't a clue of the time or how long it was until check-out. His chest tightened – a bodily reminder of his lost inhaler. Eddy contemplated his predicament. The few coins of spare change scattered on the bedside table were the last of his cash and, without a functioning debit card, he was scuppered in terms of staying put or leaving.

He weighed up his options. His room was on the ground floor, he hadn't any meds on him and the nearest thing to a sharp object was a teaspoon. He swigged down the remains of his warm and flat but palatable cola and lay back on the bed, the only sound being the pulse in his ears and a maid vacuuming in the room above. He closed his eyes. Despite sleeping for a full twelve hours, he was still exhausted. He couldn't be bothered to think this one through. He just wanted to savour the nothingness of the room. During his years of touring, Eddy had stayed in some of the world's most elegant hotels, but he felt cocooned in this anonymous space. No one knew who he was. No one outside of the hotel knew where he was. No one could contact him. He stared at the ceiling and wondered if, rather than topping himself, there was a different kind of oblivion, if it would be feasible to move in, long-term, like Elaine Stritch at The Savoy. His stomach rumbled, his nausea having finally subsided. He hadn't enough money for breakfast, but he could at least finish off the bag of Quavers from last night's meal deal.

Eddy was stirred from his daydreaming by a gentle knocking on the door. He pulled on his trousers and tentatively crept to the door, opening it just a little. There was no one, just a small paper takeaway bag left on the floor. He peeked inside and pulled out a mobile phone charger along with a note from the receptionist explaining they had a drawer full of them left behind by guests. It was a thoughtful gesture, but one which made his heart sink. He winced as he remembered offloading his troubles on the poor woman the previous evening. How he'd bored on about going to London and having a terrible time. How his credit card wasn't working and how he'd lost his charger. How he'd given away his jacket and mislaid his senior railcard, train ticket and asthma inhaler. How his journey had been disrupted because of damaged overhead wires and how the steward was a Nazi. The woman had sat patiently, listening to his woes, clearly used to having her ear bent by solitary travellers. There had been a kindliness about her that Eddy latched onto, though he held back offloading about taking ecstasy and discovering a teenager in his room. He knew that, no matter how he might try to spin that one, it was a sleazy state of affairs that reflected very badly on him. He studied the charger, disappointed to discover it was the correct fit for his phone. He wasn't sure he was strong enough to be reconnected to the outside world. Or indeed if he ever wanted to be connected again.

IS IT DAD?

'NEWPORT PAGNELL?'

Without thinking, Una threw the black coffee she'd made into the sink, complete with cup. Its handle broke off with the impact.

'What the holy fuck are you doing in Newport fecking Pagnell?'

Eddy's call had come through not long after Una had accepted she needed to be proactive and, bracing herself, had Googled *how to report a missing person*. She had been alarmed to read that a 999 call was considered appropriate, and was trying to determine whether Eddy's disappearance merited one. Contacting the police frightened her. As things stood, she could try to kid herself he was sulking or had lost his phone. Involving the police made it real, so instead she'd called Howie. And had immediately regretted it.

So when Eddy's name flashed up on her phone, she was out of her seat like a Jack-in-a-box as the dog did zoomies around the kitchen table, releasing the pent-up energy in the room. The moment she heard Eddy's familiar north Manchester accent, every muscle in her body relaxed. She slumped over the kitchen table.

'Eddy, what the fuck?! We've been trying to get hold of you.'

She listened in silence to Eddy's garbled explanation of aborted train journeys, lost phone chargers and onion rings. The quiet interrupted only by the thud of Joni upstairs, jumping from her platform bed, striding down the stairs, two, three at a time. In seconds, Joni was at her mother's side, breathless, gathering Chakakhan into her arms, bouncing her like a small baby in an attempt to calm both the dog and herself.

'Is it Dad?'

Una held up her finger to shush Joni, while concentrating on what Eddy had to say.

'Mum, is it Dad?'

Una nodded.

'Where is he?'

Una waved her hand, signalling for Joni to be quiet.

'MUM!'

Una sat, elbows on the table, her fingertips massaging her temples in the vain hope she might be able to swerve a migraine. 'Where the fuck is Newport Pagnell anyways?'

'Mum, is Dad coming home today?' asked Joni.

But Una continued to ignore her, her focus on Eddy as she tried to make sense of his blather. 'So why can't you get a cab back to Milton Keynes and get a train from there?'

Joni sat down and cradled Chakakhan, and listened intently.

'Eddy, I can transfer money into that account. It's not rocket science. Jeez.' Una covered her eyes while she listened to Eddy's response. 'That's the most mental thing I've ever heard. For how long?'

'Mum, what's going on?' Joni asked.

But Una was locked into the call. 'What? Like Elaine Stritch at The Savoy?' she said.

Una's relief that Eddy was alive was now tempered with the realisation that he might have lost his mind. 'Eddy, Queenie's dead. I've spoken to Howie. He wants you to call him straight away.'

THE MOST NORMAL THING IN THE WORLD

★

Any fanciful plans Eddy had about moving into the hotel long-term were scuppered on discovering it was fully booked that night with a hen party, a stag-do and some stragglers from the Leave Means Leave rally. The kindly receptionist had pulled a face, as though to say you're best off out of it luv. So instead he'd settled for a late check-out – an extra hour of respite in the safety of his room. Lying motionless on the bed, staring at the ceiling, he thought about his phone call with Una. Of her dropping into the conversation like it was the most normal thing in the world, that she'd spoken to Howie. It unnerved him. He hadn't factored in those two speaking to each other. Had Howie told Una about him going back to the hotel with Iiris? Or was Eddy now a member of some murky brotherhood of adulterers, where he could rely on the protection of other cheats, happy to provide excuses and alibis for their allies' extra-marital affairs? If he was, he wanted out. He wanted things to return to how they'd been before London. He may have been contemplating jumping out of his bedroom window back then, but at least his integrity had been intact.

Eddy knew his current predicament was entirely of his own making. It had been his own stupid fault that he'd become embroiled in the murk of the Jambhalabar. He was complicit in the sleaze. He fired off a short text of condolence to Howie. To wish him *long life*; a Jewish courtesy so ingrained in Eddy, that nothing – not even the events of the previous few days – could fuck with. No sooner had the text been marked as delivered than his phone rang. Howie's name flashed up. Eddy switched it off. He might have plucked up the courage to phone Una, and death etiquette may have nudged him into texting Howie, but that would be the extent of his reconnection with the outside world. He had no desire to check his texts and voicemails – despite the ping ping pinging of his phone alerting him to the fact there were very many indeed.

I WISH YOU LONG LIFE

I wish you long life, was all it said. Howie found the wording odd and even a little sinister. Without a moment's hesitation, he called Eddy back, but the phone rang just once before going dead. Howie was furious. *Sting wouldn't put up with this,* he thought, before shouting 'Fucker!' at the top of his voice, without any concern for his neighbouring hotel guests. And certainly not the young woman in the next room, who was lying on the bed, looking at the plastic shower cap she'd put over the smoke alarm on the ceiling, her window open the few inches it would allow, smoking a cigarette with one hand while turning over a painted pebble in the other, and wondering about the whereabouts of her friend.

YES

✱

Eddy's journey back, from Milton Keynes to Manchester by taxi and by train, was as uneventful as the aborted attempt two days previously had been a clusterfuck. He was apprehensive about seeing Una, but even he recognised her exasperation had been tempered with relief. He knew she had every right to be cross but, at that moment, he was supremely thankful she was at least still speaking to him. Eddy was surprised when she'd offered to meet him at the station, but this olive branch gesture had been rationalised by her explaining there had been torrential rainfall and that taxis would be thin on the ground. She'd said it as though it was no big deal, but knowing she gave at least a bit of a fuck gave Eddy a much-needed toehold onto sanity as the train sped north.

Una and Eddy drove back to the house in silence, inching through surface flooding, their diverted journey taking far longer than was usual. The atmosphere wasn't, as Eddy had feared, seething, but instead it was an uncommonly easy quiet. Even the dog was calm and snoozed in her crate.

When they finally arrived back, Una pulled up in front of the garage doors and they stayed in the car, waiting for the rain to ease. The dog, sensing they were home, woke up, her identity disc chinking as she scratched her chin. Eddy and Una stared ahead at nothing much in particular.

'How did City do?' Eddy asked.

'Three-two against Swansea. Away from home.'

'Great. That's us in the semis then.'

They sat quietly again, any awkwardness masked by the noise of the rain bouncing off the car bonnet.

'Tony rang by the way. She sounded worried,' Una said.

'I'll call her.'

'It's okay. I texted her. I told her you were on your way back.'

'Thanks.'

'Have you spoken to Howie?' she said.

'No, but I texted him. About Queenie.'

Una nodded. She looked at Eddy. 'What happened to your glasses?'

'Trod on them.'

'And your lip?'

'Not sure. I had too much to drink.'

'Looks painful.'

'It looks worse than it is.'

Una pondered his face for a moment. 'It's not like you to get stotious.'

Eddy shook his head. 'I should have stuck to the weed.'

'You could do with a shave.'

'I know.'

'Eddy...' Una turned away, again staring in front of her. The view of the garage door semi-obliterated by rain so heavy it was as if buckets of water were being thrown at the windscreen.

'...I'd like it if we could go back to sleeping together. I think it would be good for us.'

'Yes,' Eddy replied, in the smallest of voices.

He considered her face, quite lovely in profile. It was a fragile beauty that belied how brusque she could be. She remained still, her hands on the steering wheel, as he stroked a stray piece of hair back behind her ear. She didn't move into his hand, but she didn't pull away either. He'd been so dreading Una's wrath. And now this. He felt enormous love, gratitude and relief.

'I'm so sorry, Una.'

She nodded. Eddy took one of her hands cautiously and held it between both of his. He couldn't remember the last time he'd touched her, and in some ways it felt like touching her for the first time. They sat like that for a while, neither of them looking at the other, neither of them aware of the dog standing on her hind legs, studying them from her crate at the back of the car. Neither did they notice Joni watching, straining to make out what she was seeing, through the blur of rain and the slats of her shuttered bedroom window.

CRUCIFIXES AND POULTRY

✴

Eddy propped himself up, his acid reflux threatening to eat through his gullet if he didn't sit up immediately on waking. He moved his hand over to the other side of the bed, where Una lay sleeping, her back towards him, and gently rested his palm on her hip. Her body was comforting in its bony familiarity. He did this carefully, so as not to disturb either her or the dog, who was sleeping, nestled against her belly.

They had gone to bed before midnight, both of them exhausted. They hadn't had sex – not that he'd expected they would. Una had suggested they sleep together, and Eddy thought it respectful to take this to mean literally. And so they had climbed into what was once the marital bed with nothing more than the unsaid expectation of sleeping side by side. And this, for Eddy, with all it represented, was more than enough. He'd fallen asleep with just ten milligrams of Valium, half a spliff, and a squirt of lavender pillow mist to assist him. Even Chakakhan had slept calmly, perhaps sensing some kind of truce. He took a blast from one of the many asthma inhalers he had dotted around the home and thought about Tony. He knew he should have called her, but he wasn't feeling strong enough. He would choose his moment and give her a studiously edited account – a less shameful version – of his trip to London, with no mention of ecstasy or Iiris or dancing the Kung Fu. Something similar to what he'd offered up by way of explanation to Una. He wasn't sure she'd believed him, but she'd accepted his sorry tale of disrupted journeys and Newport Pagnell service station with grace.

The creaking landing floorboards alerted him to Joni, lurking at the bedroom door, peeping in and catching his eye. He gave her a little wave, recognising she'd be surprised to see her parents together in bed. Hearing her, Chakakhan jumped down and trotted off, and the pair of them headed downstairs. Eddy felt enveloped by this mundane domesticity and felt nothing but love and gratitude for his little family. He looked around the room, lit by muted light through linen curtains. It was unfamiliar after all the time he'd spent exiled in the spare bedroom. It was neat and tidy – so different from the mess and hoarding of his own space, where half of the curtain hooks had jumped off the rings and left his curtains hanging like sheets on a washing line, giving an appearance of neglect unusual in this postcode. Una's bedding was freshly laundered, unlike his own. His sheets had been on the bed for so long they held a Turin Shroud-like imprint of his body.

Eddy knew his relationship with Howie was untenable, but his private pension plan hadn't done as well as anticipated and was still a couple of years off maturation. They had savings, though, and the house was worth a fair bit. He knew old age was expensive, but if he and Una cut their cloth, if they downsized and lived a quiet life somewhere where the property was less expensive, perhaps it could work? Maybe they could move to Ireland? He'd never considered it before. He'd always felt apprehensive when travelling through countries with strong links to the church. Ecclesiastical iconography sparked atavistic alarm that he might be outed as a non-believer or, worse still, a Jew. He wondered what rights he might have, being married to an Irish citizen. Since the Referendum, he'd felt increasingly uneasy in the UK. The menace wasn't something he could quantify. It was a mood, a febrile undercurrent. He knew Una missed her family, especially as her parents aged. He doubted he'd have trouble persuading her to go. And Joni adored her grandparents – her cousins embracing her into the wider family had helped fill the gap of absent siblings. Una's childhood in coastal Sligo was a world away from Eddy's own upbringing in the suburbs of Manchester, but he'd always slept best at his in-laws' smallholding, despite his unease around crucifixes and poultry.

Slipping out of bed so as not to disturb Una, Eddy made a mental note to Google 'anti-semitism in the Republic of Ireland'. He felt an uncharacteristic spring in his step as this germ of an idea developed, a cloud lifting along with a rare release of endorphins. Having showered and shaved, he joined Joni in the kitchen – his wet hair combed back from his face, and wearing a freshly ironed floral-print shirt he knew to be one of Una's favourites. With his split lip healing, he looked shiny and polished, as though he'd been through a wax car wash.

'I was wondering where that had got to,' Eddy said, nodding at the oversized dressing gown Joni was wearing.

'Found it,' she said, pulling up the hood.

'It wasn't lost.' Eddy smiled. He liked that Joni was wearing his clothes. He cherished anything that suggested a relaxed father-daughter bond. 'Isn't it a bit big?'

'Nope,' she said, glugging milk over a large bowl of cereal, her face covered by the hood. 'Daaad?' She said, with an inflection she'd used since being tiny when she wanted something from her soft-touch of a father.

'Yeees?'

'Have you got a green T-shirt or green towel or something?'

'Not sure,' Eddy said, rinsing out the now-empty milk carton and squashing it into the recycling bin. 'Why?'

'St Patrick's Day,' she said as she left the kitchen, with her laptop tucked under her arm, and carrying a cereal bowl and a large glass of juice, she kicked the living room door open with her big fluffy slipper. 'I want to make Chakakhan a costume.'

Eddy hadn't realised what day it was. Una always liked to mark it with Joni and do something silly, usually involving the dog. That his brainwave had fallen on such a date felt auspicious. It was meant to be. *'Puh puh puh,'* he said.

He rolled a spliff on the kitchen worktop and for the first time in an age he felt his suicidal thoughts take a back seat to the unfamiliar burblings of optimism. He looked out of the window to check the weather and, though it was still drizzly, he decided a new Eddy resolution would be to give Una breaks from dog walking. He gingerly bent and clipped the lead onto Chakakhan's collar in full expectation of losing a finger, but the dog seemed chilled. Off they trotted for a walk around the park, to pick up the papers and to check out house prices, to see how feasible retirement would be.

FUN

✴

Twenty-fours hours into her self-imposed exile, Tony plucked up the courage to turn on her phone. Disconnecting from both her ex-partner and her wayward boss had helped shift Tony's anger, and her indignation was now sitting somewhere flat and fatigued. Concerns for Eddy had nipped away at her, but any comfort in seeing a text from Una that informed her he was on his way home were cancelled out by her annoyance that he hadn't bothered to call her and that she'd been left to deal with the problem of Iiris alone. So, for once, she had made the decision not to work on a Sunday. She was weary and wanted to laze about, to read, to snooze and take it easy for the rest of the day. If there were decisions to be made about her future, then they could wait. She resigned herself to a day of junk food and moping, momentarily curtailed by Fazakerley dropping his lead by her feet.

'Okay mate, but we're not going far.'

Tony negotiated her dog through puddles of rain, and the Saturday night aftermath of smashed glass and splats of vomit. Not for the first time, she considered how other people's idea of fun was rarely hers, and how isolating this could be. She hated being outdoors at the weekends. The feeling of being a bystander, watching as gaggles of people her own age – groups of friends with homes to go to – let their hair down. She'd never been good in large groups; had never been part of a gang. She felt excluded, while at the same time having no desire to join in. She wondered whether she would be better suited to old age, to a life less hedonistic and boisterous. She longed for domesticity – her own place and her own family. But right now, with her love life non-existent and an ace job turning sour, it seemed further away than ever.

It had just gone 10am, but already the bars were opening, the city gearing up for its St Patrick's Day celebrations. Tony hadn't bothered with her contact lenses and was wearing her hated bottle-bottom prescription specs. The gym in the office block wasn't open at the weekends, so she hadn't showered and her normally primped hair – damp from the drizzle and lying as flat as her spirit – had lost all of its pompadour pomp. Her downbeat look was perfectly accessorised by a compostable bag full of dog poo.

Life as an openly gay woman – even in a city known for its tolerance – had left her hyper-vigilant and alert to attack. So when someone ran up behind her and jumped on her, throwing an arm around her neck and shouting 'SURPRISE!' in her ear, she was a hair's breadth from drop-kicking them into the Rochdale Canal.

'Top of the morning to ya,' Meredith shouted.

Tony extracted herself from the head grip. 'Fuck's sake Meredith, do one will you? I nearly had a heart attack.'

Fazakerley was instantly animated, it being the first time he'd seen Meredith since Tony had walked out on her. Meredith crouched and gave him a huge hug, and the dog sneezed repeatedly with excitement, his tail wagging so hard that his back legs lifted off the ground.

'Have you missed me, big boy?' Meredith said, laughing as Fazakerley licked her face, his wet paws threatening to mess up her outfit. Tony felt a sting of betrayal and tugged him away. 'Leave.'

Fazakerley stood, his mouth open, panting, wagging his tail while Meredith rearranged her little shoulder cape and the tiny top hat perched on the side of her head.

'We're off to the pub? Come with us, to be sure.'

Tony winced at Meredith's attempts at an Irish accent, which sat somewhere between the Welsh Valleys, the Scottish Highlands and her fee-paying school in Hertfordshire. She looked across the road at a group of twentysomethings, all way too animated and loud for her downcast mood. And all, like Meredith, decked out in emerald green.

'I'm not dressed for it.'

'You literally don't have to be? Come on, it'll be, like, fun?'

That word again. Tony cast her eye over Meredith's outfit and wondered what St Patrick would have made of the micro-mini skirt, the green suspenders and the matching stockings. Her bust was squashed into – and spilling out of – a waist-cinching corset. A temporary shamrock tattoo stuck onto her left boob.

'What are you supposed to be anyway?'

Meredith stepped back, flicked her long green wig over her shoulder, hands on hips and one leg bent in the perfect flamingo pose. 'A kinky leprechaun. Obvs.'

'Obvs,' Tony said.

On the other side of the road, standing among the group of friends, a tall, raffish-looking lad in a fancy-dress mitre and cassock beckoned to Meredith to hurry, holding his hands out, palms up, to signify he wanted to escape the rain.

'I think your pope's getting impatient,' Tony said.

'Rupert! Two mins!' Meredith shouted to her friend.

Tony rolled her eyes.

'What?' Meredith said.

'Rupert.'

Meredith sighed. 'You still haven't lost that chip have you.'

'Hope not.'

'Well, we're going for a full Irish at O'Sheas. You're welcome to, like, join us? If you can bear to.'

'Nah, youze are okay.'

'Well the offer's, like, literally there.'

'I've got loads of work to be getting on with,' Tony said, pulling Fazakerley's lead.

'On a Sunday?'

Tony hesitated. She hadn't considered it might sound weird to be in the office at the weekend.

'Yep. Howie's promoting his new album.'

'I know! I saw him on, like, Graham Norton? Literally amazing. Were you there?'

'No.'

'Shame. But let's meet up, yeah?'

Meredith's persistence was annoying, but it was wearing Tony down.

'Maybe.'

Tony didn't know why she said this. Possibly it was because it felt like the only way to shut Meredith up and partly, perhaps, because that stuck-on shamrock tattoo on her left boob had rekindled something Tony hadn't realised she wanted rekindling.

'MEREDITH!' shouted Pope Rupert from across the street.

'I'll call you, yeah?' Meredith said, knocking Tony's spectacles sideways as she planted a surprise kiss on her cheek. Her scent prompted a floral flashback as tantalising as it was unwelcome.

Tony shrugged. She felt self-conscious about her appearance – so drab and unkempt compared to Meredith. She wished she'd put in her contact lenses and sorted her hair before leaving the office. She cursed her luck at bumping into her ex-lover while looking so down at heel. Meredith ran across the road to her friends. A car slowed and bipped its horn in appreciation of her outfit, prompting Meredith to perform the only Irish dance ever to use jazz hands. She perched her bottom onto the bonnet of the car, kicking her legs, squealing with delight and taking a selfie. Tony watched mesmerised and imagined what the reaction would have been if she'd sat on the car bonnet. *They'd have run me over*, she thought to herself. The car revved and screeched away, the driver tooting the horn, while Meredith gave a cheery wave and joined her friends.

Tony limped away, her leg playing up in the damp atmosphere, but feeling an unexpected buzz from the kiss on her cheek. Maybe she'd been hasty to cut Meredith so wholeheartedly out of her life. Maybe she needed to lighten up a bit. She thought about the shamrock tattoo on Meredith's left breast and smiled.

SUBLIME DOMESTICITY

✴

Eddy arrived back, his shopping bag weighted with damp Sunday papers, coffee beans and milk, and unclipped Chakakhan's lead with the confidence of a man who'd been doing it all his life. The dog shook herself dry before trotting off into the living room with her favourite toy, the squeaking eliciting a rare dog-related laugh from Eddy. He was determined to embrace this gift of gifts, this surprising armistice from both his wife and dog, which had so unexpectedly fallen into his lap – his spirit cheered further by the upturn in house prices locally.

He unpacked the shopping, the boiler firing up as Una showered upstairs. Grinding the coffee beans, he drank in this new normal and wondered how it had been possible to become so dissociated from such sublime domesticity. It was only the adverts, blaring out from the living room, that encroached on this moment of bliss. Eddy walked over to shut the door on the noise, popping his head in to ask Joni to turn the TV down a little – a sleight of hand she achieved by locating both the remote control and the volume button without so much as a glance up from her laptop. The bright screen reflected in her geeky glasses. The room was exactly how he remembered it from the last time he was in there, an hour or so earlier. Yet something was different.

His brain struggled to adjust to what he was looking at. It didn't make sense. It reminded him of having once been broken into, of gradually noticing items were missing, followed by the slow realisation an intruder had taken their things. Except nothing was missing. Quite the opposite. Something had been added to the room while he'd been away. Because there, sitting on an armchair, watching TV, legs stretched out, dirty feet crossed at the ankles, was someone he had trouble comprehending. Someone who was wearing his jacket. The same jacket he'd given her in the hotel lobby when he'd seen her two days before. It was only Iiris, with the orthodontic braces and the three fucking eyes.

171

A LITTLE MORE KISS ASS

★

Howie had woken in a funk. While escaping Viola's party had seemed like a great idea at the time, now, alone in his hotel room, with just TV, his guitar and masturbation to entertain him, he'd hit the brick wall of his creativity and resourcefulness. The previous evening, when too tired for another gymnastic sex session and too tight to fork out for one, he'd decided to write a song. He was conscious his royalty payments had suffered a downturn in recent years and, although he'd never admit it, it looked like Eddy's misgivings about the Swing classics album – that its critical reception would be lukewarm – were spot on.

'One a scale of one to Rod Stewart, how many more of these fucking cover albums are you planning on churning out?' Eddy had said in one particularly fraught exchange.

'Raoul thinks it's a great idea.'

'Raoul! Fucking Raoul! That's it now is it? You're taking advice from a man who bleaches his arsehole?!'

Howie hesitated, recognising he should have kept his association with Raoul out of their squabble. He knew Eddy believed Raoul to be a snake in the grass, conspiring to undermine and overrule him. And it was true that, since Raoul had wormed his way in, Howie had become less receptive to Eddy's management style. But he was at ease with his decision – buoyed on by Raoul whispering in his ear that he needed a younger manager. Someone who didn't bleat on about artistic integrity all of the time. Someone a little more kiss ass and a little less killjoy.

Eddy doesn't know the half of it, thought Howie, even though sometimes he unwittingly hit the nail on the head.

'It'll be country duets next,' Eddy had said.

Howie didn't dare tell him this had been the exact idea that had been mooted over a clandestine boozy Soho lunch with Raoul and a couple of his industry contacts a few weeks earlier.

And so, with a dwindling supply of drugs and the spectre of his own company stretching out for days on end, Howie tried to distract himself and use the time to write a song. But after ten minutes or so of uninspired guitar noodling, he ground to a halt and wanked himself silly into a face flannel instead.

Howie lay on the bed, bathrobe open, his flannel discarded on the carpet, feeling downcast that his go-to cure-all had failed to lift his spirits. It bugged him that Eddy had gone to ground. As the only boy child of a single mother and estranged from both his sons, Howie had missed out on male energy. Because despite the perks that came with his association with Raoul, Eddy was the nearest thing he had to a brother. Howie may be about to consciously uncouple from the most significant relationship of his life, but already, without Eddy on tap, he was feeling rudderless. He thought back over their night at the Jambhalabar. At how angry he'd been at the comparison with Morrissey. Of the revenge he'd taken – deliberately ordering seafood, knowing of Eddy's intolerance, and knowing he was too pissed and high to be mindful of the consequences. Of thinking it a hoot to ask Raoul to bring a couple of young models to their table. Of choosing the fairer-haired and more timid of the two and pushing the other – the sulky-faced one with the braces – towards Eddy. He recalled how he'd planted a condom in his jacket while he was off dancing the Kung Fu. Howie had revelled in what he'd seen as a fall from grace by someone he considered way too virtuous; in shoving the young Estonian, despite her protests, into the taxi with Eddy, who was off his tits and unawares; of slamming the cab door shut and banging on the roof to indicate to the cabbie to drive away. He'd even waved them off.

IDUNNO

'Where's your dad?' Una asked, picking up the empty cereal bowl from the coffee table.

Joni broke off briefly from her laptop screen and shrugged. 'Idunno.'

Una went into the kitchen, cheered to see Eddy had got the papers. It wasn't like him to rise before noon on a Sunday, or any day for that matter, so having the Sunday papers was a special treat. She was aware he was making an effort and these baby steps towards some kind of truce had spurred Una to make some conciliatory gestures of her own.

Having showered, she'd opened her wardrobe and scanned the rail with a heavy heart. Her preference for comfort over style had, in recent years, resulted in an assortment of shapeless garments in a palette so muddy and muted that, should she ever find herself stranded on a peat bog, there would be little likelihood of finding her. She hadn't given much thought to clothing for a long time, but something had shifted and she felt inclined to unearth an outfit more in keeping with her brighter mood. A long-forgotten wrap-around cashmere robe hung at the back of her wardrobe, still in its plastic cover, labels attached. Eddy had bought it for her one Christmas, but she'd privately decided it wasn't her, and had stored it away. Una looked in the mirror, holding the garment against her, and was surprised how the baby blue suited her, complementing her eyes and her sand-and-silver hair. She closed the curtains and turned on a table lamp, then took off her bathrobe and tried on the garment over her naked body. It felt lovely against her skin. It was a softer look than she was used to, but even she had to admit she looked nice in an outfit designed to swathe rather than swamp her. She ran her hand down her arm, comforted by the luxurious yarn and wondered what she should wear underneath. It crossed her mind that perhaps she should wear nothing. Her failing marriage and the indignities of the menopause had conspired, or so she thought, to kill off what remained of her libido. So this idea, which popped into her head, was like the unexpected arrival of an old friend. Una pushed the bedroom door shut and untied the knitted belt, allowing the robe to fall open.

Unaccustomed to seeing herself naked in a full-length mirror, her body looked curiously unfamiliar. Una considered her fifty-four-year-old figure. Although she was still much the same weight she had been in her twenties, pregnancy had left her with loose skin over her belly and her small breasts deflated. Insecurities over these changes had impacted on her self-esteem and sex life, and Eddy's insistence he thought her beautiful had fallen on deaf ears. But sleeping next to him again, after such a long time, of the unfamiliar sensation of his body heat, allowed her to be less tough on herself, less shamed by the imperfections. She thought about a time when their sex life was spontaneous, lighthearted and fun; when there was an undercurrent of desire and an unspoken understanding that intimacy was always on the cards. She lightly traced her breasts with her fingertips, her body responsive, as though it was someone else's touch. Almost imperceptibly, Una rocked her pelvis and squeezed the muscles of her inner thighs, curling her toes into the thick rug, her face flushed, her arousal unexpected. It was a delicious reminder of something that she had quietly grieved as lost.

Downstairs, the front door slammed, jolting her out of the moment. She wrapped the robe around herself, securing it tightly with the belt. Now feeling a little foolish, she ditched the idea of going knickerless and rooted through her underwear drawer, hunting for something a little less utilitarian than her everyday multipack briefs. She settled on a frou-frou lacy reminder of the days when she would actively shop for such things. She pulled them on hurriedly, slightly bashful about her choice, and tripped barefoot into the en suite, ruffling her damp hair with a towel while stretching to get her make-up bag from on top of the mirrored cabinet.

She unzipped the bag and tried to figure out the last time she'd used it – a couple of redundant tampons indicating it had been some time ago. The bag smelled wrong, of old cosmetics that should have been binned. Una rubbed her finger into a cream eyeshadow compact, turned solid with age and smudged a hint onto her top lid. It was tricky without her reading glasses. She was aware the make-up didn't go on in the same way as it once had. It had been so long since she'd worn cosmetics that her face had aged in the interim. Her eyelids were now slightly hooded, the skin a little crêpey. She unscrewed a gunky mascara, pulling out a hair wrapped around the brush – its length a reminder of the days of her thick plait. She wondered about its shelf life as she applied the gloop, crossing her fingers it wouldn't cause an infection. A decade old bottle of Jo Malone perfume still smelled good, so she sprayed it on her wrists, rubbing them together and breathing in a scent that reminded her of happier times. She rummaged and found a red lipstick, but was alarmed at the intensity of colour. It felt like a step too far, so she rubbed it off with some toilet paper. Finally, after she'd tweezered out a couple of white bristly hairs from her chin, she was done. She looked at her reflection. It was hardly a bold transformation.

'Fuck it,' she said, out loud to herself, reapplying the lipstick.

Back in the bedroom Una stood on a stool to get her hairdryer from the top shelf of her wardrobe. It had rarely been used since she'd had her hair cut short, a decade or so earlier, and she was alarmed by the smell of burning dust when she turned it on, deciding instead to let her hair dry naturally. She studied herself in the mirror. She had to conclude she looked prettier than usual and that she brushed up alright for a fifty-four-year-old.

Downstairs, Una noticed Eddy's phone on the kitchen table, and deduced that he hadn't strayed far. She popped her head around the door into the living room.

'Has Chakakhan had a wee?' Una asked Joni, outstretched on the sofa, looking at her laptop.

'Idunno.'

'Where's your dad?' she said, coming into the room for the cereal bowl and to coax Chakakhan into the garden.

But her daughter's 'idunno' seemed to be the *mot du jour*. Una rolled her eyes and gave up on the dog, who was curled against Joni and appearing in no hurry to go outside.

Una humped the bag of Sunday papers onto the table. The newspaper's front page was dominated by a massacre at a New Zealand mosque, the photos of victims – smiling snapshots taken in happy times – a terrible testament to the worst of atrocities. It was an unbearable read. Una turned the page in an attempt to shut out horrors that might encroach on the gratitude she felt for Eddy having returned home safely, in a world in which not everyone did. She felt relief at the tentative steps they'd taken towards something less fractious than the war of attrition their marriage had become. She didn't know if it was sustainable long-term, but perhaps, if they both cared enough to put in the effort, they could fix what she'd thought was beyond repair.

The torrential rain of the previous day had given way to the more customary Manchester mizzle, but Una's mood was bright. Unaware Eddy had already walked Chakakhan, she slipped on her raincoat and whistled for the dog.

Outside, Una was puzzled to see the garage doors open and the car gone, and wondered if Eddy had gone to buy bagels – a happy old tradition that had fallen by the wayside as his chaotic sleeping habits had appropriated their Sunday mornings. She thought it odd for him to leave without saying anything, especially given the upset and worry of the past few days, but she wasn't about to overthink his efforts to make things better between them. She set off for her walk anticipating what she hoped would be a smoked salmon and cream cheese bagel, along with a wedge of baked cheesecake, waiting for her on her return.

A RARE DAY OFF

★

Tony could still feel Meredith's kiss – the trace of lipstick where she'd planted her lips felt palpable on her cheek. But her comment about her being chippy had stung. She knew there was a smattering of truth in what she'd said, but she felt that someone so blessed by dumb luck had no right to say it. Would it be so terrible to join her and her friends for breakfast though? There was nothing to eat in the office. She would have to go out and get something anyway. A full Irish would certainly hit the spot. And if she tried hard to keep her snarky comments in check, she might even enjoy herself. She looked in the mirror, touching her face where Meredith's red lips were still visible – the kiss, like a spell, bewitching her. Even her annoyance at Eddy had evaporated. She decided to park her grievances, even if only temporarily, and focus instead on how best to spend a rare day off.

FRESH MEAT

★

Eddy was a terrible driver. And like the most terrible of terrible drivers, he had little insight into how bad he was. He had neither the temperament nor the hand-eye co-ordination necessary to keep the wider community safe. His mind was rarely on the road at the best of times. But driving Iiris to the station, a little stoned, wearing a spare pair of spectacles with an out-of-date prescription and mildly dazed after a mishap with the garage door, had proved particularly high-risk. He hadn't even got as far as Whalley Range before he'd managed to mount a kerb, trigger a speed camera and narrowly miss a cyclist who'd kicked off his wing mirror at the next set of traffic lights.

But Eddy was frantic. It had never entered his head, when he'd last seen Iiris on the steps of his hotel in London, that two days later he would discover her making herself at home in his living room. And that Joni, his own daughter, would have answered the door and invited her in while his wife took a shower upstairs. It was the stuff of nightmares.

On spotting a cashpoint, Eddy swerved the car, pitching up on double yellow lines, the front wheels on the pavement. He legged it to the machine and took out the full £500 daily allowance. He felt obliged, once again, to gift Iiris money in the hope that she would get out of his life. But he was beginning to have misgivings over her motives –though if she was intent on blackmailing him, she hadn't alluded to any demands. In fact, had he stopped to think about it, he'd realise she'd never once asked him for money. He just kept giving it to her. So if he was paying her off, he had yet to establish what it was he was paying her off for. He glanced in his rear-view mirror. In his mad panic to get Iiris out of the house and too impatient for the remote-controlled garage door to fully open, he'd bobbed underneath and walloped his head, causing a perfect bloody imprint of the door's edge across his forehead.

Iiris was sitting in the front passenger seat, smoking. Eddy opened all the windows from the main controls and handed her the cash.

'On a scale of one to Mark Chapman, how worried should I be about you turning up at my home address?'

Until this point they'd barely said a word to one another, beyond Iiris pointing out the bleeping would stop if Eddy were to put on his safety belt.

'I must find my friend,' she said, her eyes narrowing as she dragged on her cigarette.

'Well you won't find her at my house. And how the fuck did you find out where I live anyway?'

'It was written here.' Iiris took a folded piece of paper from one of Eddy's jacket pockets. 'These people, they put you in control of your energy.' She handed Eddy a crumpled letter from his energy provider, extolling the virtues of installing a smart meter.

Eddy snatched it from her hand and chucked it out of his window.

'Okay, this has got to stop. I'm going to drop you at the station. You need to go back to London. And Iiris, you must never contact me again. Not. Ever.'

Iiris sighed. 'I told you. I must find my friend.'

Eddy smacked the steering wheel. 'What fucking friend?'

'Zophie,' said Iiris. 'The Slovak.'

'And who the fuck is Sophie the Slovak?'

'Not Sophie, Zophie. With a zee. Zophie with a zee has apartment keys.'

'And what's that got to do with me?'

'She went with Howie Rocks.'

'And how is that my problem?'

'Howie Rocks can tell me where Zophie with a zee is.'

'Fuck's sake. It's bleeding obvious where Zophie with a zee is. She'll be back home wondering where the fuck you've got to.'

'But I do not know fucking address!' Iiris shouted.

It was the first time Eddy had seen her agitated. Animated even. Alarmed at her outburst, he shot away from the kerb.

Eddy had barely checked his wing mirror since he'd passed his driving test at seventeen, so he failed to clock the cyclist bombing up on his offside, who braked sharply to avoid being hit and jumped from the bike to save himself from being catapulted into the afterlife. An explosion of profanity dispersed into the air as Eddy took off, picking up speed down Wilbraham Road.

'Look, this isn't nice to hear,' Eddy said, clueless as to the calamity that had just been averted. 'But you have to understand that three days is a lifetime to a pop star.'

He only noticed the red light as he was almost through it, and pulled up abruptly, causing both himself and Iiris to jolt forwards and backwards. Iiris hit both hands on the dashboard while managing to hold onto her cigarette. They simultaneously fell back into their seats like crash-test dummies, and Iiris took a long draw on her ciggy, blowing a steady jet of smoke out of the passenger window.

'They're like sharks,' Eddy continued, 'they have to keep moving, hunting for fresh meat, or they die. I can guarantee Howie will have forgotten your friend's name by now. With or without a zee.'

However indignant Eddy was feeling, it was nothing compared to the cyclist who, having now caught up with him had, in a flash, reached in through the window, turned off the ignition and thrown Eddy's keys into one of the paved-over front gardens of the houses that lined the road. Then, taking advantage of the green light of the pedestrian crossing, he whipped off into the distance – though not before flipping Eddy the finger and wellying his driver's side mirror, leaving it hanging by the electrics. All of this happened so quickly, that Eddy barely had time to respond, beyond shouting a feeble and futile 'HEY!'

NOT A PIGEON

★

Howie's upbringing had been largely free of religious doctrine. His school had been Church of England, but as far as he could remember, the only nod to Christianity was the annual bloodbath over casting the nativity. Yet languishing in his hotel room, in that no man's land between end of life and funeral, he found himself thinking about the deaths of Eddy's parents. Ethel had been dead for many years, taken suddenly, just after Eddy announced his engagement to Una; the timing proof of her propensity for the dramatic. Eddy's father had died just a few years ago, remaining as silent in widowhood as he had in married life. Howie hadn't given it much thought at the time, but he recalled how Eddy had snorted when asked about Leo's funeral arrangements, just a day or two after his death and pointed out that the service had already taken place. Leo was in the ground by teatime on the day he'd died. Howie found the brevity of this custom appealing.

He recalled visiting the Katz family home following Eddy's father's passing, a nicety foisted upon him by Stina. It had been in the early days of their courtship and Stina was already pregnant – a shocker to both of them given her insistence they practice safe sex. In many ways they'd hardly known each other, but he'd been captivated and was making an effort to impress. Looking back though, he believed it to be one of the first red flags. Her assumption that he'd show his respects was a revealing indication of things to come. Of her policing of his behaviour. In that aspect, he thought, she was even worse than Eddy.

He remembered how they'd turned up at Leo and Ethel's house, a slightly tired semi in a lower-middle class north Manchester suburb. Eddy and his sister were sitting Shiva, a week-long period of mourning which to Howie's secular eye, appeared to consist of sitting on uncomfortable furniture, while receiving shedloads of overly sweet food from the community. Howie contrasted it with his own situation. While Eddy had 4,000 years of tradition to guide him – a strict set of customs and rituals to observe – all Howie had was Jean bending his ear about her well-thumbed brochure from the funeral home. It was less than forty-eight hours since his mother had died and already she was on the phone, on his case. He hadn't bargained for the workload death brought, the ludicrous event-management aspect of it, and had presumed, like everything else to do with his mother, he could leave it to his sister to organise.

'No way. Not a cat in hell's chance,' Howie said, the second the question was out of her mouth.

'I just thought you'd want to say something.'

'Like what? What would I say?'

'I don't know. You're used to getting up in front of an audience.'

While this was true, the thought of delivering a speech at his mother's funeral provoked an attack of collywobbles Howie hadn't experienced even on stage at Live Aid.

'Think of some funny stories,' she said.

'Can't remember any.'

'What about the time that coloured family moved in opposite and...'

'No,' Howie said, shutting her down. 'That was fucking horrible.'

'Language.'

Howie pulled himself up from the bed and walked over to the window.

'It was harmless,' Jean said.

'No, it wasn't.'

'Well, give it some thought.'

Howie switched his phone to speaker phone and propped it on the sill, putting some distance between himself and his sister while making it easier to smoke out of the small gap in the window.

'Anyway, what time is good on Wednesday?' Jean asked.

'What's happening Wednesday?' Howie replied, his voice weary and overburdened.

'I've made an appointment at the funeral home. We need to dot the i's and cross the t's.'

Howie couldn't believe Jean was roping him in. Absenting himself from Viola's birthday celebrations now seemed like a stupid move. He should have known Jean would do this.

'They do a dove release service,' she said.

'And how much is that?'

'Depends on how many you have.'

'How about none.'

Jean rustled through paperwork. 'A hundred and ten pounds,' she said.

'A hundred and ten quid for a funeral pigeon?'

'It's not a pigeon, Neville, it's a fan-tailed dove.'

'I don't care what it is, it's a rip off.'

'For when words aren't enough,' Jean said, reading from her brochure. 'Now, would you like to view the body?'

'Why would I want to do that?'

'Some people find it helps.'

'I'm good thanks.'

There was more rustling of paper. 'Dressing of the deceased and hygienic treatments...'

'I don't want to know,' Howie said, his voice raised.

'That's a hundred,' Jean said, ignoring him. 'Viewing the deceased is a hundred and fifty on top. Gosh.'

'I'll give it a miss, thanks. She didn't look great when I saw her dead in the hospital, so she's hardly going to look better now.'

'If you're sure.'

'I'm sure.'

'Righty-ho. Now, coffins. Solid oak or mahogany? Both look super.'

'How much?' Howie waited while Jean consulted her price list.

'It says price on application.'

'I bet it does. What else have they got?'

'Hold on.'

Howie blew the cigarette smoke out of the window into the drizzle.

'Banana leaf! Ridiculous. The world's gone mad. Cardboard? God strewth! What if it rains?'

Jean carried on reeling off options and add-ons, most of which were batted back by Howie who had lost interest. He was more focused on seeing if the smoking woman in the next room was at her window.

'And she's not going out in one of those ruddy wicker ones either.

Your Aunt Gladys had one of them. It was like sending her off in a picnic hamper.'

The window of the next room was shut and a despondency descended on Howie that he didn't know how to shake. He needed someone to guide him through all of this. He needed Eddy.

IT'S NOT BEEN YOUR DAY

✴

Within minutes of the cyclist chucking the keys, the traffic began to build up behind Eddy. Iiris remained impassive as she finished her cigarette, flicking the still-smouldering butt onto the pavement. It was raining again, and a steady light mist was blowing into the car. But with the engine off and the keys missing, Iiris was unable to close her window.

'I'm cold,' she called to Eddy, as he ran around the vehicle, foraging for his keys.

But Eddy was in no mood to bother with a woman who appeared to be some kind of jinx. He scurried up and down the pavement, trying to work out where they may have landed. He was in too much of a panic to think logically. Some of the drivers, realising this wasn't going to be a quick fix, managed to manoeuvre their way around his car onto the wrong side of the road, bypassing the traffic lights. Others stayed stationary, waiting for the traffic to move. But as the lights went to green, to red and to green again, tensions mounted. At first it was a few passive-aggressive pips on the horn, followed by longer and louder blasts. But it wasn't long before a nugget-headed man – having tired of keeping his fist on the horn – stepped out from his car. He marched over to Eddy, hitching the jeans he wore below his stomach, and that showed off the crack of his arse. His bare belly protruded from under his T-shirt like a beach ball about to pop, his feet splayed outward on account of his chubby thighs, his centre of gravity tipped backwards to counter the weight of his gut. He was eighteen stones of mottled flesh and aggression.

'Are you going to shift that car?'

'No, I thought I'd leave it there,' Eddy said, his death wish back with a bang. 'It's not bothering you is it?'

'Are you taking the piss? My daughter's got a party to go to.'

In normal circumstances, Eddy would have had sympathy with a dad tasked with getting his daughter to an event. He would have been mortified to be the reason for the hold-up, and the cause of distress. He looked over and saw this guy's little princess scowling from the car, a mini version of her father, but with ringlets and teeth. Her florid face and fury mirroring her fathers' own. Eddy didn't know who he should be more afraid of, angry dad or Little Miss Gammon.

'On a scale of one to Stanley Kowalski, what's the chances of us kissing and making up?'

Iiris lit another cigarette while the car felt the full force of beach-ball-belly-man's boot, appearing disinclined to get out of the car and into the cold, even though there was a lunatic hell-bent on trashing the driver-side panel. Fortunately, poor muscle tone and clogged arteries brought the attack to a premature end, and the man got back into his car and performed a screechy and illegal manoeuvre as inelegant as his low-slung pants, before speeding up the wrong side of the road.

Whether it was coincidence, surveillance or calls from the public, the police soon arrived, silencing car horns and disgruntlement as people settled back to revel in this turn of events. With no sense of urgency, two officers got out of their patrol vehicle and strolled over to Eddy, who was attempting to stick his wing mirror back using nothing more than forlorn hope and one of his elastic bands.

'How did the mirror get broken?' said a young constable who was so short that Eddy wondered if she needed a booster seat to reach the pedals of the patrol car.

'It was a cyclist.'

'You hit a cyclist?'

'No, a cyclist hit my car. Well, kicked it to be precise.'

The officer looked sceptical. 'So, what's the problem here? Have you broken down?'

'No. The cyclist threw my keys over there somewhere. I can't find them.'

'And why would he do that?'

'I've no idea. Everyone is so angry these days. I blame Gordon Ramsay.'

'Did the cyclist do that too?' said the officer pointing at the stoved-in door panel.

'No that was someone else. Honestly, it's reality TV and social media.

They've normalised confrontation.'

'And what about your face?' she said, pointing at Eddy's forehead.

'Remote controlled garage door.'

'It's not been your day, has it, sir.'

The second officer, large to the first officer's little, walked around to the passenger side of the car, where Iiris sat smoking. Unsmiling, she beckoned her colleague over. Eddy put the elastic band back on his wrist, twanged it and followed her to the passenger side. The larger officer squatted, to put herself at eye level with Iiris, as though talking to a child. Eddy craned to get a better view and felt a fluttering of panic on seeing the HOWIE ROCKS stone held out in her palm. Why the fuck did she still have that? And why the fuck was she showing it to them? Would these coppers make the connection? Would they figure out just which Howie it was from the ramblings of this woman-child with her stupid painted pebble? Eddy tried to earwig their conversation, but they were talking too quietly, too conspiratorially, for him to hear. The shorter of the two caught his eye. Her previous benign demeanour had evaporated.

'Perhaps it would be a better use of sir's time if he looked for his keys?'

Eddy twanged his elastic band over and over and tried to be scientific about where the keys could have landed, given the trajectory the cyclist had thrown them. It wasn't easy with his old spectacles, but he narrowed it down to a specific area. And there they were, on the paved-over garden of a red-brick semi, its windows triple-glazed against traffic noise. Eddy walked back to his car, trying to look chirpy, like it was all sorted out now so they could be on their way.

'The young lady says her friend went off with an old man,' said the larger of the two – a broad-shouldered ox of a woman, who looked like she'd put her nanna in a headlock for sport.

'He's not old. He's fifty-eight.'

The three women looked at each other, pulling faces as though Eddy had said something ludicrous. Never had the gulf between himself and younger generations felt so yawning.

'Do you know this young lady's name, sir?'

'Of course I do. It's Iiris,' Eddy said tacking on, in the hope it would add clout, 'with three eyes.'

'And how do you know her?'

'I don't know her. Not really. We met in London, and she turned up at my house... She turned up uninvited at my house and now I'm driving her to the station.'

'That's a little odd, don't you think?'

'Welcome to my life,' Eddy said, his arms outstretched.

'Do you make a habit of giving lifts to people you don't know?'

'Well I'm not a taxi, if that's what you mean. Except for my twelve-year-old daughter.' Eddy laughed, hoping his feeble dad joke would lighten the mood. But his attempt at humour fell on deaf ears.

'She says she doesn't know her address.'

'I'm amazed. She had no trouble finding mine.'

The bovine officer stood. 'How old are you luv?'

Eddy felt everything clench.

'Seventeen.'

If Eddy had been wearing a hat, he would have thrown it into the air.

'Next birthday,' she added.

Eddy felt a little deflated, but still mightily relieved that Iiris was at least legally an adult. But it didn't seem to cut any mustard with the coppers, who appeared to be increasingly curious as to what this bare-legged Eastern European teenager was doing in a car with a much older man who didn't appear to know much about her.

'Pull your car over, sir. I think we need to have a little chat.'

THE BEST OF HAIR DAYS

★

Washing her hair with a vending machine cup over the sink in the communal toilets was laborious and time-consuming, but with the gym shut at weekends, Tony had no choice. She was determined to look her best if she were to join Meredith and her friends at the pub.

If.

Her denial was such that even as she moved the plastic beaker between the hot and cold taps, she was telling herself she hadn't made up her mind yet, one way or the other. Even as she blasted her hair with her dryer, upside down for maximum volume, she was tricking herself into believing she was keeping her options open. Even as she combed through the pomade, she was convinced she hadn't decided for sure, but was simply smartening herself up. She checked her perfectly preened hairdo in the mirror. It bothered Tony that Meredith had seen her looking so scuzzy. She shuddered to think of the sight she'd presented earlier. But despite such an unpromising start, it turned out that today would be the best of hair days. There was a part of her, bigger than perhaps she was willing to admit, that wanted Meredith to be impressed by how she'd rebuilt her life. She wasn't used to having the upper hand, but was aware that even Meredith, with all of her privilege, seemed a little in awe of her new situation. For once, she wasn't the underdog and it felt great.

SHE'S NOT IN ANY TROUBLE

✶

The overpowering aroma of pine disinfectant did little to mask the smell of unwashed human that was pulverised into the upholstery of the police car. Eddy sat in silence, next to Iiris, contemplating the absurdity of his predicament. Because in the end he hadn't been arrested over suspicions of pimping, noncing or sex trafficking, but rather the roadside saliva drug test that revealed cannabis in his system. Eddy had been surprised the officer had presumed him to be under the influence. He imagined he'd presented as perfectly lucid, even if the circumstances they'd found him in were a little odd. But, in the end, there had been no crack detective work required at the scene, just the giveaway of a large spliff sitting behind his ear. He twanged the elastic band on his wrist, and wondered if they still removed belts and shoelaces in police custody.

Iiris took out a fresh cigarette packet and a lighter from her pocket.

'Sorry, luv, you can't smoke in the car. You can smoke outside the station. We're nearly there.'

It hadn't gone unnoticed by Eddy that the police officers were being decidedly more pleasant to Iiris than they were to him.

'I don't see why Iiris has to come to the station,' Eddy said. 'She was just the passenger.'

'We're aware of that. She's not in any trouble.'

He glanced at Iiris, but she was looking out of the window while turning over the cigarette packet in her hand. He wondered what she'd told the officers. And what she'd told Joni when she'd turned up at the house. And what, by now, Joni had told her mother about the young woman who she'd invited in. And what Una had made of the whole fucking fiasco. His brief dalliance with optimism, his one last attempt at a happy domestic life, seemed ridiculous to him now. Mentally, it was back to business as usual. A mudslide of melancholy oozed over him, swallowing up the goodwill of the night before.

BUTTERFLIES

Tony looked out of the office window to check the weather. It was still drizzly and, although the weather wasn't going to dampen her spirits, she was worried about it ruining her hair. She knew her compromised mobility would add a good half-hour onto the twenty-minute walk to O'Sheas, and that she was already pushing her luck if she were to get there in time for a full Irish. She considered taking her car, but the hassle of parking and of Meredith seeing she was still driving her old banger, caused her to rethink. There was something about the anticipation of sacking off work for the day, of spending time with Meredith, that had her lighten up a little on her usual frugality. She decided to treat herself to a cab. She might even have a drink. Tony sniffed her armpits, concerned her favourite shirt, a vintage Ben Sherman with a button-down collar, wasn't clean. All good. She kissed Fazakerley on the top of his head and off she set, with butterflies in her stomach and an overly cheery wave goodbye to the smiling security guard.

A PRIZE FOOL

★

If Eddy's mood could be conjured up in the form of a microwaveable meal, then the solid grey blob of macaroni cheese served on a moulded plastic plate perfectly represented his state of mind. His arrest had coincided with the dishing up of lunch – the culinary equivalent of a punishment beating.

The cell had been painted an acid-yellow gloss, though it brought little sunshine to a room lit by a flickering, buzzing, fluorescent strip. A run of glass bricks, high on the wall, failed to let in light and had the odd effect of making the room feel gloomier.

He'd accepted, without complaint, the DNA swab, the blood sample, the fingerprinting and the mugshot, though he'd put up an impassioned resistance against the removal of his belt. But the detention officer easily overpowered him – he was taking no truck from an out-of-condition sixty-three-year-old, whose criminal history started and finished with a bus lane fine. Eddy hadn't taken up the offer of a phone call. There didn't seem much point in contacting a solicitor. He knew he was guilty and may as well face the consequences.

On a scale of one to Boy George, he thought, *how humiliating would community service actually be?*

But it wasn't the judiciary that concerned him. It was Una. For all Joni's hormonal monosyllables, he feared she'd have told her mother about the young Estonian woman, who he'd bundled from the house in an unholy rush. He didn't want to drag his daughter into it, didn't want her to be a co-conspirator. But he didn't want her to bubble him up either.

Apart from outbursts of expletives from his nearest cell neighbour, the station was quiet. It was only the wheezing of his chest that threatened to drown out the mantra in his head, scolding himself for being a prize fool. He thought about twanging his elastic wrist band, but he couldn't be bothered. He took a sip of tepid tea – reeking of chlorine and as cloudy as a Bank-Holiday Monday – musing that there was more nutritional value in the polystyrene cup than the rubbery pasta dish, which sat uneaten beside him on the thin vinyl mattress that served as a bed.

Now and again, a rancid tang of undigested stomach contents cut through the disinfectant. Eddy looked at his stockinged feet, hoping he hadn't trodden in anything, having been required to leave his shoes outside the cell door. He stood, hitching his belt-less trousers, and tippy-toed to the toilet in the corner, trying to avoid contact with the floor. Grappling with his flies, while trying to keep his trousers up, defied him, and by the time his piss hit the stainless-steel pan, they were rumpled around his ankles. The disgrace was complete. He was in no doubt that, had he still had his belt, he could have done himself in before the officer whistling in the distance had checked the CCTV. It would be the police who'd find him. Not some family member at home, or a hotel chambermaid, or a dog walker discovering him strung from a tree. It would be the police who would have to deal with the consequences. And it would serve them fucking right.

UGLY ON THE INSIDE

★

Tony gripped the handrail as she made her way up the steps to reception, attempting her best sober walk for the smiling security guard. A pint of Guinness had been enough to cause tipsiness. But she was glad of this lapse in her sobriety. She'd had a good time at O'Sheas – managing to put physical distance between herself and Meredith's friends. She'd pulled up a stool at the end of a long table, her knee pressed against Meredith's in the crush of the room, and their proximity and the alcohol had relaxed her. The rancour she'd felt towards her ex had ebbed away, along with her resolve to shut her out of her life.

Tony had kept the conversation light, carefully treading the line between mischief and discretion when answering questions about Howie and her job. Meredith had never been the slightest bit curious about the nursing home, so Tony enjoyed this new-found fascination in her life. She managed to address Meredith's curiosity so she'd feel included in Tony's reconstructed world, without actually telling her a thing.

'Has he, like, had work done?' Meredith asked.

'He should ask for his money back if he has,' Tony replied, her answer semi-honest. She chose not to reveal a story of Eddy's, told in confidence, of the liposuction that had caused a whole week of studio time to be binned. Of Howie not being able to hit the high notes while in post-operative discomfort, partly from the procedure and partly from having to wear compression pants.

'He's sort of handsome though, in a, like, sleazy kind of way?'

'He's dead ugly on the inside,' Tony said, with a little more bite than she'd intended.

'In what way?' Meredith's tone was playful. 'Tell me.'

She placed her hand on top of Tony's as they leant in towards each other, to be heard over the noise. Tony laughed, not taking the conversation further, but hyper-aware of the electricity of the touch. She looked at Meredith's child-sized hand, her manicured nails, painted St Patrick's Day green. It crossed her mind she'd never seen Meredith with long fingernails before. When they'd been together, she'd always kept them clipped short. They both had. It had been a practicality, to save them causing harm to each other during lovemaking. She took Meredith's long nails as evidence that she was single; that she didn't have anyone to keep them short for.

They left O'Sheas together, linking arms and giggling, oblivious to the drizzle and the raised eyebrows of Meredith's friends.

'I should really take Fazakerley out,' Tony said, as they meandered away from the pub, off the main drag, with an understanding this warmth between them was the prelude to something. 'He'll be crossing his legs.'

'Is Howie okay with you leaving a, like, dog in the office?' Meredith asked.

Tony shrugged. 'He lives down south. Eddy's cool about it though.'

'Amazing. I'll come with you?'

Tony should have anticipated this, given Meredith's tendency to invite herself along to whatever took her fancy. But she wasn't sure it would be a good idea. Though normally fastidious about clearing away her bedding and quick to gather any of her hand-washing spread about the office to dry, her waking that morning in a low mood, followed by the excitement of bumping into Meredith, had caused her to be unusually lax.

'No, it's okay. I've got a few things I need to sort out.'

The drizzle was a little heavier now, so Tony took off her jacket and held it over both of their heads, taking care not to flatten her hair or knock Meredith's tiny top hat, and walked at a pace her limp would allow. She hadn't meant to sound ungracious. She didn't want Meredith to think she'd gone cold on her, that she was holding back.

'But I could walk Fazakerley over to yours later maybe?' Tony said. Afraid of rejection, these conversations didn't come easy. Meredith had no such qualms.

'Amazing! But I don't mind, like, coming to yours?'

Tony hesitated, chewing the inside of her mouth, unwilling to divulge her makeshift living arrangements.

'Where is home anyway?' Meredith asked.

'It's complicated.'

'Why so, like, mysterious? You're not with someone are you?' Meredith said, the laugh in her voice stinging Tony a little. As though such a thing was beyond belief.

'No,' she replied. 'Just the dog.'

Meredith said nothing, not at first. But as they walked through Sackville Gardens, huddled under Tony's jacket, both drawn to the calm away from the St Patrick's Day high jinks over in nearby Canal Street, Meredith replied. 'I'm glad.'

And there, directly in front of Alan Turing, rain running down his bronze statue nose, they kissed. And it was every bit as delicious as Tony had remembered.

UNDER INVESTIGATION

★

The last time Eddy had hopped on a Manchester bus, Marvin Gaye was alive, Jimmy Savile was a national treasure, and they still had conductors, who took cash.

With his car keys returned, but his car now impounded, Eddy had been released, *under investigation*, by an officer who clearly ran a tight ship and wanted him gone.

'On a scale of one to Dixon of Dock Green, how does your job live up to your ambition to serve the community?' Eddy said to the non plussed officer, as he handed over his belongings with the speed and efficiency of a server at a burger joint drive-thru.

Eddy wandered to the main road and to the nearest bus stop. Living for so long in the bosom of the middle classes had insulated him from the ins and outs of Greater Manchester's public transport system. He felt adrift in a part of the city unfamiliar to him.

On seeing a double-decker approach, he put out his hand, unsure if this was the correct etiquette in 2019. He had no idea, at this distance and with his out-of-date prescription spectacles, where the bus was headed. But anywhere was preferable to the chill wind blowing fine rain through the shelter.

As the driver indicated to pull in, Eddy was momentarily in two minds as to whether to board the bus or throw himself under it. The thought of ending up as nothing more than a stain on the tarmac seemed both appropriate and appealing. But by the time he'd run the plan through his head, the moment had passed, the hiss of the bus's air brakes breaking the spell. Eddy boarded. The driver paused as Eddy stood without a coat, wet and gormless, saying nothing and twanging his elastic band like some sad human banjo.

'Where to?' the driver asked, appearing a little perplexed at Eddy's ignorance of protocol.

Eddy shrugged. 'I don't know. Where are you going?'

'Piccadilly Gardens.'

'That'll do.'

And with that, thanks to the miracle of contactless payments, he set off on his journey into town.

Eddy sat at the front, in a seat designated for the elderly, confident that no one, looking at the state of him, would take issue. He peered out at block after block of brick and render housing with spartan facades and an absence of foliage, the view semi-obscured by poor vision and rivulets of rainwater that ran down the glass. Despite the blur, the journey became increasingly recognisable to him as the streets narrowed and the buildings grew taller, punctuated by a frisson of expectation each time the bus drove over tram tracks. He imagined a horrific pile-up – a tangled mess of bus and tram that would solve his most immediate of problems. Piccadilly Gardens may have been in the opposite direction to Chorlton. It was somewhere he could get his bearings and find his way home from. But he wasn't sure if home was where he would be heading.

BLAST SHADOW

Leaving Joni under strict instruction to clear the kitchen table of crafting detritus, Una went upstairs to change. She swapped her cashmere robe for some trackie bottoms and an old T-shirt – the Ban the Bomb logo having long since faded to its own blast shadow. She wrapped herself in a soft blanket and lay on the bed, weary of second-guessing what Eddy was up to.

She had a migraine brewing, the lingering phantom scent of the perfume she'd scrubbed off had prompted her to take medication and rest. Her make-up was now smeared onto cotton-wool balls and discarded into the bathroom bin. Her cosmetic bag, zipped shut and placed back on top of the cabinet. She'd no idea where Eddy had got to. He'd been uncontactable and gone for hours. But he'd used up the last vestiges of her patience and goodwill during the London trip. She knew this state of affairs was unsustainable. It was a miserable existence for both of them. She would have to face it. Their marriage was over.

A SPANNER IN THE WORKS

★

Eddy was taken aback to find Fazakerley in the office, alone, on a Sunday. But the dog, always enthusiastic with its welcomes, wasn't an unpleasant surprise. Still, it had thrown a spanner in the works. He had no problem with Tony managing her own hours, it had been one of her conditions of employment, but while the large open holdall, with clothes strewn from it may have puzzled him, it wasn't as surprising as the tuba, that stood bell down, in the centre of the room. The sleeping bag on the sofa suggested Tony must have worked late, going an extra mile untravelled by previous personal assistants. Her dedication prodded his conscience as it dawned on him that topping himself would essentially be doing her out of a job. It hadn't occurred to him to write a suicide note, but perhaps he could scribble down a quick reference instead. It would give him something constructive to do while waiting for the overdose to kick in.

He walked over to the filing cabinet in which he kept a stash of medication, some prescription, some over-the-counter – most of it trousered when helping his sister clear out their parents' home after Leo died. It was a mixture of anti-inflammatories, beta-blockers and stool softeners, all wildly out of date. Eddy figured the more the merrier. He would take the lot. At least that had been the cobbled-together plan, when he'd got off the bus, unsure of what to do or where to go next. A few minutes of wandering around the bus terminus had established that not only would suicide be the solution to his marital woes, and his disenchantment with Howie and the music industry in general, but it would also solve the problem of not being able to figure out which number bus would get him back to Chorlton. He'd lost track of how long it had been since he'd left the house, but he knew Una would be wondering where he was, regardless of whether Joni had spilt the beans about Iiris. Cold in his shirtsleeves and hungry from refusing the police station food, he stood sheltering from the rain under an M&S Simply Food canopy, his senses assaulted by an amplified busker, murdering 'Hallelujah' at a decibel level that threatened to jettison Leonard Cohen's celestial body back into the physical realm.

A plan came quickly to him, perfect in its simplicity. It was only a short walk from Piccadilly Gardens to the office. No-one would be around on a Sunday, providing the perfect opportunity to do himself in. He would barricade the room from the inside, so Tony wouldn't be the one to find him. He would neck the meds, lie on the sofa and Bob's your uncle, it would be goodbye cruel world once and for all. He was energised by this plan of action, and bobbed into Marks to pick up a butty, tickled that this would be his last meal on earth. He strode to Ancoats in the rain, stuffing the chicken tikka wrap into his mouth with no care for the acid reflux which – if he lapsed into unconsciousness quickly enough – would only kick in once dead.

Eddy was relieved to see a familiar security guard on reception; the nice smiley one who knew him and would happily wave him in. He wasn't sure how long it would take for the tablets to work, but he'd hoped to have it done and dusted by teatime. So, it had thrown him when Fazakerley had jumped off the sofa to greet him. He would need to have a rethink. He'd never been the type of boss to crack the whip or pull rank, but he hadn't bargained for this when agreeing to Tony's flexitime. He was disgruntled at this stymieing of his plan. But *fuck it*, he thought, *puh puh puh*. Needs must. He would do it anyway.

TURD POLISHER

★

In the time it took for the elevator to reach the third floor, Tony was sober. Her face was no longer flushed from alcohol, but ashen with the alarm of someone about to be rumbled. It had been the smiling security guard who'd tipped her off. He'd called to her as the elevator doors closed, letting her know 'the boss' was upstairs.

She had hesitated before entering the office, trying to affect the nonchalance of someone to whom a sleeping bag, tuba and dog were perfectly normal things to find in a professional workspace on a Sunday afternoon. But all of her faux composure flew out of the window on seeing Eddy on the floor, slumped against the sofa. Fazakerley lay next to him, licking out the empty packet of a chicken tikka wrap. She ran to him. Splots of blood were dripping from his nose, saturating his shirt. His left eye was purple and swollen shut; his fairground funhouse visage reflected in the polished bell of the tuba.

'No, Eddy! Who did this?'

It was a natural assumption to make. But the flex of her hairdryer around his ankle told a different tale. Because Eddy had never made it to the filing cabinet to gather his stash of meds and had instead stumbled over Tony's hairdryer cord – still plugged into the wall and stretched across the floor – nosediving like a trip-wired horse in a Hollywood Western, clattering the corner of the desk with the left side of his face as he went down.

Tony hurriedly wound the cord around the hairdryer before shoving it out of sight behind the sofa, tossing her sleeping bag over the back with the same sleight of hand. Eddy opened his one good eye, and smiled to see her.

'I don't suppose you've got a steak on you?' he asked, his voice nasal as though suffering from a heavy cold.

'I'll get a towel,' Tony said.

'I'm fine,' he replied. 'I just need a steak.'

'Fucking hell, Eddy, you don't need a steak, you need an ambulance.'

Tony pulled a towel from where it had been left drying over the back of a chair.

'Or frozen peas would do,' Eddy said, touching his lips as though checking they were still there.

Tony dragged her holdall out of view and picked up his spectacles from the floor.

'At least your specs are okay.'

'They're fucking useless. It's an old prescription. I think that's why I tripped.'

Tony didn't dare correct him. She knew she was culpable. Her hand trembled as she dialled 999.

'Is the patient breathing?'

'Yeah.'

'Is the patient conscious?'

'Frozen peas,' Eddy piped up in the background.

'Yeah.'

'You'd be best off taking him yourself, la,' said the Scouse operator, bonding with Tony's accent. 'There's a Paddy's Day rush on.'

The A&E triage nurse looked impressed by Eddy's injury, proclaiming 'ooh nasty', when he took the bloodied towel from his face.

'That was a garage door,' Eddy said, pointing at the gash on his forehead. 'And this was a desk,' he said, pointing at his eye.

'Too much to drink?'

'No. Bifocals.'

The nurse looked at Tony.

'An old prescription,' she said.

There was a tick-box run-through of symptoms that might indicate a more serious head injury but once the nurse established Eddy wasn't in imminent danger of a brain bleed, he was sent back into the standing-room-only waiting area. Tony meandered off to find a wheelchair and returned dragging one behind her, its heavy wheels swivelling the wrong way, the chair veering left and right.

'You have it,' Eddy said, unaware that he was dribbling.

'Don't be soft. I got it for youze.'

Eddy sat slouched in the chair, looking vulnerable and much older than his years. Tony stood next to him, checking the electronic board that updated predicted waiting times. Two hours.

'You go,' Eddy said.

'No, you're okay.'

'Honestly, I'll be fine. It'll be ages yet. I've already fucked up enough of your day.'

Tony had been fearful the one pint of Guinness she'd had at lunchtime may have put her over the limit, so they'd made their way to hospital in an Uber. Eddy with his head back, a bloodied towel pressed over his face, muttering apologies for inconveniencing her. Her phone had pinged en route, and Meredith had asked her how long she would be. Tony replied that her day had got complicated and she was on her way to A&E with Eddy. Meredith sent a crying face emoji. Tony told her she would be over later, and devil, peach and pointed finger emojis popped back up on her phone. Tony wasn't sure what these meant, but they were thrilling nonetheless.

There wasn't much chat in the waiting room, just the dulled team spirit of a disparate bunch of listless people having a rough day. Tony didn't think it was the time or place to bring up the subject of Iiris – of her turning up at the office or her being booked into The Sharples at the company's expense. Of handing her petty cash in the hope she would use it to fuck off home. None of these things seemed nearly as important as they had a day or two earlier. Her anger over the whole episode crumbled with self-reproach over Eddy's accident; she felt way too guilty and chastened by her boss's current predicament to add to his woes. What had gone on in London was none of her business, she decided. If she wanted to stay working in this job, perhaps she should learn to turn a blind eye?

'Did you know Queenie died?' Eddy asked, wiping the drool from his chin with his bloody towel.

'Ahh, when?'

'Friday.'

'She was dead old though. I wonder what her secret was?'

'Ciggies and spite,' Eddy said, lisping over each S sound, as though he'd just got out of the dentist's chair.

Tony smiled. 'I'll light her a candle.'

'I should too. Even if she did call me Howie's Jew friend,' he said, mimicking Queenie's thin, tremulous voice.

'She never.'

'She did. She was a horrible old bag really,' he said, trying to control his spittle, 'but we both helped create a monster. We had that in common at least.'

Tony laughed.

'I'm serious,' he said.

'Don't be soft.'

'It's true. I've been giving it a lot of thought.'

Tony suspected Eddy giving a lot of thought to something probably wasn't a good thing. 'So you reckon youze are to blame for Howie being a prick?'

'Not just me. He's had a lot of people enabling him: Queenie, Jean, friends, girlfriends, the Dumplings, the press... Raoul fucking Zazou.'

'You're being a bit hard on yourself.'

'I've not been hard enough.'

'I somehow doubt that.'

Eddy shrugged.

'Howie's an adult,' Tony said.

Eddy huffed as though to dispute this.

'He's a celebrity. The two things are incompatible.'

Tony smiled and checked the predicted waiting times, which had gone from two hours to two hours thirty. She wondered how long she'd be able to stand with her leg playing up. She longed to be able to sit, or at least lean against a wall.

'It can't have been all bad,' she said.

'No. But I started out polishing a rough diamond and ended up with a gleaming turd.'

Tony laughed. 'You should put that on a business card.'

'What? Eddy Katz. Turd Polisher. Sounds about right.'

They said nothing for a few minutes, as Tony thought about what Eddy had said, knowing there was some truth in it.

'Shall I call Una?'

Eddy thought for a moment. 'I guess.'

Tony had no signal but managed, eventually, to access the hospital wi-fi. But the connection kept dropping out, so she left Eddy in the wheelchair to make the call outside. As she stood under the canopy, sheltering from the rain, trying to pick up a more robust signal, a blurred WhatsApp photo of what Tony thought might be Meredith's bum cheeks arrived on her phone. She'd forgotten this was one of Meredith's saucy little quirks – how, when Tony was working at the nursing home, she'd send her photos. She might be draining a catheter bag or cleaning between the toes of an elderly resident, only to have her phone ping with a photo of her girlfriend's fanny. As much as Tony delighted in these fruity interludes, she would never send one back. She was far too paranoid about images being passed around – of them being used to blackmail or bully her. Meredith, however, couldn't have cared less.

Tony phoned Eddy's home number, but it rang and rang. She gave up and went back into the waiting room to ask for Una's mobile.

'It's zero seven something,' he said. 'I think it ends with a two two. Or is it a one one...?'

Finally, a chair at the end of a row became free. Tony wheeled Eddy over so they could sit next to each other, his swollen lips moving as he silently ran through all of the permutations of Una's phone number. Tony gazed around the room – collective hopes raised every time a nurse came to call the next patient, each person silently envious of whichever lucky bastard's ailment had been deemed serious enough to bump them up the queue. Eddy squinted at his waiting-room compatriots through his one good eye; at the mixture of couples, and families and a small sad child, whose unbroken whimpering echoed the general ennui of the room.

'Did you know that the more people you bring with you to hospital, the less serious it is?' Eddy said in his new Joseph Merrick voice, leaning in to Tony, so no one else would hear.

'How do you work that out?'

'Hospital documentaries. Seriously ill people arrive alone. But stub your toe and along comes the entire family.'

'That's probably dead sound. Maybe that's how they should triage.'

They chuckled together like a pair of old lags, Eddy holding the bloodied towel to his mouth. Tony watched an elderly couple doing a crossword together, the old man's arm in a makeshift tea-towel sling. She nudged Eddy and nodded towards them. Their sweetness made them smile.

'Have you got anyone Tony?'

She shrugged. 'Not sure. Maybe. I hope so.'

Eddy smiled as best he could, wincing at the pain in his cheekbone. 'I'm glad. We all just want to be loved.'

'I suppose,' Tony said. 'My dog loves me.'

'Mine doesn't,' Eddy said. 'Well, she's not mine really. She's made that very clear. She's Una's. I don't think she likes men.'

Tony laughed. 'Who? The dog or Una?'

'Both,' he said, with a rueful, crooked grin.

'Do you think Howie feels loved?'

'I don't think he cares.'

'The Dumplings love him,' Tony said.

'The Dumplings love Howie. They don't know Neville.'

Tony nodded. She liked it when Eddy took her into his confidence. It was one of the reasons she was so fond of him. It made her feel important. She felt bad she'd taken advantage of this trust by living in the office. She should get a place of her own. What had felt like a perfectly reasonable arrangement before the events of the day now felt like a piss-take. She touched the back of his hand.

'Talking of dogs, I'm going to have to take Fazakerley out at some point. He'll be desperate.'

'You go. Honestly, I'm okay.'

'I'm happy to come back.'

'No, don't be daft. Go. Get a taxi. Sort yourself out from petty cash.'

Tony gave Eddy a peck on his head. She didn't feel it was the time to tell him that there was no money left in the tin. Not since Iiris had turned up looking for him.

'I'll keep trying Una. If I can't get hold of her, I'll come back and get you.'

Eddy took her hand and squeezed it. 'You know I don't expect you to work weekends.'

'It's cool. It suits me.'

Tony looked at Eddy, sitting in the wheelchair with his massive swollen eye and a gash on his forehead, clutching his bloodied towel and his out of date prescription glasses. 'Well I love you Eddy Katz.'

'Love you back, Tony Dunn.'

THE CUSP OF BAD NEWS

★

Una was dead to the world, lying on her bed, cocooned in her blanket, the sound of knocking permeating her dreams. She opened her eyes, the residual effects of the staved-off migraine causing her to squint in the afternoon light of the bedroom. She tried to orient herself in that split second or so of befuddlement. As her thoughts untangled, she had the sick feeling that something was wrong. Then she remembered that Eddy was gone. Again.

The knocking continued and it took a few seconds for her to realise it wasn't a dream but someone in the real world at the front door. Her anti-social streak and Eddy's low moods meant that outside of the window cleaner coming for payment, they rarely had visitors. Friends had long since got the message not to pop by, and Joni, a bit of a chip off both of the old blocks, didn't encourage school friends to come calling either. She had no interest in their sleepovers and excursions to the Trafford Centre, and found their new-found obsession with boys an excruciating embarrassment.

Una held off for a moment or two, waiting for Joni to answer. The dog was kicking off in the hall, the yapping feeding the anxiety rising in her chest. She knew it couldn't be Eddy. Taking the car meant he had a full set of keys. Had someone come to tell her the worst? She jumped from the bed, shouting to Joni from the landing.

'I'll get it.'

How long have I lived like this? she thought, as she hurried barefoot downstairs, still wrapped in the blanket and laden with dread. Forever on the cusp of bad news.

The stained-glass panel in the front door was too ornate to offer a clear picture of the person standing outside, and Una faltered, hesitating on the staircase, her hand clutching the blanket to her chest while she digested what she saw. It was a man, dressed in black. His silhouette slightly stooped. And always, despite all the years she'd known him, a little shorter than she thought.

THE YIN TO THE YANG

★

It took effort for Eddy to keep up with the predicted delay times on the waiting room display, but squinting at it, trying to make the letters clear, at least gave him something to do. It didn't, however, take his mind off the ferrous taste in the back of his throat or the pain in his cheek – the throbbing in his face the yin to the yang of the numbness in his lips. He tried to open his left eye a little, but it wasn't possible. He wondered if he'd done permanent damage to his eyesight, but reasoned it hardly mattered given he'd no desire to stick around long enough for it to impact his life. With any luck he'd come away with a prescription for a strong opioid. Something he could use to help to finish himself off, once and for all.

It was obvious from the long waits between each patient that the A&E department was struggling to cope with the level of demand. He wished Tony was back with him, but felt guilty about pulling her out of line. Especially on a Sunday. He found her such a reassuring presence. He thought how different his current situation would be had he taken her with him. But he'd copped out. He knew Howie would have had a fit if he'd brought her, and he'd wanted to avoid drama. *Well that worked out well*, he thought. He would never have got wrecked if she'd been with him. After Norton he'd have gone back to his hotel room to have his head done in by *Question Time* and to shout at Fiona Bruce. He would never have met Iiris. He would never have wet the bed, or lost his train ticket. He wouldn't have been subjected to Burger Boy, had his wing mirror snapped off, been arrested, had his car impounded, and he wouldn't now be sitting in A&E, only able to see out of one eye. All of this because he'd pandered to Howie's dislike of a woman, whose only crime appeared to be a fondness for cargo pants. Howie didn't deserve Tony and he wasn't sure he did either.

He thought back to how he'd found the office – the tuba, the sleeping bag and the towel draped over a chair. He'd never quizzed Tony about her home life, it seemed too intrusive, and she hadn't offered any information. He'd presumed she liked to keep things private. She'd once told him that home was just her and the dog, but he hadn't enquired further as to where that home was. When he'd asked earlier whether she had someone, she'd been typically vague. She never spoke about family and he didn't like to pry. He felt uneasy now about his failure to take more interest in her life and well-being. He thought about the open holdall with clothes pulled from it. Was it possible she had nowhere to go? That she was living in the office? He made a mental note to give her a pay rise – or at least, if he was going to top himself, a great reference and a big, fat golden handshake. Finally, he heard his name being called.

'Edward Katz,' the nurse shouted.

But before he could get to his feet, from some way away, he heard a woman shout 'Eddy!'

He tried to focus on where in the crowded room the sound had come from, but the sea of faces was a blur. He hoped it was Una. Perhaps Tony had made contact? But the woman was way too enthusiastic and upbeat. Whoever this person was, her presence had caused the waiting room to sit up and take notice. Even the young child had stopped whimpering. Eddy tried to make sense of the apparition skipping towards him, but he couldn't believe his eye. Because waving her hand like a long-lost friend was what appeared to be an X-rated elf.

PROPER BAGELS

★

Una had no option but to banish Chakakhan to the garden, such was the ferocity of her reaction to Howie's surprise visit. Joni, lounging on the sofa, AirPods in, TV blaring, had been oblivious to his arrival. She looked on perplexed as her mother shut the dog outside.

'What's going on?' she said, taking out an earbud.

'Howie's here,' Una said, striding back across the room.

Joni, normally one of life's under-reactors, shot up so quickly it was a miracle she didn't get the bends.

'Why?!'

'No feckin' idea,' her mother replied as she banged the door that separated the kitchen from the living room, leaving the dog slavering at the patio window.

Una hurriedly cleared the table of the debris of Joni's costume-making, nodding at Howie to sit down.

'Making something?'

'It's Joni,' Una said, her manner occupying an uneasy place between abruptness and alarm. 'I left her to clear it up.'

Una had already told Howie, on the doorstep, that Eddy wasn't home and that she didn't know where he was or when he'd be back. But he'd asked if he could wait and for some reason – knee-jerk politeness maybe, or perhaps because his mother had just died, or simply because he looked a bit pathetic standing in the rain – she'd invited him in.

'Joni,' Howie said. 'Wow.' As though only just remembering Una and Eddy had a daughter. 'I haven't seen Joni for years. How old is she now?'

This could have been an innocent attempt to break the ice. Indeed, had anyone else asked this question, Una would have answered that Joni was twelve – maybe adding, with a roll of her eyes, that she was almost a teenager. But coming from Howie, an enquiry about the age of her daughter had triggered the kind of instinct that sees herds of cows trample dog walkers to death. She couldn't bring herself to answer. What she wanted to say was that Joni's age was none of his fucking business. That he should get any thought of her pubescent daughter out of his filthy fucking head. Her internal response was pretty much on a par with Chakakhan's demented yapping in the garden. But instead, she asked if he'd like tea or coffee.

'Yeah man, espresso?' he said, spitting his chewing gum into his hand. 'Bin?'

Una was relieved that the sound from the TV in the living room took the edge off the silences between them. And glad for the blanket, still draped around her shoulders, which cloaked her body and provided protection from the scrutiny of Howie's gaze. She was self-conscious about her bare feet, cold on the tiled floor. She didn't want Howie looking at them. She didn't want him looking at any part of her.

Una was unusually clumsy as she made the coffee, clattering the crockery stacked drying on the draining board, as she rooted around for an espresso cup. Spilling fresh coffee beans across the worktop, she sensed Howie watching her as she did her best to catch them from scattering onto the floor.

'So, I'm presuming Eddy got back safely?'

'Yep, yesterday afternoon,' Una said, a touch absentmindedly, having opened the grinder to find it full – sussing that Eddy had ground some beans, yet abandoned them, unused. She glanced at his phone, forgotten on the table and recalled the garage door having been left wide open – a stupid thing to do even in this neighbourhood, chancing the Flymo being nicked. It seemed obvious to her now that he'd taken off in a hurry.

Una hoped Howie wouldn't clock her hand shaking as she passed him his coffee, the little cup rattling on its tiny saucer. He took the drink off her, steadying the cup in a way to suggest – much to her embarrassment – he had noticed her jitters.

'Sorry,' she said. 'Too much caffeine.'

'No such thing,' he said, before knocking back the drink in one single mouthful.

'Do you want another?'

Howie smacked his chops. 'Go on then.'

Turning her back, Una was glad not to have to look at him as she made another coffee.

'I did get a text off him though,' Howie said. 'After you called me.'

Una closed her eyes with the embarrassment of it, remembering her desperation.

'Yeah, sorry about that. I was freaked out. He's never done that before. He always stays in touch.'

'Yeah man.'

He may not have been physically in the room, but an elephant-sized Eddy sat on the table between them. Howie hesitated for a few seconds, as though he was considering what to say. 'I've not spoken to him since Thursday.'

Una handed him his coffee, which he again downed in a mouthful.

'Is he avoiding me?' Howie said.

'I don't think he had his charger with him.'

'But he knew Queenie had died. Why didn't he call when he got home?'

Una hated this. Being put on the spot. Being forced to make excuses for her husband. Of having to field Howie's questions and manage his annoyance.

'He was really tired.'

She knew this was a lame excuse. And had she been closer to Howie, had there not been a rift, she would have confided in him. She would have told him of her alarm over Eddy's behaviour. But instead she continued to explain away his disappearance as no more than an unfortunate set of circumstances.

'He had a mare of a journey. Something about a replacement bus service and having no money on him. He got stuck at Newport Pagnell, the fecking eejit. He stayed over night.'

Howie snorted.

'What? Wow. It's not exactly Agatha Christie hiding in a spa hotel in Harrogate is it?'

Una smiled and shook her head, grateful Howie was able to see the funny side. She slowly peeled an apple, to give her something to do with her hands.

'How was London?' she said.

'Oh you know what these telly things are like.'

'It was a good craic. Me and Joni watched it,' she said, not about to admit that Joni had flipped the programme on by accident, for all of five seconds.

'Oh yeah?' Howie said, seeming genuinely chuffed.

'Yeah.'

'I was supposed to do the single. But there was some kind of fuck up.'

Una said nothing, not wanting to reveal that they hadn't stuck with the programme long enough to find out.

'When do you think he'll be back?' Howie said.

Una shook her head. 'Not sure. He went to get bagels.'

Howie laughed.

'Oh man, I haven't had Sunday morning bagels for years. Not proper ones.'

'Proper bagels,' Una said, smiling. 'Don't get Eddy started on that subject.'

Eddy denouncing grocery-store bagels was a family joke. Claiming they were just bread rolls with a hole in the middle. That proper bagels were a par-boiled delicacy. They were crusty, chewy and sweet, and could only be found at Jewish delis, in suburban backwaters, on certain days of the week and often, due to high days and holidays, not at all.

'He's fierce evangelical about proper bagels,' she said, relaxing a little.

Howie laughed at this shared experience.

'We'd stay up all Saturday night, then he'd drive really, really, slowly to Crumpsall for bagels, at seven in the morning. They'd still be warm. He was always so paranoid about his eyes being bloodshot and worried the old bags serving would know he was stoned and tell his mum.'

'Those old bags were probably in their forties,' Una said, her pointedness flying right over Howie's head.

'Yeah man. It was when we had that minging flat share in Hulme. Eddy was... god he must have been getting on for his mid-twenties. But he still bothered about what Ethel thought.'

'He never stopped being bothered about what Ethel thought,' Una said, cutting up the apple. Her little dig at Eddy made Howie smile.

It was dawning on her, though she couldn't bring herself to say it, that the bakery closed early on a Sunday. And even if Eddy had gone there, he would have been back ages ago.

'Was he okay?' Howie asked.

'What? When?' Una said, miles away.

'Was he okay, yesterday? When he got back?'

'Yeah. Except for a split lip and broken glasses. Said he'd had too much to drink and had fallen in the hotel.'

'Yeah man. He was a bit merry. He seemed to be having a good time though.'

Una said nothing. Eddy had given her the impression he'd had a rubbish time. She didn't know if Howie was being straightforward or mischievous, but either way it rankled.

They sat for a little while talking – Una eating the apple in slices, too self-conscious to bite into it in front of a man who she knew could sexualise anything. The subject moved on to the more neutral ground of Queenie's death.

'Was it peaceful?'

Howie considered this question, looking at the ceiling as though replaying the events of a couple of days before. 'Sort of. I guess.'

He took off his shades and rubbed his eyes. They were as small and piggy as Una remembered them, but a little pink. And for a second, it looked to Una as though he was welling up. The moment was broken by the door opening, and Joni peeking through, with Chakakhan ready for attack but held back by her collar.

'Is Dad back yet?'

'No, not yet.'

Howie stood, grinding his chair across the tiled floor.

'Wow, Joni, you were a kid last time I saw you.'

Chakakhan growled and pulled herself into the room, baring her teeth, wearing some kind of apron. Joni said nothing.

'Good costume,' he said. 'What's it meant to be?'

'A back-street abortionist,' Joni replied, picking up the dog. 'But I need to find some way of attaching knitting needles.'

'Oh right.' Howie said. 'Cool.'

Una shrugged.

'Her idea.'

'When will he be back?' Joni said.

'Your guess is as good as mine, Jojo.'

'Where's he gone?'

'To get bagels,' Una said, a little irritation in her voice.

'But that was ages ago.'

'Well, he must have gone somewhere else after,' Una said, trying to draw a line.

'What, with that girl?'

Una and Howie looked at each other, as the elephant that had been quietly relaxing on the table between them, stirred and hauled itself onto its feet.

'What girl?' Una said, trying to sound matter of fact. She put the paring knife down and pulled the blanket tight around herself.

'The one that came to see him this morning.'

'This morning?'

'Yeah.'

'Who was she?'

'Idunno.'

The elephant put on a party hat and tooted a horn.

'Did she have a name?'

Joni thought about it. 'Idunno.'

'Where'd she come from so?' Una said.

Joni screwed up her eyes, as though racking her brains. 'Idunno, but she had dirty feet.'

The elephant was now balancing on a ball and juggling with flaming torches. Howie remained expressionless, his fists in tight balls.

'And when you say girl, how old?' Una said, her tone measured.

'Like, Year 11?' Joni replied.

'A teenager? And she came specifically looking for your Dad?'

Joni had the look of someone who, while standing in the witness box, had realised they might be implicating themselves in a terrible crime. Even Chakakhan had stopped acting up and had buried her head into the crook of Joni's arm.

'I. Don't. Know,' she said, forming actual words in her desperation to shut the conversation down.

'But she left with your Dad?'

Joni turned on her heel and left the room with an exasperated 'AAAAGH!'.

The elephant set off a firework, bowed and thanked his audience, and wished them all a good night.

IT EXPLAINED A LOT

★

While Eddy knew barely anything about Tony's personal life before he got into the Uber, there was hardly anything he didn't know by the time he got out. Meredith had talked, pretty much non-stop, from the hospital to the end of his road, at a volume he found jarring, given his delicate state.

'Do you know how she got the limp?'

Eddy shook his head and immediately wished he hadn't. His X-ray had revealed a fractured eye socket, which explained the swelling, the searing pain in his cheek and the numbness in his lips. It also explained why he shouldn't have shaken his head. He'd left the hospital with a course of antibiotics, instructions to sneeze with his mouth open and to drink through a straw. There was a ban on nose-blowing for a fortnight at least and a promise of a follow-up outpatients' appointment to be sent through the post. Disappointingly, there were no painkillers, just a junior doctor enquiring whether he had any paracetamol at home. Which, of course, he did. Many packets. Stockpiled and stashed in his bedside cabinet.

'It was, like, her mum. Or was it her dad? Can't remember. But one of them broke her leg and never took her to the hospital. And now she's got one leg, like, shorter than the other?'

'That's fucking awful,' Eddy said, truly appalled at this information.

'The social services took her. Turned out she'd only ever eaten, like, crisps or something?'

'Were they prosecuted?' Eddy said, holding a tissue to his mouth, every *prrr* sound producing a spray of bloody spittle.

Meredith considered this possibility, maybe for the first time. 'No idea,' she said, shrugging. 'Did you know her real name is Tonya?'

'No, yes. I think so. Maybe.'

'After the ice-skater.'

'Strange choice.'

Eddy couldn't work out if Meredith was a malicious gossip or just devoid of a filter. Either way it was clear she had neither a volume control nor an off button.

'And she's really good on the tuba. Like, proper good. Went to music college and everything. She practises, like, all the time. It's SO annoying.'

'I didn't know that.'

How could I not have known that? Eddy wondered. Though it did explain why there'd been a bloody great big tuba sitting in the middle of the office.

'Six years! I mean who goes to college for six years?!'

Not you, I imagine, Eddy thought, though he might as well have said it out loud, because it was clear Meredith had no listening skills.

'Six years!' Meredith's mind had clearly been blown by Tony's diligence.

'I didn't know she'd been to music college,' he said, ashamed to realise it hadn't occurred to him that she might have a degree. A Master's even. That he'd made assumptions because of her broad Scouse accent and low-status job in a nursing home.

'It cost her literally, like, mega-loads? That's why she ended up at the old people's home. Sometimes she'd do nights then go to college in the day.'

'I didn't know any of this,' Eddy said, feeling increasingly uncomfortable at the revelations spilling out of Meredith, with all the sensitivity of a tabloid hack.

'Do you want to know something.'

'No.'

'When the social workers took her into, like, the children's home, she didn't speak. She'd only talk to, like, dogs?'

'Luv, this is personal stuff. She might want it kept confidential.'

But it appeared Meredith didn't understand the meaning of the word, and she carried on a pretty much unbroken stream of horror stories from Tony's early years – the older siblings she'd been separated from, the family dog she never saw again. It explained a lot, thought Eddy, except for who this fucking woman was, and why on earth Tony had her in her life.

'So, how do you know her?' Eddy said, picking up the briefest hint of a hesitation.

'She's literally my like, BFF. But we had a bit of a falling out. It's all, like, sorted now though?'

Eddy suspected it would be easy to fall out with this person – someone so free and easy with a best friend's confidences, someone who had steamrollered her way into Eddy's afternoon, insisting he needed help – her help – getting home. He was grateful when the cab turned into his road just after Meredith announced she was a singer, in a manner that suggested it was his lucky day. Such encounters were an occupational hazard – people collared him with varying degrees of nervousness or aggression, expecting interest in their talent or project. Meredith took the opportunity to launch into an unrecognisable dirge. The most dreadful foghorn sound emanated from what was an undeniably pretty face, as she travelled up and down through an aimless vocal run of off-key notes, her pointed finger appearing to follow some imaginary lie-detector test. It was the melodic equivalent of being battered against rocks in a dinghy and one from which Eddy would, at that moment, happily have jumped from, head first, into a watery grave.

'Here will do, thanks,' Eddy said, with an urgency borne of relief. He instructed the driver to pull up a little way from his house, conscious he didn't want Meredith to know where he lived. Having one stray young woman turn up at his door was more than enough for one day.

'Selfie,' she said, putting her arm around his shoulder, positioning her phone in front of them both and taking a picture before he could protest. She looked at the photo, clearly finding it hilarious, and showed it to him. It was the first time he'd seen what he looked like since the accident and it made for frightening viewing. He looked every bit as mangled as he felt. His battered, bruised and miserable face made a ghoulish contrast next to this sparkling, if demented, leprechaun. Eddy paid for the journey with his card and turned to her.

'Thanks for everything, it's appreciated.'

She looked crestfallen, as though expecting to be invited in.

'I'm sorry, I don't have any cash, but take the cab back into town. I'll make sure Tony sorts you out tomorrow. Promise.'

Her sulky pout was childlike and petulant. But any disappointment was short-lived. 'OMG, amazing! Look who it is!'

Eddy craned to look at the figure she was pointing at. It was difficult to make out with only one, myopic eye. He took his glasses from his bloodied shirt pocket to get a better look at the man walking from his house and crossing the road ahead. Blurred, but instantly recognisable in black, his slightly bent rock star gait giving the impression of perpetually playing a low-slung guitar.

'Fuck!' Eddy said, shooting down in his seat.

'Wow, he's, like, shorter than I thought?'

Meredith put her hand on the door handle, as though she was about to get out of the car.

'No!' Eddy shouted, grabbing her arm.

'Aren't you going to say hello?'

Eddy peeped out of the window until Howie disappeared from view.

'Fuck,' he said. 'I'm in so much shit.'

BITCH

Tony was relieved the smiling security guard had clocked off his shift before she'd arrived back, his replacement a less-familiar guy absorbed by his phone. She was embarrassed by the drama of Eddy's bloodied exit – uneasy this incident might become the focus of speculation and gossip around the building. But she was mainly mortified to have been the cause of Eddy's accident. She didn't know how, but she was determined to make it up to him.

Rattled by the earlier commotion and in desperate need of a piss, Fazakerley met her with unusual gusto. The office was as big a tip as she remembered – the trail of blood across the floor a sickening reminder of Eddy's misfortune. She hurried Fazakerley to the roof – his relief to be freed from the confines of the office expressed in the lengthiest of wees – and looked out over the city. Accrington brick-and-terracotta baroque was dwarfed by steely tower blocks that reflected the battleship grey of the sky and the darkening of her mood. She texted Meredith, telling her she'd be free in an hour or so, but the anticipated response – instant and enthusiastic – failed to materialise. Their tryst had lost the buzz of its earlier promise.

Tony held the phone in her hand, willing Meredith to reply while remembering her assurances to Eddy that she'd continue to try Una. She didn't want to deal with her but was feeling way too ashamed to wriggle out of the obligation. Tony rang Una, daring to hope that, once again, there would be no reply. But Una picked up.

'Oh hiya, Una.'

'Who is this?' she said, sounding every bit as scolding as Tony feared she would.

'Sorry, Una, it's me, Tony. I'm really sorry, and don't worry cos he's okay, but Eddy's had a bit of an accident.' Tony paused, anticipating Una's concern. But there was nothing. 'He's fine though. Well not fine, but alright. He fell in the office and bashed his face.'

'The office?'

'Yeah, sorry. I found him. I took him to casualty. He says he'll get a cab home. But he wanted me to tell you. Sorry, I did try calling, but there was no reply. Sorry.'

'I was asleep.'

'Sorry,' Tony said, for what felt like the millionth time.

'Okay, well, thanks for letting me know.'

Una ended the call. Tony was dumbfounded at her apparent lack of care. She hated how Una made her feel, but more than anything she hated how Una treated Eddy.

'Bitch,' she said.

HE'S AN ADULT

★

'So, who is she?' Una had asked Howie, following Joni's hurried retreat from the room.

'No idea,' he'd replied in full knowledge that it was, in all probability, the Estonian model.

Una had looked directly at him, her eye contact suggesting that she would take no shit.

'Honestly,' he added, uneasy about the paring knife that lay on the table between them. 'I swear. I've not spoken to him in days.'

'Well something went on in London. I'm not a complete fecking idiot,' she said.

Howie sighed. 'He's an adult, Una. It's none of my business what he gets up to away from home.'

He made a speedy exit after that, his leaving hastened by the throwing of a tepid cup of coffee in his face. An act of aggression so bold and unexpected, that all he could do was clean his glasses, say his goodbyes and drive like the clappers back to The Sharples. To the safety of the Annie Walker suite. To the comfort of a 1999 Barolo, a fistful of downers, and an unusually frenetic face flannel wank.

HONESTLY

★

After Howie had gone, Una checked the time. She'd been sitting there for over an hour, across the table from that bastard. It was bad enough Eddy had disappeared into thin air, but having to entertain Howie in his absence was beyond the fecking pale. But still, maybe it was worth it, she thought, placing her empty coffee cup into the sink.

'Honestly,' he'd said, following his declaration that he had no idea who this girl was.

And it had been this 'honestly' that had enraged her. The brass neck of him thinking his 'honestly' had any value. It was bad enough that she found herself living in a post-truth age, in which politicians lied to the populace as shamelessly as they lied to their wives. But she wasn't prepared to be taken for a ride in her own home, in her own kitchen, by that lying gobshite.

'I'm not a complete fecking idiot,' she'd said, despite feeling like the biggest fecking idiot in the whole of south Manchester – an area, she'd often thought, was full to the brim with big fecking idiots.

Right until that moment, Una had wanted, with every fibre of her being, for Howie to leave. But Joni's bombshell about a teenage girl had shifted the dynamics of the room. From that point on, it had been her gaze that penetrated him. All the sadness and confusion she'd experienced earlier in the day had mutated into a liberating fury. She knew she was making him uneasy. And it felt great. In a fleeting psychopathic moment, she'd imagined stabbing him with the paring knife. Instead, revenge wasn't a dish served cold, but lukewarm – in the form of a tepid coffee, slung over him, arching through the air like a slow motion frisbee. A single-origin Arabica slap in the face.

Una had stood, the empty cup in her hand, staring in astonishment at what she'd done. *Death in Venice* rivulets of coffee dripped from Howie's once trademark fringe, over his rock star shades, down his famous conk, and seeped into the black of his *Call Me Unpredictable* T-shirt.

'There was no need for that,' he'd said.

She'd laughed, despite not finding it funny, covering her mouth with her hand. 'It was only an espresso.'

For a horrible moment, Una had thought Howie was going to take his top off, but instead he pulled his T-shirt out of his trousers and proceeded to wipe his glasses clean. Without another word, he'd taken his leather jacket off the back of the chair and clip-clopped from the kitchen in his Cuban-heeled boots. He'd paused momentarily as the landline rang, but she hadn't answered it until she'd heard the front door close – surprisingly quietly, given the circumstances.

'Who is this?' Una said, still holding her empty cup.

It had been Tony – way too chipper for Una's liking – phoning to tell her Eddy had fallen in the office. Una had cut her short. She'd felt no inclination to rush over to the hospital to collect him. Because Eddy was already in the past tense. He was no longer her problem.

LUKEWARM

Tony didn't know what Eddy had clocked before his accident, whether he'd noticed the sleeping bag and the clothes. But she had to concede the tuba and the dog would have been hard to miss. Not that the tuba was a secret exactly, but she'd always hid it as best she could. Tony was uncomfortable with Eddy knowing of her musical prowess. She didn't want him to think she was engineering a career leg-up from someone with connections in the industry – even though those connections were unlikely to be of any use. Her instrument was so niche that opportunities were few and far between. Stepping into dead men's shoes being the orthodox route to a place in an orchestra.

It had taken her longer than anticipated but, having tidied and cleaned the office to the standard of a crime-scene cleaner, she tried again to get hold of Meredith. When eventually Meredith picked up, she sounded distracted. Lukewarm even. Tony, acutely sensitive to the slightest change in energy, was immediately on the back foot.

'I'm done here. What's your address?' she said, trying to reclaim some of the authority she feared had been lost through the disruption of their afternoon.

There was a silence. It was only a second, maybe two, but just long enough to swallow up all the emotional distance Tony had put between herself and Meredith over the previous five and a half months.

'I'm not there,' Meredith said. 'I took Eddy, like, home?'

Tony could hear herself breathing.

'You took Eddy home?'

'Yeah. I went to the hospital, but you'd like, gone? So I went with him to the X-Ray department.'

'You went with him to the X-Ray department?'

'Yeah, he's got, like, a broken eye socket or something.'

'A broken eye socket?'

'Yeah a broken, like, eye socket,' Meredith said, laughing at Tony's

229

parroting of everything she said.

This was horrible news. Tony knew Eddy's injury had looked bad, but this was proper GBH. The calamity was made all the more wretched by Meredith's managing to jostle her way into Tony's new job and plonk herself centre-stage of the crisis.

'How is he?' Tony asked, her voice feeble.

'He's not allowed to blow his nose for, like, two weeks,' Meredith said.

It felt inappropriate to suggest another day or time to meet. And anyway, in her heart, Tony knew Meredith had lost interest. That little window of opportunity she'd accidentally happened upon earlier in the day had slammed shut. She didn't bother saying goodbye, but simply ended the call. Tony'd had a lot of lousy days in her life but this one, she thought, was up there. Top five even. She looked at her phone, half-hoping, half-dreading, that Meredith would call her back. But, of course, there was nothing.

A FAIR COP

★

Eddy plodded down the path to his front door with the long-drawn-out trudge of a negligent tenant arriving to hand in their keys, knowing they'd blown their deposit. It was a fair cop. He let himself in for what felt like the last time, to see his coats and jackets missing from the run of hooks that spanned the length of the hall. Some were strewn on the floor, the rest spilled out of bulging binbags. That, and the sound of drawers banging shut in his bedroom upstairs, confirmed that Una knew about Iiris. The game was up.

He tugged a raincoat from a bag and rummaged in the pockets, retrieving an asthma inhaler and a packet of Rizlas. He shoved the coat back in the bag and went into the kitchen, holding his glasses up to his good eye, and noticing the two espresso cups and a splash of coffee on the table, along with a puddle on the floor. He walked quietly over to the living room door and opened it a little to see Joni stretched out on the sofa, the dog curled up next to her, telly blaring, earbuds in, engrossed in her laptop and oblivious to her dad's arrival. Chakakhan – her head wrapped in a charlady headscarf – looked at him and gave a low growl, baring her teeth. Eddy softly closed the door. He wasn't sure of the etiquette of being chucked out. He didn't know whether he should go upstairs and offer Una some kind of explanation, or just fuck off once and for all. Instead, he took a cloth and wiped the spilt coffee as best as he could with only one functioning eye. He took off his bloodstained shirt, put it into the kitchen bin and changed into a clean sweatshirt he pulled from the tumble dryer. He took a bag of draw and his grinder from a much-loved wooden box he'd bought all those years ago in Kathmandu. He picked up his phone, placed his keys on the table, scrawled a note, and walked out on his home and his little family, watched only by Chakakhan, in her pinny and headscarf, now sitting in front of the curtains on the bay window ledge, sporting the look of a dog frustrated not to have a finger to flip at him.

PARASITES

Howie showered when he got back to the hotel, his hair having taken the brunt of Una's weaponised coffee.

'It was only an espresso,' she'd said, laughing.

Fucking mad bitch, he thought. No wonder Eddy always looked so miserable, having to live with that frigid cunt. Still, it had almost been worth taking the hit, just to see her face when Joni had dropped her dad in it. If he hadn't been so worried about the paring knife, he might have stuck around to watch the drama unfold.

It had been weird, though, sitting in Eddy's house. Even more so, without him there. Howie couldn't remember the last time he'd visited. But he clocked it had been a different kitchen and that the coffee machine looked way more up to date than his own. Such things – while none of his business – pressed a particularly unpleasant and unreasonable button. It pissed him off there were people who took a wage or percentage from money generated by his career. Even if they had actively boosted the coffers from which they'd all benefited. *Noses in the trough*, he'd whinge on to anyone who could be bothered to listen.

Eddy's state-of-the-art coffee machine was the latest in a long list of resentments, that had rankled him over the years. It was one of the reasons he'd cast adrift his original band – going solo as a tactic to rid himself of a bunch of schoolmates he considered freeloaders, cashing in on his talent. His shabby behaviour towards industry professionals had created an increasingly long list of people who refused to work with him. So now, with his office reduced to just Eddy and Tony, any other work was farmed out to a disparate bunch of freelancers who didn't give a shit about him or his career. *Parasites*, thought Howie. Getting rid of Eddy was long overdue.

STAY HERE

✴

Tony jumped when her phone rang and she allowed herself, for a nanosecond, to believe Meredith might have had had a change of heart. But it was Eddy, his speech still peculiar from the injury, letting her know he was on his way over in a cab. *Perhaps he's coming to sack me*, she thought. It would be the perfect finale to round off the shittiest of days.

Eddy's eye looked even worse than when she'd last seen him at the hospital. She helped him off with his coat and tried to be upbeat, to make the abnormal normal, shooing Fazakerley out of the way as she guided him to the sofa.

'Mr Magoo,' he said.

'Who?'

'Mr Magoo. It's a cartoon.'

Tony hadn't a clue what he was talking about but plumped the cushions to make him more comfortable.

'I've made you a tea,' she said. 'Will you be able to drink it?'

'I'll have a go.'

'I hear you met Meredith,' she said, with her back turned to him, stirring his cup. Grimacing.

'I did, yeah. She's quite a handful, isn't she?'

Tony laughed. For all of Eddy's woes, he always had a way of making her feel better. She turned to him. 'She told me about your eye socket. Fucking hell Eddy.'

'Yep. I'm not allowed to blow my nose for a fortnight.'

Tony whistled. 'That's a big ask. God Eddy, it looks dead painful. Have they given you anything for it?'

'Paracetamol.'

'Seems a bit lightweight.'

'That's what I thought.' Eddy smiled crookedly as Tony passed him his tea.

'I've put an extra sugar in.'

'Ta,' he said, blowing on it to cool it, as best he could with numb lips.

'I can't believe she turned up at the hospital. I'd told her where I was, but I'd no idea she'd do that, honest,' Tony said.

'It's okay. It was funny I suppose. She sang me a song.'

'Oh god.' Tony was genuinely mortified. 'As if you hadn't suffered enough.'

Eddy took tiny, tentative sips of tea. 'Sorry to put you to trouble,' he said.

'It's no trouble.'

'I didn't mean to intrude on your day.'

'Eddy, it's your office. You're hardly intruding,' Tony hesitated before adding, 'I'm the one who shouldn't be here.'

'I'm glad you are. I wasn't sure what to do. Una's chucked me out.'

'No way. When?'

'About an hour ago. My stuff's already in binbags in the hall.'

Tony's strange, strained phone call to Una earlier now made total sense.

'She had good reason,' he said. 'I was half-expecting it.'

Tony said nothing. She held the sugar bowl, teaspoon in hand.

'Something happened in London. With a girl,' he said.

Tony put another teaspoon of sugar in his cup, and stirred it for him. 'Oh Eddy.'

'No, not like that. At least I don't think so. I was off my tits and off my rocker, so who fucking knows?'

With a great sigh, Fazakerley flopped onto the floor.

'I took her back to the hotel, Tony. Why the fuck would I do that?'

'And Una found out?'

Eddy nodded slowly, as though barely able to believe it himself.

'The girl. She turned up at the house this morning.'

'No, you're joking me,' Tony said, clattering the sugar bowl down.

'Yep. Joni let her in.'

'Joni. Oh, Eddy, no fucking way.'

'Yep. I panicked and got her out before Una came downstairs. But I suppose Joni will have told her by now.'

Tony hesitated, gathering her thoughts. 'Was she called Iiris by any chance?'

'Iiris. Yes. Iiris,' he said.

'With three eyes,' they chimed together.

'She turned up here, on Friday.'

'Here? The office?'

'Yeah, she came looking for you. I tried to get hold of you.'

Eddy groaned, exasperated, then put down his tea and rested his head back on the sofa.

'Fucking hell. I'm going to end up a hashtag."

Tony took his senior railcard wallet out from the desk drawer and handed it to him.

'She had this. And your jacket.'

He sat ruminating for a few moments, as though trying to make sense of it all. 'But how the fuck did she find out where I worked?'

'The address was on the bill from the hotel,' Tony said, passing it to him. 'It was in your pocket.'

Eddy unfolded it. 'Shitting Nora. I don't even like Pringles.'

'I'm sorry, Eddy. I put her in The Sharples. I didn't know what to do. She said she'd nowhere to stay.'

Eddy pulled his senior railcard and the return portion of his train ticket from the wallet, the ticket now stamped as used. 'There it is. Fucking hell.'

'I told you,' Tony said.

'Told me what?'

'To let me send the tickets to your phone.'

'It wouldn't have made any difference. My phone was dead.'

'Ah. Next time I'm coming with you,' she said, trying to lighten the mood. There was an awkward silence while she tried to think of something to say. 'I got her some leggings on petty cash,' she said eventually.

But Eddy was distracted.

'I feel like sending that ticket to that fucking steward,' he said, putting the wallet down.

'And I gave her money so she could get back to London,' Tony continued.

'You did?'

'I'm so sorry Eddy. I didn't think for a minute she'd show up at your gaff.'

Eddy attempted to laugh, but it was too painful. 'I gave her money to go back to London as well. This morning.'

'Fuck's sake. She must be minted. Where's she now?'

'Haven't a clue. I got arrested driving her to the station.'

'Go way!'

Tony sat next to Eddy, her arm across his back, as he explained – painfully and at length, occasionally dabbing his mouth with a tissue – how his day had panned out. Of altercations with cyclists and neo-Nazis. Of keys flung in gardens and the police turning up. Of drug tests and arrests. Of congealed macaroni cheese and his car being impounded. Of finding his way to Piccadilly Gardens but not knowing how to get back to Chorlton. Of a busker murdering 'Hallelujah'. Of a chicken tikka wrap. Of falling in the office. Of Meredith arriving at the hospital and her impromptu sing-song. And – what was surely the final nail in his marital coffin – of seeing Howie coming out of his house.

'Fucking hell, Eddy, I thought my day was shite.' Tony blew out her cheeks.

Eddy picked up the railcard wallet and pulled out the photo of Joni and found the condom tucked behind. Tony tensed, wishing she'd thrown it away.

'What the fuck?'

She said nothing.

'Tony, I've not bought a johnny in years. I'm fucking married. We were trying for a baby since 2001. Why the fuck would I have a johnny?'

'You're asking a lesbian?'

'Honestly, Tony. Someone's put that in there.'

Tony wanted to believe him, but the jury in her head was still out.

'Fucking hell, there's some dark shit going on,' Eddy said, putting his head in his hands but finding it too painful.

'It'll sort itself out.' Tony knew, as the words came out of her mouth, that she was talking bollocks.

'Una will want a divorce and I wouldn't blame her.'

'Nah, don't be soft,' Tony said, rubbing his back.

Fazakerley spread out at Eddy's feet, his chin resting on his foot.

'You just need to let the dust settle,' Tony said. 'Explain what happened.'

'I took a sixteen-year-old model back to my hotel room and she followed me to Manchester. That's what happened. Oh, and I've got a johnny tucked behind a photo of my daughter, inside my old person's travel pass. Fucking hell, Tony, it's creeping me out, never mind Una.'

'At least the johnny hadn't been used,' Tony said, knowing she might be stretching the limits of a glass half-full.

'I'm not some dirty old man Tony.'

'I know you're not. Eddy, she's not going to chuck you out over one stupid mistake.'

'I wouldn't bet on it. John Denver divorced Annie and she filled up his senses like a night in the forest.'

Tony had no idea who John or Annie Denver were, but thought it best not to ask and passed him his tea. 'You need to talk to her.'

'Tony, I can't even get my laptop to talk to my wireless printer.'

'Shall I book you into The Sharples for tonight?'

'Best not.'

'No, you're right. Fuck. Iiris could still be there I suppose. I could ring and find out if she's checked out. In fact, I should do that anyway.'

Eddy stared at the cup in his hand.

'How about The Lowry?' she said, struggling. Having run out of platitudes and small talk. 'A nice balcony room with a view over the Irwell? I mean it's not exactly Lake Como, but it'll give you and Una a breather. You must be knackered.'

Eddy remained silent, but it was a horrible quiet. Tony's brunch with Meredith felt like a million years ago now. He placed the cup of tea back on the side table. 'Tony, I don't think I can be left alone tonight.'

Tony shivered and Fazakerley bristled. It was as though something fiendish had come into the room. She pulled at a throw folded on the arm of the sofa and put it around Eddy's shoulders. He shuddered and hugged it to himself. Tony made a miniature sign of the cross, surreptitiously, with a quick darting movement of her forefinger. They sat in silence for what felt like an age. Finally, he cleared his throat. Tony knew what was coming and was willing him, with prayers to any random saint she could think of, not to say it.

'I think if I'm alone, I'll kill myself.'

Tony knew he'd disclosed something sacred. Something which he might never have told anyone else, might never even have said out loud. Something which, now it was out in the open, she couldn't unhear. She felt out of her depth and frightened, but she also knew, at that moment, that she was the only thing keeping him on the planet. That Una was too angry and Joni was too young. That his parents were dead and his sister lived abroad. That she didn't know who his friends were, and suspected there weren't many. And Howie... well, she could pretty much guarantee Howie would find the whole thing a giant ball-ache and would actively make things worse. Whether she liked it or not, the buck had stopped with her. She knew she would have to come clean about her living arrangements.

'Eddy, I'm so so sorry, but me and Fazakerley, we've been sleeping here.'

'It's okay,' he said, rubbing the top of her hand. 'I thought you might be.'

'I know it looks like I've been taking the piss, but I hadn't anywhere to go. It's only temporary. I'll sort something out.'

'Honestly. I'm not bothered. Well, not bothered you've been staying here. I am bothered you've got nowhere to go.'

'You should stay here too. Just for tonight. We can figure something out tomorrow. You have the sofa. Me and Fazakerley will sleep on the floor.'

'Don't be daft,' Eddy said. 'I'll sleep on the floor.'

'Eddy, stop it. Look at the state of you. Honestly, have the sofa. I'll be okay on the cushions. Get some sleep. Things will seem better in the morning.'

He didn't reply and she was glad. She was trying to appear in control, like cabin crew on a plane going through turbulence, exaggerating calmness to mollify the passengers. She set about shifting the furniture, leaving a respectful distance between the sofa and her makeshift bed, and arranging it in such a way that Eddy wouldn't be able to leave the office without stepping over her and waking her. Relieved the windows didn't open, she discreetly hid the kitchen knife. And when all that was done, she lay in her sleeping bag in the draught from under the office door and crossed herself. She knew she'd be able to keep him safe overnight. But, after that, all bets were off.

A JOB WELL DONE

✳

Una picked up the note from the table. *Car impounded, will sort.* This, along with the keys, confirmed Eddy had been to the house while she'd been upstairs. She screwed the piece of paper and flipped the lid of the bin, faltering as she pulled out Eddy's bloodstained shirt. It was her favourite; one she'd picked out for him when they were in New York. It felt like a hundred years ago. She'd always liked him in it.

She had a momentary wobble, a fleeting pang of heartbreak that she overrode, before she shoved it back in the bin along with the note, slamming the lid shut. His broken eye socket and seized car might have raised more questions than answers, but Una was done. If she was going to throw Eddy out, she had to stop caring. She had to not care about the bloodied shirt and his injury. She had to not care about his emotional state. Most importantly, she had to force herself not to care about the stash of medication she'd found in his bedside cabinet.

Earlier, Una had marched into the hall, gathered together Eddy's coats and jackets, and shoved them into black binbags, so starting the swift but brutal process of ridding Eddy from her life. Throwing him out made all the more doable by not knowing who he was anymore.

His room was a tip, but it was gratifying to see the binbags fill with clothes picked up from the floor and pulled from drawers – his belongings a chaotic mix of clean and dirty T-shirts, underwear and odd socks. The empty coat hangers rattled and jumped off the rails as she banged the wardrobe doors in a rackety marital exorcism. Bed linen, stretched and grubby from night sweats and a lackadaisical attitude to laundering, were pulled from the bed. Pillows still in pillowcases were destined for landfill. In normal circumstances Una would be meticulous about donating to charity and recycling, but her determination to expel all things Eddy left no space for social conscience. All she wanted was to end her marriage and to have Eddy gone. If torching the place hadn't been fraught with health, safety and insurance issues, she would have done just that. The energy generated by her humiliation, of hearing about that fucking girl in front of Howie of all people, was so intense she could have burnt the entire place down with just one blast of her fiery breath.

Una tossed the debris from on top of his bedside cabinet into the holdall from the London trip, sneezing from a month's worth of dust. She made no distinction between asthma inhalers and sweetie wrappers, his pile of crime paperbacks going the same way as snotty tissues. Getting on her hands and knees, she opened the cabinet door. But instead of the expected clutter, the cupboard was empty save for about a dozen boxes of over the counter pain relief medication, neatly piled like a Damien Hirst installation. It seemed an excessive hoard. Una considered this for a moment. She thought about Eddy's botched suicide attempt and how he hadn't taken enough pills. At the time she'd found it reassuring – proof he didn't want to die. But perhaps it was simply proof he hadn't known what he was doing. And that since then he'd been stockpiling medication so that next time he'd get the job done properly.

Unusually for their income bracket, the Katz-Coynes were a one-car household. So the note from Eddy, informing her their car had been impounded – a state of affairs she could make no sense of – added to her list of grievances and woes. Her intention had been to ferry his belongings to the council tip first thing the next morning, so she was maddened by this hitch in her plans. She bumped his belongings down the stairs – the hall now full of bulging binbags – took his keys and opened the garage door. It was a good-sized space that would easily house the bags until the car was returned home. She dragged them out, one in each hand, back and forth and piled them one on top of another, then dusted her hands at a job well done. Chakakhan watched from in front of the voile curtain while Joni watched from behind.

A FELLINI MUSE

*

Howie wouldn't usually agree to meet a woman in a hotel bar. At least not a mysterious one who'd turned up unannounced; one who had arrived in reception and asked that a call be put through to his room. Years in the spotlight had instilled a legitimate fear of being hunted down by journalists, stalkers and Dumplings. They were a canny lot and the trick was to stay one step ahead. But this woman had managed to convince reception staff she was genuine and he was grateful for the distraction. He accepted the call. He took in her voice – the vocal fry indicating youth and piquing his curiosity. Her accent was difficult to place. English, posh, but with a Valley Girl twang. She explained, cryptically, that she knew Eddy. Howie was intrigued and agreed to meet her, putting aside his reservations along with a clean face flannel.

The receptionist pointed out the woman sitting at the bar. She had her back to him, her blonde hair smooth, her tight shift dress hugging a Fellini muse silhouette. Howie had hung around the fashion world long enough to spot the signature red sole of a Louboutin stiletto, wrapped around the legs of the high stool. Any doubts he'd been harbouring evaporated as he approached her, his swagger turned up a notch as he anticipated her face. He touched her lightly on her shoulder and she turned, revealing herself to be Fifties Hollywood starlet beautiful. Howie's gaze alternated between her wide smile, her big doe eyes and her cleavage. Her breasts as perky and adorable as a basket full of puppies.

'Howie,' he said, extending his hand.

'Meredith,' she replied. 'Amazing.'

I'VE DONE THIS

✱

Joni had seen the binbags in the hall when she'd gone looking for her mother to find out what was for tea. She'd pulled one open to reveal a familiar jumble of outerwear. It was obvious what was going on. Her father was being thrown out because she'd told her mother about the girl with the dirty feet.

'I've done this,' she whispered. Her hand shook slightly and she tugged a familiar coat from one of the bags – an oversized camouflaged parka that Eddy said he'd bought for *when the revolution kicks off*. Like all of her Dad's quips, she hadn't known if he was joking. She'd had her eye on this particular jacket, even though it was massive on her, and she'd occasionally try it on. Joni took it upstairs, followed by Chakakhan, and both of them faltered outside the spare bedroom door, listening to the clatters and bangs of Una, effing and jeffing as she binned Eddy's things. Joni hurried into her bedroom, climbed the ladder to her high-rise bed and stuffed the parka down under the duvet. Keeping it safe for her Dad.

SIGNATURE DRINK

✳

Still stewing over the flung coffee and being ghosted by Eddy, Meredith was just the shot in the arm Howie needed. He pulled his bar stool close. They sat face to face, their legs interlocked with an intimacy that belied their fresh acquaintance. There was some frivolous small talk in which Howie ordered a neat Scotch, all the time checking out this absolute peach, already settled with a cocktail and looking ravishing in the soft light of the bar.

'So how do you know Eddy?' he said.

'Well, I don't? Not really. I found him in, like, A&E? All by himself. He told me his assistant had brought him, but that she'd literally gone home?'

'Tony,' Howie rolled his eyes. 'Yeah man. It doesn't surprise me. She's on probation. I think we're going to have to let her go.'

Meredith said nothing, but anyone looking out for such signs would have noticed a flutter of amusement travel across her pretty-as-a-picture face.

'So why were you at the hospital?' Howie asked. 'Nothing serious I hope.'

Meredith tapped him on the end of his nose. 'Nosey,' she said.

Howie didn't give a flying fuck about why she was at the hospital. He was way too distracted by the brief but electric touch, and by her knees either side of his, her legs slightly apart, her dress stopping mid-thigh. He imagined sliding his hand under the fabric.

'He's got a broken eye socket,' she said. 'It's, like, literally gross?'

'Oh yeah?'

Howie feigned interest but he was distracted by her hand, now resting on his leg.

'He said he'd, like, fallen?'

'He's been having a lot of falls lately. I'll have to get him one of those emergency button things old people wear round their necks,' Howie said, blabbering in an attempt to quell his mushrooming erection.

Meredith took hold of his hands and studied his rings. 'They're so cool. I like jewellery on, like, men.'

Lots of people commented on Howie's chunky rings. One of them – a glass eyeball – was something of a trademark. But when Meredith noticed them, he felt validated. She turned his hands over to study his palms. 'Amazing,' she said, tracing a line across his right palm. 'You fall in love, like, so easily.'

Howie said nothing. He was enjoying her touch and the feeling of the blood rushing straight to his genitals.

'You're very creative? You let your heart, like, rule your head. Literally.'

'Toadally.'

'What star sign are you?'

'Scorpio.'

Meredith gasped. 'Amazing. Elusive and secretive with a sting in your, like, tail? Wow. I've never met a Scorpio I didn't, like, like?'

She took his right hand in both of hers. 'This,' she said, looking him straight in the eye, 'is your dominant hand.'

She giggled and the erotic subtext threatened to make Howie ejaculate in his trousers, right there and then. Meredith rested his hand back on his thigh.

'How did you know I was staying here?' he said, his voice strangulated.

'I followed you?' Meredith replied, with a playful what-are-you-going-to-do-about-it chuckle, her up-speak inflection making it sound like a question. This was something Howie generally found annoying. In Meredith, though, he thought it adorable.

'You followed me?' Howie replied, enchanted by her pluck.

Meredith looked directly into his eyes and removed the strawberry that sat between two scoops of pink ice cream on her cocktail. 'I saw you coming out of Eddy's house and got the Uber to, like, chase you?'

She bit into the strawberry, tugging the stalk, her lips plumped by the fruit. Howie was transfixed.

'I had no idea,' he said. Nor did he care. He was delighted to have had her follow him. Anyone else and he would have called the police. But Meredith? Well, she could follow him straight upstairs to his hotel bed.

'But why were you at Eddy's?'

'I took him home. I felt sorry for him? He looked like such a, like, mess?'

'He always looks a mess, to be honest.'

Meredith laughed. He liked her laugh. Moreover he liked that she laughed at his jokes, which was more than Stina did. She hadn't found anything he'd said funny for an age. He liked Meredith's accent too. She was well-spoken, as his mother would have said. He was known to be partial to *posh totty* – a turn of phrase he applied to any young woman with long vowels – and had a reputation for bedding the wasted aristocratic socialites who moved in showbiz circles.

'I just thought you ought to, like, know?' she said, placing her hand on his knee.

'Yeah man. Toadally. But he's not my responsibility.' Howie shifted slightly in order that Meredith's hand might move further up his leg and found himself rewarded with a gentle squeeze of his mid-thigh.

'Your car is so cool. What make is it?'

'Aston Martin Vanquish, six-litre coupe,' Howie said, as though reading from *Auto Trader* magazine. 'Eight-speed automatic transmission.'

'Sick colour,' Meredith said.

'Man U red,' he said, winking.

'Amazing.'

This time Howie didn't have to move for Meredith's hand to creep up his thigh. She knocked back the last dregs of her cocktail, her hand resting just inches from his bollocks.

'What are you drinking?' Howie asked.

'Meredith's Fruity Bum-Bum.'

'Meredith's Fruity Bum-Bum?' he said, laughing.

'It's my, like, signature drink?'

Howie raised his hand to beckon one of the bar staff. 'A Fruity Bum-Bum.'

'Meredith's Fruity Bum-Bum,' she said, having already trained the staff to make a drink that was neither on their radar nor their cocktail menu.

'That Uber guy wasn't happy about tailing you,' Meredith giggled.

'You were going really, like, fast? But I told him I would, like, give him a fifty pound tip if he managed to keep up? That literally changed his mind.'

Meredith thought this hilarious and, oh, how Howie was enchanted. She was, at that moment, the perfect woman; the ideal mix of youth, sass and glamour, and giving off every kind of signal that she was sexually available. He couldn't take his eyes off her. He had bored of Stina's slender, flat-chested frame. The supermodel stature that had first attracted him had become an embarrassment as the press made mischief, photographing the couple from angles that would only exaggerate the difference in height.

'You're very naughty,' Howie said, preoccupied by her touch.

'I am, like, naughty. I'm a very naughty girl.'

And with that, her hand, so tantalisingly close to his crotch, moved and cupped his scrotum, giving it a long lingering squeeze. Howie's eyes rolled so far back into his head that he thought he'd found a contact lens he'd been missing since 2002. And, in that moment, he forgot his dead mother, his sister and her funeral pigeons, his displeasure at Una and the flying espresso. He forgot how cross he was over Eddy's disappearance and the state-of-the-art coffee machine. He forgot about the dismal sales of *Call Me Unpredictable*, of the trip to London, of the missing Estonian and the Slovak hiding in her room. All he cared about was Meredith Pruitt's hand, cupping and squeezing his ballbag – the pleasure enhanced by the phone vibrating in his pocket as a text came through. Had he'd bothered to check, he'd have seen, in no uncertain terms and with a smattering of Swedish swear words, Stina pointing out that he'd forgotten to wish Viola a happy birthday.

THE BLACKEST OF SLEEPS

★

Seeing Tony curled in her sleeping bag with Fazakerley by her side, it struck Eddy that the only thing between her and a shop doorway was her job. The irony wasn't lost on him that while she was ducking and diving, trying to keep body and soul together, all he wanted was to die. He also, at five o'clock in the morning, wanted a piss. Tony had left a table lamp switched on, for which Eddy, with his compromised sight, was grateful. He walked across the room with the wariness of a much older person, fearful of a repeat of his earlier stumble. The dog was already standing before he got to the door.

He hadn't slept well. In fact he wasn't sure he'd slept at all. The sounds of the puking, tin can-kicking St Patrick's Day stragglers in the street below were unfamiliar to him. It was so different from the suburbs, where only the occasional cat fight or randy fox would break the quiet.

He had nodded off, once or twice maybe, only to be woken by the snorts of his blocked-nose mouth-breathing. At home he'd have watched TV or read a book. But lying on the sofa in the office, he had only his overthinking to entertain him. Mostly he replayed the day. He wondered where Iiris was, his paranoia suggesting she might be on the other side of the door, like some B-movie haunting, cigarette in hand, asking about the whereabouts of her friend. He checked his phone for word from Una – even her scolding would be preferable to silence – but there was nothing.

Tony stirred as he approached, startled at the figure nearing her.

'Where you going?'

'The loo.'

'I'll come with you.'

Which is exactly what she did. She walked to the toilet with him, the dog tramping behind. Both of them stood outside the door. He thought it not dissimilar to being monitored by CCTV in the police station, he felt scrutinised and infantilised, but he was touched that she cared.

'We'll figure out how to get your car back in the morning,' she said, settling back into her sleeping bag.

'Thanks, Tony. I'm sorry to drag you in to all this. I'll see you right.'

'It's fine,' Tony said.

But Eddy knew it wasn't. He lay down on the sofa, trying to find the best position for breathing, wondering if he'd have the guts to kill himself in the morning. Or whether he should get the car back to Una first.

Finally drowsiness descended on him. And, for once, without the aid of pot or pills, he fell into the blackest of sleeps.

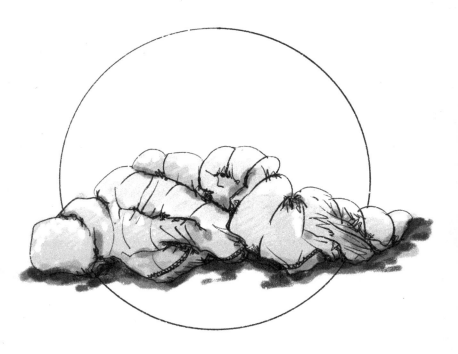

SOD THE LOT OF THEM

★

Una knew that adolescence would change the relationship she'd enjoyed with Joni. That breaking away from parents marked a normal transition to adulthood, and she should accept being frozen out of her daughter's life. If she was lucky, and if she could resist the urge to become overbearing and intrusive, it would be a temporary state of affairs. Their relationship would shift and settle into something less testy and more adult with time. But it appeared that chucking Eddy out had sped up the process of separation, as Joni now refused to say one word to her in the kitchen before school. All attempts at conversation were met with stony silence. Una hadn't dared ask her if she'd spoken with her Dad. She knew not to go there. *Sod the lot of them*, she thought. If Joni didn't like it, she could go and live with her father. Let her deal with his moods. At least this was how she'd felt when Joni slammed the front door so hard that Una had gone to check if the stained-glass panel was still intact.

By mid-morning though, Una was feeling decidedly less bullish. Her mood veered between wanting to dig in her heels and wanting to beg forgiveness from a child who'd gone to bed with nothing more nutritious than a bowl of Cheerios. Una had also forgotten to feed the dog. And failing to eat anything herself had led to another scorching migraine that had kept her awake for most of the night. She was both knackered and wired, desperate for solutions to problems that weren't instantly solvable. She was also aware that while binning Eddy's stuff was cathartic for her, it must have been awful for Joni to witness. She felt wretched. How had she managed to so spectacularly fuck everything up? Her conviction the previous evening that she could return to acting and rebuild a new life melted away faster than a Wibbly Wobbly Wonder on a hot summer's day.

A PRAYER TO ST SEBASTIAN

✴

By the time Eddy woke, just before midday, Tony had been online to research collecting impounded vehicles – a bureaucratic palaver that would require picking up documents and car keys from his house. How this would be possible, while keeping him safe, she didn't know. She hadn't left the confines of the office since he'd confided in her, except to escort him to the toilet. The absurdity of it. Of standing outside while her boss took a long, noisy wee. It had freaked her out when she'd discovered him trying to get out of the office. It had been the worst kind of wake-up – to be immediately on guard, adrenaline pumping. Briefly, a little later, she'd hurried Fazakerley onto the roof while Eddy had snored on the sofa, his face half-purple from the fall. She hoped he'd be feeling brighter when he woke, and she had everything crossed that all he needed was a good night's sleep. She felt weighted by the gravity of his confession, but shouldered it with the seriousness it merited, helped in part by a prayer to St Sebastian.

CLEARING HER DESK

★

Una was unsure how to react to Tony's call. It was only a few hours into their unratified separation and she was uncertain of the etiquette.

'Hi, Tony, you okay?' she'd said, forcing herself to be more upbeat and less brittle than the day before.

'Una, Eddy's here. At the office.'

'Right, so.'

'He needs the keys and some documents so he can pick the car up from the pound.'

Una felt disarmed. As much as she didn't want to talk to Eddy, she wasn't sure she liked having to go through an intermediary either. She felt demoted, as though her status had nosedived overnight.

'What does he need?' she asked.

Una didn't know what Tony had been told, but it was obvious that they were operating on the understanding that she was now the ex. And, as such, she no longer had an automatic channel of communication to Eddy.

'Photo ID. So, a passport or driving licence.'

'Okay.'

'And proof of address.'

'What? Like a utility bill or something?'

'Yeah, so long as it's in Eddy's name and it's recent.'

It felt so weird. This boring, formal, polite negotiation.

'Sorry, Una, this is such a pain, but he'll need the MOT certificate and insurance details too.'

'Christ, what a ball-ache.'

'I know. There's more. Sorry. They want proof of ownership, so the V5C document.'

Una could hear Eddy saying something in the background. She wanted to ask Tony to put him on the phone but felt like she no longer had the authority. It felt like the marital equivalent of clearing her desk.

'Hang on,' Tony said.

Una could hear, but not make out, a muffled conflab between Tony and Eddy. She hated this secrecy and felt affronted by this twentysomething's intervention.

'Eddy says the car's registered to you which might complicate things. I need to find out if he can collect it or if you have to.'

'Oh great.'

'I've got the page in front of me. It shouldn't take a mo.'

'Where is the pound, so?' Una said.

'Erm, looks like somewhere round Ardwick, I think.'

'And how much is all this costing?'

'150 quid. Oh, hang on, no, it's 170 if it's after midday.'

'Which it will be.'

'Yeah. Looks like. Oh, got it, here it is.'

Tony read from the webpage: 'If the legal owner of the vehicle can't go to the pound in person then someone can collect it on their behalf. The person collecting the vehicle blah blah blah...' Tony trailed off as she read it to herself. 'Okay. Got it. Eddy can collect it but he'll need a signed letter of authority from you, and a copy of your passport or driving licence so they can check it's your signature.'

'Fuck's sake.'

Una had a rare craving for a cigarette, despite having given up years before.

'So, why was the car impounded? Or aren't I allowed to ask?'

'Erm, the police said it was causing an obstruction.'

'The police?'

'You'd be better asking Eddy. He's here, next to me. Do you want a word?'

'No, not really,' Una said. She didn't want to talk to Eddy with Tony sitting beside him, hearing their conversation. Even if it was about fucking V5C documents.

Eddy mumbled something and Una heard Tony whisper, 'No, she doesn't want to.'

'So what's a good time?' Tony said.

'For what?'

'To pick up the paperwork?'

'Not sure. I think the printer's out of ink. I might have to get some.'

'Okay, so how about you ring me when you've pulled it all together?'

'I suppose.'

'Great.'

Una didn't know how she'd react to Eddy turning up for the documents. Maybe she could leave them in an envelope on the doorstep. Or would that be immature? Perhaps Tony would come and collect them? Una felt a sting of indignation. She didn't want this go-between coming to her house.

'Actually, Tony, I'll drop them off so. I've got to come into town anyways.'

It wasn't true, but Una was grateful to have some mundane chore to fill her day and mop up her nervous energy.

'Oh, okay. If you're sure.'

'Yeah. I'll get the tram in.'

'Great. That works. I could photocopy them here.'

Una thought about this. She didn't want to run into Eddy, but she could wait in reception.

'Okay. But I'll need to get back for Joni.'

'Yeah sure.'

Una considered her new status. She would have to learn to negotiate a way through all of this; find a way to disconnect from Eddy while co-parenting Joni. It hadn't crossed her mind until now that it was never going to be possible to fully break free – not when they had a kid together. This realisation felt crushing. She could freeze Eddy out of her life for sure, but Joni would always be shuttling between the hostile parties like some school-age emissary, burdened with concealing the details of the other's new life. She hated these complications. The last time she'd broken up with anyone she'd been in her twenties. They'd said their goodbyes and that had been the end of that. Una picked up Chakakhan and carried her into the study to set about collating paperwork – a dreary activity on a dreary Monday, and one much in keeping with her mood.

THE FUCKING MONKEES

★

The worst thing had been telling Eddy that Una didn't want to talk to him. Until she'd phoned, Tony had persuaded herself that for someone with a busted face on a suicidal bender, he'd seemed a little brighter. But Una's rejection had visibly upset him.

'Did she seem angry?' he asked, dabbing his un-blowable nose with a tissue.

'No, not especially. I think she felt dead awkward.'

'Did she ask after me?'

'Not exactly,' Tony said, hesitating, but unable to lie outright.

'Did she mention Joni?'

'Only that she'd have to get back before she got home from school.'

'Do you think I should text her?'

'Text who? Una?'

Tony was finding the interrogation exhausting. Her spirit was flagging as she tippy-toed through the minefield of booby-trapped questions.

'No, Joni,' he said.

'Yeah, why not?'

'I don't know what she knows. Perhaps I should talk to Una first.'

Tony was fearful that any exchange with Una might not end well. And then what? 'No, let's get the car back before we do anything else,' she said, hoping to buy some time. Time in which she hoped she'd figure some way through this mess.

Eddy's insistence that he'd be okay to drive back to Chorlton from the car pound was, Tony presumed, part of his self-destructiveness. With his old bifocals and his left eye shut, there was no way he was safe to be on the road. She needed to persuade him to let her drive – even though she was uninsured – partly as a public service, but also because she was terrified to let him out of her sight. She had no idea what the plan was once they'd dropped the car off; whether he'd come back to the office or not, and if they'd both be sleeping there indefinitely, with the office becoming some garment district hipster doss-house. What she did know was all her ideas were short-term and she was fast approaching the limits of her resourcefulness.

'I need a spliff,' he said.

'The alarms will go off if you smoke in here.'

'It's okay. I'll go onto the roof.'

Tony was now so far out of her depth that she feared she might be the first person ever to drown in a third-floor office. Keeping Eddy safe wasn't just gruelling, it was going to be impossible. She would have to come clean.

'I'm worried about you Eddy.'

He said nothing.

'Really worried. I think you need to get help. Not me. Professional help. I'm so sorry. I don't know what I'm doing.'

The words, delivered in a semi-frantic tone, came across more bluntly than intended. Tony feared that she sounded like she wanted rid.

Eddy sighed. 'I'm sorry. It's not your problem. None of it is. Not me or the car. I shouldn't have dragged you into this.'

'No, Eddy,' Tony said, her alarm escalating. 'That's not what I'm saying. I'm dead happy to help. I want to help. I just don't feel qualified. I think I might be making things worse.'

'You've never made anything worse.' Eddy lost his struggle with composure. Little boy tears ran down his messed-up face.

Tony felt dreadful. Dreadful and culpable. Eye injury aside, she was aware that if she hadn't booked Iiris into a hotel, maybe she'd have fucked straight off back to London and not turned up at Eddy's house. Tony passed him a box of tissues and Fazakerley curled up at his feet. She'd heard people often felt better for crying. She hoped this was the case.

'Look, once we've got the car back to Una, we can work out what to do.'

'I'm fucked Tony.'

'No you're not. It's just a bad patch. We have to believe things work out in the end Eddy. We mustn't give up. We have to keep going.'

'Things will work out for you. You're one of the sanest people I've ever met.'

Tony guffawed. 'Well no one's said that before.'

'No, I mean it. And you've got your whole life ahead of you,' Eddy said, before remembering to add the requisite, *'puh puh puh.'*

'Eddy, you could live for...' she quickly did the sums in her head, 'another thirty years!' She sounded astonished.

'Oh fuck don't say that,' he said.

They both smiled, and Tony relaxed, ever so slightly. She was desperate to believe these little humorous interludes might signal an upturn in his mood.

'Right this minute, I'd settle for being able bend over without needing an antacid,' Eddy said, attempting to lace his shoes.

'Here, let me,' Tony said, kneeling in front of him, feeling every bit the mother to his small child.

'Sorry. Thanks. Where do you think Iiris is?' Eddy said.

'Estonia, with any luck.'

'I'm scared she'll show up at the house again.'

'Nah, she'll have gone back down to London by now,' Tony said, stopping herself qualifying it with a 'surely?'

'I fucking hope so. Why did she come here though?' Eddy said.

'She was looking for her friend?'

'Yep, Zophie.'

'Zophie with a zee,' they chorused together.

'So, where the fuck is Zophie with a zee?' Tony said.

'Probably in my living room watching the telly.'

Tony snorted. 'Apparently Zophie with a zee has the keys to their flat,' she said.

'Yeah, I know. I can't believe ol' three eyes travelled all the way to Manchester because she didn't have her fucking front door key.'

'Or her phone.'

'Why couldn't she use a phone box?' Eddy said.

'Gen Z. That's like asking you to send a telegram.'

'I guess.'

'And, anyway, Zophie's number would have been in her phone.'

'Course.'

'I expect it seemed like a logical thing to do. I think she thought she could find Zophie through you and Howie.'

'Fucking hell, does she think we all live together or something? Like the fucking Monkees?'

Tony didn't get the reference, but she got the gist.

'I thought it was brave. In a mental sort of way.'

'I know,' Eddy said. 'That's what frightens me.'

'She'd only been in the country for three days.'

'Three days?'

'And she couldn't remember where the flat was. Other than it was near a bus stop.'

'Well, that narrows it down a bit.'

'That's what I said.'

'Fuck. So she really was stranded. I thought she was stalking me.' He sat thinking for a few moments. 'Thanks for putting her in the hotel.'

'I didn't know what else to do with her.'

'Still, it was kind.'

'Yeah, well, sorry it backfired,' Tony said, pulling a stupid-me face.

'It served me right.'

'I don't think you're cut out for skulduggery, Eddy.'

Eddy shook his head.

'I don't know how Howie manages it. All that plate-spinning. No wonder he hasn't written a decent song in years.'

Tony carried on chatting, asking about aftercare for his facial injury and talking about her memories of Queenie in the nursing home. It was blather, but she was thinking on her feet, trying to steer the conversation away from anything to do with Una, Joni or home. She didn't want to trigger him while they endured the agonising wait for Una to turn up in reception. Tony hadn't any strategy to deal with this and prayed that divine intervention would come along and save the day.

Which it did. In the form of a phone call from the school.

GERREMOFF

★

Una, Joni and Eddy sat alongside each other in the headteacher's office like a three-piece condiment set. But it was Joni, sat in the middle, arms folded, her face as sour as oxidised wine, who was definitely the vinegar.

Eddy had taken an instant dislike to Mr Cockbone, the head of school – a man who rejoiced in a name that any sane person would have ditched the minute they entered the teaching profession. But Mr Cockbone appeared to be someone who thrived on conflict and Eddy recognised in him a particular breed of twat from his own schooldays. He imagined this smug bastard had a sadistic streak which, in times gone by, would have been satiated by the thrashing of small children. Eddy's hackles were up even before he'd sat down.

'There was an incident at lunchtime,' said Mr Cockbone, a waxy-faced man with pores as open as ripe Emmental. 'Involving your daughter.'

'Which was?' Eddy said, deliberately downplaying his alarm.

'Joni removed the caretaker's ladder, leaving him stranded on the roof.'

Eddy snorted, partly on account of his nasal problems, and partly in admiration of his daughter's pluck. It wasn't that he found it funny exactly – it was more the surprise of it. Joni had never been in trouble before. She was too much of an oddball to be teacher's pet material, but she liked to keep her head down and preferred not to draw attention to herself. Mr Cockbone caught Eddy's eye. The antipathy he'd harboured towards Joni now shifted to her father.

'Sorry,' Eddy said, dabbing snot with a tissue and trying not to smirk. 'I can't blow my nose for a fortnight.'

'Is this true, Joni?' Una said, looking way more shame-faced than her daughter.

'Yep,' Joni said, dangling and jiggling her slip-on pump from her toe. Her arms and legs so tightly intertwined that all that was needed was a Boston fern and she could have passed herself off as a macramé plant hanger.

Eddy hadn't planned on seeing Una when she turned up at reception with the paperwork. But just as she'd arrived, the school had called, informing her of Joni's misconduct. Fortuitous timing saw them sharing a cab, anxious to discover the nature of their daughter's predicament, privately aware their marital woes would no doubt have played a part in her plight. It was a tense but silent journey, and one which had seen Eddy ponder how quickly he and Una had become self-conscious strangers. Still, he thought, it was better than sharing an Uber with Meredith Pruitt. At least Una was unlikely to burst into song.

Mr Cockbone flashed a look at Eddy that signalled he'd made assumptions about this family. Eddy's appearance suggested some kind of punch-up. Una was wearing a baggy old jumper, her face pinched from the dregs of her migraine and from the drama of the previous few days. And Joni was a bit of a misfit, out of step with her peer group; a surly child, talked about in the staff room with some wariness, as a bit of a loner.

'Oh there's no question that she did it. I saw her with my own eyes. As did all those standing at the bus stop, filming it on their phones.'

Joni shrugged.

'Joni,' Una said, astonished that she would do such a thing.

'What your daughter has to understand is, when she's in uniform, she's an ambassador for the school.'

'It's a polyester sweatshirt, mate,' Eddy said. 'It's got about as much gravitas as a string vest on the Golden Mile.'

Being back at school, any school, invariably provoked this response. It was the reason Una had banned him from parents' evenings. And he could sense her now, next to him, squirming.

'What happened Jojo?' she said.

'What happened was she took the ladder away,' Mr Cockbone said, puffing out his chest like an irascible bullfrog.

'Wasn't it heavy?' Eddy said to Joni, reprising his role as the man who missed the point.

'A bit.'

Mr Cockbone raised his voice. 'She could have killed him.'

'Bit overdramatic,' Eddy said.

'Stop it,' Una said, flicking him with the back of her hand. Her embarrassment cranked up ten notches every time he opened his mouth.

Eddy was aware that in terms of winning Una back, this wasn't going well. But he presumed that ship had sailed. He was surprised, however, to find this particular aspect of new-found bachelorhood quite refreshing.

'He could have fallen,' Mr Cockbone said.

'And if shit were cheese there'd be more of it eaten.'

Una groaned, her sigh the verbal equivalent of someone throwing in the towel.

'Mr Katz,' Mr Cockbone said, clearly unused to dealing with people uncowed by his status. 'What Joni did was extremely dangerous. I've spoken to Mr Fletcher and he's livid. He wants a written apology.'

'He had it coming,' Joni said.

Eddy, Una and Mr Cockbone looked at her. All of them were caught off guard.

'It served him right,' she added.

'How come, Jojo?' said her dad, 100 per cent behind her, regardless of the facts.

Joni uncrossed her legs and pushed her shoe back on. 'He heckles the girls.'

'Heckles the girls? In what way?' Una said, pulling herself up in her seat.

'When we walk past, he calls out things.'

'Like what?' Una said.

'GERREMOFF!' Joni shouted, causing all three adults to jump.

'Ah, an old-school pervert,' Eddy said, noting the colour drain from Mr Cockbone's Swiss-cheese face.

'Did you know this?' Una asked, pointing her finger at Mr Cockbone.

He stretched his neck as though his shirt collar had become too tight. 'Not the specifics, no.'

'Meaning?' Una said.

He said nothing.

'But you had an idea?' Eddy said.

'We call him Fletch the Letch,' said Joni, to her father. 'Everyone does.'

'Mr Katz, or can I call you Eddy?' Mr Cockbone said, his authority fizzling out like a damp Roman candle.

'No. Let's keep this formal.'

'Sorry. Mr Katz. Mr Fletcher has been with us for some years and...'

'I wouldn't boast about it, Jeez,' Una said.

'...he's a valued member of staff.'

'So, on a scale of one to the BBC, just how many sex pests do you have on your payroll?' Eddy said.

'I think we're getting off the point.'

'I think we're getting right to it. You've got some nonce on the premises, letching after young girls. Yet it's my daughter who's the one in shtuck.'

'Exactly,' Una said.

Being backed up by Una came as such a surprise that Eddy did a cartoon double take, glancing at his wife, half-expecting to discover she was talking to someone else.

'I'll look into your daughter's allegations, but none of this changes the fact that what she did was foolhardy in the extreme.'

'He was sexually harassing a twelve-year-old child,' Eddy said, emboldened by Una's support.

'I'm not a child.'

'Just for argument's sake,' Eddy said to his daughter, 'let's say you are.'

'As if,' Joni muttered.

'I'm sorry, but I'm going to have to suspend her. It'll give her time to reflect on her actions.'

'Yes!' Joni said, punching the air with her fist.

Mr Cockbone didn't look at her and instead addressed her parents. 'It's not a holiday. She'll be given work to complete. I'll mark it myself.'

'And what about your man? Is he going to be suspended to reflect on his actions?' Una said.

'I'll talk to Mr Fletcher. See what he has to say.'

'Try talking to the kids. See what they have to say,' Eddy said.

The family Katz-Coyne didn't notice Joni's fellow pupils watching from their classroom windows as she marched out of school, flanked on either side by her parents, in solidarity, to a waiting taxi. Nor were they aware that Joni had, in the space of one lunch hour, acquired legendary status as that weird Year 7 kid who'd taken that creep Fletch the Letch's ladder away, leaving him marooned on the roof.

DAMAGED GOODS

Tony knew Meredith was fickle, but even she'd been surprised at the speed with which her ex had discarded her. Her loss of interest as rapid as a child with a funfair goldfish in a plastic bag. Tony wished she'd binned that effing birthday card. It was her own stupid fault. Even the relief of Eddy going home had left her conflicted. Tony thought about him dashing off with Una to Joni's school. Witnessing the sudden coming together of his little family had prompted a sadness that caught her off guard. Eddy and Una rushing to their daughter's side had hammered home just how alone she was in the world. Even Fazakerley's watchful presence couldn't modify her belief that she was destined to live forever on the margins of other people's lives, doomed to live out her days alone, with only domesticated animals offering solace. It felt so inevitable. This job she loved was bound to go tits up. She felt foolish to have had aspirations and wished she'd kept her stupid ambitions in check. She looked over at her tuba, poorly disguised behind the Swiss cheese plant and felt more ridiculous still. Her virtuosity had been something she'd taken quiet pride in. But even at school she'd known – when allocated a dented old tuba the same height as her eleven-year-old self – that her music teacher had made a muggins of her. Assigning her an instrument that no one else wanted to play. The fact she'd excelled at it had surprised everyone, not least of all herself. It mattered to be singled out as exceptional at a school not known for its achievements and by teaching staff who'd dismissed her as damaged goods. *Maybe they'd had a point*, she thought. Any forays into a richer, more fulfilling life than the one she'd been born into were bound to end in disaster. It seemed so obvious to her now that people needed luck and support to get anywhere in life and she was convinced her luck, such as it was, had just run out.

THE MOCKERS

★

Making the appointment a morning one had been asking for trouble and, true to form, Howie rocked up a good three-quarters of an hour late. Yet despite the solemnity of the occasion, and the early start, he was surprisingly chipper. He knocked on the window of the funeral home, a cigarette hanging from the corner of his mouth, and gave Jean and the funeral director a cheery thumbs-up.

'Someone got out of the right side of the bed this morning,' Jean said, coming outside to usher him into the office, her floral outfit giving the appearance of a seed packet of winter-flowering pansies.

Howie flicked his still-burning cigarette onto the pavement and followed her inside. He'd never been in a funeral home and had imagined an aspidistra on a stand, a ticking clock, a stuffed raven, the faint odour of formaldehyde maybe. Instead, the light wood and pastel decor was more Sylvanian than Addams Family. In fact the only gothic thing in the room was Howie's hairdo, and even that had a couple of millimetres of white roots showing.

The funeral director stood to shake his hand. 'Did you have any trouble parking?' She was a solid, short-waisted woman with a low centre of gravity, whose musculature suggested weight training. Someone for whom parking was a bog-standard ice breaker.

'Yeah man, toadally,' Howie said, trying not to grind his teeth, having downed amphetamines and caffeine in order to make the appointment, and mindful of a cracked veneer. 'I put it in a residents' space round the back.'

'It's a sports car. Like James Bond,' Jean said. 'What is it again our Neville?'

'Aston Martin Vanquish, six-litre coupe.'

The funeral director gave a non-committal nod.

'Eight-speed automatic transmission,' Howie added, sensing the boast hadn't gone down as well as he and Jean would have expected.

'It might be an idea to put it in the Aldi car park or it could get keyed.'

Howie was relieved to have an excuse to leave Jean and the funeral director while he went to shift his car. But not before he'd scaled down the floral tribute and vetoed everything Jean had set her heart on, from joining her and Gordon in the funeral limo to honouring his mother's wish to be seen out to 'I Remember You'. Poor old Frank Ifield binned along with the solid mahogany coffin and the fan-tailed doves.

'But it would be so lovely to see them soar into the heavens,' Jean said, her voice quavering a little.

'Yeah man, before they come back to earth and get pecked to death by other birds.'

'You're making that up.'

'No, I'm not,' Howie said, laughing. 'They can't survive in the wild.'

'And who told you that?'

'A friend,' Howie replied, disinclined to tell her it had been Meredith Pruitt. Meredith who, he'd discovered, was quite the animal lover, even though her professed veganism seemed to embrace a fair bit of room-service sausage, bacon and egg.

Jean raised her eyebrows, disapproving of the friend who'd put the mockers on her fan-tailed doves – the same friend who'd been in bed with Howie for the previous forty-eight hours.

A LOADED QUESTION

★

Tony had given up calling Eddy. He never picked up and wasn't responding to voicemails. She didn't know if his silence was a good or bad thing, but a few days after he'd returned home, she hit on a strategy designed to entice him out.

Iiris checked out Monday, she'd texted, adding a thumbs-up and three eyeball emojis.

Monday? came the immediate response.

Yeah. Four nights + deep clean surcharge cos of smoking

Eddy didn't reply, but Tony plodded on in the hope of engaging. *Maybe needed to wait til Monday to get address for her flat*

Eddy replied with a question mark.

From her agency

I guess

You going to Qs funeral?

There was a delay, before he replied. *When is it?*

Dunno. Want me to find out?

Pls

'Have you spoken to Eddy?' was Howie's opening gambit when Tony finally plucked up the courage to call.

She suspected this was a loaded question and was immediately on the back foot. But fears over landing Eddy in it were dodged by a clattering so loud that Tony had to take the phone from her ear. A squeal, a crash and a woman's giggling revealed Howie had company.

'Careful,' he said, his voice slightly muffled.

'Sorry?'

'Not you.'

Tony was relieved for this intervention. The distraction allowed her to steer the conversation away from Eddy.

'Do you need help with the arrangements?' she said.

'What arrangements?'

'Queenie's funeral?'

'Nope. My sister's doing it.'

'Jean?'

'Yeah man.'

'I know her from the nursing home. A bit anyway.'

Howie said nothing.

'I used to see her when she visited Queenie.'

'Right.'

'I'll come,' she said, hesitantly. 'If it's okay?'

'Come where?'

'The funeral?'

'I guess,' he said.

The conversation was proving to be every bit as excruciating as Tony had envisaged. 'Is it at Stockport crem?' she said.

'Yep.'

'When?'

Howie sighed, as though the questions were exhausting him.

'Thursday.'

'Oh, right, that's sooner than I thought.'

Howie said nothing.

'I suppose it's a quiet time of year,' she said.

'What?'

'January's dead busy. It quietens down in spring. I found that out in the nursing home. It's like people hang on for Christmas or something, then give up the ghost in the new year...' Her voice trailed off with the realisation that her observations might be insensitive to the newly bereaved.

'Sorry,' she said, cringing. 'What time's it start?'

'Dunno. Midday. Early afternoon. Something like that.'

'Oh. Okay. Cos I'm sure Eddy'll want to be there.'

Howie sighed. 'Hang on.'

Tony waited for what felt like an age, aware of muffled talking in the background.

'Twelve-thirty. Then back to Jean's for the aftershow. Tell Eddy

I expect him to be there.'

'We all grieve in our own way, I suppose,' she said to Fazakerley, after coming off the phone.

But the dog was unconcerned. Fast asleep. Sprawled half-on half-off the sofa. Tangled in his blanket, like *The Death of Marat*. She thought about the limited wardrobe options packed in her holdall, and suspected low-slung cargo pants and calf tattoos weren't going to cut it at a funeral. Fazakerley opened one eye, vaguely aware he was being spoken to.

'C'mon, mate. Best get down the chazzers.'

SCHMATTBUSHBY

✱

The funeral director had been right when she'd warned Howie his car might get vandalised, though she'd under-estimated to what extent. Not only had the Aston Martin been keyed, but it had also been graffitied – an old-school cock and balls spray-painted across the passenger-side door. Howie had driven back from the funeral home unaware of the damage, and had travelled up the A6 and through the centre of Manchester oblivious to the hilarity his predicament was generating; ignorant of the fact his car would soon be trending on social media yet lucky the tinted windows disguised just which cock it was who was driving it. It took a smirking valet at the hotel to point out the problem. Howie was livid and returned to his hotel room in a foul mood. But his agitation was short-lived. A precision hand-job delivered by Meredith, his own personal penis whisperer, soon put him in a better frame of mind.

Though promiscuous, addicted even, Howie was a lazy and inconsiderate lover. His libido may have been out of control, but his tastes remained pretty vanilla. But ever since that first evening, when he and Meredith had snogged like teenagers in the elevator to his hotel suite, he'd been locked in a glorious cycle of sex, drugs and round-the-clock room service with a woman who he'd soon discovered, was sexually proactive with a penchant for kink. It was exhausting, in the best possible way, but what Howie lacked in stamina, he compensated for with uppers. Meredith had no such problems with endurance and shagged with the vim of a nitrous-injected dragster. Howie was cock-a-hoop to have this young woman treat him as her own private petting zoo. He'd even agreed to some entry-level bondage – happy to indulge her, so long as none of it required standing for any length of time.

'Okay, you're going to need a, like, safe word?' Meredith said as she gaffer-taped his wrists to the headboard, having popped home briefly, a couple of days in, to collect a surprisingly large wheelie suitcase of lingerie and sex toys.

'I dunno,' he said, mulling it over. 'Help?'

'Don't be silly,' she said, twisting his nipple.

Howie squealed. Meredith laughed at his distress and blew on him as though to make it better. Howie found the sensation exquisite. It crossed his mind that he might look into getting his nipples pierced – like Meredith, with her little bars. She obviously liked her intimate piercings. She'd even had her fanny done, as Howie had discovered when he'd cracked a porcelain veneer the first time he'd gone down on her. He wondered what Stina would make of him having nipple rings at the age of fifty-eight. She'd no doubt think it ridiculous and yet more proof of a mid-life crisis.

'It has to be something you wouldn't normally, like, say during sex?' Meredith said.

Howie wasn't sure he'd ever said 'help' during sex. He suspected all that might be about to change.

'Okay, got it,' he said, with the self-satisfaction of a man who'd finally had an original idea. 'Sir Matt Busby.'

'Amazing.'

So, Sir Matt Busby it was, ringing out from the Annie Walker suite at the slightest hint of discomfort. Howie was in heaven, having torrid sex with someone who didn't charge by the hour. But what he enjoyed more than anything was that Meredith didn't need to be made love to. It was one of his bugbears and why he preferred fucking strangers. He found sex with Stina gruelling. Not because it was strenuous, but because he couldn't deliver the tenderness and emotional connection she craved. Meredith, on the other hand, appeared to view sex – and indeed life in general – as purely recreational.

In the short time he'd known her, Howie had discovered Meredith did little paid work. He'd learnt the hard way of her singing ambitions. But still, he thought, lots could be done in post-production these days. He genuinely believed that despite her foghorn voice, she had the tits and sass to get somewhere in the business. He'd make a few phone calls. Get Raoul on board. He'd even joined in with her, buoyed by alcohol and uppers, following her insistence they could record a duet.

'Literally A Star is, like, Born?' she'd said, demonstrating her impressive ability to hold a conversation while bouncing on his dick.

After a week or so of sleeping, eating and fucking, Howie's relationship with Meredith had transitioned from fun and furtive into something less fleeting. And, like all the corniest of adulterers, he saw putting her on the payroll as the perfect cover while he figured out how to best break up with the mother of his child. This plan of action gained traction when Tony rang to discuss funeral arrangements – her worthy offers of help in stark contrast to the fun he was having with Meredith. He'd only answered the call on the off-chance Tony'd had word of Eddy. But instead she'd waffled on about his mother's funeral, reminding him how she knew Jean. Howie was disturbed that she had a connection to his family, preferring not to be reminded that the office PA came to the job via the dementia wing of a nursing home, that she'd had a role in the personal care of his mother. It felt too intimate and gave credence to his belief that Tony lacked the glamour he felt the position warranted. Meredith, on the other hand, had the sprinkling of stardust he thought necessary for the job – an attribute she had proven even as Tony was on the phone. She'd performed a strip – a kind of a dance of the stained hotel towels, streaked with Howie's hair dye – which had culminated in her twirling sideways and crashing into the breakfast trolley. An opened bottle of champagne glugging onto the carpeted floor.

'Careful,' he'd said, pressing the phone to his chest to muffle her giggling. Putting his finger to his mouth to shush her had prompted Meredith to stick out her tongue and stamp her foot. Howie found her childlike petulance delightful and blew her a kiss, while Tony bored on about the funeral.

'Perhaps you could work for me?' he'd said later, his interaction with Tony having strengthened his resolve.

'Literally?' she said, naked, save for a stethoscope.

'Yeah man, toadally. You could be my PA.'

'That's so cool. I would be, like, such an amazing PA?'

'Tony's got to go. I don't like her attitude. You could travel with me. We could do this more,' he said, waggling his penis at her like a Happy

Monday with a lone maraca.

'What about Eddy?' Meredith said, snapping on a latex glove for reasons that weren't immediately apparent.

'What about him?' he replied.

'Won't he, like, object?'

'I'm the boss,' he said.

She rolled him onto his side and instructed him to draw his knees to his chest.

'Eddy's past it. I need someone younger,' he said, as he lay curled with his back to her, stretching to get a slice of cold toast that had been on the trolley since breakfast. 'I'm working on it. I'll tell Eddy once the funeral's out of the way.'

'Cool', Meredith said.

Howie munched on the remains of his breakfast, vaguely aware of Meredith squelching a tube of something onto what he was about to discover were her index and middle fingers.

'Schmattbushby!' he spluttered, his safe word mangled by a mouth full of toast as Meredith – without so much as a please or a thank you – hit a spot only previously explored by his urologist, and rooted around his prostate with the fervency of a mudlarker at low tide. Howie couldn't decide whether to be scandalised or grateful as Meredith ferreted around his jacksie with such relish that he was surprised she hadn't brought a trowel. He was unable to make it stop and not sure he wanted it to. His mouth clenched with the rigidity of a condemned man in an electric chair, while his penis jumped about like a sprung fire hose. His ejaculate shot across the bed and hit the breakfast trolley with a punch that almost took out the teapot. Meredith squealed with laughter and removed her glove.

'Schmatt fuckin' Bushby,' he sighed, as the munched remains of his toast and the bitten-off half of his previously-cracked porcelain veneer dribbled out of his mouth and onto the hotel pillow.

IN CAHOOTS

✦

Eddy lay on the bare mattress, his head supported by the sweatshirt he'd fashioned into a makeshift pillow. The parka Joni had pulled from a binbag served as a blanket. He had no immediate plans to ferret through his personal effects to retrieve any more of his things, even though his socks were beginning to niff as badly as his unwashed body. He'd decided he liked the room spartan like this. The lack of stuff suited his nihilistic mood. Personal possessions he'd amassed over his lifetime had become meaningless clutter. He was happy for Una to chuck everything he owned into a skip. He wanted nothing.

Hostilities between himself and Una had plateaued. There'd been no discussion regarding his returning home, no indication of whether this was a temporary or permanent arrangement, just an understanding that the best thing for Joni, while she was suspended from school, was that both her parents be present. Even so, Eddy had seen little of either his wife or his daughter since they'd sat united in the headteacher's office – he'd only occasionally encountered them when venturing outside of his bedroom to scuttle to the bathroom or when making the briefest of trips downstairs to peruse the fridge and pick at leftovers. He felt uneasy in their presence, suspecting they were talking about him; mother and daughter in cahoots, bonded in disapproval. Their silence when their paths crossed proof of their contempt. But, as disturbing as this was, he had other, more pressing concerns.

Eddy still hadn't spoken to Howie. And each passing day had made meaningful contact less likely. But he couldn't have cared less. Iiris's shock visit had left him hyper-vigilant and broken sleep had helped cultivate fears she would return to the house. His startle reflex was on a hair-trigger, and Tony's text informing him that Iiris had checked out of The Sharples was of little comfort. Where she had gone was anyone's guess. Eddy hoped it was London. Better still, Estonia. But he feared it was Chorlton-cum-Hardy.

DO NOT DISTURB

✳

The reception staff were unfazed at Howie's booking of a ground-floor family room – of him adding it to the bill, while retaining the Annie Walker suite on the top floor. Those same hotel employees who had, over the course of the past ten days, quietly clocked the comings and goings of the young woman with the Kewpie-doll face. The one he'd told them was his niece. The same woman they'd watched on CCTV, being fingered by him in the elevator.

The arrival of Stina and Viola to The Sharples signalled a pesky hiccup in Howie's rollicking sex bender and he hadn't been there to welcome them when they arrived at the hotel. Instead, he was stretched out on his bed, enjoying the panoramic view of Meredith's bare bottom repeated to infinity in the panels of the mirrored bathroom as she brushed her teeth. He was playing with himself under his harem pants as Stina's text pinged through, announcing their safe arrival. Knowing his girlfriend was a few floors away in the same building, prompted him to follow his erection to the bathroom and to stand behind Meredith as she gargled with mouthwash. Intercourse was as rapid as rabbits in a field where there's a farmer with a gun. Howie's pants were around his ankles and the whole thing was over faster than it would have taken to put the Do Not Disturb sign on the door.

THE TINIEST OF HESITATIONS

✳

Given the hotel's fashionable reputation, the family room at the back of the building was a poorly lit disappointment. Overlooking a row of dumpsters and overshadowed by a multi-storey car park, the cramped room suffered from a lack of regard Stina hadn't anticipated when arriving in the stylish foyer.

'*Förbaskat,*' she said, shutting the door behind her and recognising that despite being very pleased with itself, this hotel felt no obligation to cater for young children.

'Was that a swear, momma?' Viola said, pulling off her shoes and climbing onto the sofa bed that butted against the double divan, happily settling down with Bebisbjörn the bear and the TV's remote control.

Ever the pragmatist, Stina tried to reconcile herself to this box-ticking afterthought of a room – in all likelihood the only one allocated to travellers with kids. It would only be for two nights after all. But though she was prepared to tough it out, she knew Howie would be far less amenable, and anticipating his displeasure put her on edge. She looked at the room service menu. It had been a long journey and they were hungry, but she couldn't stomach eating from a tray in such a gloomy space.

'Let's go,' said Stina.

'Where?'

'To eat.'

'Pizza!' Viola said, thumping the air.

'*Kom nu,*' Stina held out her hand. 'Pappa will be looking for us.'

The brasserie wasn't overly busy, but, even so, Stina and Viola were seated away from other diners by staff mistrustful of a young child's ability to behave. They'd hardly been at the hotel an hour and already Stina was counting the minutes until she could hit the road home. She checked her phone, her food going largely uneaten while Viola chomped her way through a side plate of fries – the only child-friendly dish on the menu.

Howie hadn't replied to Stina's text informing him of their arrival. Nor had he replied to her next one, letting him know they were in the Terry Duckworth room on the ground floor. Neither had he picked up when she'd called him, the phone ringing out before clicking onto voicemail.

'*Hej hej*,' she said, doing her best to sound upbeat. 'We're having something to eat in The Weatherfield. See you soon.'

Stina wondered if there'd been a misunderstanding. Perhaps Howie hadn't realised she'd be arriving during that afternoon. It wouldn't surprise her. They'd hardly spoken two words to each other since Viola's birthday. Just the odd text regarding logistics.

She dragged out the meal for as long as she could, but eventually they set off back to their room. She paused at reception. 'My partner's staying here, but I can't get hold of him. He was supposed to be transferring to the Terry Duckworth today. Can you see if he's checked out of his room?'

'Sure,' said the receptionist. 'I can help with that. What's their name?'

'Howie Howden. Thank you.'

It was only the tiniest of hesitations, but Stina picked up on the fleeting alarm that passed over the receptionist's face.

'Let me see. Howden.'

Viola hugged Stina's legs and Stina ruffled the child's hair as the young man tapped at a keyboard hidden from view behind the desk.

'Is there a problem?' Stina said.

'No, our system's just running a bit slow,' he replied, his cheeks flushing. 'Erm, so it looks like he hasn't checked out yet. Would you like me to put you through?' he said, nodding at the phone on the desk.

'No, thanks. What room's he in? I could go and get him.'

The receptionist looked back at the screen. As if working out what to say or do. And Stina knew, before the young man found the backbone to tell her it was the Annie Walker suite on the top floor, that she mustn't go there. Not with Viola. She knew they must go back to their own room and wait.

EN FAMILLE

Una could hear him. The migraine thump behind her eyes had stopped her checking the illuminated alarm for the time, but the silence of the street outside suggested it was the dead of night. She knew it was Eddy. Chakakhan's grumbling had alerted her to him moving about the house, coughing and clearing his throat, his asthma playing up. She kicked off the duvet. It was chilly but, despite being out the other side of the menopause, she still had trouble regulating her temperature, the change of life having blown her body's thermostat. She lay on the bed, aware of a draught. The faint rattle of her window suggested the front door was open. It wasn't unusual for Eddy to be wide awake in the night. Or to be outside having a spliff. But normally he'd smoke in the back garden or, when the weather was bad, lean under the cooker hood with the fan turned on. She wondered when the last time she'd joined him for a smoke had been. She'd never been as committed to pot as he was, but she'd enjoyed the occasional toke back in the day. Before she felt it imperative to stop. To have her wits about her all the time.

Una hadn't meant for him to return home the day after throwing him out. But the incident with Joni had pulled into focus the need to rally for their child. Though she was loath to admit it, being with Eddy at the school had felt empowering. Having him face down Mr Cockbone and stick up for his daughter was the Eddy she knew of old. She was proud of him for fighting Joni's corner, for refusing to be cowed by the head teacher's status. The memory, which she'd replayed over and over, made her smile and nudged at a fondness for the man she was determined to divorce.

But since they'd arrived back in a taxi, *en famille*, Eddy seemed to be avoiding all contact. And yet she'd catch him lurking outside the living room door while she and Joni watched TV or hear Chakakhan grumble, having sensed him standing on the staircase when they were eating in the kitchen. Several times Una had gone into the hallway, only to see him scuttle back upstairs. She'd also been surprised to find, at one point, he'd developed a sudden interest in gardening and was outside pruning a forsythia bush. Una had hammered on the window for him to stop, aware that however well-meant this foray into horticulture was, he was cutting it back at entirely the wrong time of year.

'It's still in flower,' she'd mouthed through the window.

But he struggled to lip-read with his one functioning but short-sighted eye, and had continued to hack at the bush with a pair of blunt secateurs.

Una went outside, gripping Chakakhan in her papoose. The dog had gone nuts.

'You have to wait until it's finished flowering,' she'd shouted over the noise of the dog.

'Oh,' Eddy had said, having one final go at a branch.

'You could mow the lawn if you're looking for something to do.'

Eddy had gazed at Una with the dunderheaded look of a tourist without a phrase book. 'Right,' he'd said.

But the lawn had remained un-mowed, and the once-glorious forsythia bush looked increasingly bedraggled over the coming days. Una was convinced that Eddy was determined to reduce it to a stump by stealth. Perhaps, she thought, that was what he was doing now, in the dead of night. She got out of bed, pulled on her dressing gown and set off downstairs with Chakakhan tucked under her arm, navigating the steps barefoot in the darkness.

'What the actual fuck?' she whispered to the dog, on seeing the front door wide open, the hall illuminated by the bright outside light.

Una squinted and reached for the dark glasses she kept on a side table – one of the many pairs she had dotted around the house. She wriggled on some wellies and stepped outside. The garage door was open, casting a long beam of light down the driveway. She could hear movement from inside. She shushed and stroked Chakakhan, aware the dog's low-grade grumble was a precursor to a barking fit that would wake the neighbourhood.

'Eddy,' she said, her whisper audible in the silence of pre-dawn. 'Eddy?'

The noises stopped.

'Eddy?'

Una walked slowly towards the door, her breathing heavy. 'Eddy.'

'Hello?'

'Eddy, what the fuck?'

Eddy was brandishing a long-handled brush. The un-battered side of his face looked surprised to see her.

'What the fuck? It's the middle of the night,' she said.

'Sorry. Did I wake you?'

'What in Christ's name are you doing?'

'There's a bat.'

'A bat? Where?'

Eddy scanned the room as best he could. 'Must have flown out,' he said.

'Why the feck are you in here anyways?'

'I was looking for a suit,' he said, poking at the binbags, squashed between the car and the wall, with his brush. 'For the funeral.'

Una paused, a little shamefaced to have put him in this position. 'Ah right.'

'You coming?'

She shook her head. 'Nope,' she said, conscious that the one silver lining from the last two weeks was that Eddy was in no position to ask that she join him. 'How you getting there?' she said.

'Driving.'

'With that eye?'

Eddy shrugged. 'I'll be careful.'

'What time will you be back?'

'Dunno. There's a buffet back at Normal Jean's after.'

Una snorted. Him making her smile, caused her resolve to waver a little. She considered offering to drive him. She could always sit it out in the car, and did a quick calculation of how long it would take. But she realised it wouldn't be possible. It was Joni's first day back at school after the suspension and she felt it important to be home when Joni returned. She looked at the binbags, at Eddy rummaging for a suit, and felt uncomfortable that he had to do this. Had she not been trying to control the dog, she would have helped. They could have picked over the bags together, as though it was a perfectly normal husband-and-wife activity at three in the morning.

'I'll leave you to it, so.'

Back in her bedroom, Una felt dreadful. Like the world's biggest bitch. She was fast coming to the conclusion that ending her marriage wouldn't be the dispassionate exercise she'd envisaged. Eddy, for his part, seemed remarkably compliant. But his willingness to get out of her life, putting up no argument and making no pleadings to stay, brought more hurt than relief. His making it easy for her – whether by accident or design – was making it much harder. *Maybe he does have someone else*, she thought. But even Una, still unsure of what happened in London, had to admit it unlikely that Eddy had taken to shagging around. Throughout all of his absences, when away on tour, his fidelity had never been in question. If she was being entirely honest, she would have to concede it hadn't been the girl coming to the house that had enraged her. But more the glee in Howie's eyes on finding out.

Whatever had gone on in London must have been some kind of aberration, but finding the words to confront Eddy eluded her. Talking it through, as husband and wife, was unimaginable after so many years of bottling things up. Besides, the situation with Joni and the school had muddied those particular waters and she felt only able to cope with one crisis at a time. But however shamefaced and culpable Una was over the whole binbag episode, she was secretly gladdened that Joni had become a little clingy. She'd even tagged along to collect the car from the pound, so turning a ball-ache of a chore into a girls' day out with a trip into town and a burger for lunch, where Joni had announced, over the cauliflower option, she'd become a vegan. Exclaiming, with the certainty of youth, she would never wear or eat animal products again. Una knew her well enough to suspect this might be true. Each evening, they would binge-watch Netflix series, and Joni would take it upon herself to educate Una in her favourite programmes. Talking over episodes of *Stranger Things*, explaining plot twists and turns as though her mother was incapable of following them herself. Una was happy to act the eejit; prepared to let her concerns of whether it was suitable viewing for a twelve-year-old slide, just for this reconnection with her daughter.

FROSTY

★

It had been around nine o'clock in the evening when Howie finally rocked up to greet his little family, knocking on their door with the dull thud of a melancholic milkman. Meredith's promise of a quickie, should he give Stina the slip, became increasingly tempting as the night wore on. He'd brought little more than his outfit for the funeral with him, having neither the energy nor the inclination to pack up and decamp all his things. Stina's greeting had been low-key, her manner distant. Viola had been warmer, jumping from the sofa-bed and trampolining across their mattress for one of Howie's wooden hugs. It was well past her bedtime, so Stina had little option but to switch off the light and get into bed herself. Howie so resented this aspect of parenthood, of having even the most basic of freedoms curtailed. Not being allowed to turn on the TV for fear of waking the child vexed him. The whispers and the tippy-toeing were yet another tedious feature of a role he was unfit to play.

It had been strange lying next to his official girlfriend after so many frisky nights in the Annie Walker. There had been no bodily contact between them, despite being sardined together in a bed that Howie suspected wasn't even a regular-sized double. Stina had rolled away from him, and hardly moved a muscle, despite his fidgeting and noisy chomping on hotel mints in an attempt to mask his tobacco breath, the room semi-illuminated by him looking at his phone. He didn't normally suffer from claustrophobia, but cooped up with Stina's long limbs and Viola's snoring had him climbing the walls. In a strangely prudish break from tradition, he'd noticed she'd changed for bed in the poky shower room, locking the door behind her. A belted bathrobe had been wrapped tight around her waist, despite the short distance to walk across the floor. But any chance of a good night's sleep had been scuppered by the crashing of a 2am kerbside glass collection, the constant bleeping of the nearby car park barrier and the general wide-awakeness of his fucked-up body clock. He was dreading the funeral and the gathering back at Jean's, and the prospect of another night in the Terry Duckworth with a girlfriend as frosty as Uppsala County in the spring.

'Where are you going?' Stina asked, as he got out of bed and pulled on his harem pants.

'For a smoke. Can't sleep.'

IN ON IT

✳

Sometimes, when Eddy peeped through the shuttered blinds in his daughter's bedroom, adjusting the tilt rod to open the slats just enough to monitor outside his home, he would see her. Bold as brass and as clear as day. Standing at the end of his drive. Stamping out a cigarette. Her bony frame swamped by his jacket. He'd given up on his broken glasses – while actively suicidal and with one eye swollen shut, there seemed little point in making an optician's appointment. But despite his poor eyesight, he could see Iiris with twenty-twenty vision, returning to torment him.

With each passing sleepless night, these visitations became more frequent. A large forsythia bush, in glorious full bloom, offered the ideal hideout during the day. After dark, tree branches heavy with blossom and backlit by streetlamps, would cast Iiris-shaped shadows across the front lawn. The stone gatepost finial ball assumed the perfect outline of a human head. It wasn't long before Eddy's paranoia tapped him on the shoulder to inform him the entire suburb was in cahoots. Vehicles that slowed, in a road made narrow by parked cars, were monitoring his movements. Passers-by, dog walkers and schoolchildren were conspiring against him. The postie, banging the front gate, would see Eddy scuttling downstairs to intercept the anticipated hate mail and blackmail. A car horn, a child shouting, even a barking dog were all evidence of the community's disapproval. All of them disgusted by the funny business that had taken place down in London. Every last one of them. In on it.

Eddy had tried several vantage points in the days since his return, but Joni's bedroom, specifically her platform bed, offered the best daytime view through his binoculars – held skew-whiff and telescopic to his good eye. Opening the slatted blinds at the perfect angle and as vigilant as a barrelman in a crow's nest, he watched, eye peeled, the comings and goings below.

After several nights of wakefulness, Iiris had got into the house, appearing behind him in the bathroom mirror as he splashed cold water on his face. Iiris with three eyes, whispering, 'where is my friend?' so close that he could feel her breath on the back of his neck, before she disappeared like a music hall magician when he turned to confront her.

It was inevitable, as his precarious toehold onto sanity worked its way loose, that he would become fearful of her hiding in his bedroom. And so the doors of the empty wardrobe were left open. His curtains were folded on the floor. His bed dismantled. His mattress upended. A bedside cabinet was laid face down in case Iiris managed to fold herself into tiny pieces and secret herself inside it. It didn't matter that he had nowhere to sleep, because outside of the occasional head-nod lapse, he was twenty-four-seven combat-ready.

After dark, when Joni had gone to bed, he would move downstairs to keep up surveillance. At other times, he would stand on the doorstep or patrol the garden, a semi-psychotic, pot smoking night watchman. As hauntings went, it was entry-level Stephen King, with neither Una nor Joni seemingly aware of Iiris's presence. But even that conundrum could be reasoned away when, the night before Queenie's funeral, as he rummaged in the garage looking for his suit, he witnessed Iiris shape-shifting, swooping above him in the form of a bat. Una not being able to see her was proof Iiris had singled him out for special treatment. That whatever demonic mischief she was up to, it was him she was out to torment.

HIS FAVOURITE COLOGNE

✳

It hadn't escaped Stina's attention that Howie'd had his roots done. It was the first thing she'd noticed when he'd turned up at the door. This fortnightly chore that had been hers throughout their relationship was the reason she'd come armed with dark towels and a box of his preferred blue-black dye. She knew his refusal to have it done professionally was grounded in shame, that going to a salon would be too public an environment for something so personal; that this signifier of mid-life was something he struggled with. Whatever, the significance of his freshly tinted hair was not lost on her.

She'd hardly slept a wink all night. The room had been airless and imbued with the warm gases of the scores of disappointed travellers who'd been allocated this space. A persistent hum that came from somewhere in the bowels of the hotel had bored into her skull with the commitment of a Renaissance trepanner. Maybe it was the acoustics, or maybe it was cursed, but there was something about the room that amplified sound and dread. It hadn't occurred to her when she'd set off in her little yellow car for Manchester that they'd be making their own way to Queenie's service. She'd supposed there would be a funeral car. Maybe if she and Howie had been in more meaningful contact, he would have told her his car had been vandalised and was in for repairs. Perhaps he'd have mentioned they wouldn't be joining Jean and Gordon in the funeral limo. Had she been aware of this, she would have thought to bring the Lexus – pristine, garaged up and laughingly known as their family car. Its low mileage indicative of how little they did together.

When eventually she'd heard the sound of Howie's key card opening the door, she'd shut her eyes and feigned sleep. She had no intention of asking where he'd been for the past few hours, but the resinous scent of his favourite cologne was evidence of him having showered. Notes of frankincense, palisander and patchouli betrayed, rather than concealed, his deceit.

AS IF

✱

It was around 7am when Una heard Eddy treading quietly up the stairs. She was conscious he'd had no sleep, but wondered how much she'd got herself. She felt shattered from such a disrupted night. Wired and worried, her concern for Eddy, Joni and her ageing parents had flashed in sequence through her brain like diabolical traffic lights. But she needed to get up. It was Joni's first day back at school following her suspension, and she'd promised to drive her to avoid being swamped by questions from schoolkids on the bus.

She rested her forearm over her migrainey eyes and wondered, for the thousandth time, whether she should move Joni to a different school. But where? Maybe she should go home to Ireland and lick her wounds in a place that wasn't so hell-bent on going to pot. She knew it had problems of its own, but return visits had suggested a country committed to progress. England had become such a backward-looking, unhappy place. All that was needed was a return to flammable nightdresses and polio, and its pig-headed regression would be complete. Going home to Sligo would not only solve the problem of Joni's schooling, but it would also address a desire to be closer to her parents. A couple of her sisters lived local to them and kept her posted as to how they were muddling along. But it didn't sit well with her, this care by proxy. She could feel time slipping away. Her parents appeared to age exponentially with each visit. She'd never fully overcome the anxiety she felt each time the phone rang, dreading that one day it would be THAT call. But for the move to be possible, she would have to tackle the thorny issue of custody. She knew Eddy would want meaningful access but she was troubled by real concerns over his ability to cope. The wretchedness of divvying up her young daughter's life as though she was some kind of sharing platter saw Una pull the duvet over her head. The enormity of ending their marriage seemed crushing and complex.

Sensing an approaching postie, Chakakhan jumped from the bed and pressed her nose against the bedroom door, hackles raised, poised for attack. The letterbox clattered, prompting Eddy to hurry back downstairs. She tried to envisage a life without him. She wasn't sure she still loved him, not romantically anyway, but she found it impossible to sustain hatred. It was while wrestling with these conflicting emotions that – like all the best and worst of ideas – a solution pinged fully formed into her head. It was obvious. Eddy should come to Ireland with them. Did people do that? Take their exes with them when they moved house? Chuck them into the van along with rolled-up rugs, house plants and garden furniture? How would it work in the event of either of them hooking up with new partners? *As if* she thought. She had no wish to start afresh and adapt to a whole new set of foibles. At her age she'd be taking on a person with a lifetime of baggage; their own children maybe; grandchildren even. The idea of ex-wives, of step-children, of blended families felt impossible and exhausting.

Picking up the vibrations of some future imaginary partner, Chakakhan jumped back onto the pillow next to her and growled. Yet still, the thought of relocating to Ireland nipped at her. The north-west of England had been her home for much of her adult life, but it was the north-west of Ireland that called her to her now. She propped herself up and put on her dark glasses to scroll through properties in County Sligo on her phone, curious to find out if the sale of their house in Manchester could fund two homes in the area she'd been raised. Her squinted eyes focusing on anything that looked like it had at least two fields between herself and the next human. She was surprised to find the place she'd always thought of as a backwater as a teenager, in which she'd been bored out of her skull and from where she'd plotted her escape, now looked a blissful proposition. *An affordable county*, said the estate agent's blurb. *A hidden gem*.

THE ODD COUPLE

★

Eddy expected the letter to be old-fashioned hate mail – words cut and pasted from magazines and newspapers. It didn't occur to him that someone as young as Iiris was unlikely to do something so analogue; that the modern-day stalker wouldn't need to put in the leg work of their lo-fi predecessors; that cutting out, gluing, buying stamps and envelopes, walking to letterboxes had been superseded by effortless digital hounding. Instead, the letter was a summons for a speed awareness course, his car having been caught on camera the day he'd fled the house with Iiris. It demanded he reply within twenty-eight days to confirm who was driving. He threw it in the bin. Twenty-eight days was a meaningless concept for a man who'd given up on life. He hadn't shaved. Or showered. A dark linen suit pulled from a binbag in the middle of the night was creased to fuck, but he put it on anyway. He'd also rescued a moth-damaged Crombie of his father's. His shirt needed ironing, he couldn't find a tie and his open collar accentuated the motif of neglect. But none of it mattered.

When Una returned from dropping Joni at school, Eddy was ready to leave for the funeral.

'You going already?' she said.

'I want to get there early. I don't want to be rushing.'

Una looked quizzical. Eddy had never been early for anything in his life.

'Will you not at least put a comb through your hair so?'

Eddy looked at himself in the hall mirror, took a bite from a slice of cold buttered toast with one hand while he flattened his bird's nest hair with the other. He didn't see a problem.

'The state,' she added, picking dog hairs off the coat.

'It'll do,' he said.

Una passed him the car keys. She shook her head but, still, there was none of the residual hostility he'd come to expect.

'Are you sure you won't get a cab?' she said.

'No, I'll be careful. Promise.'

Una held up her hands as if to say, okay, you win. But Eddy took heart from her concern. 'Did Joni get off alright?'

'Hard to say. Think so. But Eddy, we need to talk about what we're going to do.'

'About Joni?'

'About everything.'

'Righto,' he said. He left the house, closing the front door softly behind him, the prospect of such a conversation sealing his early departure.

Mindful of his poor eyesight and the letter about the speed awareness course, Eddy drove slowly to the crematorium. He leant forward in his seat, never exceeding fifteen miles an hour, oblivious to the tailbacks and bad temper of drivers as he pootled along on a breakfast of marijuana and cold toast. He arrived a good couple of hours early and waited in the car park, observing the precision-timed cycle of hearses arriving and leaving – a steady carousel of human misery.

'Where is she? Where is she? Where is she?' Eddy said to himself, his one eye on the lookout for Iiris with her three. Wondering if she was going to turn up to the funeral and bang the window like the final scene in *The Graduate*.

With this in mind, the gentle knocking on his blind left side caused him to start. Tony waved and gestured for him to lower the window.

'Very smart,' Eddy said, looking at her funeral suit.

'Ta. Sue Ryder.'

Tony stepped back to show off her outfit. 'It's a bit tight though. I won't be able to stuff my face at Jean's. You going?'

'I guess.'

'If I'm going mate, youze are too.'

Eddy was relieved to see his buddy. Her presence took the edge off his anxiety.

'Your eye's looking a bit better,' she said.

'Hmmm, maybe. It's a bit more yellow today, I think,' he said, looking at himself in the rear-view mirror.

'It matches Howie's car,' she said, nodding over to where Stina had just parked. Howie got out and flicked a cigarette butt into a shrub.

'Fuck,' Eddy said, shooting down in his seat.

'It's okay. He hasn't seen you. He's too busy checking his reflection.'

Tony rested her forehead on her forearm, against the car door frame to give the appearance of being deep in conversation, all the while keeping lookout for Eddy. 'Is that Stina?' she asked.

'Not looking.'

'Wow. She's loads taller than him isn't she?'

'Sore subject that. What's he doing?'

'Hitching his kecks. Eating a chewy. Ignoring the kid.'

Tony gave a running commentary of Howie's trudge towards the crematorium until the arrival of the hearse signalled it was time to go in. She linked Eddy's arm and they walked into the chapel, onlookers unable to distinguish who was steadying who. Jean turned and gave a half-smile but couldn't disguise her disapproval of the odd couple being ushered into the row behind her. Stina looked around and mouthed a friendly *hell*o, nudging Howie to indicate that Eddy had arrived.

ARE YOU A BOY?

✱

After the service, back at Jean's bungalow, Stina sat on the toilet lid, wondering how long she could eke out this interlude from the awfulness of Queenie's wake. She'd done so much work on her self-esteem over the years, determined to move on from the timorousness of youth. But the funeral, and now this gathering, had found her shrivelling under the microscope. Tearful from lack of sleep, she felt singled out and picked on. She leant back against the cistern and closed her eyes, placing a finger against the side of her nose. The buzz of the extractor fan masked the sound of her alternate nostril-breathing – a yogic technique she occasionally employed to calm herself – though any hope of finding sanctuary in this pine-fresh refuge was scuppered by someone trying the door.

'Sorry,' she called out, hoping to sound normal. 'Coming.'

Stina flushed the toilet to add authenticity to this snatched moment of respite, then washed her hands with the bar of lavender soap that matched the decor of the pristine bathroom. She unlocked the door, embarrassed to discover a queue of people waiting outside. She apologised as she went back into the lounge, trying to control her emotions, hoping to see Eddy. Instead she saw Howie, who'd come back from his smoke in the garden, sitting in Gordon's armchair, a bottle of sherry in hand. She dearly hoped he wasn't getting pissed and looked away, focusing instead on Tony and Viola. The child's face a mess of blue icing and hundreds and thousands. She watched as Viola stuck her tongue out as far as possible, trying to lick any remnants from her chin, while handing the screwed-up fairy cake case to Tony.

'Lovely. Ta,' Tony said, taking it from her.

Stina laughed, grateful for the comic relief. The exchange helped her compose herself.

'*Å nej*,' Stina said, joining them, as Viola licked her hands and wiped them dry on her velour jumpsuit. 'Who gave you the cake?'

'Auntie Jean.'

Stina rolled her eyes.

'It's her skin,' she said to Tony. 'I have to be careful what she eats.'

Stina wiped Viola's scrunched-up face while the child watched through googly glasses and patched eye as Tony placed several cocktail sausages and Scotch eggs onto a napkin. Winking at Viola before meticulously wrapping them, she stuffed the bundle into her jacket pocket.

'Are you a boy?' Viola said.

'Viola!' Stina was mortified.

'It's okay, I get this all the time,' Tony said, laughing and turning to Viola to explain. 'No, I'm a girl.'

'*Gerhl*,' Viola said, without malice, copying Tony's Liverpool accent.

'I'm Tony, by the way,' she said to Stina.

'Yes. I'm sorry,' she said, placing her palm on her chest. 'Stina.'

They shook hands, the formality slipping easily into a light but natural embrace.

'Mind yourself,' Tony said, touching Stina's elbow to steer her out of Jean's path.

'Strewth!' Jean cried, hurrying to the aid of an elderly man whose slice of Victoria sponge was sliding from his paper plate onto the floor.

Stina and Tony smiled at each other and rolled their eyes, both on the same page.

'No Eddy?' Stina said.

Tony shook her head and checked her phone. 'He said he'd be here. I hope he's okay.'

They looked at each other and nodded, their faces betraying their concerns. And with that the two women – mismatched physically in every way, yet entirely in sync – moved across the room to the window. But there was no sign of Eddy. Just Agnieszka, hurrying down the drive.

TOO HANDSY

*

No one batted an eyelid when Tony excused herself early.

'Sorry, I've got to get back to me dog,' she said, feeling obliged to explain her departure to the roomful of guests.

Not that they cared. Apart from Stina, not one of them had engaged with her. Her leaving had prompted little more than the most wishy-washy ripple of byes. But she was glad to escape the disapproval of that lot and, anyway, she was distracted. Eddy still wasn't answering his phone.

As Tony drove away, her backfiring exhaust ricocheting around the cul-de-sac like a Sergio Leone gunfight, she reasoned it would be no big deal to go via Chorlton to check on Eddy. Stuffing her mouth with the snacky food she'd trousered earlier, she glanced back at Jean and Gordon's bungalow, and wondered if there was any truth in what people said about pampas grass in front gardens. She shuddered, spitting out a cocktail sausage into the palm of her hand. She thought about Viola, asking if she was a girl, and smiled. Tony was used to that kind of confusion, and it was never hateful in children. Adults, on the other hand, would often misgender her deliberately. Gordon had done it himself, earlier, asking if she'd like a drink and calling her 'fellah'. She'd clocked him, circulating, being way too handsy. *Gordon the Groper*, she thought. *Fucking perv.* She'd seen Stina's discomfort and had struck up a conversation to shield her. She ruminated on how lovely Stina was and how at ease she'd felt talking to her. She was baffled as to what she saw in Howie, but her own involvement with Meredith demonstrated that, when it came to matters of the heart, she was in no position to judge.

Once on the main road, Tony was jolted from her daydreaming. Aware of someone waving at her from a bus stop, she slowed slightly. It took a heartbeat to process it was the Polish woman who'd helped serve teas back at the bungalow and one heartbeat more to accelerate away. Tony was embarrassed about her clapped-out old car, with its smell of wet dog and the spat-out cocktail sausage and pilfered Scotch eggs on the passenger seat. She was ashamed to offer this stranger a lift, so instead she stared straight ahead, hoping the woman hadn't noticed her hesitancy. A quick glimpse in her wonky rear-view mirror revealed she was standing in the road, watching Tony's car disappear from view.

SOME WOMAN

★

Zoned out of the TV blaring in the background and invisible behind voile curtains, Una had been gazing out of the window, lost in thought, when she spotted the woman, her head bobbing up and down over the wall like a child's pull-along toy. Una tipped the sunglasses from the top of her head onto her nose. She had one of her migraines coming on, her headaches made worse by bright sunshine and a clenched jaw.

'What the actual fuck?' she whispered, primarily to herself but also to the dog, whose grumbling threatened to blow up into a full-scale barking fit. Turning from the window, she threw her phone into Joni's lap as she lay flopped on the sofa, watching *Family Guy* on TV.

'Call your Da and find out where he is.'

Joni groaned, exhausted from her first day back at school. 'Can't you call him?'

Una turned to look out of the window, see-sawing Chakakhan in her arms.

'Mum wants to know where you are,' Joni said to Eddy, having wearily dragged herself upright and called him on the mobile.

'She's looking round the bloody gatepost now,' Una said.

Joni took the phone from her ear. 'Who?'

'Some fecking woman. Watching us.'

Joni stood to have a look, but Tony had ducked back down.

'Give us the phone,' Una said, moving back into the room in order to calm the dog, who was now in full psycho-pup meltdown.

Joni passed it to her.

'Eddy.' Una's voice was a little shouty over Chakakhan's barking.

But Eddy was gone.

NOW WHAT?

✶

When Tony drove down Eddy's street on that sunny spring afternoon, she was taken with how beautiful the cherry trees were. Thinking it must surely be optimum blossom day, she wondered if she would ever have the money to live in an area like this. It seemed incomprehensible.

Despite her taped wing mirrors sitting at the wrong angle, Tony skilfully manoeuvred her car into what appeared to be the last space in the postcode, her textbook parking skills testament to the teenage joyrider who'd taught her in stolen vehicles. She'd spent hundreds of hours driving the East Lancs Road in cars, vans and even once a milk float. She'd explored the flatlands of Cheshire in a footballer's Ferrari, which they'd left abandoned but undamaged, with only a half-sucked Chupa Chup stuck to the leather upholstery to indicate the age of the driver. Tony dreamed of owning a more reliable car. Her own was held together with little more than gaffer tape and prayers to St Christopher. She remembered the Mini Convertible that Meredith's parents had bought for her birthday, the keys in a gift box, the car wrapped in a bow. It was the same car Meredith had written off, having flipped it onto its soft roof – an accident she'd walked away from, like most things in her life, blasé and unscathed.

Doing her best to appear nonchalant, Tony ambled along the pavement, trying to figure out which was Eddy's house in a road where properties had names instead of numbers. Eventually she spotted it. *Belhaven*. Peeking out from behind a substantial stone gatepost, she took in the ornate gingerbread woodwork trim along the guttering, the stained-glass panel in the front door and the garden crammed full of daffodils which bobbed in the light breeze and late-afternoon sunshine. The road was so peaceful, with just a yappy dog cutting through the spring birdsong and the faint drone of a distant jet beginning its ascent into Manchester airport. She wondered how Eddy could be so unhappy when he lived in a place like this.

'Now what?' she said to herself.

As plans went, this one hadn't been particularly well thought through. She considered knocking on the door but didn't relish meeting Una in person after their cringey telephone interactions. She looked over at the bay window, the voile curtains concealing all but the faint glow of a TV screen. In her mind's eye, when cooking up her cockamamie idea, she'd imagined seeing Eddy's car in the driveway. She'd have been reassured and taken herself off back into town. She'd factored in neither on-street parking nor a garage, with its roller door firmly shut. As Tony stood, clueless as to her next move, she tuned into the familiar refrain of an Eddy fag and asthma coughing fit coming from the garage.

'Ace,' she said to herself.

And with her mind now at rest, she limped back to her car and set off home to the office.

CLARITY AND CALM

✱

It hadn't been Eddy's intention to take his life that afternoon. In the garage. At his home address. It breached even his own careful protocols. Until that moment, he'd been determined to avoid scenarios that might have Una or – *puh puh puh* – Joni chance upon his body. Even at his most despairing, he'd been able to recognise the trauma such a discovery would inflict upon those he most cherished. But sitting in his car while on the phone to Joni, parked on top of the crushed Flymo and perched perilously close to his wit's end, he'd overheard Una telling his daughter there was 'some woman' lurking outside their home. Eddy was left in no doubt that his worst fears had come to pass.

Iiris.

And that was that. He turned off his phone and switched on the engine, the radio bursting into life with Howie's god-awful swing version of 'Begin The Beguine'.

'Fuck's sake,' he said, his hand instinctively reaching for his heart.

He jabbed the off switch and felt a refreshing sense of purpose. The decision, far from being an act of desperation, came from a place of clarity and calm.

'I'm done here,' he said.

As meditative states went, it was a pretty grim one, but his brain, for the first time ever perhaps, cut him some slack. All of the panic, the second-guessing, the over thinking subsided. Nothing mattered anymore. But it hadn't occurred to him their car had a catalytic converter; that attempting to take his life in the garage would be about as efficient as putting his head in a modern-day gas oven.

The ingestion of car fumes into his asthmaticky lungs sparked a ferocious coughing fit, reigniting atavistic concerns for his orbital floor fracture. He scrabbled to switch off the ignition, caught between a death wish and doctor's orders. He pressed the garage door remote control on his key fob and clambered from the car, scrabbling over binbags full of his clothes and the mangled remains of a hover mower. He ducked out from under the rising roller door, spluttering into the fresh air and sunshine.

He bent over, hands on knees, sucking on his inhaler as best he could with a broken face, and only straightened once his coughing had subsided. He scanned the surrounds expecting to see Iiris, but the only sign of life was a neighbour's cat trotting to greet him. It rubbed itself against his leg and Eddy bent to stroke it, taking another tentative puff on his inhaler. His cat allergies instantly triggered. All snot and spittle, he wiped his nose across the sleeve of his old dad's Crombie, pulled the elastic band from his wrist and pinged it across the lawn.

TOO WEIRD

Una was still looking out of the bay window when Eddy came into view. He walked to the front gate, peered up and down the road as though expecting someone, then ambled slowly back to the house. He looked out of shape, stooped and dishevelled, his black eye the perfect finishing touch to his derelict appearance. She was surprised to see him home so early, but more surprised still to see him give the neighbour's cat an affectionate ruffle. In all the years she'd known him, he'd always given cats a wide berth, his allergies another in a long list of tiresome maladies – some real, some imagined – that impacted on their daily lives.

'Oh Eddy,' she said to herself, seeing him wipe his nose on his sleeve.

She noticed him take off his elastic band and fire it across the lawn. The cat chased after it, and she smiled at what she supposed was a playful ruse to get it away from him. The band had always seemed such an idiotic thing to her, and having him twang it in her presence had pissed her off from day one. She'd felt policed by this visual reminder of his fragility; annoyed that whenever they'd had a disagreement, he'd snap the band in what felt like a passive-aggressive ploy to shut her down.

But now, seeing the state of him – her crumpled husband so beaten and defeated – and watching him being kind to the cat, she felt an unexpected tenderness. She wanted to rush out and enfold him, tell him everything was going to be okay. But it had been so long since there'd been any spontaneous intimacy between them that she held back. It would be too weird.

Having come into the house, Eddy didn't pop his head around the living room door to say hello as he usually did before hanging his coat, taking off his shoes, throwing his car keys onto the hall table and going upstairs to freshen up. It was a routine that had hardly changed in years. But Una thought nothing of it. She went into the kitchen, wondering what they'd have for tea. Opening the freezer, she wished she'd made more of an effort when she'd last been out shopping, and had bought something more substantial than oven chips and fish fingers. She took a bunch of takeaway menus from a drawer, thinking it would be good for all three of them to have an evening in together. They could watch a film with a pizza maybe. She was tired from the drama of the previous couple of weeks, but felt a line needed to be drawn. She'd be fifty-five in a few months and was conscious she'd reached an age that her younger self would have believed decrepit – just a few short years from a milestone that would once have signalled retirement. But Una felt she hadn't even got going yet. She drew comfort from her folks being in their eighties. Their advanced age suggested it possible she might have another thirty – forty even – years ahead of her. She couldn't bear the thought of squandering them. She clicked her tongue in an effort to distract Chakakhan from sniffing along the bottom of the hallway door and called to Joni to choose a pizza. But there was little chance of her daughter hearing over the TV. Una went into the living room and the dog raced past to the door that adjoined the hall, scratching at it, barking to be let out.

'Pizza,' she said, handing a menu to Joni, who folded her arms, refusing to take it.

'Vegan, duh,' she said, shaking her head.

'They do vegan.'

'Really? Cool.'

Una went back to the window while Joni chose her pizza. The dog's rising agitation alerting her to the possibility of someone skulking outside.

'What's Dad having?'

'His usual I expect.'

'Margherita extra olives,' they chorused together, and Joni rolled her eyes at Eddy's predictability.

Una pulled back the voile curtain to get a better view of the street.

'Vegan Rustica,' Joni said, chucking the menu onto the coffee table. Turning back to the TV.

'Please?' Una replied.

'Please,' said Joni.

Una scanned the pizza menu but couldn't concentrate. Not with Chakakhan's scratching at the door competing with the noise of the TV.

'What's up baby?'

Una had intended to pick up the dog and go outside to see what was bothering her. But as she opened the door, Chakakhan shot up the stairs. Una sighed and studied the menu, unable to decide whether to have the Napoli or the Formaggio, if she should order arancini or not. Or maybe she should have the Vegan Rustica, like Joni. As a show of solidarity and acceptance of her daughter's new vegan status. Then, still no nearer to making a decision and with no particular sense of urgency, she plodded up the stairs to see what was going on.

LIVING IN THE MOMENT

★

While Una had been downstairs, resolving to seize the day, in the room above her, Eddy had conceded defeat. His exhaust fumes effort might have come to nothing more serious than a hacking cough and biliousness, but his determination to end it all had not gone away.

He'd let himself into the house in a state of stupefaction. Trance-like, he'd taken off his shoes and placed them neatly side by side, hanging up his father's Crombie. It would have been hard to ignore the sound of the TV leaking out of the living room but if he did hear it, it gave him no pause for thought. He knew Una and Joni were in the house. But they'd become an abstract. No more than a potential fly-in-the-ointment interruption to the task in hand. There was no time to linger. No time to contemplate the devastation he was about to wreak on the family he adored. No time to reflect on the harm he would visit on a daughter he would ordinarily have done anything to protect. No time to consider the seed he would plant in her head, that she was not worth sticking around for. No comprehension of how this might play out in years to come, of angry grief expressed through screwed-up relationships with men. Even if he'd had the time to reflect upon any of this, it would have made no difference. Because his belief that his family would be better off without him bloomed around him with the toxicity of a 9/11 dust cloud.

At the top of the stairs he scanned the landing and reviewed his options. He hadn't a plan beyond needing to get things done as quickly and as efficiently as possible. He looked into Joni's bedroom. Her blinds were half-open and slatted shards of light spread out like spindly fingers over the scrambled mess of her room. Eddy had given no consideration to how, in the days, weeks and years to come, this moment – his decision to end it all in the bedroom of his precious and only child – might be picked apart. How the brutality of it would be beyond the comprehension of those he'd loved, desperate to understand why he'd chosen this time and this place. But Eddy didn't have a choice. Because whatever life events, genetic predispositions or metastasising melancholy had propelled him towards this dénouement, he was, for once, in a very un-Eddy space. He wasn't thinking. He had finally achieved the impossible. He was living in the moment. And it was a terrible thing.

Eddy walked across the cluttered floor – a mish-mash of discarded clothes, bags and school books. Something squeaked as he trod on a heap of what appeared to be dirty laundry. He picked up his bathrobe – the one Joni had appropriated – and took Chakakhan's squeezy toy from the pocket. He squeaked it – the sound an absurd Marx Brothers accompaniment to the unfunniest of scenes. He pulled the belt from the robe and tossed it over the top rail of the scaffolding bed, knotting it securely. The bed that Joni loved. The bed she'd helped design. That same bed that now provided the perfect gibbet for her doomed father.

There were no angels, no walking into the light, no dead relatives there to greet him. Just the din of what sounded like an aircraft taking off.

This is quick, Eddy thought, as he slumped forward, the belt tightening around his neck.

Then, blackness.

WELL IMPRESSED

*

'Sherry, Neville?'

Gordon waggled a bottle of Bristol Cream, his grinning face reflected in Howie's mirrored lenses. He knew Howie hadn't clocked him watching him, in the kitchen with Agnieszka – Howie's moving forward and Agnieszka stepping back, her finding herself pinned against the dishwasher. He'd seen it with his own eyes. *Weyhey*! he'd thought, feeling privileged to witness an actual real-life presidential pussy grab.

Howie had held up his hands, laughing, like he'd won at cards. Agnieszka had pushed him away. She'd still been holding a tea-towel. Her look of bewilderment had tickled Gordon. The incident had put a spring in his step, as he continued to the bathroom to apply a topical antibiotic to his arse crack. He'd always fancied Agnieszka. It had been the reason he'd offered discounted driving lessons. He liked being in close proximity to her when she got nervous, slapping the dashboard with the palm of his hand to surprise her with an emergency stop. He enjoyed the feeling of power he exerted with his dual controls, sometimes pressing the brake ever so slightly – his little joke – the unexpected jolt making her squeal. He would help her with her seat belt, his faux chivalry giving him the opportunity to cop a feel. But a pussy grab? Well, that was premier-league groping. Gordon had been well impressed.

Having finished in the bathroom he went back to the kitchen. Keen to mentally re-enact the scene he'd found so titillating. Neither Agnieszka nor Howie were there, just Casper in his basket, nibbling at a hot spot on his hind leg. Gordon opened a large sharing bag of crisps and stuffed a handful into his mouth before setting off back into the living room. He knew he'd never tell Jean about what he'd seen. No, it would be his and Howie's dirty little secret.

'Bottoms up,' he said, winking, as Howie took the bottle of sherry. And off Gordon trundled, clinking his drinks trolley around the room.

TOASTING MARSHMALLOWS

★

She didn't see him at first. A quick scan of the half-lit room revealed nothing but the untidiness created by a twelve-year-old girl. Una opened the blinds and cussed the daughter who'd crossed her heart and promised to keep the room clean if her parents allowed her a platform bed.

'What a feckin' hole,' she said.

It was only later when looping this scene over and over that Una wondered how it had been possible to miss him. Eddy's crouching body leant forward, as if sitting round a campfire, toasting marshmallows. How odd he looked to her. His face scarlet and puffy. As though he'd been crying.

'Oh Eddy,' she said, stepping towards him. The pizza menu still in her hand.

But he didn't acknowledge her. Nor did he respond to Chakakhan delightedly pinging about the room, squeaky toy in mouth. It had been the dog's persistence that had prompted Una to open the living room door. Chakakhan had taken the stairs two steps at a time – a surprising feat for such a small animal with bowed legs and a low-slung undercarriage. It had been her phenomenal hearing and possessive streak that had motivated her. The squeak she'd heard when Eddy stood on her toy was pitched at the exact frequency necessary to cut through the background noise of *Family Guy*, traffic on the outer ring road and a Boeing 737 coming into land five nautical miles away.

'Come on, Eddy. Enough so,' Una said, stepping across the debris on the floor, intending to console him with a hug.

It was only then she saw it: the belt from his dressing gown stretched taut from the scaffolding pole and pulled tight round his neck.

Thinking back, she didn't know how long it had taken her to heft his dead weight upwards, to wedge her knee under him as she tried to slacken the ligature. And how, having done so, she didn't have any hands free to untie the knot. She didn't know how long she had balanced him there, desperate, trying to figure out what the hell to do next. Even as she attempted, one-handed, gibberish profanity falling from her mouth, to pick at the knot tied to the scaffolding, she was forging some story, stringing together some different version of events to tell her daughter. To explain why her father was dead.

PART FOUR

*

Early April, 2019

A BETTER PERSON

★

Howie had been back home in Surrey for three days when Jean's call came through. He seldom answered the landline on the grounds it was only ever cold calls or family, neither of whom merited the walk across the room to pick up the phone. Had Stina been there, she would no doubt have answered, and Howie would have waved his hands and mouthed *not here* to the rolling of her eyes. Instead, he was spreadeagled out across the huge L-shaped sofa, having not long returned from his emergency dental appointment, his new veneer turned around within hours, his lips still a little numb from the anaesthetic. Stina had gone to collect Viola from school, and he was enjoying having the house to himself. Just him, a weed vaporiser and Cantona, the favourite of his cats. The languorous vibe complemented by Miles Davis through £30,000 worth of speakers. Bliss. It was the perfect conditions for a wank.

Face flannel at the ready, Howie rooted around in his harem pants, causing both his penis and Cantona to stir. Ever alert to the possibility of furry rodents, the cat grabbed at the movement beneath him. Howie nudged him away, his dormant knob flickering into life at the familiar caress of his right hand.

The answer machine clicked onto Stina's recorded message – officious, and in perfect English, but signing off with the Swedish '*tack*'. Howie tutted. They weren't speaking, having fallen out on the M6 toll road on the way back from Queenie's funeral.

'Fucking clown car,' he'd said, as they'd queued in Stina's yellow Peugeot to pay at the booth.

Howie shrank in his seat on seeing an adjacent motorist do a double take, catching his eye. 'Why the fuck didn't you bring the Lexus?'

'Why does it matter?'

Howie had said nothing. His bladder was beginning to call out for a comfort stop, but he'd neither the piss bottle nor the pluck to brave public toilets.

'Anyway, I thought you'd be driving back in the Aston,' she said.

'I told you. It's getting a respray.'

'You told me when I got to Manchester. What did you expect me to do? Drive back home and swap cars?'

Howie had brooded while Stina sorted the toll charge. 'Should have flown back,' he said.

He hadn't heard what she'd muttered. But he knew it was in Swedish. He'd said nothing. The combination of Stina's little car and a restless night spent in a tiny hotel room, listening to his daughter's mouth-breathing, had put him in the foulest of moods. He'd intended to nip up to Meredith again, while Stina and Viola had breakfast, but he'd fucked up. Exhaustion had got the better of him and he'd fallen back to sleep, winding up on the motorway without so much as a bowl of cornflakes or a hand-shandy to set him up for the day.

'I don't know why you didn't stay in Manchester 'til the car was ready, if driving home with us is such a chore,' Stina had said as they pulled into the services, Howie's bladder and nicotine withdrawal by now overriding all other concerns. It wasn't like her to argue in front of Viola, but the kid had been oblivious – engrossed in an iPad cartoon, headphones on, hugging Bebisbjörn the bear.

'I've got to sort THIS out,' Howie had replied, pointing at his broken tooth. The much-needed dental appointment forcing his reluctant return south. 'I'll fly back up Tuesday to get it,' he'd said, in full knowledge that the car wouldn't be ready until later in the week.

The journey had continued in silence, Howie was more comfortable after managing a stealth piss in a thicket at the service station picnic area. Stina had barely said a word to him since, despite his attempts to pick a fight, consciously or unconsciously hoping she'd flounce out and give him respite from what he felt was an annoying crusade to make him a better person.

The familiar shrill tone of Jean cut through '*So What*' at a pitch that jarred with both his tinnitus and his burgeoning erection. Normally he'd have turned the music up to drown out her out, but there was something in his sister's inflection that caught his attention. Indignation may have been her default setting, but Howie recognised she was unusually strident. One word fired out of the answer machine and shot straight across the room, scoring a direct hit into the centre of his hippocampus, the jolt propelling Cantona off the sofa and out through the door.

Agnieszka.

Howie's hand-job halted mid stroke. He muted the music. He could just make out the gist. Agnieszka had disappeared. Left work without so much as a by your leave...

He picked up the phone.

'Jean.'

'Pinch, punch, first of the month!'

'Yeah man,' he said. His lips still a little rubbery from the dentistry.

'What's this about your cleaner?'

'Well, it's the most extraordinary thing. I haven't seen hide nor hair of her since mum's send-off. She vanished into thin air halfway through the afternoon, leaving me with all that clearing up to do.'

'Have you rung her?'

'Well that's what's so peculiar. Her phone's still here. And her coat.'

All trace of marijuana evaporated from Howie's body. Any lingering hint of an erection gave up the ghost. He was, in an instant, stone-cold straight and flaccid.

'She's normally so reliable,' Jean said. 'Twice a week for five years she's turned up regular as clockwork.'

Howie rubbed his head with his fingertips. 'Have you tried ringing any of the contacts in her phone?'

'It's switched off.'

'So turn it on.'

'I make her switch it off when she comes to work. It says it needs a code.'

'Why do you make her turn it off?'

'Neville, I'm paying her to clean, not chinwag with her friends,'

Jean said, adding, with the timing of Frank Sinatra, 'in Polish.' The syllables stretched to emphasise her disdain of Agnieszka's mother tongue.

Howie chose to let this go.

'Is there anyone else you can ask? Does she have a husband?'

'I very much doubt it. There was some hard-luck story about a man from Denton, but I don't remember the details. She lives up that way somewhere with her young son. That's as much as I know.'

'Maybe she had to get back to the kid?'

'But why not say something? I'm not a monster, Neville.'

Howie ran his tongue over his repaired front tooth, zoning out of the conversation, Jean's voice now white noise. He cast his mind back to that afternoon. To Agnieszka. To the thrill of the pussy grab. He'd done the same to random women countless times before. He thought it a hoot. Only once had it backfired when his under-estimating the right hook of a Geordie lass had resulted in a broken nose. But even that had proved to be a positive, bestowing him a tough-guy image that distracted from his lily-liver. He'd never given this behaviour a second thought. It was, after all, just a bit of fun.

'NEVILLE.'

Howie realised Jean had been shouting his name. 'Yeah man.'

'Anyway, I've put her things in a bag on the doorstep. If she hasn't come to collect them by tomorrow, they're going in the wheelie bin. Five years and this is the thanks I get.'

A clumsy conversation followed regarding Queenie's belongings, which, after her long stay in the nursing home, amounted to no more than a laundry bag of clothes, a biscuit tin of costume jewellery and an envelope stuffed with family photos.

'Is there nothing you want, Neville?' Jean asked, incredulous. 'Nothing at all?'

No. He didn't want anything. What he wanted at that exact moment was to get back to Manchester and back into bed with Meredith Pruitt.

SPOILSPORT

For a horrible moment Tony thought her unease over Iiris's stay had been justified, believing the young woman had managed to run up a bill of thousands of pounds during her gratis weekend at The Sharples. The end-of-month total made no sense. But an itemised breakdown saw her blameless. Her room service statement showed no more than a few cans of Diet Pepsi and a phone call to Estonia. The heft of the bill was Howie's. But even so, it didn't add up. Stina had told her they planned to drive south the morning after the funeral, yet it would appear the Annie Walker suite was still in use. Perhaps there'd been a change of plan and no one had bothered to tell her. It wouldn't come as a surprise. There'd been no word from Eddy since the funeral and she was the last person Howie would keep in the loop. She cast her eyes over the bill, detailed to the last boiled egg. A life of penny-pinching had made her hypersensitive to such expense and excess. It was pretty obvious from the nature of the room service that Howie'd had company. And that he'd hardly left the suite at all.

Then she saw it.

And once she'd spotted one, another jumped from the page. And another and another. At least one a day. The same four words repeated over and over. At twenty-five quid a pop.

Meredith's Fruity Bum-Bum.

The clippered hair on the back of her neck bristled in tandem with Fazakerley's hackles. The dog stood to attention, aware of an incoming threat. Even in those first few seconds, Tony was manufacturing some implausible narrative which would account for why that particular cocktail had turned up on Howie's room service bill. Some scenario that explained how, in the months since their break-up, Meredith had managed to get what she called, her *signature cocktail*, onto the bar menu of a fashionable Manchester hotel. It was a cocktail that a smitten barman had invented for her – a mixture of champagne and vodka, sugar and passionfruit liqueur, mixed berry purée with two pink scoops of ice cream. Tony remembered how she'd called the barman a *dirty bastard* when he'd shoved a big, ripe strawberry between the two scoops with his forefinger, declaring the concoction Meredith's Fruity Bum-Bum. And how her disapproval had been undermined by Meredith squealing with delight and declaring it *amazeballs*, insisting he invent a cocktail for Tony too. And how hilarious Meredith had found it when he'd handed her the drink – a Kahlua, Baileys and ice cream gloop that had the look of a poor-performing turd on the Bristol Stool Chart. Tony had told the pair of them to fuck off, which had only increased their mirth. Meredith sliding off her bar-stool, helpless with laughter when the barman had announced it would be called 'The Spoil-Sport'.

It had only been after they'd broken up that Tony had recognised her role in the relationship was as Meredith's stooge. She recalled the times she would fight her girlfriend's corner, only to end up the butt of the joke. But not one of the humiliations she'd endured during their time together, not even the betrayal with the sports science student, compared to this – to the bombshell discovery that Meredith might have hooked up with her boss.

Tony's eyes flitted over the statement searching for further clues. The first Bum-Bum showed up on the 17th March. St Patrick's Day. The same day that Meredith had escorted Eddy home from the hospital. The same day she'd gone lukewarm on Tony. The same day she'd told her she couldn't meet as planned, because something had 'like, come up'. Tony slapped her laptop shut, not knowing what to do with such a huge surge of adrenaline. Had she been better on her feet, she'd have run for miles to outpace her internal dialogue. Instead she circled the office, Fazakerley's eyes fixed on her unsteady gait. She knew she'd no claim over Meredith's life. That they weren't a couple and hadn't been for some time. But none of this cut through the intensity of her outrage. She was collateral damage in some star-fucking mission that Meredith had set her mind on, when hearing about the new job. Tony pulled up Meredith's Instagram account on her phone. And there she was. Bare-shouldered, in bed, wrapped in crisp white hotel sheets, Fruity Bum-Bum held up, cocked as though toasting her own success, her phone reflected in Howie's trademark shades, perched on the end of her nose. #thesharples #mybestlife.

'Can you put me through to the Annie Walker Suite please?' Tony said, trying to sound less unhinged than her ragged breathing suggested.

The phone rang and rang.

'Hello?'

The voice sounded groggy, as if just woken, even though it was mid-afternoon. But there was no mistaking it. The familiar sleepy insouciance confirmed that the birthday card, the invite to the pub, the sudden fucking interest in her life had all been ruses to get a foot in the door. The whole snide chain of events fell into place like a one-armed bandit lining up for a triple cherry jackpot.

'Hello?' Meredith repeated.

Tony paused, realising she had no clue as to what she was going to say.

'Hello?' Meredith said again, a hint of annoyance in her voice nudging Tony off the blocks.

'So does he know you're me ex?'

'Excuse me?'

'Howie. Does Howie know you're me ex?'

Meredith was silent.

'Cos you know he hates me guts. Just warning you, it might not go down well.'

'Tony.'

'Finally. You get me name right.'

Meredith groaned, as though she was pulling herself up in bed, already finding the confrontation a chore.

'So you're straight now, are you?' Tony said.

'Straight?'

'Yeah. You've decided not to be a lesbian after all? You've knocked that on the head then?'

'No one cares about those labels anymore Tony. I'm like, pan?'

'I'll tell you what you are, girl. You're a fucking chancer. How's that for a label.'

'You see this is why air signs should, like, stay away from water signs.'

'Do you know about his wife?'

Tony heard Meredith sighing, possibly even yawning.

'They're not actually married?'

'Do you know he's got a little kid?'

'All this grudge-bearing. It's very like, un-Piscean.'

'I was sleeping in me car after we broke up.'

'Poor Tony. Literally always the victim.'

'Fuck you Meredith. I thought me luck had changed. But then you turn up like some fucking jinx and shit in me nest.'

'Tony, how is it any of your business?'

'You're shagging me boss. You've made it me business.'

'But you don't even, like, like Howie. What did you say he was? Ugly on the inside?' Meredith said, mimicking Tony's accent.

Tony fell silent. She'd been so careful, so professionally guarded when chatting to Meredith about her job. But it was true. She had said that about Howie. What a fucking idiot.

'You're right though,' Meredith continued, unable to contain her glee. 'He doesn't like you. Doesn't like your, like, attitude?'

'Me attitude?'

'Literally. I hate to be the one to tell you this but he's not, like, keeping you on?'

Bullseye. Every cell in Tony's body reverberated with the impact. Her voice was reduced to the futile peep of a day-old chick heading towards a macerator. 'That's not true. Eddy would have said something.'

Meredith laughed.

'Eddy doesn't know. And anyway, he's getting the, like, sack too? Howie says he's past it.'

In the blurry aftermath of Meredith's big reveal, Tony wondered if such a shock to the system was survivable, whether the force of the blow had sparked some rampant malignancy that would finish her off in the months to come. That she would be brought down by some vicious, paralysing illness that had originated not from a kink in her DNA, but from Meredith's bastard delight.

Fazakerley plodded to Tony, prompting a long-standing concern over who would take care of him if she were gone. There was no one. She ruffled the dog's head and felt the unfamiliar prickle of tears stinging her eyes. The sensation alarmed her. She blew out her cheeks, attempting to control emotions that had been suppressed since childhood. But none of the coping mechanisms she'd manufactured since choosing silence as a five-year-old helped her organise her mess of thoughts, to disentangle her dread of the future from humiliation at the hands of her ex.

And there it was. Boom. Howie's text, the knock-out uppercut to Meredith's left hook. Sacked in two weirdly formal sentences. No suggestion of regret to take the edge off the bombshell. *Your contract is terminated with immediate effect. This decision is final.*

SORROW AND DIGNITY

★

It was quite a turnout at the crematorium. The same chapel in which people had congregated to say goodbye to Queenie was once again inadequate for the throng. The appeal for just close family to attend had gone largely ignored. Genuine mourners were outnumbered by those hoping to catch sight of the pop star known previously for his music, but more recently for his high-profile arrest.

At the main gates, Death-Stare Maureen headed up a cluster of die-hard Dumplings, rallied together to show solidarity for a man they considered innocent. His most ardent devotees a silent contrast to the scrum of press photographers, who jostled to get a snap of the shamed but defiant star, hunched in the back of a funeral car. Camera flashes and shouts of 'Howie, this way!' Upstaged the uber-fans that whimpered with the thin warble of a Methodist Church choir. Random onlookers stood both across the road and in the road, with a couple settled on a small patch of grass at the entrance, making a day of it, with sandwiches and a blanket spread out on the ground. All it needed was a couple of tricoteuses de la guillotine and the picture would be complete.

Howie, his gaze fixed forward, caught no one's eye as the car inched past at the requisite five miles an hour, his hand held by his supportive new girlfriend and recent tabloid sensation, Meredith Pruitt, her hair blow-dried smooth into an expensively coiffured chestnut-brown side bun. Howie's head was sunken into his upturned collar. Hers was turned to the cameras, with an expression intended to convey both sorrow and dignity, all in one well-rehearsed pout. Howie was glad to have her as a distraction. With Eddy gone, Tony sacked and Stina back in Sweden, what remained of his inner circle had melted away on hearing of his arrest. Both Raoul and the manager he'd lined up had proved every bit as false-hearted as he'd have known them to be, had he bothered to scrutinise their motives.

A NON-JUDGEMENTAL TREASURE

✱

It would have been odd for Stina to attend the funeral but, still, her absence was noted. It was hardly surprising given Howie's arrest, along with the revelation that he was banging a twenty-five-year-old – news of which had been leaked to the tabloids, perhaps by a Sharples employee but more likely by Meredith herself. Photos, gleaned from her carefully curated social media presence, featured on page after page of Fleet Street rags. Her beauty, youth and exhibitionism a potent mix for newspaper editors looking for the next young woman to drool over and chastise.

During this time, the only person Stina could think of to turn to, the only person dependable enough to field press interest and give practical support, was Tony. Sacked by Howie the day before his arrest, her level-headedness – while organising everything from Viola's withdrawal from school to the cats' relocation to her parents' home in Sweden – had revealed her to be a non-judgemental treasure. Stina had employed her on a temporary basis to facilitate the move and the women spoke often. Stina was surprised by the ease of this new connection, and found herself looking forward to their calls.

'Did you know he was unfaithful?' Tony asked, during one of their late-night heart-to-hearts.

Stina hesitated, mulling it over. 'I didn't know, but I knew, if that makes sense.'

'Yeah. It does.'

'I can't work out if I was naive, stupid or delusional.'

'You and me both,' Tony said, thinking about her infatuation with Meredith.

'Maybe he expected me to turn a blind eye.'

'Who does he think he is? Prince Charles?'

Stina laughed. 'Probably. But that's not a relationship, that's an arrangement.'

'Maybe he's one of those people who thinks it's not really cheating if you don't get caught.'

'I guess,' Stina said, her hollow laugh underscoring her sadness. 'But even if you don't find out, it changes the relationship. It's like a spell's been broken. It's probably why we stopped sleeping together.'

'Oh, right.'

'I've never told anyone that. We still shared a bed, but the sex had fizzled out. I thought it was me. I thought it was tiredness, being a mum. Or familiarity.'

'Maybe it was his stinky fag breath,' Tony said, quickly following it up with, 'sorry.'

Stina laughed. 'You're not wrong. But I think it was because deep down, I knew.'

Such confidences were given up easily to Tony, despite the two women barely knowing each other. They'd found common ground in their shared association with Howie and Meredith, and they had many conversations like this, Tony's kindness touching Stina's heart at a time of isolation and shame.

MEMORY LANE

★

If Howie's mood could be conjured up in the form of a microwaveable meal, the solid grey blob of porridge served up on a moulded plastic plate perfectly represented his state of mind. His arrest had coincided with the dishing up of breakfast – the culinary equivalent of an early morning firing squad.

The police had arrived at 7am on the day Howie had planned to fly to Manchester to pick up his car. He'd been crashed out on the music room sofa, having not shared the marital bed since arriving back from his mother's funeral. The cats had scattered at the banging on the door. A uniformed search team had marched in while a detective spelled out the allegation.

'What?!' Howie had said. 'WHAT?!'

He'd thought it was a drugs raid. He'd been half-expecting one for years. Even in the depths of REM sleep he'd have one ear cocked for the bang on the door. And here it was. Despite only waking a minute or so earlier, he'd done a quick mental inventory of how much weed and coke he had on the premises. It wasn't much, a small amount that he reckoned would add up to little more than a slapped wrist. His heart had been racing when they entered the room, but more from the surprise of it than the fear of being in serious trouble. But by the time he'd been read his rights, Howie had known this was huge.

'Who? What? When? Where? Why?'

Howie had felt it necessary to offer up the ornate wooden box from Rajasthan that held his drugs, thinking he could somehow deflect the obscenity of the allegation towards something more in keeping with his rock'n'roll image. Like some kind of trade-off. An off-the-cuff plea bargain. Take them to the drugs and they might drop the charge of rape.

In normal circumstances, Howie could tune out the ringing in his ears, his tinnitus neutralised through a process of habituation. But, as the officer set out the charge, he'd lost the ability to filter noise. The distant whirr of the grass being cut on the golf course and a bin lorry bumping along the road outside had become an intolerable din – topped only by Stina, in the adjoining room, repeating over and over to the officers tramping through their home that her four-year-old daughter was asleep upstairs. As though somehow this might stop the nightmare in its tracks. Howie had stood, wanting to go to her, to tell her it was malicious nonsense. That he was being framed. But the officers had told him to sit down.

'It was my mother's funeral last week,' he said, unsure of what leverage this might give him. None, it turned out.

A detective had led him away, shielding Howie's matted bedhead as he'd ducked into an unmarked car. His silk harem pants, hanging off his arse, mismatched with the Cuban-heeled boots he'd been allowed to pull on, sockless.

The police had processed Howie like any other arrestee, with a detached professionalism that belied the leaking of his mugshot just hours later. The normal sheen of stardust had been absent from a photo that was the personification of mortification, umbrage and panic. The press – cock-a-hoop to get their teeth into such a story – had sent news of his arrest around the world. And in the days that followed, among the pages and pages devoted to fact, speculation and lies, they reported that Stina had 'fled' to Sweden. On that count, they weren't wrong.

Howie hadn't been informed, until sitting at the interview table, who'd made the allegation.

'Ms Golobova,' said the officer.

Howie looked blank.

'Who?' he said, genuinely baffled.

'Are you saying you don't know this person?'

'Toadally.'

The lawyer – who'd arrived within an hour of Howie's call – held up his finger as if to silence him.

'Sorry, no comment,' Howie said.

'From...' The officer checked their notes. 'Žilina.'

Howie offered up his hands, as a gesture of his bewilderment. Convinced it was some kind of set-up.

'Zophie Golobova,' said the officer. 'Sixteen years old. From Žilina in Slovakia.'

Howie's face betrayed the clatter of the penny dropping.

'For the purposes of the tape, Mr Howden is nodding his head.'

'Raoul,' Howie said in little more than a whisper.

'Who?'

'Nothing. I mean, no comment.'

'I'd like to talk to my client,' the lawyer said.

Howie lay in the cell, the stiff polyester sheet pulled over his head. It was a crude attempt at privacy while he replayed the events of that night at the Jambhalabar, events that his short-term memory bank hadn't even bothered to file. His forgetting of Zophie an indication of how little importance he'd attached to the encounter. But the cell, the solitude and the shock of the arrest forced him to take an unlit scuttle down memory lane.

He remembered the introduction. How he'd indicated to Raoul he preferred the lighter-haired of the young models being directed to their table. Her English wasn't as good as her sulky-faced friend with the braces. The one he'd steered her towards Eddy. Zophie had been the more timid of the two and it hadn't taken much alcohol to get her tipsy, and the wine he'd topped her up with had gone straight to her head. He remembered how she'd stumbled as she got in and out of the taxi, the difficulty he'd had negotiating her onto his boat. How the slight swell of the Thames had caused it to rock a little, and how she'd stumbled onto her knees, her long legs tangling as she'd tried to stand. How he'd hoisted her under her armpits, her head lolling, her shoes falling off as her feet dragged pigeon-toed across the deck. How he'd lugged her into the cramped bedroom, cursing as he banged his elbows on the narrow door jambs, her limp body a dead weight despite her small frame. Of how testy he'd become on discovering he was all out of condoms, having planted his last one on Eddy for a laugh back at the club. And how he'd spat on his hand as a rudimentary lubricant and fucked her, bareback and mechanically. Her lying on his bed, blacked out in an alcohol-induced stupor, taken as her consent.

AN UNWITTING ACCOMPLICE

The arrest had floored Stina. She remembered the night in question, but could offer no alibi as she went over and over the events both in her head and in a police interview. She returned briefly to England to cooperate with the investigation, following Howie's release on bail. But it did him no favours that she hadn't seen him for two weeks after the date of the alleged attack. Their phone records confirmed that they'd barely spoken. And her account of him turning up late to their room at The Sharples, only to slip away 'for a smoke' in the dead of night and not returning for hours sounded way more sinister than she'd intended. She hadn't spoken one word to him since the day the police came to their house. She had nothing to say that couldn't be communicated through his lawyer. His choosing Meredith's apartment as his bail address was confirmation, if it were needed, their relationship was over.

It transpired there was little forensic evidence of value in their home. Howie's leather trousers revealed nothing more than the secretions of a man who forwent underpants. Stina had laundered his clothes – stinking of cigarettes and stale cologne – on a hot wash. As requested, she'd dropped off his jacket at the drycleaners. She felt culpable and foolish to discover she may have been an unwitting accomplice.

'Do you think he did it?' Tony asked Stina one night, both women stretched out on their beds in different countries, an hour's time difference apart, yet on the same page.

'I don't know,' she admitted, Tony's candour allowing her to be totally frank. 'I want to believe he didn't, but hand on heart, I can't say for sure.'

Stina had raked over every detail of their life together, looking for clues. But she knew that Howie's privilege, of having anything he wanted, could have encouraged a belief he could take what wasn't his. It was a crushing thought. But, whatever the truth, she had just two choices. To stick by a philanderer or to stick by a rapist. She chose to stick by neither and had returned to Sweden at the first sign of the press setting up camp outside their home.

FORTY MILES NORTH

✱

Tony felt uneasy to be in the kitchen that Howie and Stina had shared. She boiled a kettle for the removal guys while tapping a tin of pet food with a spoon to rally the cats. Stina had told her that Howie seemed more upset over losing custody of them than he had of being separated from Viola. But the tacit spectre of his uncertain fate deemed him an unsuitable candidate for their ongoing care, and Tony had been tasked with arranging their transport to Sweden.

The removal company were boxing up Stina and Viola's belongings – a modest vanload, gathered before her swift getaway. Tony had helped, folding knitwear into moth-proof bags, holding the garments to her face, marvelling at their softness and at a life in which you could be spoiled for choice as to what to wear each day. It was a strangely intimate exercise as she got to know Stina through her things. Outer garments treated with care, undergarments hurriedly bagged up. Tony didn't want the removal guys to handle items so personal. She found it strangely embarrassing, noting Stina's preference for thongs. She remembered the occasion Meredith had cajoled her into trying one on.

'For a laugh,' she'd said.

Tony had attempted to neutralise the cruelty of it by laughing along. Meredith had been almost tearful with mirth as Tony had stood in front of her, exposed. Naked save for the scrap of lace. Feeling like netted salami.

Viola's jolly bedroom contrasted sharply with the rooms of Tony's childhood, where safety glass and fire escapes betrayed the social care aspect of spaces that were sorry facsimiles of family homes. Tony had been surprised to discover Viola's beloved Bebisbjörn had been left behind.

'Is she sure?' Tony said to Stina, their phone calls now amounting to several a day.

'She left it for her daddy,' she said, each word interrupted by a sob. 'She said he'd be lonely without us.'

Both women knew Howie was undeserving of such an offering.

But that, after a lifetime of bounty, this small bear might be his most meaningful gift.

Stina was leaving all the furniture. Most of it, like the house, was Howie's, and she wanted a fast and clean break. Howie's disgrace, and the police's rifling through her possessions, had seen her resolve never to step foot in the property again. She'd been required to return to England just once, to provide a witness statement. She managed the round trip in a day – her journey facilitated by Tony who'd picked her up and dropped her off at the airport in the bright yellow Peugeot gifted to her by Stina. Tony'd had butterflies in her stomach at the arrivals gate, but Stina had seemed genuinely delighted to see her. Her face had lit up with her gapped-tooth smile, her embrace had been heartfelt. Tony felt blessed for this silver lining that had appeared from the most sombre of clouds.

'Have you spoken to Meredith?' Stina asked as they drove to the police station.

'Only once. I needed her address to send up Howie's guitar and bi-focals,' Tony said, a catch in her voice as she added, 'and Bebisbjörn.' This new-found tearfulness was taking some getting used to, but she felt comfortable around Stina, and under no pressure to curb emotions that sat so close to the surface.

'I know,' Stina said quietly, touching Tony's arm as she changed gear.

Tony brushed away a tear, marvelling at how comforting these small acts of kindness, which had been so rare in her life, could be.

It was just a few miles from the airport to the police station, a journey that took them past the Airbnb apartment that Stina had rented for Tony while she organised her move.

'There it is,' Tony said, pointing to a grand house set back from the road, a magnificent star magnolia in full bloom dominating the front garden.

'Oh, it's lovely. I'm glad. Are you able to practise your tuba?'

'I go into Bushy Park. I don't think it's allowed, but Londoners are mental. I'm there pumping out the Carnival of Venice and they walk past acting like they haven't noticed. In Liverpool, they'd be joining in.'

Stina laughed.

'Dogs usually stop to have a look though. And a few deer have come for a nose.'

'I've never been to Liverpool.'

'You should go. I'll take you.'

'I'd like that.'

The two women continued the journey deep in thought. Stina eventually broke the silence. 'Have you spoken to Howie?'

'You're joking, aren't you?' Tony said, snorting. 'He hardly spoke to me before all this, never mind now.'

'He knew you had the measure of him.'

'I don't know about that,' Tony shrugged. 'God, I wish I'd had the measure of Meredith. You know I have to go through her now? She's his PA apparently.'

Both women shook their heads.

'How does she sound?'

'Like Ursula the Sea Witch,' Tony said.

Stina laughed. 'Excuse me?'

'She's got a new voice.'

'A new voice?'

'Yeah. Low and serious,' Tony said, mimicking Meredith's new baritone. 'Like she's pretending to be a grown-up.'

'Well at least one of them is. *Jösses.*'

'They deserve each other.'

It was a cliché of course, but one that rang true. However uncomfortable she felt regarding her history with Meredith, she was savouring the liberation of moving on. The realisation that her ex was unworthy of her love saw the distress of the betrayals lose their charge. Though she did wonder, in conversations with Stina, how Howie would handle being holed up in Meredith's apartment – his hideaway from press interest and the address he had to stay at as a condition of bail.

'Badly,' Stina said.

As she drove away from Stina and Howie's house for the umpteenth time, it occurred to Tony that as much as Meredith would be enjoying the attention, she wouldn't be cut out for prison visits. And if Howie were rearrested and charged, he would soon discover the limitations of her love. Tony waved at the police officer stationed at the front gates. It was a thankless responsibility to maintain order between the press, the public and the Dumplings. Angela with the dimples had proved to have quite a temper on her; while Little Cheryl, now decidedly less bubbly, spent each day sat on a folding picnic chair, draped in a blanket, clutching a framed photo of Howie like a mother of one of Argentina's disappeared.

As Tony to and froed over the next few days, she became used to the photographers shouting and jostling; of their pushing themselves onto the bonnet, hoping for a money shot. Instead their pictures captured nothing more titillating than a large, unfazed lurcher-type dog, who gazed back at them from the front seat of Tony's bright yellow car. For all of the shock and distress of the previous weeks, Tony was optimistic. The alarm of Meredith's slap-in-the-face revelation, that Howie was to sack her, had proven to be short-lived. Stina's stepping in with an offer of temporary work, along with the corking perk of a dog-friendly Airbnb – a sunny garden flat in Hampton Wick, situated between the park, the river and her cat feeding duties at Stina's former home – had solved her immediate housing crisis. But it had been the offer of an audition, to provide six months' sabbatical tuba cover at the Royal Stockholm Philharmonic Orchestra, that had her dare to believe that her luck had finally changed. The promise of a toe in the door to an orchestral career, saw her desperate to find someone to tell.

'I'm just forty miles north of Stockholm,' Stina had said, sounding delighted.

Tony knew this. A Google search had revealed the train journey cost just a fiver, and took thirty-seven minutes on a high-speed link.

'Fingers crossed you get it!'

But Tony already had sensed that something in the universe had shifted. The sensation of her disjointed, chaotic life, falling into place was unfamiliar to her. But she had a hunch things were finally on the up and this was an opportunity that would go her way.

BRAZEN

Howie left police custody a good two inches shorter than when he'd arrived. His Cuban-heeled boots taken for forensic analysis and swapped for cheap plimsolls. He'd been released on bail pending further investigation, his overseas properties deeming him a flight risk. He'd been allowed to return home to collect a few things and to meet with his lawyer before driving to Meredith's Manchester apartment in the family car. His mirrored shades and piss bottle had never been more necessary, given the public's obsession with the case. He'd said his goodbyes to the cats – Cantona, rubbing his head against his own – the horror of his situation laid bare by the knowledge he may never see these much-loved creatures again. Losing his cats' uncomplicated love was a reminder that life as he knew it was over.

Howie drove up north, sick to the stomach, the promise of frolics with Meredith bringing little cheer. The discovery, on his arrival, that her apartment was shared with a posh boy called Rupert was a detail she'd failed to impart.

'Who the fuck is that?' Howie said, pulling her into the galley kitchen, his voice a stage whisper.

'Rupert?'

'Rupert?' he said, incredulous. 'What, like the fucking bear?'

'What is it with you northerners and Rupert?' she'd said, in what was their first crossed words. 'It's literally, like, a perfectly good name?'

Howie hadn't noticed before, that Meredith pronounced perfectly *parfectly*. This fizz of irritation was new. He took himself to their bedroom, shutting the door on a living room that felt way too small for his problems and Rupert's long legs. His sulk so entrenched that, within twenty-four hours, Rupert and his belongings were gone.

It was a typically-sized modern two-bedroom apartment but, unused to compact living areas and without access to outside space, Howie felt caged. It disturbed him to think that, should the rape allegation stick, he'd be spending many years in spaces far smaller than this – and sharing with characters way more problematic than Rupert.

Howie railed against the discomfort of his domestic situation and the injustice of his felonious one, insisting to his lawyer that Zophie's motives had to be financial. Revenge for her being dropped by her agency. That she intended to carve a career for herself off the back of what he insisted was a consensual if pedestrian fuck. He accepted he'd cheated on Stina. He would hold his hands up to that.

'But I'm no rapist,' he said in a Zoom call to his lawyer. Meredith's fairy lights and bunting a chirpy backdrop to a grim exchange.

'Did she consent?'

'She came with me to the boat. What did she think would happen?'

'But did she consent?'

'Yes.'

'She consented to sex?'

'She came with me to the boat,' Howie said, this time less forcefully. It slowly registering that Zophie's joining him hadn't bestowed him with some sexual power of attorney, free to make decisions on her behalf. He held Bebisbjörn tightly, the bear sitting on his knee below the table.

'They've got nothing on you,' said his £1,000 an hour lawyer. 'Hold your nerve and brazen it out. It's your word against hers. We've got your back.'

The lawyer was right. Forensic evidence gathered from the houseboat proved nothing. His unwashed bedding revealed copulation had taken place, but his insistence that it had been consensual was hard to disprove. CCTV that showed him leave the Jambhalabar with Zophie supported his claim that she was a willing participant in his age-inappropriate philandering. Even the surprise coming forward of the minicab driver, who gave a sworn statement that the young woman had appeared disorientated when dropped at the station; that Howie had seemed unconcerned over her welfare; that he'd waited at the golf club until his partner had driven past in her bright yellow car had painted a picture of someone snide and dishonourable, but had failed to establish guilt – a fact Howie's lawyer, standing on the steps of his Marylebone offices and pumped up by the bagging of this nice little earner – was at pains to emphasise. Reading from a carefully drafted statement, which said that his client would 'strenuously fight this bogus claim', he reminded people 'Mr Howden has not been charged with any crime.' Howie stood silently next to him, prompting bystanders to remark, 'He's shorter than I thought.'

FOAM AND GLITTER

✶

Una looked out across the bay, from the window of a house considered turnkey-ready by the smart young estate agent at her side. The foam and glitter of a Seamus Heaney ocean a reminder of how Eddy had always relaxed when staring at the sea. Things would have worked out so differently, she thought, had they made a home here.

'We've had fierce interest in it,' she heard the agent saying, tuning into the familiarity of the Sligo accent. 'Dubs and Brits buying second homes. Even our American friends. Is that what you'll be after?'

Una shook her head. 'No,' she said, noting the lack of trees in the surrounds, their absence suggesting the strong winds she found so exhilarating.

It wasn't the house of her dreams. In the thousands of hours she'd spent thinking about this move she'd visualised something older, more characterful than this white-rendered slab from the Celtic Tiger boom that jarred so with its surroundings. The house stood alone on a long stretch of rocky scrubland, the low-maintenance patch of lawn and gravel out front suggesting much the same aesthetic on the inside. But it was a good distance from its nearest neighbour and came with a sizeable plot of land, ensuring no future encroaching into her physical or mental space. It was a soulless ex-holiday let, meagrely furnished by an owner with an eye on profit margins and hygiene. The easy to wipe clean dark leather sofa; the shiny tiled floors, vertical blinds and whiff of disinfectant according it the air of a veterinary practice. It was a house that, like her, just needed some life breathing into it. But oh, that view. Nothing but the Atlantic ahead. The next house as the crow flies the shoreline of Newfoundland.

'So, you're wanting to come home then?' the agent said.

Una nodded, a catch in her throat. She felt ridiculous to be fighting back tears, standing next to a stranger, in this blandest of rooms with the most epic of views. But tears hadn't been far from the surface lately. Everything that had happened had left her so thin-skinned she believed the only things that held her together were her baby-blue cashmere robe and magical thinking.

'I'm wanting to look out at the sea,' Una said, the paucity of soft furnishings causing her voice to bounce off the walls.

'Well, one thing we're not short of is coastline, that's for sure.'

Una pushed open a window and a blast of sea air danced across her synapses. The pop of bliss it brought sold the house on the spot. She touched the top of her head – a reflex action – to flick her sunglasses down onto her nose, but found she'd either forgotten or mislaid them. It was okay though. She didn't feel headachy. In fact she hadn't had a migraine for days. Not since she'd given her statement to the police; a blow-by-blow account, in the most minuscule detail, of how Howie had assaulted her almost a decade ago. On the hottest day of the year.

THAT WOMAN

★

It had been the coming forward of Agnieszka that had done for Jean, the police turning up at her bungalow for a witness statement, wanting to know what had gone on at Queenie's wake. Jean knew nothing, Gordon kept schtum.

'Do you honestly think my brother would have anything to do with that woman?' Jean's stress on *that woman* packed with all of the indignation of a sitting president. Her insistence that Agnieszka must be out to make mischief, to extort money from Howie, was surely the only plausible explanation.

Jean had gone to bed that night on an empty stomach, having scraped her tea into the bin. She fell into a hypoglycaemic coma in the early hours before slipping silently away at dawn. Agnieszka's accusation that Howie had assaulted her in the kitchen, on the day of Queenie's funeral, had been the final nail in what was, at least, a mahogany coffin – chosen by Gordon, safe in the knowledge such a traditional and solid casket would have had Jean's blessing. Two doomed fan-tailed doves were booked, along with flowers spelling 'MOTHER' – a nod to the absent son who hadn't made the journey from the other side of the world. Howie's instinct had been to miss the funeral, but his legal advisors had calculated that such a familial tragedy, the death of an only sibling, might help garner sympathy and support, his attendance reinforcing his insistence he had nothing to hide.

A TENDER BLUR

✶

Perhaps Chakakhan hadn't cared if Eddy was dying or dead. Or maybe leading Una to Joni's bedroom had demonstrated the kind of canine pluck that sees animals awarded medals. Either way, that little dog had saved the day.

Seeing Una grappling with Eddy's limp body had triggered a predictable response. Chakakhan sank her teeth into his stockinged foot with such force that, despite being seconds away from irreversible brain damage and a few seconds more from death, Eddy had been jolted back to earth – to Manchester, to Chorlton, to Joni's bedroom, to Una hefting him upright and the excruciating pain of the tiny dog's shark teeth buried gum-deep into the boniness of his ankle.

Una said she couldn't remember how the knot had been untied. But the muscles spasms in her back, in the days that followed, suggested a fierce struggle. The trauma causing her memory to fragment.

Physically, Eddy had got off lightly. The bruised larynx that caused his speech to remain a raspy whisper for a good four weeks afterwards was less bothersome than his throbbing foot. Mentally though, he was still fragile and tearful; shame-faced to have put Una through such a shocking ordeal, and mortified to have done so in Joni's bedroom. He'd been determined not to seek medical attention.

'At the very least you need a fecking tetanus,' Una had said as she'd cleaned his ankle with an antiseptic floor wipe, her hand trembling.

But Eddy had been frightened that he'd be sectioned if he asked for help. And more fearful still that cutbacks to services would mean there wouldn't be help to be had. Consequently, they'd told no one, his hoarse voice passed off as laryngitis, his painful limp a sprain. But at least this time, if the ship was sinking, then both of them would go down clinging to the wreckage together.

In the hours following Eddy's attempt, they'd sat together as a family –

Eddy and Una's pizzas uneaten, still in their boxes on the coffee table, in front of the TV that both were staring at, but neither were watching. Joni was enjoying her Vegan Rustica, oblivious to the tragedy that had been swerved in her bedroom a short time before. The weekend passed in a tender blur, Una not leaving Eddy's side and Eddy afraid to let her. With his room still dismantled and neither of them having the energy or motivation to put it together again, Eddy was back in the marital bed, sleeping soundly courtesy of diazepam, marijuana and a nightly nip of Tullamore Dew. Una found sleep more fitful, her prior belief Eddy wouldn't kill himself, shattered by his attempting to do so right under her nose.

Una took a ramshackle approach to Eddy's care. With no medical training, and completely out of her depth, she cobbled together a primitive alarm system to alert her, should he get out of bed in the night. Threading the tie from her pyjama bottoms through the button hole of his pyjama top. The makeshift umbilical cord was a surprisingly successful contraption – the only downside being them shuffling together to the toilet when either of them need to pee, stepping over Chakakhan in the dark, stretched across the bedroom door.

Eddy's coming clean about the London fiasco hadn't been the shouty experience he'd dreaded. The showdown he'd so worried about – the recriminations and finger-pointing he presumed would end in divorce – turned out to be a gentle confessional. Eddy found much comfort in those long conversations that first weekend. Detailing how he'd found himself embroiled in a scene with a sixteen-year-old Estonian model had seen some of his darkness lift. Una found his story both sickening and preposterous. Her sympathies lay entirely with Iiris, who she viewed as an exceptional young woman, full of ingenuity and pluck – someone able to converse in a second language, unafraid to travel alone to strange cities. In fact, she was the only person to come out of the sorry tale with integrity intact. Eddy was less convinced, but he knew to keep his mouth shut. Even so, the absurdity of it all had at times seen Una laugh out loud.

'But you don't even like Pringles,' she'd said, spitting her coffee back into her cup.

But if Eddy was relieved to have Una's forgiveness, he was more relieved still to discover he'd been sacked by Howie. The two-sentence text popped up on his phone, when he finally felt able to switch it back on, in the days following the suicide attempt.

'Did you not get me voicemail?' Tony said, being the first person Eddy thought of to call.

'Sorry, no. I've had my phone off.'

'What's wrong with your voice?'

'Nothing. Just a sore throat.'

'How's your eye?'

'Getting there. I blew my nose on Sunday.'

'Congratulations.'

'Thanks. I've got more good news,' Eddy said.

'Go on.'

'Howie's sacked me.'

'Shit. No way. You okay?'

'It's a weight off, to be honest.'

'What will you do?'

'Dunno. Ireland maybe. Me and Una have been talking about it. Fresh starts and all that.'

'Wow. Ace.'

'How's things with you?'

'Great. His majesty sacked me too.'

Eddy hesitated. His glee felt horribly inappropriate. He knew how she needed and valued the job.

'Oh fuck. What? I'm so sorry. The bastard. When? What did he say?'

'Yesterday. He didn't say anything. He texted me.'

Tony read out the message. It was identical to his own.

'The fucker just copied and pasted. What a complete arsehole,' Eddy said. 'Tony, I'll work something out. What do you need me to do?'

'Nothing. Honestly. I've got the swivel chair in me car and I've given the Swiss cheese plant to the nice security guard. The dead smiley one.'

Eddy laughed. 'Take whatever you want. But seriously...'

He didn't know exactly how he could help her, plunged as he was into such an abrupt retirement. But he felt honour-bound to make amends for Howie's conduct. Yet, before he could say anything, Tony interrupted. 'Eddy, Howie's been arrested.'

'WHAT? When?'

'The bizzies turned up this morning. Dead early. Stina told me. He's in custody. Being questioned.'

'Questioned about what?'

There was a pause, just long enough for Eddy to flop into his chair, not knowing anything, while expecting the worst.

'Rape.'

Even without being informed that the victim was a sixteen-year-old Slovak model called Zophie, away from home for the first time; even without hearing the sorry tale of incapacity and stupor and the weight of a man on top of her; of her hangover, then the herpes; even without mention of a little houseboat in Chertsey; even without being told it was Iiris who'd coaxed the story from her through her barricaded bedroom door and that both women were now back in their respective countries, having been sacked by their model agency on the say-so of Raoul; even before Eddy discovered it had been Iiris who'd contacted the police; that it had been those little and large Manchester officers who'd set the ball rolling for Howie's arrest; even without this knowledge, Eddy knew the accusation to be true.

PART FIVE

*

Early May, 2019

GOOD CHIPS

✱

The bench had a small plaque screwed to it, dedicated to the memory of a Tadhg Ó Súllieabháin 'who'd loved it here'.

'Tad-hig O Sulli-e-ab-hain. O Sullieabhain. O Sullieabhain?' asked Eddy, pronouncing all the Bs and Hs. 'Is that it?'

Una laughed. 'Not even close. Tige O'Soolawoin. Or O'Sullivan if you want to be an arse.'

'Tige?'

'Tige. As in tiger,' Una said, never failing to be amused by Eddy's commitment to learn every word he came across in the Irish language.

They sat, sharing a bag of chips, as Eddy savoured the crisp, onshore breeze that intensified the flavour of salt on his lips. They watched the waves break and the sand martins flutter in and out of breeding burrows in the weathered banks. Joni was in the distance, stopping and starting as Chakakhan ran in front and behind her, yanking the lead. Eddy thought how she looked like a kid again – zig zagging between childhood and adulthood as erratically as Chakakhan darted between the rock pools and the incoming tide, the dog kicking off at any seagull that dared come near. The scene was crystal-clear through his brand-new specs. A handful of wet-suited surfers rode blustery waves, but otherwise, there were few people about. Just a couple of dog walkers and someone flying a kite – its diamond silhouette soaring, lunging and looping the loop, its ribbons catching the same currents the seagulls free-wheeled in the late spring sunshine.

The house they'd viewed was set a fair way back from this place. Fears of coastal erosion, rising sea levels and a repeat of the 1755 tsunami had prompted Eddy to stipulate that, as much as he'd love a sea view, if he were to sleep at night it would have to be a distant one. They'd accepted an offer on their Manchester home even before it went on the market, agreeing a chunk off the asking price to get rid quick.

'You okay?' Eddy asked, squeezing Una's hand.

She nodded. 'You?'

'Yeah,' he said.

'Sure?'

They asked this a lot these days. The tectonic plates of their relationship having shifted and settled somewhere less likely to quake.

'Yeah. I am. I feel I'm being pieced back together, like...' Eddy screwed up his eyes trying to think of the words. '...a Kintsugi vase.'

Una snorted.

'Don't laugh,' he said nudging her, the mood between them playful. 'I mean I wouldn't go putting any water in me, obviously, but yeah, I think I'm going to be okay.'

And this time, he believed it to be true. He still relied on his old friends marijuana and valium to help him through the inevitable wobbles. But in a few short weeks he'd made much progress, the barbed edges of his anxiety smoothing like ocean glass as plans took shape. He knew he'd have to come to some kind of accommodation over his relationship with Howie. His devoting his professional life to someone who didn't deserve it was no doubt going to be costly in terms of analysis. But his promise to Una that he'd commit to talking therapies was acknowledgement of the work ahead. Her finally opening up about what Howie had done to her on that hottest day of the year had helped him make sense of the past decade, of her withdrawing from him. That one brief act, possibly long-forgotten by Howie, had poisoned the well of their marriage.

It was probably a stretch to think he'd ever be happy-go-lucky, but his apocalyptic world-view seemed less extreme in light of rising temperatures, the Ebola virus and global current affairs. He hadn't been entirely honest with his GP about the extent of his mental collapse, but the ten-minute appointment had hardly been conducive to the baring of souls. A prescription for an upped dose of the antidepressant he hoped to wean himself from had been filled, but not taken; a referral to a psychiatrist so far in the future as to render it meaningless. The elastic band had been discarded, but the breathing exercises were helping – the knot in his stomach slackening as he stopped second-guessing the sincerity of Una's love.

'Good chips,' Eddy said.

'Grand,' Una replied, tucking in.

He whistled to Joni.

'Chips!' he shouted, his croaky voice mended. Holding her wrapped portion above his head.

Joni whooped and ran towards her parents with the joyful bounce of a child taken out of school in term time. Una laughed at her daughter's exuberance as Eddy's phone pinged. He took it from his pocket.

'Oh.'

'What?'

'Howie's been rearrested.'

'When?' Una said, sounding unsurprised at the news.

Eddy continued to read the text. 'Early this morning. Had to happen.'

He was right. Because in the days following Howie's press statement on the steps of his lawyer's office, more women had come forward – each with stories that corroborated Zophie's version of events. There'd been just one or two at first but as word of these developments filtered into the public realm, the volume of accusers increased exponentially. Allegations went back years, forming a chronicle of entitlement. The goosing and the groping had gone unchecked, the pawing unpunished. The free pass celebrity had afforded him had licensed its escalation. Behind the scenes, police were building a devastating case – each woman providing details only those at the receiving end of Howie's libido would know about. The impact of these assaults had reverberated through his victims' lives – stories of shame and loss of esteem, of careers upended, ambitions thwarted, relationships soured. The women discovered there was strength in numbers. Able to voice their truth, it soon became clear that, despite what Jean, the Dumplings or his lawyer had hoped or believed, Howie's world had fallen apart faster than Harvey Weinstein's bathrobe.

Eddy blew out his cheeks and shook his head.

'Who's told you?' Una asked.

'Tony. I guess Stina will have told her. I don't think it's public yet.'

Eddy texted back, thanking Tony for letting him know. Wishing her luck. 'She starts that tuba gig tomorrow,' he said, putting his phone back in his pocket.

Una smiled.

'How long's it for?'

'Just six months. But it's a serious foot in the door.'

'Fair play to her.'

Eddy nodded and held out the bag of chips. Una took one and caught his eye.

'What?' he asked.

'I wish I'd told you about, you know, what Howie did to me.'

Eddy nodded but couldn't think of anything to say. Una put the chip back in the bag and sighed.

'You know, I don't think he thought he'd done anything wrong.'

'Probably not,' Eddy said, a catch in his voice.

'I've replayed it a million times over the years. What I should have done. Screamed? Called the cops? I dunno.' Una paused for a moment, and then, speaking in barely a whisper, she said, 'but I was holding Joni.'

Eddy brushed a tear from his healed eye, his glasses lifting from his nose. Una nodded towards her daughter, who was laughing and spinning in circles as the dog ran around her at the end of its lead. 'I was so proud of her that day at school. Standing up for herself. But it still got her suspended. What kind of message does that send out to young girls?'

'It's all so fucked,' Eddy said, offering up the chips again.

Una took one. 'You know what the really stupid thing is?' she said. 'I thought I had to protect you from what happened to me. In some mad way I even thought I had to protect fecking Howie.'

Eddy sighed. 'I'm so sorry Una.'

'It wasn't your fault.'

'It kinda was. I should have paid more attention. Asked questions.'

'Ach, we all should.'

They sat, gazing ahead, as Joni neared.

'You know sometimes I'd feel the atmosphere change,' Eddy said.

Una looked at him. 'In what way?'

'Backstage. I've been thinking about it a lot.'

'How do you mean?'

'I'd go into the green room and feel the temperature drop. The mood would alter. They'd fire looks at each other.'

'Who would?'

'Howie. Raoul. Guys Raoul would bring along. Howie's kind of age, you know? In high spirits. Coked-up. And there'd be these young girls, just standing around. I felt like some old fart. I'd show my face then fuck straight off back to the hotel.'

Una stopped eating.

'I'd often recognise them,' Eddy said. 'Big names. A-listers. Always loud. Really loud. But the girls had a different energy. Kind of bewildered I guess. I never got it until now. Stupid.'

'In plain sight and all that,' Una said.

'It was so fucking normalised.'

Una nodded. 'People expect stars to behave that way,' she said. 'Like it's weird if they don't.'

'Howie the womaniser. Fucking hell, I must have heard that ten thousand times. He's a bit of a lad. Boys will be boys.' Eddy shook his head. 'Christ, he was two times winner of *The Great British Shagger*. They gave him a fucking trophy.'

'Playboys,' Una said.

'Studs.'

'Lotharios.'

'Ladies' men.'

'Ladykillers,' Una shuddered.

Eddy blew out his cheeks and put his arm around his wife's shoulders, pulling her into him and kissing her on the top of her head.

'I love you Una Coyne.'

'Love ya back, Eddy Katz.'

Joni arrived breathless and rosy-cheeked, while Chakakhan cleared the area of any seagull hoping for a chip.

'Gross,' she said, pulling a face at her parents' display of affection. It was something that had become more normal of late and which Chakakhan, if not Joni, had got used to. 'What are they cooked in?'

'Vegetable oil,' Eddy said, 'I checked.'

'Cool. Budge up.'

The three of them sat squeezed together on the bench, eating their chips, popping open their cans, mesmerised by the view so loved by the person whose name Eddy had struggled to pronounce.

'Tige. Tige. Tige O'Soolawoin?'

'You got it,' Una said.

'To Tadhg Ó Súllieabháin who loved it here,' Eddy said, toasting him with his fizzy drink.

Una smiled and clinked her can against Eddy's.

'Good chips,' Joni said. 'When are we moving?'

'Hopefully by September. In time for the new term,' Una said.

'Cool.'

'*Puh puh puh*,' Eddy said.

'Yeah, *puh puh puh*,' Una and Joni chorused. And they laughed as Chakakhan barked for a chip.

THE END

MICHELE HOWARTH

THANKS

✱

With huge love and gratitude to those who have cheered me on, most especially my early readers who were so generous with their time – Paul Abbott, Rowan Aust, Jill Boughey, Julian 'fave' Bovis, Janine Bullman, Sean Conway, Carol Croom, Jimmy Dowdall, Nigel Durkan, Jenny Eclair, Susan Ferguson, Audrey Golden, Cate Halpin, Jenny Landreth, Lynne Mackay, Andrew Male, Harland Miller, Carol Morley, Benjamin Myers, Kate & Pat O'Connell, Marie Phillips, Cara & Judy Rodway, Rose Rouse, Jon Savage, Lemn Sissay, Adelle Stripe, Mark Thomas and Nicholas Treadwell – if they were sceptical they didn't show it and for that I am grateful.

Thank you so much to those creatives who agreed to work with me and who took Glitterballs to another level. Yes I'm looking at you Richard de Pesando, my ace designer, who more than nailed the 'sleaze and threat' brief and who will no doubt ask me to shorten my words of gratitude to fit neatly on a page. Credit for Glitterballs coming in under 150,000 words goes to my candid yet kind mentors/editors: Sally Orson-Jones and Rufus Purdy. Their enthusiasm for Glitterballs meant more than they probably realised. Thanks also to my eagled-eyed proofreader Kathryn Myers, who has made me second-guess those eagle-eyed and second-guess hyphens. Thanks a million to my dream audiobook narrator Stephen Hogan, for saying YES, and to his agent, Neil 'Voice Squad' Conrich for twisting his arm on my behalf. I feel very fortunate to have all of your names attached to my novel.

Heartfelt thank-yous to the cousins O'Toole, Stephen & Gavin for casting their legal eyes over my manuscript. It's comforting to have you in my corner and to know that there are at least two people in my wider circle who can countersign a passport photo. Thanks also to Graham Bartlett for guiding me through police procedural and to Orna Ross for co-founding the Alliance of Independent Authors – without such an extraordinary resource, Glitterballs would no doubt still be languishing in the slush piles of literary London.

Thank you to those friends and strangers who answered ridiculous questions about everything from the career paths of tuba players to the colour of wheelie bins in Chorlton-cum-Hardy: Ed Bicknell, Kate Bielby, Martin Carr, Katie Chatburn, Chris Clare, Tammy Cohen, Karl-Johan Elf, Deborah Faulkner-Moscrop, Mike Garry, Felix Good, Conall Gormley, Stewart Levine, Gill Mills, Alfie & Tam Pickard, Maisie Rashman and Jane Ray.

Thanks to those organisations, teachers and fellow students who gave support and feedback, most especially Carol Croom, Simon Crump, Amanda Faber, Rosemary Griffiths, Jericho Writers, Lee Wetherley and Debbie Young. To the content providers of a thousand free online webinars, I salute you.

Special mention goes to my writing buddy Michelle 'with two LLs' McDonagh who had to listen to me rant, whinge and bore on, on an almost daily basis, since I finally pulled my finger out to write this effing thing back in 2020. Not sure I'd have got to The End without you Michelle. Ta very much to my intrepid roving ambassadors, Rowan Aust and Susan 'sferg100' Ferguson, for moving and shaking on my behalf. Massive respect to Lisa Barbaris and Max King III for their benevolence in an industry not known for it's generosity of spirit or purse. But mostly thank you to Elliot, to whom I dedicate this novel. This is for you Ellie and our own happy ending.

Werner Herzog, helping with edits.

GLITTERBALES

spent his life running away from the expectations of his family and yet somehow he'd managed to run flat onto his face into a trap set by his mother's reach. Howie dragged himself reeling over? kkk dkr f, a⌀ ⌀⌀ Bdahbbj aeafffed on about work pressures and possibly needing to go back down South. Jean, seemingly oblivious to his problems, forged ahead.

"They do a store release service."

"And how much is that then?"

"Depends on how many you have."

"How about you."

Howie waited while Jean rustled through paperwork, his phone resting on the windowsill, switched to speakerphone to put some distance between them and to make it easier for him to smoke out of